# ALSO BY KATIE GOLDING

*Fearless*
*Wreckless*

8/22

# RELENTLESS

## KATIE GOLDING

sourcebooks
casablanca

*For Morgan.*
*Thank you for sharing your bus seat with me.*

Published by Sourcebooks Casablanca, an imprint of Sourcebooks
P.O. Box 4410, Naperville, Illinois 60567-4410
(630) 961-3900
sourcebooks.com

Cataloging-in-Publication Data is on file with the Library of Congress.

Printed and bound in the United States of America.
POD

# AUTHOR'S NOTE

Content warnings for this book include: alcoholism, mentions of childhood physical abuse, and medical trauma.

The characters in this story are dealing with some very traumatic personal histories, some of them still ongoing. And while their romance is the primary focus of the novel, I want to make clear that these themes are mentioned and addressed inside. If you are a survivor of abuse or if you are/know someone struggling with addiction, perhaps both, I pray nothing I've written causes you additional hurt.

Every year, thousands of children are subject to the horrors of abuse. The Childhelp National Child Abuse Hotline is staffed twenty-four hours a day, seven days a week with professional crisis counselors who provide assistance in over 170 languages. The hotline offers crisis intervention, information, and referrals to thousands of emergency, social service, and support resources. Please, if you see any signs of abuse in someone you know or if you yourself are involved in an abusive relationship, get help right away.

1-800-4-A-CHILD (800-422-4453)

# Chapter 1

WHAT THE HELL WAS I THINKING LAST NIGHT?

My hungover head throbs with a vengeance as I glance toward the bright-as-hell light coming in through the windows. Turns out I'm a dumbass and forgot to pull the curtains closed before I passed out. Wonder how many people saw the X-rated show that went down in here? My hotel room is on a higher floor, but that doesn't mean anything with the almighty power of today's camera phones. At least it can't be on YouTube yet, because Billy would be beating on my door to ream me out for risking my sponsorships. Or he'd send Frank, our manager, to do it.

I scrub a hand through my hair, blowing out a stream of air for the millionth time in my disastrous life. Who am I kidding? No one gives a shit what I do.

*Except* for maybe this girl. The naked woman on the pillow next to me moans and stretches luxuriously my way, her eyelashes fluttering open and a smile teasing her lips. Fuzzy memories of last night flash through my mind: the end-of-season awards ceremony, the bikes and the medals, the music and fountains of champagne between whiskey shots sipped from my secret flask. Stumbling past the press corps back to the hotel and up to the room, where I unzipped her green sequin dress and she shredded my tux and rode me like I was a Moto Grand Prix World Champion, even though I'm not.

A guilty grin dares to stretch across my mouth—talk about getting lucky. She's freaking *gorgeous*: the kind of woman I always swore I got but my redneck ass only ever really dreamed of. All smooth skin and long eyelashes, brown hair that's long in the front

and short in the back, and with the sweetest curves. And she definitely knows how to use them.

Her freezing-cold hands start exploring the finer aspects of my
chest, and *Christ, what's her name?* Stella? Sabrina? Definitely
started with an S.

"Buenos días," she purrs in Spanish, and that makes a lot of sense
considering we're in Valencia, but I just...I remember her being
German for some reason. "¿Descansaste bien?"

I don't know what that last part means, but I smile real pretty
and run a tentative knuckle down her prettier cheek, soaking up
the way she leans in to my touch. Even better, she's not really waiting for an answer as she starts kissing her way up my outstretched
arm and across my good shoulder. I'm certainly not about to stop
her to ask for a translation. I hadn't been laid in *weeks* before last
night.

Too much time traveling between motorcycle races, bouncing
between so many countries, I'm gonna have to get another passport
soon. And too many rodeos when I'm home in Memphis. Too many
bulls to remember all their names, too much drinking to cover the
pain of getting bucked, and too many managers trying to help me
make better decisions.

As far as I can see, I'm doing just fine on my own. Especially
when one of those icicle hands of hers drops way below the sheet
line. I cough out a grin, nearly lurching into the ceiling in the best
way—*buenos días* indeed.

"You are so big, Billy," she growls in a sultry accent, and I lurch
again. But for a brand-new, super-sucky reason.

I tug her hand away from my already-wilting cock, scooting back
on the bed and my throat starting to itch like my digestive system
just shifted into reverse. Because why wouldn't my hangover decide
to kick my ass even worse when I'm already down?

"Billy? I'm not Billy."

Sexy-Sa-Something's staring at me like I'm the one who's done
something wrong, even though she's in my hotel room calling me
the wrong damn name.

*Christ, I hope I wasn't aware of this mix-up last night.*

She scrambles for the bedsheet, clutching it to her bare chest until she's covered. Apart from one gloriously dusty nipple. "Then who are you?"

"I'm Mason." No spark of recognition, no nothing as she blinks those thick black eyelashes at me. "Billy King's little brother."

Her hand flies to her mouth, a whole bunch of horrified Spanish being muttered behind it.

"And what did you think I was Billy for anyhow? He's blond," I snap, "and...tall."

Her eyes dart to my dark hair, then over my shorter, brawny body she spent all night kissing and touching, and she's getting it. But she isn't happy about it.

She shoves at my chest, cursing me out in Spanish before she switches to English. "¡Dios Mío! Is that why you were at the award party? For your brother?"

"Are you—Why were you there? Party crasher?"

She looks just as offended as I feel. Especially considering the number of orgasms I recall her having. And that's not even counting all the ones I was too drunk to remember.

"I'm a model. For Blue Gator." She smooths her hair until it's all sleek and sharp, and okay, now that she said it, I'm pretty sure I've seen her on the paddock holding an umbrella in one of those little outfits before. "Do you even race moto?"

"Do I even—*oh*, I see how it is." I scoff as I get out of the bed, my dick totally depressed and all but useless. "For your information, I do race. MotoPro, baby. And I'm the best damn bull rider in the state of Tennessee."

As long as we're not counting the Cornucopia Exhibition. And everyone just *loves* to talk about last year's Cornucopia Exhibition. The one where "I" got eight seconds on Smashbox.

Worst day of my whole fucking life.

"Where?"

*Awesome.* As soon as I find my feet, I nearly lose my lunch from the world swirling and tilting in circles. I place a steadying hand on the nightstand littered with condom wrappers—thank God—and empty little liquor bottles. *Oh no*. That's gonna be on the bill.

It takes me a good thirty seconds before I can straighten myself and start looking for my clothes. Not that I can seem to find them: the room's a freaking wreck. I don't even want to know what that lamp's gonna cost. But I'm definitely sure to hear about it.

I swear, this is what I get for trying to be a good brother. I should've known better than to spend all night celebrating Billy being crowned Moto Grand Prix World Champion. *Again*.

I came in sixth. And sixth isn't nothing when you're racing motorcycles against the fastest people on the planet, on the toughest racetracks they can throw at us. But no one ever seems to care about where I finished. Should be used to it by now—that's what happens when you're born to be second best.

"Well…" Sexy-Sa-Something now sounds more curious than regretful and is still sitting wrapped like a present on the mattress hanging crooked off the box spring. Guess that explains why my lower back is killing me. "Who do you race for?"

I set right an upturned desk chair and find my hat, setting it on my head and starting to feel a little more human. I always think better under my black Stetson. "Dabria. I ride for Dabria Corse." Where the hell are my pants? My red duffel bag is empty and my stuff's scattered, but there's gotta be some underwear somewhere. *Shit*, not that I remembered to wash any.

Commando it is. Once I find my Wranglers.

"Dabria? Are you Lorelai Hargrove's teammate?" Of course, that name she knows. Then, in an announcer voice, she adds, "The First Woman of Moto."

I swallow a burp that tastes like tequila and something a little dirtier, and I should probably wash my hands. Soon. "Yeah. I'm her teammate. Or was. She's moving to Women's Moto. For MMW."

Sexy snuggles her bedsheet as I pick through the tangled bed-spread on the floor, pure gossipy joy on her face. "Are she and Massimo Vitolo really together now? After all those years of fighting? I knew their rivalry was all a publicity scam."

"Yeah, they're together now, but it wasn't a scam." *Oops*. I need to shut up. My mouth's been known to be a little big sometimes, and it's safer to stay quiet. Not that I've quite learned how to do that. "And Billy's probably about to be married, so pass that through the...grapevine." I barely edit out the word *groupie* in time.

She gasps, looking oddly offended. "He cheats on his girlfriend?"

"No!"

*God, if that gets back to Taryn...*

I stop my clothes search and wrench myself vertical, and *God*, my lower back is really killing me. I hope I didn't hurt myself; it's gonna make my bull ride on Saturday even more risky.

I turn toward Sexy, my hands desperately indicating to myself. "You slept with me, Mason. Not Billy. Remember?"

She slumps on the bed we all but broke, suddenly disappointed again. "Oh, right."

Geez. And so much for finding my pants. Actually, you know what—

I let out a sharp whistle that catches her off guard, Sexy popping up straight on the bed as her eyes go big and her hands go slack. I smile innocently. Then I grab the sheet she's clutching and rip it away from her, sending her tumbling back into the pillows with a squeal and a giggle. *God, what an ass she's got.* Still, I wrap the sheet around my waist like a good boy.

This was a mistake. I think? Rules seem kinda fuzzy on mistaken identity.

The muffled theme from *Star Trek* starts interspersing the steady sound of giggles and not getting dressed, and I follow the sound of Captain Kirk's voice encouraging me to go where no man has gone before. Even though the nightstand says I was all up in that last night.

A pile of pillows turns out to be the culprit hiding a green sequined dress and a mound of my wrinkled black tux, and I dig out my cell phone. When I check the screen, a wide smile cracks across my face: the most gorgeous woman I've ever seen in any hemisphere—apart from the one in my bed—is smiling at me in an expert selfie, a little camera icon asking if I want to accept the video call.

Um, *fuck yeah* I want to accept this call. Guess my good behavior is finally paying off.

"I, uh, I gotta take this. It's my...manager."

Sexy-Sa-Something waves a sleek tan limb at me, can't really tell whether it's an arm or leg. Don't stay to find out. I dart past the crooked mattress and leap over the shattered lamp, the bedsheet clutched in my fist around my hips and trailing behind me as I hit the hallway. The door barely swings shut behind me before I swipe my thumb across the phone screen. I didn't miss her, did I?

My pulse jumps triple the speed as the screen pixelates and then catches up, my eyes gorging on the blue sky and *Chiara Freaking Martes* beaming at me in a purple knit scarf with her layers of brown hair cascading around her face like she's in an Italian shampoo commercial.

*Goddamn*, she's so pretty. How did Massimo ever leave her for Lorelai?

"Well, hi." I drawl the words as smoothly as I can, country boy charm turned all the way up high. But my voice doesn't work right, and it comes out sounding a lot more like I'm speaking Klingon instead of English.

"Congratulations!" Chiara cheers. "Sixth place, Mason. That is fantastic!"

*Did she just—?*

I fall back against my hotel room door, naked under a see-through bedsheet and still half-hard from another woman's hand. But I'm so touched that for a second, I think I might cry.

Chiara called me to say congratulations? She knows what place I finished?

No one ever cares where I place—if they even remember that I race at all.

Then the wind blows where Chiara's at, catching a lock of hair across her nude lipstick, and there's no half about my hardness anymore. This bedsheet was a bad idea.

I know it for sure when a door opens across the hall, an older couple coming out of their room and stopping dead in their tracks at the sight of me. The husband flares red the more he absorbs my bare body, black Stetson, and white bedsheet. I scramble to bunch the sheet better over my erection while still holding the phone, but it's too late. He huffs out something in a different language that doesn't exactly sound approving, ushering his wife back into the hotel room and slamming the door. *Whoops.*

I look back to my phone screen to find Chiara quietly laughing like she must've heard that. "Yeah...I'm sorry to ask this, but can you hold on?" I wait until she nods, then I stick my phone between my teeth and address my situation.

This is so embarrassing. I've spent *years* drooling over Chiara Martes from afar in the Moto Grand Prix paddock, but she was always off-limits. Massimo "No Mercy" Vitolo has warned me to stay away from her before. Except I don't see why he gets a say— Chiara's best friend or not—so I don't really care to ask for his permission or for his blessing.

I'm not my righteous big brother, and I've never been known for making the best decisions. I'm known for making the *wrong* ones.

I finally get myself situated enough to look back at my phone and nearly get in trouble all over again. Chiara reaches up to tuck her chestnut hair behind her ear, another naughty lock daring to caress her cheek, and I love the wind, just, *so much.*

"Did I call at a bad time?" Chiara asks in her fancy Italian accent. She sounds so sincere that it melts me on the spot.

I swallow thickly to make sure my voice works right this time. "Nah, not at all. I'm real glad you called." At least now if I die on my Saturday bull ride, I'll get to take this with me to the grave. But I'm not planning on dying; I'm planning on *winning.*

All that grace of hers slips into a mischievous smirk, and when she looks pointedly toward my bare chest, a blush darkens her high cheekbones that could satisfy my ego for the rest of my days. "Good. You raced so wonderful yesterday. So fast and so fearless. I thought Lorelai was going to hit you in that turn or push you out, but nope!" Chiara's whole gorgeous face lights up, the sharp angles of her jaw tilting up with triumph. "You were never afraid."

"I uh…" I was scared shitless, truthfully. "Thank you, for saying that."

"Of course."

Chiara takes a sexy sip from her espresso cup, tilting her head at me when she's done and waiting since it's my turn to say something. Except I still can't believe she's on my phone right now! Luckily, she takes care of moving along our stalled conversation.

"I would like to see you."

Yeah, she really takes care of it all right. Blood pumps heavily from my chest to my lap, growing thicker as she bites her bottom lip.

"Before you leave Europe to go home to America."

Italy isn't exactly on my way home to Memphis from racing in Spain—not that I really care. "That right?"

"Yes," she says, no bashfulness or beating around the bush about it. "Lorelai says you are nice, and you are a very successful racer, so someone at Dabria must think you are trustworthy. And you asked for me to call you, so here I am." She shrugs with a bright smile, and I'm *sunk*.

She's hot as fuck, and I seriously did not expect her to be this sweet. Especially to me. She doesn't even know me, and I didn't know a woman as pretty as her could *be* this sweet. I mean, the country girls I grew up around are almost always pretty, but they're also usually kinda mean. I think it's because all their fathers are assholes.

"I think we should have a date," she says. "I will cook. You can come to my apartment in Ravenna. Unless that is a problem?"

"No problem." I mean it too. Come hell or high water, I'll be there.

"Perfect. I will text you the address." She blows me a kiss through the screen that's terribly cruel, and I'm absolutely gonna have to do something about this situation she's got me in before Frank or anyone finds me. "Congratulations again, Mason. Ciao!"

I smile like a lovesick dope. "Bye."

I wait until she disconnects the video call, struggling to keep my feet on this earth as I weigh out my options:

Be a good boy and go home to Memphis, win the rodeo like my father wants. *Or...*

Sneak off to Italy and go see Chiara.

Yeah, it isn't really a choice.

I turn toward my room, but my palm hasn't even hit the handle yet when the door next to me opens, my brother coming out into the hallway.

*Damn it*. He's just gonna *love* this.

I tighten my jaw, holding on to the last of my dignity. And my bedsheet.

"Oh-ho-ho-ho." Billy lets out a low chuckle, coming fully out into the hallway. All tall and perfect, perpetually sober, and freshly showered. There isn't a single wrinkle in his pearl-snap shirt or his pressed Wranglers, and I wonder if he was ironing them in his black Stetson, Ariat boots, and his underwear no more than two minutes ago.

"You sound like the Santa Claus from hell." My head starts to pound all over again under his abuse of Old Spice cologne.

He gleefully eyes my bare chest and bedsheet sarong with the blue eyes we share from our jerk father. Right before he takes a long-armed swipe at my hat.

I reach up out of instinct and almost drop my bedsheet in the process, my big brother cracking up laughing as I scramble to hang on to the last bits covering me. "Stop, dick! We're not twelve no more."

I barely get myself decent again before Taryn comes out of their room looking like an advertisement for How Ex-Beauty Queens Should Travel: a layered cardigan over a flowy tank top and yoga pants and her long blond hair tied up in a shiny ponytail. No one ever expects her to be such a damn shark on the Superbike circuit too. But Taryn is not to be trifled with.

Billy instantly takes the duffel bag hooked on her shoulder, threading it over his.

"Okay, we have to be at the—oh good Lord, Mason." Taryn waves her airplane tickets and passport at me like my nudity is contagious. "Really?"

"Hey, I did y'all a favor." I hook my thumb toward my hotel

room door. "This girl was trying to sleep with Billy, and I ran interference."

My brother's pale face loses what's left of its color. He whips toward Taryn. "Honey, I was with you the whole night—"

"Shut up. I know you were." Then she zeroes in on me. All her country girl meanness out in force. "You"—and it's a sharp as fuck *you*—"have got to stop doing that. We all know this isn't the first time this has happened, and I expect better of you, Mason."

Boom.

The shame sours my already flipping stomach, and I open my mouth to say something back to her. But I only catch my brother's palm across the back of my head. "Shut up. Don't talk to Taryn that way."

"I didn't say nothing!"

"Yeah, but I know how you think."

I take a step toward the finger he's pointing in my face and get a blast of cool air across my nether regions. "Shit!" I whirl to look at what happened, and the end of the damn sheet is caught in the door. The rest is all over the hallway floor, now lying around my ankles.

"Mason!" Taryn hisses, my brother groaning as I scramble to pick up the bedsheet and retie it around my waist.

"What?" I can't help it. I smirk at her and throw in a wink for good measure. "I told you when we all met that I was bigger."

Taryn puts a stilling hand on Billy's growling chest as our manager, Frank, comes half jogging down the hall, checking his watch. "Oh good, y'all are—Mason, what the hell?"

"Oh, don't worry, Frank." Taryn offers a spiteful snort. "He's been busy saving my and Billy's relationship."

Frank looks more confused than usual. Probably because Billy and Taryn have been obsessed with each other since the first time he saw her barrel race and she told his bull-riding ass to get lost. That was almost two years ago now—longest relationship I've ever had was three weeks in high school that turned out to be two and a half weeks too many.

"Well, save it on the plane," Frank says. "We gotta go."

"Aren't we waiting for Lorelai?" Taryn asks.

He shakes his head. "She and Massimo are staying in Valencia for a few days before going back to Italy. It's just us."

Well, isn't that going to be helpful? "I'm, um, I'm gonna catch the next flight." I try my best not to notice the reaction on Billy's face. Not that it's easy to ignore when someone's eyebrows shoot that high.

It's Taryn who says, all patronizing, "Mason, it's real nice that you met someone, but you can get laid at home. Now let's go."

"Goddammit, that isn't what's going on." Even though I'm kinda hoping it is. "I just...there's something I gotta go do, and I'll be home in a couple of days."

The three of them share concerned looks before Billy turns to me. "You've got a rodeo on Saturday. A big one. Everyone's gonna be pissed if you miss it. And we're already on thin ice with Blake after the Cornucopia Exhibition as it is."

Oh, he just had to bring that up?

*Never gonna get those eight seconds back, I swear.*

"I'm aware of that. I'm a grown man, same as you, and I know my schedule. That's why I'll be home by Friday." Flights depending. "I just need a minute."

Billy and Taryn look at each other for a long time. "Well," Taryn says, because based on their extended eye contact, they're having some sort of secret mental conversation. Since when did that start happening? Just because they bought that big-ass ranch they make me work with them every time we're home in Memphis... *Whatever.*

"Couple days." Billy sounds like he's already begging for mercy. "I know it's not—"

"Hold on just a frickin' minute here," I interrupt. "You're not invited."

Billy turns toward me, standing as tall as he can and puffing out his chest. Still ever the star pitcher and starting quarterback and champion tie-down roper. "You're not going alone, whatever you're about to do."

I scoff heartily with the full breadth of *my* chest. I'm still the only person in the world who can catch his fastball, and *I* was the one who ran in the winning touchdown when we won the State Championships. He also doesn't ride bulls anymore. Not officially anyway. He just ropes calves like that's the same or something.

Billy's hat tips lower.

Frank checks his watch again. "We don't have time for this shit, we're already late. Mason, you coming home or not?"

I gather up my bedsheet and stare up at my brother. "I'm not." Then I knock on my hotel room door. Because I forgot to grab the key before I came out into the hallway to talk to Chiara.

"Fine." Billy sneers, gesturing to the room. "If she's so important that you're gonna miss a rodeo for her, what's her name?"

"I told you, I'm not gonna miss the damn rodeo. And *her* name is Sandra."

The door swings open. All of us look at Sexy-Not-Sandra, who is thankfully dressed and glittering in green sequins. She shakes back her brown hair, staring straight at my brother. "Sabella." Then she jerks her pointy chin at me. "And he is Mason. The best bull rider in the state of Tennessee."

"Ha!" I point at my brother, nearly losing my bedsheet again before I remember to grab it while still hanging on to my phone.

Sabella giggles and holds open the door for me, her shoes in her hand and a small black clutch under her arm, bless her. I slide past her inside the room, happily taking the kiss she drops on my cheek before she slips out into the hallway, heading for the elevator.

What a lady she is. Gonna have to remember her, just in case I make it back to Spain. With the bull I'm supposed to ride on Saturday, that's kinda iffy.

"See ya at home, Brother," I call over my shoulder.

"Wait! I thought you and she were—"

I kick shut the door behind me.

When I finally free myself of the tangled bedsheet, I drop it onto the messy-as-fuck floor. Kiss my wonderful, wonderful phone and toss it onto the still-crooked mattress, not even caring when it slides off and thumps onto the carpet.

"Hell yeah!" I shout to the room, doing a couple naked fist pumps for good measure.

Chiara Martes called me. And off to Italy I will gladly go.

I dare anyone try and stop me.

# Chapter 2

I NEED BIGGER BOOTS.

That's all I'm capable of thinking as I stand here in the kitchen I probably shouldn't be in. In the country I'm not supposed to be in either. As far as anyone knows, the closest I've ever been to Ravenna, Italy, is when we're racing our motorcycles in Rimini. And technically, that was true. Till about twenty minutes ago.

"Mason," Chiara says, and my eyes nearly roll back into my skull at the twangy twist of my name under her Italian accent. Cannot get enough of that shit. "Do you think this is enough pasta?"

She peeks over her shoulder from in front of her stove, biting that delicious-looking bottom lip. She's impossibly even prettier in person than she is through a phone screen, wearing a strappy white dress showing off her creamy shoulders. I'm even further ruined by the thin necklace clasped closely around her long neck. I want to remove it with my teeth.

Chiara giggles at my silence, the sound summery and sweet despite the chilly November air, and it faintly registers in my soggy brain that she asked me a question. I should probably find an answer. But I can't remember what she asked; all I can do is smile. "Huh?"

"Come here, please." She waves toward herself as though her English isn't perfect, along with everything else about her. She's been the sweetest and most polite hostess *ever* since I got here twenty minutes ago, and it's totally throwing me off my game. I'm not used to being courted. The country girls back home in Memphis don't roll that way—at least none of the ones ever interested in me.

My boots thunk heavily on Chiara's wood floor, muffling on a geometric area rug before I stop beside her and have to look up a little to meet her eyes. My truck is on thirty-six-inch tires, and my best boots give me another four, but that still isn't enough for Chiara in high heels—all that long brown hair swinging gorgeously down her back, her legs going on for days, and the purple and blue flowers on her dress begging for their petals to be plucked.

I make the mistake of looking down, and she's wearing an anklet that matches her necklace. My jeans start to get a little tight in the front and *Christ, I've gotta get myself under control*. Think of baseball. Think of Mama. Think of Adam's hog giving birth—*ugh*.

"Is this enough pasta?" Chiara's eyes drop to the amount she has cradled in her hand, a patient smile on her lips.

My eyebrows pop so high, my black Stetson shifts back on my head. "You're asking me?"

She shrugs a single delicate shoulder. "Well...yes."

I look hard at the long, crunchy noodles. What's the right answer here? Agree? Act like I know something? All I can think is how much she smells like Thanksgiving: all cinnamon and nutmeg and everything warm I wanna snuggle inside for, like, forever. "Uh, yeah, I guess that's enough?"

My indecision seems to please her. "Good." She dumps it all into a pot of boiling water, then waves her hand over the words, "I can never decide and always make either too much or too little. Not that either is really a crime. After our cheese aperitivo and bruschetta, the pasta is only the first course. Then will be the salmon."

*Courses?* My head is spinning.

Never had a woman cook for me before. Other than Taryn when I'm crashing with Billy. Most women I date usually ask where I'm taking them to dinner, and they always mean the kinds of places that don't have decimal points on the menus. If I never have to pay for a lavender-flavored dessert again, it will be too soon.

"Anything I can do to help?" *Mama would be so proud.*

Chiara's already set the glass-top table for two with plates, cloth napkins, and silverware, and I feel like I'm in another dimension. Isn't it usually up to the man to do this stuff on a date? I am really failing here. And I'm usually good at dating. It's one of the things I do best.

"Yes." She smiles and grabs a spoon from a drawer, then stirs a sauce that's more orange than red and smells like nothing I've ever smelled before. "Tell me: what do you think of this?"

She holds out the steaming wooden spoon, and my mouth is watering for a dozen different things in front of me and none of them sauce. But a low moan instantly curls through my throat from the stinging heat and layer of flavors I hadn't been expecting.

"*Wow*. That's...really damn good," I get out with a chuckle. Chiara redips it and takes a taste herself. "What do you call that?"

"Vodka sauce."

*Figures.*

"It is more of an American dish than something Italians typically cook. We do not mix cream with our tomatoes. But Lorelai made it for me once, and I really like it. Also, I use grappa instead of vodka because it is stronger. That reminds me..."

Chiara smiles with a wink and disappears around me, returning with two stemless glasses with clear liquid in them that doesn't smell like water. *Oh thank God.*

She raises her glass to mine, clinking them together. "Salute."

"Salute." I probably say it wrong. Because Chiara smiles really big as she takes a drink from her glass like she's sipping on sweet tea, and mine hits my throat like a goddamn freight train.

"You like it?"

I nod, truthfully. "Feel like if I breathe too close to your stove, I'm gonna set the place on fire, but yeah, I like it." I am definitely gonna have to get me some of this before I go home. I just got notified of the bull I'm gonna ride on Saturday, and it's either gonna be really good or really *bad*. If I'm not celebrating like crazy come Sunday, maybe they can drink it at my funeral in my honor.

Chiara giggles. My jeans get a little tighter. "It is grappa morbida. My and Massimo's favorite."

My jeans get a little looser.

"Yeah, I bet," I offer by way of a polite response, then throw back the rest of the glass.

I've been racing against Massimo Vitolo for years, and he *would* like a drink that looks like water and kicks like a mule. He races that way, talks that way, and just *is* that way. Quiet till he's cruel. A threat you forget about until he passes you by and takes your flag. The kind of guy who's used to getting what he wants and being first and doesn't take kindly to sharing space.

But he's still screwing around in Spain with his girlfriend, Lorelai, for the next few days. So I don't think I need to feel guilty for standing in his apartment or having dinner with his roommate. His super freaking *hot* roommate. As long as Chiara isn't using me as a way to get back at him for breaking up with her...

*Damn it.*

With the full power of the grappa I just downed hitting my system, I stare her straight in the face. "Look, Chiara, I'm just gonna say this outright. 'Cause that's kinda what I do."

She cradles her glass in her hand, tilting it all relaxed against her chest with no sign of nerves in her eyes, even though my pulse is ticking up like a bomb's about to go off. But then again, I know me, and I know what I'm about to say. And *risk* by doing it.

"I know you and Massimo were together for a long time, and I know everyone says you're fine being broken up now and that you like Lorelai a whole lot. And maybe you do, and maybe you don't. But either way, I'm not Massimo. And I'm never gonna be."

Chiara watches me for a minute, then she takes a small sip of her grappa, a grin curling the corners of her lips. "Is that correct?"

"That is correct."

"Well then, who are you, Mason? What are you like? I would like to know." She winks afterward, and okay, at least she's not mad.

"Well...I'm honest. For the most part," I quickly amend, Chiara snickering a bit. "I don't pretend to know more than I do. But I know more than most people expect me to."

"Yes, I bet you do." Her full lips curve around the phrase in a way that's every definition of tempting, her honey eyes blazing and locked with mine. Doesn't help when she reaches over and softly squeezes my upper arm, and I can distinctly feel each and every stroke of her thumb through my shirt. I don't quite know how I got here. I definitely don't know what I did to deserve it—I'm the one drooling over *her*. "Anything else?"

"I drink whiskey, not vodka." I take a small step closer when I can't resist any longer. She's like a damn drug. "Don't mind a little smoke now and then."

"And how are you with women?" She tilts her head. "Soft? Slow? Or are you rough?"

*Oh, I like the way she says rough.* "You're really asking me how I make love?"

"Yes."

I nod, slowly, unable to resist a smile; I can't believe this woman is real. That we're actually having this conversation.

Chiara pulls in a breath as I dare to reach really closely around her waist, setting my empty glass on the counter behind her and checking whether she's okay with me touching her. I think she will be soon. And I like soon. It's a whole lot better than never.

"I make love like I'm dying," I answer her. "Because when I'm not racing motorcycles, I'm riding bulls. And to be honest, I'm kinda surprised I made it this far." Chiara smiles like my answer is exactly what she wanted to hear, and it takes all my flimsy integrity to add, "But I don't mess around with taken women, Chiara. And I don't like being used by them to make other men jealous."

She bites her lip, a flush in her cheeks painting her guilty. "I am not taken, Mason, and I am not trying to make anyone jealous. He and I were together, yes, but that was a long time ago, and we are just friends now. We will always be friends. But we did make an agreement that I would never date the other moto racers. It makes him uncomfortable—he says it's distracting to his racing."

No need to clarify who "he" is; we both already know.

"Well…" I drawl. "Who said anything about dating?"

Chiara laughs loud and clear, and my cheeks are almost starting to hurt from her making me smile so damn much. She's got a *great* laugh, the kind that makes it impossible not to laugh along with her.

"Nah, seriously though. That's important for me to know. It's not gonna stop me, since I think it's your call who you choose to spend your time with. But that's definitely something I should be aware of, and I appreciate you telling me."

She's smiling just as bright as she was before, her fingers starting to toy with the pearl-snap buttons on my shirt. Yep, we're definitely okay with touching.

"Does still make me wonder, though…"

"Wonder what?" she asks.

"Why'd you invite me here? If you knew he wasn't gonna like it?"

Chiara thinks on that for a second, then shrugs one creamy shoulder. "He may be my best friend, but it does not mean we have to agree on everything. He worries too much, always has. But I don't think any of his concerns should apply to *you*. He and Lorelai have known you for a long time—"

"They have," I agree.

"And Lorelai always says such wonderful things about you. How nice you are—and fun. What a good teammate you were to her. And she was the one who gave me your number, so if Lorelai thinks it's a good idea, I don't see why Massimo should worry about it. He trusts her. She trusts you. So I think we can make an exception, in your case."

Damn, I may have to buy Lori some flowers or something. I'm kinda touched.

"I mean, I can't really disagree with any of that. It's just…" God, I'm totally gonna blow this date. "As long as you and I are clear that I'm not the 'long-term' kind of guy. So I don't want to cause any problems for you, seeing as…"

Chiara beams at me. "It's not going anywhere? Don't worry, Mason. I'm counting on it. I'm not looking for anything serious. Just a little fun with someone who isn't going to ask for autographs from my friends. And you seem like the perfect guy for that."

I try to control my nervous chuckle. "Well, I don't know about the perfect part, but the rest is pretty much me." I definitely won't be asking for Massimo's autograph anytime *ever*.

Chiara scoots a little closer. "And I take it you've never been in love?"

"No, ma'am. I've never been with a woman long enough for that."

I don't know what about that convinces her to slide her palm slowly up my chest, over my shoulder, and around to the back of my neck, but I'll take it.

"Good," she says, and good is right.

*Don't choke the throttle, don't choke the throttle…*

"You can, uh, you can kiss me just as soon as you're ready."

*Damn it, I choked it.*

Chiara cracks up laughing, but I meant what I said—I feel like I'm gonna fucking burst if I don't taste those red lips soon. "Oh, I like you, Mason. You are honest."

"I really try to be." Speaking of… "Chiara?"

"Yes," she whispers, her eyes locked on my lips and her fingers doing delicious things to the nape of my neck. *God*, she's so pretty.

"I'm not that hungry."

"Me either."

Her hand on my neck goes flat and pulls me toward her, and she don't gotta ask me twice. I capture those delicious red lips with mine, instantly moaning at how soft and full and round they are. Curl my arm around her flower-petaled waist to pull her tighter against me, loving every bit of pressure her body grants against my hateful zipper.

She's somehow even softer than she looks: all graceful hips and supple breasts, swells of curves in all the best places. Her tongue steals its way into my mouth, stroking sinfully against mine, and my envious dick is quick to swell in my jeans. I'm definitely down for all things dirty—I may have bombed the first half of this date, but this is the part where I never fail to impress.

I reach up to take her glass from her hand, setting it on the counter behind her as my lips trail to her silky cheek. Chiara grasps at my shoulders as I nudge my knee between hers, listening to her whimper in pleasure as I nibble and tease her neck. It only takes me a second to find the zipper on the back of her dress and get it all the long way down.

She giggles at the sound, squirming a bit. But only so her thigh can better hitch itself up on the outside of mine, her hands still tangled in my hair and my hat long gone. I guess on the floor behind me. "You are fast, Mason King."

"Well, yeah," I mutter into the skin over her bare shoulder. The thin strap that was there is now caught in my fingertips, my lips tracing the line where it was in my way just a second ago. "That's kinda how I win all them motorcycle races."

Chiara laughs again, goose bumps rising on her skin as I blow a cool stream of air over the spot where I've been kissing. I wonder where else she's getting goose bumps.

I leave a last hungry kiss on her shoulder before I lean back to see her eyes, soaking up how flushed and breathless she looks. She's also totally cool with me tickling my fingertips under the hem of her skirt and up the outside of her thigh.

Yeah, she gets them there too.

"I get my orgasm first," she says with a smile, pointing a manicured finger at herself. Her nail polish matches her lipstick, and I fucking *love* it.

"Yes, ma'am," I agree. "Absolutely, no question."

"Fantastic."

I snort as she digs her red nails in the front of my shirt and tugs my lips back to hers, Chiara making easy work of my pearl-snap buttons and moaning her way through stroking her palms down my bare chest and over my hips. I've never been more thankful for every stupid workout circuit I've ever done than I am right now.

The second my shirt hits the floor, I tug carefully at the straps of her dress, peeling it down her chest to reveal a black-and-tan bustier presenting me with soft mounds of flesh. "God*damn*, girl." A soft moan escapes my lips as I duck my head to her breasts, tonguing out a dusky nipple from behind the sweetheart boning and sucking until it's hard for me.

Chiara gasps and captures my jaw in her hands, pulling my mouth back to hers and kissing me furiously. I fist my hand in her dark hair, kissing her even harder until her head is tilted back and her throat is at the mercy of my palm, and *God, how is this even happening?*

Feels like I've been dreaming about this moment ever since I saw her at that sponsor party in that blue backless dress.

I boost her up onto the counter, Chiara laughing as I turn off the burners under the boiling water and sauce, then duck under the hem of her skirt. I happily take control of her thigh and hook it over my shoulder. *Holy fuck, she's not wearing panties!* I growl hungrily and kiss my way up her inner thigh, right over the thin script that reads *Wild One*, and she isn't laughing anymore.

"God, Mason, yes," she pants, opening herself up to me, and I swear, just hearing her say my name that way is gonna satisfy my ego for the rest of my days. She's so much better in real life than any fantasy my feeble brain ever came up with. So much *nicer*.

Chiara shifts toward me as my kisses sneak toward the Promised Land between her silky thighs, my dick screaming in my jeans out of pure spite, and I'm seconds away from being in carnal heaven with Chiara Freaking Martes when I hear a woman laugh loudly in the hallway outside the apartment. A woman I've known for years and who should be in *Spain*. Not Italy.

Worse: she isn't gonna be alone.

Chiara's body goes rigid beneath me like she must have heard it too, and sure as shit, a deep male voice rumbles something I can't make out on the other side of the door a second later.

*Uh-oh.* If Massimo finds me like this, it won't be a bull that kills me, that's for damn sure. A bull won't get the chance.

I extract myself from Chiara's skirt and drop her hiked leg faster than I can get my 4x4 into gear. But Chiara doesn't just look frustrated at being interrupted—she's ghostly pale and already down from the counter, scrambling all panicked to scoop up my hat and shirt from the floor and shoving both at my chest. "Go to my bedroom!" She reaches back to zip up her dress after tucking back in the nipple I tongued out.

"Seriously? You want me to *hide*? I thought you said Lori—"

"Lorelai is one thing, but him finding us like this is another. Please, Mason!"

With the urgency in her eyes, I don't dare argue further—I bolt around the corner from the kitchen into the rest of the apartment. Three shut doors are my options. Which one is her bedroom?

The fateful turn of the lock on the front door gets my ass into a higher gear, and I dart for the room on the left, praying it's the right one.

*How the fuck am I gonna get outta here without him finding me?*

"Massimo! Lorelai! You're home!" Chiara calls out, and I wince to myself as I do my absolute very best to close the door as quietly as possible. Not the first time I've had to hide in a woman's bedroom, but I haven't done it since high school and I'm a little rusty. Closet still best? I don't know if I can still fit under a bed. My dick definitely can't right now.

It takes my eyes a second to adjust in the dark, but I turn toward the room revealing a whole bunch of *no* places to hide. Unless I squeeze between the gaming chair and under the desk covered with a computer monitor and some really nice streaming cameras. Huh.

Doesn't look to be a closet in here, just an armoire with frosted doors. Not much room for anything else: there's an overstuffed accent chair that looks really comfy, a nightstand littered with a lamp and pictures and charger cords, and a bed that's been freshly made. Doesn't even have that many throw pillows. *Shit... Is this even Chiara's room?*

I thread my arms through the sleeves of my shirt as I creep over to the nightstand and pull open the top drawer, peering inside. Instantly, I spot a hairbrush with rubber bands twisted on the handle, and something that looks like it takes DD batteries and could get you in trouble in an airport if you're not careful. I let out a sigh of relief and shut the drawer. Then I take another look at the room that's bad-freaking-ass and smile real damn wide. Until I hear Lorelai exclaim from the living room, "We're engaged!"

My stomach drops all the way to the bottom of my boots, and I freeze in the middle of Chiara's dark bedroom. This just went from bad to *way fucking worse.*

# Chapter 3

*Chiara Martes—November*

Could my luck get any worse?

My body is still a panting mess from the rush of the last five minutes, and I am, like, 98 percent sure I didn't get my nipple all the way back into my lingerie. (Based on Mason's face, it was totally worth the outrageous amount I paid for it.) At least I somehow got my dress rezipped before the front door swung open. But my heart is still pounding so loud in my chest that even though Lorelai basically screamed it at me, I'm not quite sure I heard right:

*We're engaged.*

She flashes a teardrop diamond ring at me from the doorframe, Massimo pressing a kiss to her curly hair, and I actually *feel* my slack jaw fall open another inch. And it's not that I wasn't halfway expecting this after the last six months of them being together, but I just...

I never thought he would propose to her without talking to me about it first.

We're supposed to be best friends—inseparable since we were six, roommates for most of our lives, and we tell each other *everything*. We always have. Until now, I guess.

I look to Lorelai's smiling face and hurry to find a smile for my own. "That is so—Congratulations!" I cheer as happily as I can, and I try to mean it. For all our sakes.

At least I actually like Lorelai. A lot. (No one believes me, but I do.) She's fast and fierce, and she doesn't take his shit. She's perfect for him, and she deserves to have her fairy tale. They *both* do. And *I* deserve to get astronomically laid for being a really freaking good friend. Preferably by someone who actually knows what the hell he's doing and who burns bright enough to help pull me from the gaping black hole swallowing up my life.

The infamous playboy of the paddock, personally recommended by Lorelai herself, seemed too good to pass up. Joke's on me, I guess.

I rush over to kiss her cheeks and hug her, and when she squeals and wraps her arms around me, squeezing tight and the air around her lemon and sweet, it's impossible not to feel the pure joy radiating from her. The tremors of hope and goose bumps of excitement, the bright open future of possibilities for the life ahead of them.

*I'm just not sure where I fit into it anymore.*

"We couldn't wait to get back and tell you." Lorelai squeezes me again, then leans back, her tiny hands strong on my arms and her brown eyes huge as she looks up at me. "And I could really use your help, from top to freaking bottom."

"Lorina, she is probably busy," Massimo mutters, but she just keeps going.

"I can shop for clothes and stuff like no one's business, sure, but you're so much better at decorating and party planning and organizing all that kinda stuff than I am. And you know both of us so well, and I'm gonna be totally slammed with all the extra testing for MMW I have coming up... Please, Chiara? I can't imagine trusting anyone else with something this important. Please say you'll be our wedding planner?"

"Oh my goodness!" I exclaim on autopilot. "Of course I will."

*Why* did I just say that? What is the matter with me?

"Oh, thank God!" She hugs me again, so much relief in the tight squeeze of her arms that I start to feel a little bad about not wanting to do it. "Wait a minute." She leans back and looks me over. "Why are you all dressed up? And what are you cooking that smells so good?"

Nervous tingles start fluttering from my shoulders to my fingertips, and I pull my hair over my shoulder and start finger combing out some of the tangles. If there is a God, Mason will be in my bedroom and not Massimo's. "I, um..."

It doesn't take Lorelai any more time to put it together; as the world's fastest woman on a motorcycle, she pretty much lives her whole life at two hundred miles per hour. "Oh no! I'm so sorry!" She turns toward Massimo, dropping her voice to a harsh whisper. "I told you we should've called to warn her we were coming home early. She's on a *date* right now."

"I did call her," he says at his normal volume in Italian. "When you were using the bathroom at the train station. She didn't answer her phone."

Um, yeah, because I was trying to get laid.

"My phone is off," I confirm to Lorelai in English before they start fighting about it.

"I thought you were twitching again," Massimo mutters in Italian, adjusting his bag on his shoulder. "Or whatever you call that gaming thing you do."

Does he mean streaming? I cross my arms, my irritation with him starting to brew even steeper. Not only did he *not* tell me he was proposing, but he really doesn't know what it's called? I have to juggle all his social media, his website, his finances, placate his mom and comfort his little brother and deal with everything here, and he can't spend five minutes to learn the—

"And we're really sorry that we interrupted your date," Lorelai adds with emphasis, nudging him with her elbow.

"Yes, I am really sorry." He shuts the front door they left open. He engages the lock, probably out of habit. Then he unlocks it. "So where is he anyway? Stuff him in the kitchen cupboard?"

Lorelai laughs, glancing around the apartment as though she's searching for clues. Then she spots one, pointing at the red Dabria duffel bag on the floor. Perfectly matching the one she's carrying. "Mason," she calls out like we're playing a game, "you can stop hiding now."

I wince. He is *never* going to call me again after this.

Something sharp ripples through Massimo's shoulders, and I ignore it. Pointedly. He's getting *married* to another racer, so why can't I date one? And Lorelai didn't seem to see it as a problem—she knows how Massimo feels about this, and even so, she was all too happy to pass on Mason's phone number. Along with a firm warning not to let his reputation scare me—that yes, he's a bit of a lothario, but at home in Memphis, he's a certified nerd. And that is 100 percent my catnip. Tell me he's a genuine cowboy on top of it, all belts and buckles, riding bulls and two-stepping the night away? Yes, I will take his number, please. And he wants me to call him when?

"I wasn't hiding," Mason drawls a moment later, his cowboy boots landing heavily on my wood floor and coming up behind me. I sink into the sound—how firm he walks, not at all hesitant. Men always tiptoe around Massimo. "I was grabbing a hair tie for Chiara."

He stops beside me and hands me a ponytail holder with a blue-eyed wink, his shirt rebuttoned and tucked neatly into his jeans behind his cowboy belt buckle. No evidence of my practically tearing his shirt off him less than five minutes ago. Not exactly my fault—he's a lot better kisser than I expected him to be.

*Don't think about his abs, don't think about his abs...*

*Or other large, thick, and very defined muscular things...*

Mason turns to Massimo and Lorelai, extending his hand. "I hear congratulations are in order."

Massimo looks directly at me, indignation blaring from his eyes as he shakes Mason's hand. He lets it go almost too fast to be polite. Lorelai practically jumps onto Mason in an attack hug.

He laughs and swings her around, Massimo grunting and walking off toward his bedroom. But warmth surges through me—they seem so comfortable with each other. Especially when Lorelai doesn't like that many people. And she really doesn't like to be touched. But they spent the last year as moto teammates after all. And from Lorelai's stories about growing up in Memphis, it sounds as if they knew each other long before that. Maybe even as kids.

Mason sets Lorelai down, both of them beaming with happiness. "I'm so excited for you, Lori," he says in his thick southern accent, taking a final fist bump from her. "Truly."

"Thanks, Mason. And...if you could wait to tell Billy and Taryn—"

"Oh yeah, that's no problem." He winks at me. "I was never here."

I toss my hair disappointedly—meaning he's never going to come back. Great. Why does everyone get to have sex in this apartment but me?

Lorelai squeezes his arm. "Thanks. And I'll, uh, get out of y'all's way." She beams at me, taking the same path Massimo went.

Mason clears his throat, scrubbing at the back of his neck as somewhere behind us, a door softly closes. I hug my arms over myself. "Um…" I have no idea what to say to him—how to explain my reaction earlier or to begin to apologize for Massimo's reaction now. I'm also very aware of the fact that *Mason's* aware that I'm not wearing underwear.

"I should, uh, probably get going."

*Thanks a lot, Massimo. Again.*

Mason grabs his duffel bag, hooking it over his shoulder and heading for the front door before I can find another option to present him. I do have the good sense to follow him out into the corridor, though.

"Mason, I am so sorry about this." As soon as I close the front door behind me, I instantly regret my wardrobe choices—*God*, it's so freaking cold! At least we're alone out here. As long as my neighbor doesn't come out and start getting involved. "They were supposed to be in Spain for another two days at least—"

"Oh, it's no problem." He gestures vaguely to the door. "These things happen."

He's being so sweet about the whole mess, and it makes me melt even more. Not that he'd ever know based on my inability to stop shivering. Stupid wind. "Where will you go?"

"I'll just grab a hotel somewhere. I was already planning on it."

It brings a blush straight to my cheeks. "Mason, when a woman invites a man to come to Italy for dinner on his way home to America, it is more than a little implied that she is inviting him to stay the night with her. And we both knew that."

Mason grins at the ground. "I like that you said that." The corner of his black hat lifts just enough so I can see his blue eyes sparkling with mirth. "You just…said it."

"Well, yes. I am also honest. For the most part."

Mason smiles so wide that he has to bite his bottom lip to stop it from growing wider, and he's so damn cute. I can't resist taking a step closer to him, breathing in his sleek cologne. I wonder how much he'd jump out of his skin if I started messing with his belt buckle. Most men say they like forward women, until the woman actually starts being forward.

"I hate that you are leaving already…"

He jumps a little, but not as much as I expected. He doesn't stop me either—just checks to make sure we're still alone in the corridor, a smile tugging at his lips and sending adrenaline rocketing through my veins. "I hate it too. I enjoyed being here."

I stretch my fingers dangerously down the length of his zipper, loving every place it's thick and straining instantly hard against my hand. A low moan rumbles from Mason's throat, his wide palm settling on my lower back and tugging my hips against his. He tilts his head like he's going to kiss me, but all I get is the whisper of his lips against mine, his erection trapped under my hand between us.

Mason may not be taller than me, but he's broader. Absolutely stronger. I bet he could *ruin* me without even trying, and I want him to *try*.

"You're kinda making it impossible for me to go, Chiara." His voice is low and gravelly and rough, and I *love* it—crave it hoarse from calling my name and moaning over my body.

"Then stay."

I steal a soft kiss from his lips that's every definition of luscious, my other fingertips light on his square jaw and hungry for the steel of his shaft. Mason groans as he rests his cheek against mine, nuzzling my ear and neck. Then he curses under his breath and lets me go, stepping back from me. "I can't."

I'm freezing again at the sudden loss of him, and I instinctively hug my arms around myself, back to shivering on my own. What did I do this time?

Mason clears his throat, looking and gesturing at the floor between us. "Look, I like you a lot, Chiara, but it isn't right that I stay here. Not now."

"It is not ideal," I admit. "But I promise to be quiet if you do."

He doesn't play along.

"No, it isn't just that." He looks at me closely, *too* closely, and never blinks once when he says, "I'm sorry. About Massimo and Lorelai."

My head jerks back. "What do you mean?"

"Their getting engaged."

I swallow, a hollow pain throbbing deeply through me. I should be used to it by now—the distance growing between me and Massimo. Best friends or not, I've spent my entire life slowly losing him to the circuit, his fans, the world. But the fact that he's moved on with Lorelai to the point that he would get engaged without telling me... It hurts more than I knew was possible.

Still, I bat away Mason's words, smiling as though everything is fine. (It has to be fine.) "I am very happy for them."

"Yeah... Maybe you are, and maybe you aren't. Either way, I'm sorry."

I toss my hair, trying to let the icy air calm my mood, because I'm not about to get in an argument with him about this. That is *not* how you get a man into bed. "Well, I am sorry that you are leaving. Especially without having eaten any dinner."

Mason gives me half a smile. "It smelled real good. And I appreciate all the trouble you went to."

"It was no trouble," I mutter.

I'm doing a terrible job of hiding how disappointed I am. But I am disappointed. I was really looking forward to tonight. And tomorrow morning. I had *plans*. Multiorgasmic *plans*.

Mason touches his hat. "See you later, Chiara." Then he turns and heads down the corridor and disappears down the stairs, and that's it.

No kiss on the cheek or anything. He's just gone. Like all the others.

So much for Move On Attempt #6.

# Chapter 4

*Chiara Martes—November*

I'VE BEEN STARING AT MY BEDROOM CEILING IN THE DARK FOR over an hour, still terribly unsatisfied after taking out an entire squad in *Black Ops* and then spending some quality time with my favorite vibrator. Twice. Would've been once, but I turned my phone back on and texted Mason to make sure he found a place to stay. As an answer, I got a selfie of him shirtless in a comfy-looking bed—the pillows behind him extra plush so he must be in a hotel. Probably a nice one.

Hence the second round of masturbation.

*Why didn't he invite me to his hotel room? I would've gone over there...*

I groan and turn over in my bed for the millionth time: disastrously single. With sleep definitely out of the picture, I return to weeding through Massimo's social media notifications clogging up my phone. Yawn, groan, and "like" the responses from the other Moto Grand Prix riders and the official team accounts. All while ignoring the endless comments of "ride me, daddy" and "dump that wreckless whore."

*Do they really think that's going to work?*

It takes me nearly twenty minutes to report all the nudes and block most of the spam, but I give up when the barrage of sexual invitations to my best friend gets dirtier and dirtier and the insults to his girlfriend get worse and worse. It's exactly why I've been managing Massimo's social media accounts—and nearly everything else—since the day he needed it.

He'd never be able to resist responding to all that. The man is way too emotional and registers at a solid eleven on the protective scale. But I don't mind helping: I live on the internet, and he's my oldest friend. My first *everything*. The boy who saved me and the man I was happy to support as he risked everything for us. He just… happened to fall in love with *her*.

He's always been in love with her, and I knew that. (I did.) I've known it for ten years, since the first time he met her, raced her, lost to her, and came home and told me all about her. And with them being together now, he's still *my* best friend.

The guy who calls me every day to talk about everything and nothing. Who works on the bathroom pipes in the apartment we've been sharing ever since we moved out of his mom's house. And it's important to me, really important, that he's happier now. Smiling again. But something else has changed in the last few months, and it's not just his mood.

He's relying on me less and less. Booking his own flights and trains and hotel rooms, and it shouldn't mean anything. But it means *every-thing* when there's this *space* growing between us, and it's tearing me apart. Because there's not a goddamn thing I can do to stop it.

I lock my phone and set it on my nightstand, frustrated as all hell that I allowed myself to believe that nothing would ever change. I should have known better. I always knew I was in the way. Always. I just have no idea how to cope with losing my partner in crime, my soul mate, my best friend. He makes moving on look so easy, and I just can't figure out how to do it. If I'll ever find someone to replace his role in my life, to become for me what Lorelai is to him.

He's the only family I have left.

There's a light tapping on my wall, the one shared with the kitchen tile, and I groan again. But I don't hesitate to throw back the covers and get up. I do glance at my pants and wonder if I should bother. Never used to.

Whatever. My shirt is long enough to cover my panties. And I'm wearing bikinis, not a thong, so my ass is covered. Not like it really matters when he's more than seen it before but…

*Ugh*. I have no idea what the rules are anymore. Not that we've ever been all that good with boundaries.

The apartment is dark and nearly silent when I head out of my room, tying my hair up into a messy knot. I follow the sound of someone puttering around in the kitchen, not surprised to find Massimo at the stove in his boxer briefs. A golden swell of light from above the oven is hitting his abs and shining on his hands, currently using tongs to carefully remove a small glass jar from a steaming baking dish.

I nearly sink to the floor. Budino al cioccolato.

"Hey," Massimo says softly in Italian, looking over at me.

"Hey."

He reads my oversized T-shirt and snorts at the pun, then goes back to what he's doing. I head automatically to the silverware drawer to grab two spoons. A stack of bowls and the whisk he used to silently hand beat the eggs, cream, and chocolate together are piled in the sink, but he'll do them in the morning. He always does when he does this.

The part that stings is he usually only pulls out the cheer-up-Chiara-with-midnight-chocolate-pudding trick when I'm sick or if I just got dumped. Possibly fired. Very occasionally when he does something that he knows is going to piss me off. I never thought he'd have to make it for me because he's engaged. I wonder if he did.

Massimo crosses behind me and heads toward the refrigerator, and I glance at the steaming bain-marie. The recipe easily makes a large batch, but he only baked one serving, and a really terrible little smile sneaks onto the corners of my lips.

It helps a little, a lot, too much, that this is still just *ours*.

He closes the refrigerator, and I head to the table, setting the steaming budino on a coaster and taking my normal spot. Massimo is standing next to me in a moment, taking one of my spoons and scooping out a small white dollop from a mixing bowl. He holds it out to me, and my eyes roll back when I taste it.

"You made banana meringue too?" My mouth is already watering for more. It's so light and perfectly balanced, even though he prefers the flavor to be stronger.

"Hmm."

Now I feel guilty. He's pulling out the big guns.

He drops a giant dollop on top of the chocolate budino, then carries the rest back to the refrigerator before he sits across from me. Massimo waits for me to take the first bite, as always, failing to hide a hopeful smile behind the spoon he tilts against his lips.

"Oh my God," I can't help but mutter in admiration, my spoon dipping through banana peaks and fluffy, hand-whipped chocolate. It melts thick and rich on my tongue, and I'm in *heaven*.

Massimo moans deeply all through his bite, slowly pulling the spoon from his lips before he points it at the budino. "I am amazing."

I can't help but laugh, even though I try to keep my voice down. I don't want to wake Lorelai—I'm having too much fun fighting off Massimo's spoon for my next bite. "Stop! You're hogging it all."

"I didn't make this for you," he whispers back with a wink.

I curl my legs under me and settle comfortably in my seat, letting him have the next few bites. "You're so selfish. But then again, you've always been."

He shakes his head, mumbling, "I am selfish." And with the way he says it and swallows afterward... Something hot and indescribably angry flares in my chest.

I take another bite of meringue in an effort to sooth it. "Will you and Lorelai live here? After you're married?" His eyes flash up to mine, and it's not fair that he gets to look this hurt when I'm the one who had to ask. "Or will you move back in with your mom?"

*Please say yes.*

*Please say no.*

It's always been my job to be his gravity—to keep Massimo anchored to real life away from the lights and the cameras, the fans and the groupies. It was easier when we were broke, completely buried under his late father's debts, and we couldn't afford to take lavish vacations, splurge on fancy clothes, or any of that stuff. But with Massimo's full salary finally at his disposal and with Lorelai now in the picture...it's getting harder.

He shakes his head. "Lorina needs her own space. There's, um, there's a house we're going to look at in a couple of days."

I blink, stunned. He's buying her a house? A whole freaking house?

Massimo looks up at me, and my heart seizes in my chest at how heartbroken he looks. I don't understand until he adds, "It's...an hour from here, Chiara."

I nearly drop the spoon.

I want him out now. I want to seal the doors. I want to run to his room and shake Lorelai awake and demand to know why she's taking my whole life away from me.

And this is how he's telling me that he's moving out? Over *budino*?

With a thick swallow, I reach over and scoop another bite of chocolate onto my spoon. That is shaking. Really shaking. Because I already know, this is probably the last time we'll ever sit together like this. At midnight, all alone. Just warm chocolate between us and our whispered secrets. "What does your mom say?"

Massimo groans, his next bite bigger than his last. I let my evil smile show this time.

Maria Vitolo has hated me since I was eight and told her I wanted to be an explorer when I grew up. She still took me in when I needed and let me live in her house, be a part of their family, but we never really got along more than that. Mostly because her biggest fear is that someone will take her precious son away from her, and I was the ultimate threat until someone worse came along: a curly-haired American woman from Memphis, Tennessee.

"She's fine now that she knows we're staying in Italy."

*I bet she is.*

He taps his spoon against the edge of the budino glass, then abandons it. "I wasn't trying to keep anything from you, by the way."

I can barely swallow. "Okay."

"I almost called you so many times. It was just...there was so much going on, and then she said no—"

"She said *no*?"

He nods, a shadow of pain flitting across his features. "Yeah. But then she asked *me*, and we were already coming home, so..."

"Hey, it's fine." I force a quiet chuckle. "That's really romantic, by the way."

He rolls his eyes. "Stressful."

"*Ha.* Wait till we start planning your wedding, star."

Massimo tries to hide a wince by scrubbing a hand back through his hair.

I take a bite of budino, watching him closely. "You may as well just say whatever it is you're thinking. You know I'll get it out of you eventually." Seriously, he can't keep a secret from me for anything. Learned that when I was seven and he broke my favorite lunch box.

"You don't have to plan the wedding, Chiara."

I gape at him like I'm offended, but he doesn't flinch, his eyes still piercing mine.

"You have your own life, your own stuff to do, and I know that. Lorina just...she knows how important you are to me, and she wants to involve you. But you don't have to do this. Or anything, if you don't want. It's...it's whatever you want to do."

I tug uncomfortably at the end of my T-shirt, kind of wishing I had opted for pants. "It's fine." I crack a teasing smile. "I'm used to managing your life by now. Might as well organize your wedding too. Someone has to keep up the standards."

He leans forward on the table, resting his cheek to his fist. He stays there for a long time before he speaks. "I don't deserve you."

I reach over and take a small bite of banana meringue, grinning as I eat it defiantly. "You never have."

He sits up and takes my free hand in both of his: his grip strong but not controlling and always warm. "I would have nothing without you. You know I know that, right?"

I'd have nothing without him either. Probably wouldn't even be alive. "Hey, you're the one on the moto, not me."

"But I never would have made it there without you."

I laugh to break the tension. This asshole may make me cry if I don't. "Oh, now you admit it?"

Massimo smiles, and that's the cruelest thing he could ever do. He's so beautiful when he smiles. "It's your turn, Chiara, and everything you want, I want for you. To meet someone, fall in love, the whole thing."

I'd feel a lot better about him saying that if I didn't know him so damn well. "But…"

"But not with Mason King."

I pull my hand away from his, sitting back in my chair with a scoff. "Right. Because you want me to be happy with anyone except the one person I actually like. Just because he happens to race moto."

Massimo scowls as I get up, collecting our spoons and the budino, then carrying them over to the sink. I throw everything in with more force than is strictly quiet.

"I may not have a perfect track record here," he admits. "And maybe if he didn't race, then that would be fair. But you and I agreed: I didn't date your friends, and you promised not to mess around with the other racers. So what happened to that? The rules suddenly change, and no one told me?"

I whip around. "You changed them. You are getting *married* to another racer. Why is that perfectly fine for you and not for me?"

"Because it's *distracting*, Chiara. I'm going 335 kilometers per hour out there, and now I have to think in every curve, every battle, about how the guy I'm diving for is someone you care about. You know how hard that was to deal with when I was racing against Lorina. You're really going to put me through that again? Having to choose? And before you even bring it up," he warns, "I know she gave you his number. But you didn't have to use it."

I look a little closer at his face, and it all becomes so much clearer. "This isn't even about the racing part, is it? This is about *him*."

Massimo groans, sitting back in his chair. "It's both."

"Both?"

"Yes, both," he says. "I know him, Chiara. I know him very well, and he's not the right guy for you. You deserve someone who will be here, every day, every night. Who cares about the things you care about and who will put you first. And not only is he never going to be around because of moto, but he's…"

"He's what?"

"He's too unpredictable. He's dangerous."

I scoff—what a hypocrite! "Excuse me," I say, gesturing to his bedroom.

"This is different," Massimo says. "Her risks are calculated. Mason doesn't listen to the officials. Doesn't pay attention in the riders' meetings. He pals around with that asshole Santos Saucedo, and with him constantly reeking of whiskey, I am *this close* to proving he's got a drinking problem. You really want to go down that road again?"

I stare at Massimo, amazed he would go that far. Not only is it way below the belt to bring that up, but an accusation like that could ruin Mason's whole racing career.

"Wow," I deadpan. "Does Mason kick dogs and steal from old people too? What about kids—is he mean to little kids? Come on. Don't hold back."

Massimo flips me off. "I am not lying about this. And I'll tell you something else: he is with a different sponsor model every single night, Chiara. He's not going to give you what you want or anything close to what you deserve. He is only going to use you, and then he'll be gone."

My temper is blazing, and it takes everything I have to keep my voice steady. "You have got to stop doing this."

"Doing what?"

"The same thing that you always do." I have to take a breath when my voice wants to crack. "Who is good enough for me, huh? Who?"

He doesn't answer. Because in his eyes, the answer is no one. And that's all well and good when it comes from the fact that he loves me, and he wants to protect me and see me happy. But when no one is good enough, it leaves me right where I am. With *no one*.

"Exactly. I'm going to bed."

I push away from the counter with every intention of storming back to my room and slamming the door behind me. Let him explain it to her.

"Hey."

I whip around, hissing, "What?"

"Can we call a break here?" He's still sitting at our table in the dark, covered with tattoos and the same guilty pout he's been wearing since he was six and sneaking extra communion crackers from our priest. (He always gave them to me, always.) I also sat with him for every hour of ink that's on his body, usually feeding him pizza while they needled the color into his skin. Half the dates down his ribs are for me.

He taps his fingertips on the table, and the longer I look at him, the harder it is to stay mad. He needs a shave and a haircut, and he came home with a huge bag of laundry that I can nearly smell from here. But that's normal for the end of the circuit, when he's been racing in Asia for the past month straight before the last showdown in Spain.

Seems like I've spent most of my life waiting for the ends of Novembers. When he's finally home for more than a week, and we spend all of Christmas playing video games with his little brother, Dario, eating endless courses of delicious food made by his aunts in the kitchen at his mom's house while his cousins squabble in the living room.

I wonder if I'll still be invited—when he's married to her and no longer living with me.

"I don't want to fight," he says. "I've missed you."

"Yeah, I've missed you too." My voice is thick with the truth, and I hate it: that it's true, that he can hear it. Even worse, that Mason was right. I haven't been ready to stop missing Massimo.

I hope, one day, I will be. But I just don't know when that day will come when he keeps scaring off every guy who dares to come close to me.

And I keep letting him.

# Chapter 5

*Mason King—December*

"YOU'RE WRONG."

"I'm not wrong," Blake tells my brother. They're leaning against opposite walls, arms crossed toward each other, and ignoring me stuck right in the middle. I scoff from my seat on a bench, my knees bouncing with nerves as we all do our best to distract ourselves from what's coming. "He totally leaves the helmet on. It's part of his religion. You *don't* just take off your helmet as a Mandalorian because you want a little action. Trust me."

"Just because you wouldn't," Billy mutters. "You probably don't even take your damn boots off."

The other guys scoff and laugh as my brother and my best friend keep debating *Star Wars* dogma over me. Some of the best bull riders in the world are in this room, wrapping gloves while sitting on folding chairs, others standing, leaning against the white-painted brick walls. The whole place smells like sweaty cowboys and too much Icy Hot, and it reminds me so much of my high-school locker room before a big football game: all of us nervous, all of us waiting. And usually, everyone talking to Billy while forgetting I exist until it's time for me to score us a win.

"I bet it smells like old milk in there," someone with a Brazilian accent adds.

The guy next to him chuckles. "You know it."

They get back to chatting away about the economy back home in Brazil, while other guys start doing yoga on the floor like stretching is gonna matter when a two-ton bull stomps on your rib cage. If I listen real closely, I can hear the crowd in the stadium just down the tunnel.

Can't wait to get out there—they're my people, and they *love* me.

Everyone else pretends not to notice time ticking away until a gorgeous girl comes around the corner wearing tight jeans, a belly shirt, and a headset over her ponytail. "Mason King? They're ready for you."

"Yeah, he's on his way." Billy grabs my vest and pulls me up to standing before I get the chance to decide for myself. "Don't let him get in front of you." He speaks without meeting my eyes because he's too busy checking over my vest and tugging at my chaps again. Everything is tied and tight, ready to go. Because after I did it the first time, he double-checked it. Twice.

"Yeah, because that's something I'd let happen on purpose."

He hands me my helmet, my glove on and my rope in hand. Then my brother's palm cups the back of my head and he pulls me in close, leaning his forehead to mine. No one else in here says nothing about it, because they're all gonna be praying come their turn too.

I take my hug from my brother and a nod of good luck from the rest of the guys. We all want to be the best, but no one wants to win because someone else got hurt.

*Time to ride.*

We turn and follow the girl down the tunnel toward the arena. Nothing I haven't done a hundred times before, but my heart's still beating the fuck out of my chest in the best possible way. I can already smell the dirt and the bull, and I can't even focus on the girl's ass, I'm so wound up with all I know is coming.

It's the same way I feel before a race, when my bike's rumbling beneath me and the track is glistening, my hand itching for the throttle. I'm already anxious to get back to the circuit and my stored bike. We don't start testing until February, and it's gonna be a long, slow, boring winter. It always is.

My brother checks behind us in the empty tunnel, then fusses with the button on the cuff of his shirtsleeve. He jerks his arm and passes me my flask, stepping in front of me in case the girl happens to turn around. I take a swig, then pass it back to him, neither of us saying nothing as he tucks it back into his shirtsleeve and buttons it closed in one smooth motion.

I blow out a breath. They don't make big brothers better than Billy. I should probably tell him that. He's always been a better brother to me than I've been to him. But I've really been working on that lately, trying to do a better job about staying out of his and Taryn's way.

It's sucked a lot, not having him across the hall and ready to ride shotgun to my latest bad idea. I just don't exactly know what I'm supposed to do during my downtime now. When I'm not thinking up something fun for us to do, now that there's no *us*. He still answers when I call him, and he's bailed me out of trouble once or twice when I needed. But it still makes me feel like Peter Pan when he lost his shadow.

Billy claps me on the shoulder, and he doesn't let go. "You got this, man. He's gonna blow straight outta that gate, I promise you. Just lock down, and wait for him to spin."

"Okay."

I'm feeling almost as tall as him as we come out of the tunnel and into the lights, when I finally see the crowd that's started calling my name. *Mine.* Not Billy's.

The arena is sold out, thousands of people standing and cheering, kids reaching from the railings because it's *my* autograph they want. And no matter how many times I get bucked, no matter how many concussions I've had, this is the part I can't quit the most.

The chance to be better, to be first. To be seen. To *matter*.

Taryn comes running over from where she's been waiting for us. She gives me a quick hug, but her arms are tight with stress. "Be so safe." She says it like coming back is my call. But rodeos are hard for Taryn, and she hates watching me ride bulls. It means a lot that she comes to watch me anyway, though. I probably should've told her that at some point too.

I don't remember ever wanting a sister, but I'm glad I'm getting Taryn as one. She's good at it.

I let Taryn go, and she immediately takes Billy's hand while hugging his arm like she can't get close enough to him. "See you in a minute," Billy has to shout at me over the noise. Then he smiles and claps my back, running off with Taryn toward where they'll be watching, along with everyone else.

"I tell you, Brad, that tunnel is one of the longest walks on earth," the announcer's voice booms through the stadium. "Let's give Mason King another round of applause. What do you say, folks?"

I look up at the rest of the rodeo arena, spotlights flashing and swirling, and when I start walking farther inside, smiling and waving, the roar of the crowd is like a chorus at my direction.

There are worse ways to die.

Problem is, there's a really good chance I'm about to die. And it's gonna hurt. It's gonna hurt *bad*.

"Hey, Jimmy," the announcer says, "I ever tell you that I had the pleasure of watching Mason get eight seconds on Smashbox last year?"

"I heard that was a hell of a ride. And, folks, if you turn your attention to the jumbotron, you can see exactly what Brad's talking about for yourself."

The crowd *oohs* and cheers as they replay last year's Cornucopia Exhibition, but I don't look at the screen. That isn't me up there.

I look instead over at the chute, at the bull that's bucking and pissed the hell off and reminds me so much of Smashbox that my stomach wants to flip. It's not Smash, though. Today, it's Raptor that's gonna try to gut me.

I hook on my helmet and walk toward my triumph...or my death. Maybe a couple broken bones, if I'm lucky. I don't count on anything less than that. I only pray that my suffering isn't long. Be it painkillers or a broken neck.

*Don't choke the throttle, don't choke the throttle...*

My fist tightens on the rope in my hand, the announcers still going on and on about my past bull rides and all the glory I've brought to my family and the place in history I've carved for myself. The crowd is getting settled in the stands, a hip-hop remix of a country song playing overhead as Raptor keeps kicking at the chute. But all I can hear is her laugh in my head.

The gate crew makes a path for me. My hands land on the steel gate, the cold metal shooting awareness into my body and my breath coming hard into my lungs.

I should've kissed her before I left. What was I thinking, just walking away like that?

"All right, folks," the announcers call. "He's getting ready. Any minute now!"

I climb the gate easily, swinging a leg over and looking at Raptor, brown and white and bucking because he wants to be the best. Don't we all. He arches and looks back at me, his eyes locking with mine and huffing under blunted horns.

Fuck this fucking bull.

"Get him, Mason!" The gate crew cheers me on, helping me as I climb onto Raptor's back before I think better about what I'm doing. The hands of three different guys press on my shoulders and chest with all their combined strength to steady me. But Raptor bucks and shakes them all loose, my stomach lurching with the roller-coaster movement as I hold on with all I got.

He settles fast with nowhere to go, and I clench my jaw and my nerves, tugging at the flank strap over my palm and digging in my heels. Everything in me is screaming that I'm never gonna see her again as the crowd roars me along, my buddies hovering over me as I hit at my fist, making it as tight as I can. It's all muscle memory at this point, and *eight seconds*.

That's all I gotta last to see her again. Eight short seconds.

———

Chris Stapleton's latest hit is blaring through the hot and sweaty air of the Round-Up, my brother and Taryn showing off in the middle of the dance floor, and my last shot of whiskey tipping me right into where I want to be on a Saturday night. I deserve it too—got a clean eight seconds on Raptor, brought home a brand-new buckle, and nothing worse than a sore back and headache. Exactly like I wanted.

"Hey, Mason," a woman walking past me says. She's standardly beautiful for a country girl, and named...Nancy? Natalie. Maybe November?

"Hey," I say back, giving her half a smile and tipping my hat at her.

She smiles and keeps walking with her friend, and I've definitely been down that road before, but I don't recall wanting to drive it twice. Matter of fact, if I recall, she lived way out by Sheldon Summer's farm, and that's in the middle of freaking nowhere. Took me forever to get home that night. Or morning.

I look back to the busy dance floor, bobbing my head to the beat of the country music and leaning against the bar as I take a pull off my beer and continue scoping out my prospects. Neon beer lights are shining on dozens of blond heads, all sleek and shiny, but I've always been partial to brunettes. Curvy ones. I shake my head at myself—I gotta get over this. Which means I should also probably stop watching Chiara's YouTube videos. And Twitch streams. And scrolling her Instagram.

I've typed out, like, nine different texts to her, but I always chicken out at the last second. Keep telling myself there's no point when she's there and I'm here, and it was only ever a hookup that never really hooked up. No way she's looking for a round two with me, not after I left her in the cold like that. But there's just something about her... something that makes me wanna press Send anyway. And not on the "wyd tonight" ones—more like the "have a good day" ones.

*Bad idea. I already know it.* Stuff is just gonna get me in trouble.

The song ends to a splatter of applause, Billy twirling out Taryn a final time as people around them hoot and holler because they've gotten really good at dancing over the last couple years. Like I'm not a good dancer too, but it's all about your partner. How much they trust you. And Taryn trusts Billy a lot.

They head over as a new song starts, and I order a water and shot of Fireball. "You look ridiculous out there," I tell my brother, nearly having to shout over the noise before I wink at Taryn. "You should get yourself a real dance partner."

"Oh, like you?" Taryn flicks her hair over her shoulder.

"Damn right."

Billy laughs and takes the water and shot from the bartender.

"You want it on your tab, Billy?"

"Yeah, that's fine." He hands the shot to Taryn, who throws it back and blows out a cooling breath. Billy doesn't drink. Never has. Says I drink enough for both of us, and he's right.

"Come on, Taryn," I whine. "One dance. None of these other girls are as good as you."

She rolls her eyes and looks at Billy. She's competitive as hell, which is half the reason why she's so dangerous on a race track. In the barrel racing arena too.

"Whatever," my brother says with a laugh, leaning against the bar and taking a drink of his water. I tip my hat at him, setting down my beer. Then I take Taryn's hand and lead her onto the dance floor, the crowd starting to really get going with the new song playing.

"You really couldn't find someone else you wanted to dance with?" Taryn says as we start dancing—a slow shuffle just so she can get used to the way I feel and my rhythm, which is lower and faster than my lanky brother's.

I shrug off her question. "I've danced with all those girls before."

She gives me a look like she's not surprised. "You're gonna run out of road one day, Mason."

"So you've said before."

She opens her mouth like she's gonna yell at me, but she stops. "I just...you could do better." She nods like she's satisfied with herself, and it's not the worst thing she's ever said to me, but it's not the best either.

I try to let it go. I really try not to fight with her, but we don't always get along the best. But that's mostly been my fault. She's a little too easy to rile up.

"Oh, I can do better," I tease her. "And when are you gonna make an honest man out of my brother? You know he's crazy about you." The mortgage he's paying on their eighty-acre ranch is even crazier.

Pink floods her cheeks, happiness radiating from her as I switch up our rhythm a bit. She's letting me lead her a little more, but not by much. "That's between me and Billy," she says firmly, but there's no denying the smile in her voice.

"Right." He's been carrying our great-grandma's ring in his pocket for months now. Whatever's stalling their getting to the altar, it isn't him. "You ready to do this?"

She checks around, repositioning her grip on my shoulder and her other hand in mine. "Yep."

I wait for the beat to change, then we go for it—Taryn spinning out and shimmying back toward me, slowly stalking around my shoulders as I tip my hat at her and play it up. We earn a few claps and some whistles, my hands finding hers and going to spin her back in. But she turns left when I expected her to go right, and we crash into each other *hard*.

"I thought you were going left," she says, regaining her footing.

"No, *right*." I finally give up with a groan, turning her around so we're back to a normal starting position.

"My bad." Her eyes drift toward the bar and Billy like she's already bored of me. Then she squeals out, "Adam!" She's gone in another instant, cutting through the crowd and leaving me on my own. I slap my hands down by my side—I didn't even get a whole dance in. Now I'm getting ditched for Adam, the Wonder Vet. Some Saturday night this is turning out to be.

I head over as Taryn stretches up to hug Adam, then lets him go so he can shake Billy's hand. "How you been, buddy?" Billy says.

"Oh, you know, not too bad. Just opened up a second location. Juniper's pissed."

I barely resist rolling my eyes. Just what this town needed: another veterinary office. And yeah, I bet his office manager Juniper is pissed. I've known her since junior high, and she's usually mad about something—computer updates, the existence of daisies, the weather forecast. Adam stitching us up in his back room when doctor's offices are out of bounds. She was *furious* when I didn't call her again after our single bad date last year.

Adam glances at me. "Muskrat."

"Dr. Doolittle," I sneer back.

He narrows his eyes, hating his nickname from varsity football just as much as I hate mine. But he started it, and I thought we were supposed to be adults now?

He looks back to Billy, he and my brother and Taryn talking about horses and foals and ranches and a whole bunch of stuff that I don't really care about. Not that anyone bothers to ask my opinion on the best organic feed or the newest tractors. It's fine—while they're not looking, I order two more shots of Fireball, put 'em on Billy's tab, and throw them back.

*That's better.*

"I'm gonna head out," I tell my brother.

He looks at me over his shoulder. "Fine. I need your help at the ranch tomorrow, so plan on being there at eight. Not ten thirty. We're starting at *eight* a.m."

Sure we are. "Yep." I tip my hat at Taryn, flip off Adam, then head for the door and the cool night air. I barely get three steps into the parking lot.

"Hey, Mason!"

I turn at the woman's voice. The easy smile and curves heading my way are familiar, but how I know her or where I met her has completely escaped me. She stops close enough that I can tell exactly what kind of beer she's been drinking all night, and when I glance down, there's little pink vines stitched across the toe of her boots. Don't remember those. She may be new.

She tucks her hair behind her ear, shifting her posture so everything falls into place *just right.* "Early night, huh?"

It's after midnight already… "Yeah. Jet lag."

"*Aww.*" She steps closer, staring at my lips. "That sounds rough. But on the upside: more time for pillow fights."

There's no mistaking the meaning in her smile, and I chuckle while looking her up and down as though I'm tempted. I should be. A couple weeks ago, it wouldn't have even been a question. "You are not wrong about that. But can I…maybe ask for a rain check? I've got a meeting real early in the morning."

*Yeah, with a whole bunch of chores and a probable hangover.*

Her shrug is pure grace, but there's a slight twinge of disappointment in her voice. "Sure."

"Thank you." I touch my hat her way. "Be safe getting home."

"You too, Mason."

It isn't far to my parked truck, and I take out my fob, pressing the button so it'll auto start and the heater will kick on. The engine instantly growls to life, throaty and deep as it lopes like a dream. Just makes me miss the hell out of my bike.

I barely touch the electric running board as I climb up into the driver's seat, dumping my phone and wallet in the cup holder. Buckle my seat belt and catch a glimpse of Pink Boots in my rearview, but I don't even get my truck out of Park. I check Chiara's Instagram first, seeing if she's posted anything new.

Lucky me, because she's got a couple fresh shots of her in midnight-black ripped jeans—one from the front and one from the side—and I am in love with this woman's ass. There has never been a more perfect one in the world, and it's not fair that it's way over there in Italy, and I'm stuck in freaking Memphis.

I lock my phone and drop my head back against my seat.

*Don't text her. Don't text her. Don't text her.*

I don't know what's wrong with me. Why I can't seem to get over something that was basically nothing. Maybe I *should* go get Pink Boots and take her home. If it would fix...whatever this is. But I really, really don't want to.

I just need some kind of sign. That this isn't just me, and it isn't nothing.

My phone vibrates, a new notification popping up.

*chiara_m42 liked your photo.*

A wide grin shoots across my face, my heart rate skyrocketing. I scramble to double-check that it was really her, and she really just hit that heart icon. But it really was and she really did, and *that's it*— I'm done pretending that we aren't still thinking about each other. I throw my truck into Reverse and peel out of the parking lot. As soon as I get home, I'm texting her.

# Chapter 6

*Chiara Martes—December*

I PULL MY LEGS TIGHTER INTO MY BODY, FEET PLANTED ON THE SEAT of my gaming chair and fully bundled in sweatpants and a hoodie— only my feet, hands, and eyes exposed. But sitting like a snail snuggled in my favorite pajamas isn't helping my grumpiness. Do all weddings really look the same? Like seriously—who decided that white was *the* color? And what's with all the brides wearing their hair down these days? Don't they realize it's going to be a hot ass mess once they start dancing and partying at the reception? Ugh.

I continue mindlessly scrolling Instagram, incredibly sad that I can't use any of the colors I like or ever convince Lorelai that she'd look way better in a halter than long sleeves. But that's more up to the church and not me. Stupid covered shoulders rule.

**m.king_motocowboy:** Saw that 👀

I gasp in my empty bedroom at the DM, totally and completely busted. Because maybe while I was doing research for Lorelai's wedding, I also maybe sorta wandered over to Mason's account and… liked his latest photo like a total *creep*. But it's possible I'm a little bit addicted to scrolling his Instagram. And his TikTok. There's just something about the way he smiles, like he's always standing on the verge of chaos and the world isn't turning quite fast enough for him.

Crap, I don't know what to do. Respond? Don't respond? (Definitely respond.)

**chiara_m42:** I was hacked
**m.king_motocowboy:** Sure you were

A bunch of really-not-getting-it butterflies flutter in my stomach. I should *not* care this much that Mason is messaging me. But it's kind of hard when he's so hot, and it's felt lately like there have been a dozen signs everywhere pointing me toward texting him. All the times his name comes up when talking to Lorelai about random wedding things; that guy at the restaurant the other day wearing the same cologne Mason wears; my dress from our date staring at me every time I open my armoire. But I keep reminding myself that he's not the kind of guy who wants random "have a great day!" texts from a woman he flew five hours to see and then didn't even get to sleep with.

Another message comes in:

m.king_motocowboy: ??? 42=answer to everything?

A bright smile cracks across my face. Love that he got that joke in my screen name.

chiara_m42: Yep. And don't forget your towel

I get a string of laughing emojis before his next message comes in.

m.king_motocowboy: You up for a video chat?

My jaw hits the floor. *Video chat?* I'm a snail in sweats. I have no makeup on. Like, less than none. I glance at my room behind me, and there are glasses and a bowl of cereal on my nightstand from last night, my bed is a tangled mess of sheets, and oh my God, this is so not ideal. But when weighed against the knowledge that it's late in Memphis and he's probably in bed, shirtless…

I pull down my hoodie hood and attempt to address my rat's nest, but there is no saving my hair. So I swipe my fingers under my eyes, blow out a couple calming breaths, then switch over to WhatsApp.

He answers right away, my screen filling with a tussle of short dark hair, suntanned skin, and that sexy-as-hell verge-of-chaos smile. Behind his bed is a dark-blue wall that's so navy, it's almost black in the low lighting, and I wonder what color his bedding is?

What I wasn't expecting was the wire-rimmed glasses that somehow make his eyes even bluer. I'm officially in serious trouble.

"Morning," he says.

"Hi." I can't seem to stop smiling, but he can't either, and I kind of love it. That whatever this connection is between us, he feels it too. "I didn't know you wore glasses."

"Oh, yep." He reaches up to adjust them like he forgot he was even wearing them. "Our secret. Billy got Lasik a few years back, and I was supposed to get it too. But when he came out of the room, he said he could smell his eyes burning the whole time, and I just couldn't go through with it."

I can't resist a quiet laugh, trying to keep sitting up tall in my gaming chair even though I'm completely melting at his country drawl. It's been so long since I've heard it, I was starting to wonder if I'd imagined how rich and deep his voice was and how warm it makes me feel. "So you normally wear contacts then?"

"Yeah. Not the colored ones, though."

Interesting. His eyes are blue enough that I wouldn't have been surprised.

"What are you still doing awake?" I ask him. "Isn't it, like...two a.m. in Memphis?"

He shrugs. "Couldn't sleep." Then he jerks his chin at me with a smirk that is a direct attack on my sensibilities. "What are you doing up so early? Besides stalking my Instagram."

I roll my eyes, hoping it disguises the heat I just felt rush into my cheeks. "Wedding research. Tell me, what do you think of these flowers?"

I text him an image of the *one* centerpiece I don't totally hate. We shall see what Lorelai thinks of it, though. She and Massimo just went for a run, and they should be back in the next half hour. Hopefully with some cappuccino. Pastry wouldn't hurt either.

"You're asking me?" Mason says. "About wedding centerpieces."

"Well, you don't have to answer. It was just a question."

What is it with men and being allergic to giving their opinion on flowers? Massimo's response to everything is "Looks great. Ask Lorina."

Mason blinks at me, then scrubs a hand through his dark hair, his voice breathy over the words, "Sorry, I just... You keep asking my opinion on stuff, and no one does that."

There's a harsh truth to his words, and I watch him for a long time, the way he shifts back against his headboard, filled with books stacked every which way like he's running out of room. The quick rise and fall of his Adam's apple when he swallows.

"No?" I say casually.

"Nah. Everyone usually tells me what I think."

My friend intuition goes on high alert, and I wonder if he has anyone to talk to. Not someone like his brother, who probably messes with him constantly. And not like his manager, who has his own motives for how he responds. But someone who's a real friend. Who listens and tells it to him straight. I'm so lucky to have my fire team of Aria and Elena. And Lorelai. And Massimo. *Always Massimo.* But Mason...he may not have anyone.

I forget the flowers, settling more comfortably into my chair. "I expect that is true, yes, when you ride for Dabria. As it is for most of the moto racers." He flinches, like my words were the last thing he expected to hear. I tilt my head and explain, "After so many years, the fans, the sponsors, they all seem to forget the work they have done to build you into your brand. It becomes very difficult for them to remember that you are still a regular person underneath your leathers. So yes, I expect they do tell you what to do. All the time."

Mason stares at me, a million thoughts visibly racing behind his eyes, but I don't blink. I'm no stranger to the demands of the circuit, even if other people only ever see the privileges: the cities the racers travel to, even though they hardly see them because they're too busy competing. The money they win and then get to spend on physical therapists and experimental orthopedic surgery. Based on the scar on Mason's shoulder, he's no stranger to the operating table.

"Can I ask you something else?" I venture.

"Yeah." He clears his throat when his voice gives him away. "Shoot."

"Do you even like it? Racing moto? Riding bulls?"

"I, um…" He swallows and shakes his head like he's never been asked that before. "It's what I do. It's what I've always done."

I eye the books on his headboard—all fantasy romance novels, apart from the spare science fiction and contemporary. "What about school? Did you go to university?"

He shakes his head again. "Nah. My grades were pretty good in high school. But my father said I didn't need to go into debt just to…" He trails off, a roll of his eyes sending a sear of pain through me for whatever words he was told that have clearly never left him. "I was already busy racing and riding bulls, and I already knew how to work ranches, so there'd always be work for me when all my other careers went belly-up. That's what he said, anyway, and that was the end of it."

My eyes pop: *When* all his other careers…? Oh my God, his father sounds like such an asshole. To have your whole future dictated because someone you loved didn't believe in you…

I wink at Mason as though I'm not completely pissed off on his behalf. "Good thing you are such a good moto racer, then."

"Nah, I'm not really that good of a racer. People just expect me to be because of my brother. Now, bull riding? *That* I'm damn good at. Best in the state. Probably because Billy retired," he adds with a chuckle.

I don't laugh. There's nothing funny about what just came out of his mouth.

"Mason," I say seriously, "maybe no one has said this to you yet, but I will. No one just *gives* racing contracts to other people's little brothers. I have watched moto all my life, and it takes a very unique person to do what you do. And do not forget: as of Valencia, you are the sixth fastest rider in the world. The *world*, Mason. That is *not* nothing. So never question whether you deserve to be on that grid, because you won your spot in Moto Grand Prix. Fair and square."

He's breathing hard, his eyes locked with mine. It takes him a long time to speak, and when he does, his voice is choked. "Chiara, I don't...I don't know what to say. *No one* has ever said that to me before."

"Well, they should have."

I mean that too.

Mason shakes his head, scrubbing a hand over his jaw before he kind of slaps his hand down like he's totally lost for words.

"What?" I ask.

"Nothing, I just...I don't know why I'm talking so much."

"Because I asked you to."

He halfway laughs to himself, adjusting a pillow behind him so he's more comfortable. "Tell me something about you. Something real."

I switch positions on my chair so I'm crisscross applesauce. "Like what?"

"I don't know," he says. "What do you do? For work or fun. I mean, I know you're into gaming, obviously, but what else?"

"Oh..." I bat away his words. "I am boring. I have no life."

He scoffs heartily. "I highly doubt that."

"It is true. I serve food. Take photos when I can. Oh, and I manage Massimo's social media, and technically I am his stylist still? I don't know. I'd have to check the last title we filed with the sponsors. Nothing very exciting." I lean closer, whispering into the phone, "I refuse to live one of these big important lives, where people put their hopes and dreams on me." I shudder. "I just want to play video games, read comics, and eat. Oh, and travel."

"Oh yeah?" Mason perks up as though that's the epitome of a happy existence. "Where have you been that you like?"

Here comes the embarrassing part. "Um, I've been exactly nowhere. But I think in a past life, I must have been an explorer. Someone like Ida Pfeiffer or Jeanne Baret." I chuckle at myself, but Mason's the one not laughing this time.

"Gimme just a second," he says.

"Um, okay."

He disappears from the screen for a moment, then comes back

with a spiral notebook and a ballpoint pen, writing something across the top before he looks up at me, poised to notate. "Okay, top ten places you wanna visit in this world. Go."

I light up, listing off on my fingers, "Okay, um, Times Square in New York. Eiffel Tower. The Great Sphinx and pyramids in Egypt."

Mason nods, writing them all down. "What about Tokyo?"

I point at him. "Good one. Basically all of Asia."

Something sharp flickers across his face, but it never enters his voice. "And you gotta scuba dive the Great Barrier Reef."

"Yes," I say emphatically, then add, "and sail around Malta."

"You okay with heights?"

"Yes, no problem."

"Then skydiving's a must."

God, wouldn't that be a dream? "Oh, and I want to go to one of those gigantic music festivals."

Mason peeks up. "Comic-Con?"

I go dead still. "That goes to the top of the list. The top, Mason!"

"Okay!" He laughs, crossing it out and writing it above Times Square.

I smile at him. "How many is that?"

"Nine."

I watch him for a second, taking in the shadow of stubble on his jaw, the smoothness of the tan skin on his neck and chest. The scar on his shoulder. "An American rodeo."

His grin widens before his eyes drop to my lips, Mason shaking his head a bit when he looks down. "That isn't exactly a wonder of the world or nothing."

"Oh, I bet it is."

Pink floods his cheeks, his voice quiet. "When, um, when's your birthday?"

I arch my eyebrow, a little suspicious of his question, but still answer, "December."

"December what?"

"Seventh," I say with a chuckle. "Why?"

"'Cause." He starts to chuckle along, telling me, "You're definitely a Sagittarius."

Damn straight. "And you are...?"

"Aries. Practically textbook."

I gasp with a grin, because not only does that explain *so much*, but that makes us a perfect match, astrologically speaking. Both of us blunt, adventurous, and driven by passion. If you believe in that sort of thing.

Mason winks at me. "Hell yeah for fire signs, baby."

Heat flames my cheeks, and I do my best to ignore the electricity crackling through my veins. But he's a perfect storm of everything I like. *Of course he's an Aries.*

I get an incoming text of the bucket list we made, something warm spreading hot through my chest at the careful way he wrote everything in short, boxy handwriting. "Thank you, Mason," I say softly. "This was a good idea."

He snorts. "No one's ever accused me of that before. But it was my pleasure. And I hope you get to see these places. Real soon."

Yeah, me too. Slim chance on that ever happening.

Mason tosses away the notepad, and when his eyes come back and lock with mine, the quiet between us grows thick. Because I can absolutely tell when he switched to asking about places that he and Massimo and all the other racers visit every single year. Countries I've never seen.

"Can I ask you something else?" he says.

My heartbeat takes off. He's going to ask me about Massimo. Everyone always asks about Massimo. "Sure."

"You, um, you ever feel like you're a character in someone else's story? Like, you're living a life that doesn't necessarily revolve around you. And you're just kinda...along for the ride?"

The question catches me so off guard, a shocked laugh comes from my lungs. "I know exactly what you mean."

A wave of relief floods Mason's eyes (or maybe it's just vindication). And as much as I love that he asked me at all, something in me aches for him. That he feels like he's only ever there to serve someone else's purpose. It's not a feeling I'd wish on anyone—especially him. But being the little brother of World Champion Billy King, I'm sure he feels like that a lot. Probably has for a long time.

"Well, don't you…" he stammers, scrubbing a hand back through his dark hair. "Don't you think it's time we start being our own main characters?"

A wide smile takes my face as I consider that, then nod. "I do."

"Well then." Mason clears his throat, a devilishly cute grin curling the corners of his lips. "Let me know if you figure out how we're supposed to do that."

I can't help but laugh, hugging my crisscrossed legs closer into my body. "Same here."

A knock on my door whips my head up. Massimo peeks inside my room, and I tuck my phone against my chest, my thundering heartbeat probably blaring through the phone speaker directly into Mason's ear. "Hey, we brought you breakfast," Massimo says in Italian, passing over a tall cup that floods my room with the scent of dark-roasted coffee. Next is a wax paper bag with something inside that looks like a flaky pastry. "You're on the phone already?"

"Florist," I squeak out. "I'll be done in a minute."

"Cool. I'm going to go shower. Want to queue us up a race on *Gran Turismo* when you're done? Oh, and the guy at the shop said to give you his number." He digs in his pocket, then hands me a napkin with a name and phone number jotted in black Sharpie. "Again."

*Dude really isn't going to get the picture, is he? This is, like, the fourth time…*

I pop open the top on my coffee. "Still sore about your loss last night, huh?"

Massimo gapes at me. "You cheated!"

Not even close. "*You* need to learn to check your tires before you race. Can't believe you're this lost without your pit crew."

He narrows his eyes, then swipes the pastry bag from my desk, dangling it above his head out of my reach.

"Hey!"

"Take it back."

"Okay, fine. You're the greatest racer ever, and I cheated."

"Thank you." He gives me back my breakfast with a smirk. "Ten minutes. Then we're racing." He ducks out and shuts my door behind him, followed by the muffled sound of him and Lorelai talking before she laughs and the shower turns on. Must be nice.

I uncover my phone from my chest and look at Mason on my screen, a questioning look in his eyes because once again, I totally panicked. And hid him from Massimo.

*Good going, Chiara.*

"Sorry," I say in English, holding up my coffee as evidence. "Breakfast delivery."

He watches me for a long time, like he's got a million words on the tip of his tongue. Maybe questions, possibly confessions. Instead, I get a goodbye. "Take care of yourself, Chiara. And I hope you have a good day. That you make it about *you.*"

A bright smile lights up my entire being, and I swear to God, the next time he calls me, I will do better. No hiding, no panicking. Because Mason deserves so much better than that. "You too, Mason. I hope you get some sleep."

And I really mean that. I do.

# Chapter 7

*Chiara Martes—January*

"HELLO? EARTH TO CHIARA?"

I snap back into reality and look up at Lorelai, dressed in a wedding gown and standing on a pedestal inside this stuffy and hot bridal boutique. "Sorry."

She snorts, fussing with the lace-covered bustier as the attendant repositions the clips cinching the dress. She also sneaks in a lip snarl at Lorelai's shaved undercut. (She actually tied her curly hair up for once instead of letting it just fall all over her shoulders and down her back.)

"Where were you?" Lorelai says to me. "You keep zoning out."

"Oh just..." Thinking about my bucket list video chat with Mason. And not realizing that he is apparently *never* going to text or call me again. I don't know why I'm surprised—I've hid him twice from Massimo, and what guy wants to be shoved aside like that? None. The answer is none.

I shrug a shoulder at Lorelai, trying to smile at her in the land of never-ending whiteness, gowns ready to attack from the racks and pictures of runway-model brides all over the walls. I can't imagine myself in any of them—do people get married in shorts and T-shirts? Probably not in a Catholic church, but I can't see me getting married in a church either.

*Figure out a willing groom first, Chiara.*

"Just thinking about the wedding. How beautiful you are going to look."

"Yeah, okay," she deadpans, then looks to the mirror again. She's unfairly stunning in the long silk sleeves, Italian lace, and fitted bodice. It's been a struggle to find anything that doesn't swallow her petite frame, but this one really suits her well. Unfortunately for me and the exhausted gown assistant, Lorelai sighs, slapping her arms down by her sides. "This is all wrong. I think you're right and I'm going to have to do a custom gown."

"Okay. Not a problem. We can absolutely figure this out."

Uh, more like a *huge* problem. I set aside the stack of veils I've been mindlessly playing with, then take out my phone and pull up my planner. I don't know who we're going to find to do a custom design on such short notice. Either way, I start a new note to myself, titling it Wedding Nightmare #12.

Lorelai sighs again, but her voice cracks the second time. "Why can't just one thing go right? I don't have time for this!"

I glance up as she darts off the pedestal and into the changing room, a flash of her gown's long silk train burned in my eyes like a shooting star. I leap up from my chair. *Whoa.* I swear to God, I just saw tears in her eyes. What is going on? She was fine five seconds ago...

I hurry to pass off the stack of veils to the sales lady, then knock softly on the door to the changing room. I wonder if I should call Massimo to come over here and magically solve whatever the problem is. He's good at that. Always has been. "Lorelai?"

"Chiara?" she says softly. "Could you unzip me, please?"

I slip into the room, finding her back to me, arms hugged around herself and her eyes more than a little red in the mirror she's facing. "Of course." I go stand behind her, then start the long process of unhooking all the buttons.

She sniffles and swipes at her eyes, and I do my best to pretend not to notice. She hates crying in front of me. In front of anyone, I think. But I'm sure being openly vulnerable was never an option for her, not to get where she is in her racing career.

I pause long enough to hand her the box of tissues that someone left on a chair in here, because the dressing room could easily seat dinner for six, with plenty of space for ball gowns as wall decorations. Lorelai takes a tissue, dabbing at her eyes. I go back to the buttons. God, there're so many.

"It's just been all this stuff with MMW," she mumbles. "All the back and forth to Munich lately, the extra testing, the crashing when it doesn't go right..."

I nod along. Massimo is always exhausted the first few weeks after the circuit ends, and she's had to go back out on the road instead of recovering. "It's been a lot, what you're doing. Building something new from the floor up. That is a lot of pressure."

"Exactly," she says, meeting my eyes in the mirror. "And yeah, Werner offered to use a test rider because he's, like, the nicest manufacturer rep ever, but I just don't trust anyone else to get it right, you know? I mean, how is someone else supposed to tell them how my bike is supposed to feel for *me*?"

"They can't."

She gestures in agreement. "And it's like no one understands what I'm going through: dealing with an untested bike for a new team while trying to prepare for the normal circuit stuff, and it's not like it's *easy* to just move from the U.S. to Italy and change my religion because his freaking mother...*ugh*." She grits her teeth, but she's quick to downshift into sadness again. "I just, I miss my family and my horse, and y'all don't have bacon-egg-cheese breakfast sandwiches in every gas station on every corner... And now I have to find a dress designer and squeeze in time to get fitted and..." Her lips twist, brown eyes welling up with tears again.

I gently squeeze her shoulders. "We have time. We will get it all sorted out."

She nods, dabbing at her eyes again, but her breaths are shaky like it's taking all her resolve not to break down completely. I go back to finishing the buttons, then unzipping the zip.

"I don't know what I'd do without you, Chiara." She turns around, holding on to my shoulder as I lower the gown and she steps out. "Seriously."

I don't know what to say. I'm too busy trying not to gasp at the bruises on her body—patches of black and blue on her hip and shoulder, the road rash on her arm and her side. I've seen worse, known worse myself (got the pics to prove it), but it's been a long time, and I had *no idea* this was under her blue jeans and long-sleeved shirts.

The testing must be going worse than I thought.

I rise and wave her off as I start to hang up the dress among all the other ones that didn't work. "You, Lorelai, would be just fine. Just as you have always been, because that is who you are. Strong. Wreckless."

"Thank you," she says behind me. Then she blows out a breath and mutters, "God, I look like I've been hit by a car." I peek over my shoulder, and she's checking out her bruises in the mirror, shaking her head. "The salesgirl totally freaked when she was helping me get dressed earlier. Told me to leave him, not marry him."

I clasp a hand over my mouth. I didn't think about it until she said it, but after everything he and I went through, for anyone to even *imply* that he would...

Lorelai's eyes lift to mine, the color draining from her face when she spots my reaction. "Oh, Chiara... I'm so sorry. I didn't mean to—"

I wave her off. I wish it would erase the cold tingle of anxiety fluttering down my veins, but that'll disappear eventually. It always does. "It's okay. I'm okay."

"Are you sure?"

"Of course." I start gathering up her clothes, fixing her shirt so it's not inside out. I wasn't even sure how much she knew about my childhood, my parents, but I'm guessing he's told her more than I thought. At least I didn't have to break the news to her—I hate talking about it. The pitying looks and the way people change afterward.

"I really shouldn't have said that." There's a gentleness in her voice that I've never heard before. It takes me a minute to realize it's shame.

I take a centering breath, then wink at Lorelai. "Said what?"

Relief floods her shoulders, and she reaches for her jeans.

She seems to be feeling better once we leave the bridal boutique and get in my car, finally fixed and back to purring like a kitten.

(Thank you, Massimo.) The sun is shining brightly through the windows, which I roll down halfway so she can feel the air against her face and swirling through her hair, now back down and the clip disappeared.

She's absolutely back to smiling when I start driving a little too fast on the freeway out of Ravenna, and she laughs when I downshift without warning and punch it to speed around a slower car, heading out into the countryside.

Their new house is way out in the middle of freaking nowhere.

"Do you have any more of those biscotti from this morning?" She gets her fill of the wind, rolling her window up and turning on my car's heater. I roll up my window too. Though I leave a small crack at the top—she's so aggressive with the heater sometimes. She is aggressive in all things, though.

"Yes. In my purse." God, why is traffic so annoying today? I speed around another car, then cringe and get that heart-racing, stomach-sinking feeling when I see a cop parked on the side of the road up ahead. *Please don't get me.*

Lorelai reaches into the back seat to grab my purse—a pastel pink one she brought back for me from Valencia. "I swear, I feel like such a jerk. I don't even know what's been up with you lately."

I glance at her as she turns forward in her seat, breaking off a piece of chocolate biscotti and then handing me the other half. Double-check my mirrors, and thank God, that cop is still sitting there.

"How's the new job been going?"

I groan, then take a bite of the biscotti I scored from the cooks during my last shift. "Working with Aria and Elena is cool, but I hate serving. People act like getting their coffee order wrong is a war crime."

"That sucks." She shudders, and I can't help but laugh at the idea of her taking orders—woman wouldn't last five minutes before she snapped at a customer. She keeps nibbling on her biscotti for a minute before she adds, "So whatever happened with you and Mason?"

I nearly slam the brakes. "What? Why?"

"Because you haven't said anything about him since Massimo and I interrupted y'all's date." She shifts so her back is to the door, leaving me nowhere to hide. "Or is there someone else new in your love life?"

I scoff, winking at her before I pull off the highway and turn onto a smaller, windier one. "Just you, gorgeous."

She laughs, but she's got a knowing edge to her voice. "Everyone and their secrets."

"What secrets? I tell you everything."

"Oh, don't worry. It's not just you. Taryn says Mason's been acting weird lately."

My heart rate picks up, and I check my mirrors. There's no one else on this road. "Oh?"

"Mm-hmm. Said he's been all quiet and going around with a big smile on his face. Weirdest thing. Taryn thinks he met someone."

I stare straight ahead at the road, my hands locked on the steering wheel and my palms starting to sweat. *Oh yeah? Then why isn't he calling me?* Unless it's not me...

I mentally shake my finger at myself. *Get some damn boundaries, Chiara.*

I should probably also update my Tinder profile. Tonight.

"Maybe he did." I shrug at Lorelai. "And good for him."

She keeps staring at me. "And you haven't heard from him?"

"I have not." Honestly, not for a month now.

"Hmm. I really thought y'all would've hit it off."

"We did," I explain. "But you know how Massimo is about me dating the other racers. He was really upset that I went behind his back—"

"I'm the one who gave you Mason's number! And in fact, I even *told* Massimo I did it. Behind his back my ass."

"Well, either way," I tell her, "he went right back to the whole 'distracting him' thing, so it's probably best for all of us that it didn't go anywhere."

"That's ridiculous." She turns forward again to look out at the road, a determined scowl on her face that usually precedes a first-place podium.

"Please do not get into a fight with him about this," I beg her. "It's not worth it. I swear it's fine."

"If you say so." She shrugs, then innocently starts picking at her fingernails. "Anyway, I've been thinking that all this wedding stuff would probably be a lot easier to coordinate if you were to come on the circuit with us."

My head snaps her way, already fully aware of exactly what she's doing. "Lorelai…"

"What?" Her grin grows bigger with every word. "Is there any reason why you can't come?"

"Because I…have to work."

"No, you don't. I'll pay you a salary to be my wedding planner, and then you don't have to worry about it."

"No," I say firmly, pointing at her for extra measure.

"Come on! That's totally normal. People pay their wedding planners."

"Not when they are friends. I will not accept that."

She huffs and slumps in her seat. "Fine. But then why won't you come on the circuit with me?"

*Uh, because he's going to think I'm stalking him?*

"You say we're friends, Chiara, and I thought we were. Good friends. Well, I need my friends with me right now."

I gape at her. What a low blow! "You know I want to help you with this, but I can't…" …come up with a valid excuse that doesn't concern Mason. Especially when I keep hearing his voice in my head:

*"Don't you think it's time we start being our own main characters?"*

"Look, I'll handle all the arrangements," Lorelai says. "You can stay in my RV with me, we can talk wedding stuff in between practice sessions and press corps, and you'll get to see some sights instead of serving coffee all day. Massimo and I will have to stay glued to the track for the most part, but you don't, and I thought you wanted to travel more?"

She's got me completely backed into this corner, and based on her smile, she knows it. It really would be easier to plan the wedding from the circuit; texting her questions and waiting for her to respond to my emails while she's been testing in Germany has been a nightmare. And yes, I'd obviously love nothing more than to visit Malaysia, Qatar, Thailand, Argentina, Spain, and all the other countries they're about to blast through. But...

"Please, Chiara? Let someone do something nice for you for once."

I blow out a breath, looking back to the road. Maybe Lorelai is doing more than a little bit of scheming, but I do believe she has my best interests at heart. And she could use an extra friend right now—we both could. And we *are* friends.

God, I wonder what he's going to do when he sees me in the paddock. Smile? Freak out? Call security?

"He is not going to like this."

Lorelai tilts her head and smiles at me. She doesn't blink. "Which he?"

"Massimo, of course."

Mason, of course.

*Both. Of course.*

"He'll be fine," she says. "Trust me."

# Chapter 8

*Mason King—February*

"THAT IS TOO FAST," SANTOS TELLS ME IN HIS THICK SPANISH accent, busy dealing out autographs as quickly as he can for the crowd packed around us. Around *him*, really. We're both in leathers, knee and elbow sliders on, but as far as this crowd is concerned, he's the only racer here. "As soon as you cross under the second DHL sign, downshift."

"Downshift? That early?" That seems way too soon to start slowing for turn one. The straight before it is long and full throttle, and I'm supposed to work on *not* choking it. Seems to me like I should hold the speed as long as I can.

"Yes." He never looks up as he trades one press photo for another. "Second sign. Slow in, fast out."

*That's what she said.*

I snort to myself as his Sharpie keeps trying to slip out of his sweaty fingers, but I don't mind the sweltering humidity of Sepang, sticking thick to every inch of my exposed skin and soaking through my leathers in search of the rest of it. Feels like being at home in Memphis but on the other side of the world and with *way* better food. Plus, there's just something about sweating like this, like it's some kind of detox for my soul. And God knows, my soul needs it.

Santos passes off the autograph he just signed for a guy wearing an orange Hotaru T-shirt with Santos's name and number on it—because that ain't cool as shit—then squints at me through the sunlight. "You up for poker with me and Giovanni tonight? He says he wants a rematch."

*Yeah, I bet he does.* I always have way too much fun cleaning out his and his boyfriend's wallets. It's one of the best parts of being back at the track.

"Sure thing. Tell him I could use a little extra cash—" I cut off when I get attacked at the knees and glance down to find a little girl hugging me. She's wearing a baseball cap with my number, and how freaking adorable is that? I steal Santos's Sharpie so I can bend to sign her hat. "Well, don't you look like a future Lorelai Hargrove?"

She beams up at me like I'm a worthy hero. Poor kid; she'll figure it out eventually. "Lorelai's my favorite! After you, of course..."

"*Aww*. Same here." I wink at her, and she cuts through the crowd and runs off toward her father, enthusiastically showing him her hat. He swoops her up safely onto his shoulders, and I turn back to Santos with a smug grin, letting him yank the marker back out of my fingers.

"Thank you, everyone, but we must stop here." Santos does his best to politely wave off the next person shoving one of his official press photos in his face. But he's right: we gotta get to the track for the next shakedown session.

"And we really appreciate y'all for coming out," I remember to add at the last minute. I tip my sponsor-coated Stetson at the crowd, Santos and I heading back to the garages.

The paddock is packed, buzzing with sponsors and officials and mechanics, as everyone preps for the next practice sessions, testing new parts and new riders for the new year.

"You want to meet us at about eight?" Santos asks. "Giovanni will not be done from debriefing until at least seven."

"Yeah, that's fine." I squint toward the clock tower, trying to see what time it is now. But then something catches the corner of my eye, and I might be more dehydrated than I thought.

*No way did I just see...*

"Actually, I might need a rain check." My eyes scan the paddock, and sure enough, walking away is a long pair of legs, a well-worn pair of Chuck Taylors, and a confident-but-relaxed sway of an ass that I would know anywhere. I blink in a daze as she tosses her long brown hair and turns a corner, disappearing into a crowd of Yaalon crew people on their way to the garages.

"What? Why?" Santos glances the direction I'm looking, then narrows his eyes at me. "Irresponsible as always. You need to be more focused."

I roll my eyes. He *loves* to lecture me about staying away from sponsor models and umbrella girls. "Downshift on the second DHL, yeah, I got it."

Santos flips me off, but that's just Santos. Talking shit is his love language; they don't call him the Hurricane from Spain for nothing.

I start to cut a path through the crowd and leave Santos in the dust—if only it were that easy on the track—my heart pounding in my chest as I head the direction I think she went. My racing boots echo in the tunnel as I turn the final corner, but I stop short when all I see in the open walkway are crew people and officials. *Damn it.* I really thought I saw—

"Psst!"

My head whips toward the sound coming from a cracked-open door to a janitorial closet. A smile snaps across my lips. I glance around to make sure no one's watching me. But like usual, no one is.

I slip through the door, shutting it behind me and bumping into a person in the dark.

*Cinnamon…*

The light flicks on above me, and I'm face-to-face with Chiara, smashed front to front in the world's tiniest broom closet. There's barely any space to move; each wall is covered by a bunch of industrial shelves stacked to the ceiling with packages of napkins and paper towels.

"Hi." She smiles at me, her layered hair spilling down her shoulders and everything about her deliciously casual. She looks like a million bucks in a plain white T-shirt and blue jean shorts, and I have no idea what to say.

My pulse is so fast that I can feel it thumping in my knees, my whole throat locked closed at the surprise of seeing her, and I don't trust it. She's too pretty. Smells too damn good. Plus, it's really fucking hot outside, and I haven't been drinking as much water as I should.

"Are you real?"

When she laughs, I know it for sure. My brain couldn't ever come up with something that sounds as sweet as that. And it's been trying, a lot.

"Yes, Mason, I am real." She reaches up to peel off my hat and set it on a shelf. A huff of a breath bursts from my lips, and I can't help it—I take her gorgeous face in my hands and kiss her beautiful lips, and I kiss her *good*. It's been almost three months since I've had the pleasure of doing that, and it's been a long fucking three months.

But then I realize what I'm doing—that I'm kissing her, and I didn't ask for permission or wait for any kind of go-ahead. I kinda just attacked her, and the single thought makes me freak out so much that I jump back, letting her go. *Shit!*

Chiara stares at me. I wait for the cursing I deserve. Possibly a slap.

She smiles instead, her hand on my neck pulling my lips back to hers, and *oh thank God*. She's not mad. In fact, she moans and hooks her arms underneath mine, gripping the back of my shoulders as she tugs me closer, and I hope she's okay with staying in this closet for, like, a while. I don't see me wanting to leave it for any reason, anytime soon.

"Hi, cowboy," she breathes against my lips, a smile in her voice as her soft palms come up to cup my jaw. Her thumbs sweep over my cheeks like I'm something special, her teeth scraping my bottom lip as she kisses me a little slower and more deliberately, and I still can't believe that she's real, that she's *here*.

"Hiya, trouble," I breathe back, soaking her up as much as I can until she pulls back for real this time.

She chuckles softly as her fingertips trace my lips, like that felt as good for her as it did for me. "I wasn't sure if you saw me. But I am really glad it was you who followed me in here."

"Yeah, me too." I nip at her thumb, my palms greedily smoothing themselves down her sides and over her back, hungry to remember her. "And…what are you doing here?"

"Stalking you."

I crack up laughing, Chiara's smile brightening even further.

She loops her arms around my neck and tips her forehead to mine, her nails playing with the hair at the nape of my neck like it's the most natural thing in the world. And it feels like it.

"Lorelai asked me to come. To help her with wedding stuff while she is at the circuit."

That doesn't exactly make sense to me, but I don't give the slightest bit of a damn. "That's fucking *awesome*."

Chiara blushes, shrugging a shoulder. "So you are not mad then?"

A deep sigh falls from my lips. I hate that she'd ever even worry about that, especially when I can't seem to stop smiling. I trace away a lock of hair caressing her cheek. "Nah, girl, I'm not mad." I'm, like, the most opposite of mad I could ever be.

That perks her right back up. "Good."

Oh, we're way past good. We're *great*.

I steal another kiss from her smiling lips, then nuzzle my way into her neck, breathing her in and letting it lift up my soul. It ain't all that's lifting either. "Can I see you tonight?"

Sepang is amazing, and I already know she's gonna *love* it. We're also not that far from Kuala Lumpur, and I don't know what to do first: shopping at the badass Mitsui Outlet Park or take her go-karting. Maybe after, we could ride out to Bagan Lalang Beach... Or maybe not. Whatever we do, it's gotta be at night, since I got practice and testing all day and boring press junkets in between. But I'll think of something.

"I don't know, Mason."

"What? How come?" I lean back to see her eyes. "You came to *me*."

Chiara runs her fingers through her hair. "I came to help Lorelai. And Massimo would be really upset if he found out. He very specifically does not want me to date you."

"Why? What's he got against me?"

She gets a sexy little twist to her lips. "He says you're... dangerous."

Been called worse. Much worse. Hell, I almost take that as a compliment. "Well, isn't that for you to decide?"

She bites her lip, taking a minute to respond. "You really don't have other plans?"

"Nope." I wink at her. "Come on. Sneak out with me tonight. Nothing dangerous, just some good food, some dancing, and maybe some light karaoke."

She grins and shifts her weight. "All right. Just tonight."

"Yeah," I growl happily, tugging her hips against mine and stealing a kiss from her lips. "Can't wait."

The two-minute buzzer goes off outside, muffled through the door and calling me back to the track. But with the way Chiara is smiling at me, like she's looking forward to tonight as much as I am...

I can't seem to let go of her. Just feeling her in front of me again, her hands on my arms and watching her eyes as she watches mine. Her gaze drops to my lips, her breath quickening as the tension between us grows until I desperately need to kiss her again and would rather die than do it wrong.

My pulse is thundering in my veins, but Chiara is sweet and patient with me as I take my time leaning in, savoring every moment until I capture my prize. Her soft hands cradle my cheeks, pulling me in and kissing me deeper. Slower. Letting me lose myself in each passionate stroke of her tongue until she bites my bottom lip and pulls on it.

I don't quite remember backing her against the shelves. But I know it was definitely her idea to wrap her leg around my waist. A brilliant idea it was too.

"God, girl, you're driving me *crazy*." My fingertips sink into the back of her thigh while I press myself against her, Chiara moaning and rocking against me.

"You started it."

A low chuckle rumbles out of me. "Not even close, trouble."

"Okay," she pants out, "that's fair." She tugs my lips back to hers, and it takes her absolutely nothing to get me going full throttle. My dick is iron in my leathers, desperate to close the distance between me and what's under those little shorts, and for the life of me, I cannot figure out why we're still in this damn storage closet.

"My RV ain't far," I whisper, but my brilliant idea has the exact *opposite* effect I'd hoped for.

Chiara groans, the sound low and frustrated as she drops her leg, stopping me. "We can't."

*No, no, no.* Not again. "We can, I assure you. And I bet we can do it *well*."

Chiara blushes, but her palm settles on my chest, and that's that. She's still kinda breathless, though. "I wouldn't bet against you." Then she hands me my hat, a bright grin lighting up her beautiful face. "But for now, you are going to be late for practice."

"Oh, I'm already late."

Chiara giggles as I steal another kiss—or three—then let her push me out of the broom closet. "Go," she whispers. "You have to go race."

I hook on my hat, tilting it at her. "I'll text you tonight."

The door shuts between us, cutting off the sound of her laughter. A whole bunch of other voices slam into me, and it occurs to me that I'm in public again and there are people everywhere. *Shit!* This is exactly how I got banned from Long John Silver's. And Walmart.

I don't think anybody here noticed what just happened, though. They're all looking at tablets or clipboards or talking to each other while hurrying to their next marketing meeting.

An announcement blares overhead that is definitely not a good sign for the future of my racing career, and I take off toward my garage, running inside my pit box to find my bike ready to go and my crew looking all sorts of pissed off. Worse, a camera crew is outside, a reporter clearly relaying my disappearance to the whole world.

*Well, damn.* Guilt settles thick in my stomach. I know how hard my team works to make sure I'm safe out there, that my bike is liquid fast in the constantly changing conditions. And they've been working overtime in preparation for this shakedown.

"Sorry, I'm sorry!" I call out. My crew chief, Marco, glares at me from where he's supervising them removing the tire warmers, but he mostly seems relieved that I showed up at all. That's not entirely fair; I'm far more likely to miss a rodeo than I am a moto race.

I throw down my hat and turn for my helmet, and I run straight into my brother's chest.

"Where have you been?" Billy barks at me, his phone pressed to his ear.

The hell? What is he doing here instead of already on the track with everyone else? He's gonna miss practice if he doesn't hurry. And why is he on the phone with Taryn *now*? Can't they stand not speaking for five freaking seconds?

He hangs up his phone just as I hear my voicemail message play on the other end. *Oh.* "Frank and I have been looking everywhere for you," he says. "There's practically a damn search party on the paddock for your dumb ass."

I smirk at him. "Well, I'm here. So you don't need to worry your pretty head about it."

He leans closer and sniffs me, his voice low so no one else can hear. "You sober?"

"Nope, three sheets." I grab my gloves and tug them on before Billy hands me my helmet.

*Hard right turn one, harder left turn two, swing right turn three full throttle, ninety-degree turn four...*

My brother rolls his eyes, apparently unimpressed by my joking. But he already checked me with his damn bloodhound nose; he knows I haven't been drinking. "Whatever. Just get your head in the game."

"Don't you have your own career to worry about? Or was that last rumor about you retiring supposed to be a secret?"

He grits out a cursed something or other and jogs around my side and then out of my pit box toward his own garage. About time. If I'm already late, Billy is gonna be even later, but I didn't ask him to be my babysitter. If he misses practice, that's on him.

"Mason, let's go, let's go!" Marco claps his hands and waves me toward him. The announcement for the next shakedown session blares through the stadium, and I dart toward my bike and swing my leg over.

My manager, Frank, runs into the pit box all out of breath. "Oh, thank Christ, you're here." He puts his phone back in his pocket like he's been blowing up my voicemail too. That's gonna be fun to delete later.

"Where else would I be?" I flip down my face shield and rev the throttle so I can't hear his irritated reply. Marco drops my back tire off the stand, and I blare past my manager out into pit lane. I catch a glimpse of Chiara watching from the fence line as I pull onto the track, the wind blowing her hair around in a way that is far sexier than it should be, and it feeds the fuck out of my ego that she's here. Watching me, maybe even cheering for me...

Until Billy comes up and cuts around my side so he can take the lead—*show-off*.

We weave through the lineup and take our places on the grid, my starting spot three blocks behind my World Champion brother and one behind Massimo. The unforgiving Malaysian sun beams down and glistens off the track, and I narrow my focus on the backs of their tailpipes, knocking my fists together and doing my prerace routine for good luck.

Sepang is a battler's paradise: the wide track perfect for overtaking, whether you're bullying your buddies out of the apex in one of the ten high-speed corners or slipstreaming in one of the long-*long* straights with the throttle as open as you can get it. Nothing more fun than playing chicken at 210 miles per hour, and this is it: the start of the *best* year of my career.

World Champion or bust. All or nothing.

My eyes lift to the clock tower as the announcer says a bunch of shit that melts on the humid wind, the toes on my boot aching to shift and my wrist itching to twist. Numbers count down as my heartbeat speeds up, muscle memory already kicking in to control my breathing while I go through the coming turns in my mind.

*Man, I can't wait for tonight...*

I smile wickedly under my face shield, sweat trickling down my back and everything in me ready to *go*. Massimo's blue helmet peeks my way.

*Dangerous, huh?* I act like I'm blowing him a kiss.

He turns forward, sinking low over his handlebars and shifting his weight for the launch.

*Time to ride.*

# Chapter 9

I DIG DEEPER INTO MY CURRY NOODLES, LEANING AGAINST A WALL under the large blue Jalan Petaling sign and soaking in the harmonic chaos of tourist chatter, bartering stall vendors, and a whole bunch of different music. I'm a world away from Memphis, and I couldn't be happier about it. I'm even happier about the way my shakedown test went today.

Rounding my second year of racing for Dabria, my bike is really starting to come together. Can't wait for the first official race in Qatar in a few weeks. There's a first place trophy sitting there with my name on it, and Billy—and everyone else—will just have to deal with it.

The streetlight changes, and I glance up at the crowd of people moving toward me and straight for the entrance of the night market. Nope. I poke a bit more at my noodles, trying not to be too impatient. I'm a good forty minutes from the circuit, and I had a solid thirty-minute head start. Still, she's fifteen minutes late.

It's fine. If she doesn't show, she doesn't show. I can handle it.

*I'm gonna handle it by dealing with shit-talking Massimo.*

"Starting without me?"

I choke and cough on my noodles, looking up to find Chiara standing in front of me. I didn't even see her in the crowd, but she's definitely in front of me and definitely drop-dead gorgeous. I barely remember how to swallow.

*She came.*

"Well…" I have to clear my throat to get my voice to work. "Fancy meeting you here," I drawl with a wink.

"It is *such* a small world," she plays along. Like I didn't text her specific instructions on how to get to the bus stop from the circuit, how long the ride would take, and where I would be waiting.

Apparently, the Massimo issue is more serious than I realized. She texted me this afternoon freaking out that we can't be seen leaving the circuit together or coming back together, and no one is allowed to know. Decoy mission it was.

I don't know what Massimo has decided is so damn dangerous about me, but it's bad enough that Chiara is adamant about keeping this on the down low. Not bad enough for her to no-show, though— which I'm taking as a compliment of the highest order.

I must've done something right during our failed date in her apartment.

"Well, since we bumped into each other," I say innocently, "wanna hang out?"

Chiara laughs, tucking her hair behind her ear, and I have no idea how I'm *not* gonna spend the whole night staring at her. But I should probably try.

*On second thought…* If this is the only chance I get with her, I'm going for it.

I hook a finger through her belt loops and bring her a couple steps closer. Chiara melts the rest of the way against me, her hands landing comfortably on my chest and her grin as wide as mine feels. "Hi."

"Hi," she says back, and there's no way not to kiss her. Just once, softly.

"I am…*really* glad you came."

"I am too." She looks up at the entrance to the market, so awe-struck that she doesn't even seem to notice the flood of people around us. "This is incredible. I can't believe I'm actually *here*. I have never seen anything like this."

"Well, we're fixing that." I squeeze her hip, then let her go and hand her my nearly finished bowl of noodles.

Chiara wastes no time taking a bite, followed by a loud moan and her pointing at the bowl with the chopsticks. "Oh my God, this is *so good*. I am so hungry. Can we get more of this? Is it close?"

"Yeah, we're fixing that too." I indicate the entrance of the market. "Two things. First, anything you want, it's yours, but you gotta let me do the haggling. Unless that's something you'd rather do yourself."

She shrugs, taking another bite. "Go for it. *Mmm*, is this curry?"

"Yeah. Second thing: we're trying one of everything when it comes to food. Which means...no more of this."

"Hey!" She chuckles and hurries to take the final bite before I steal back the bowl and toss it into a nearby trash can. She covers her mouth, her words mumbled. "I'm starving, Mason."

"And I'm gonna feed you, I promise. Now, your phone." I hold out my hand, palm up, and she stares at me. Arches an eyebrow at my palm. But she produces a cell phone from the back pocket of her shorts and hands it over.

"Mason, you should know that my phone is my heaven and earth, my spouse and only child, and if you hurt it—"

"I ain't gonna hurt it." I back up a bit and open her camera. "I'm gathering evidence."

"Oh." Chiara smiles and strikes a quick pose, and *God, those legs...* "Evidence of what?"

"That you were here." Snap a couple extras of her tossing and playing with her hair, because everything she does is ridiculously hot. *Everything*. "Got it."

I head back to her, acting like I'm gonna give back her phone. But I sneak in a quick selfie of us first. I want evidence of that too.

"Wait." She places her hand on my shoulder, producing the world's most adorable pout. "I wasn't ready."

And I...may be in trouble here.

"All right, all right." I hold up the phone again, Chiara coming close enough that her cheek is against mine, my arm finding its place around her waist and pulling her in closer. It's almost scary—how natural she feels against me. How right we look together.

She takes her phone back and swipes through the pictures, and I am immensely proud of the smile it brings to her lips. "Oh, this is great." Her voice goes a bit soft as she beams at me. "I was here."

"You *are* here." And I'm the luckiest guy on the planet, because I get to be here with her. "You ready to have some fun?"

"Hell yeah." She tucks her phone into her pocket, meets my high five, and cracks up laughing when I tug her into my arms and dip her—dip her *deep*. Chiara's eyes are electric as her grin never quits and her gaze drops to my lips, and I slowly lower my mouth to hers.

"Welcome to Kuala Lumpur."

---

"Are you sure you wanna do this?" My gaze is locked with Chiara's, and everything about me is dead serious. This could be a really bad idea, and I should know. That's kinda my specialty.

"I have never been so sure of anything." Chiara's honey eyes are wide and adrenaline drugged, but she looks so much like she means it that I don't have any choice but to trust her.

It's her call.

"Okay."

She takes the shot I hand her and throws it back, then kisses the hell out of me and climbs the stage, grabbing the mic from the emcee. "Hello, KL!"

The karaoke bar is already whistling at her gorgeous legs and long brown hair, wild and messy from us walking around all night. But the bar crowd quickly goes from intrigued to losing their freaking minds when "Intergalactic" by the Beastie Boys starts to play.

They whistle and clap along to the beat, their drinks rising in the air as their phones shine on her like spotlights, Chiara already playing with them as she dances to the intro. But it hits a whole other level when she starts busting off the first verse, not even needing the monitor because she already knows the whole damn thing, and never have I seen anything like her. Nothing as free, nothing as cool.

She's slaying both me and the crowd with every roll of her spine and pop of her hips, dealing out lyrics like she wrote them. And as I cheer her on from backstage, I'm completely mesmerized at how much fun she is—like seriously, Chiara may be my new favorite person to travel with. Billy always whines about how nothing's the same as at home, but Chiara wants to try everything that's different and leave no experience undone.

She's not afraid of anything, as far as I can tell, and she's still destroying the bar that's louder for her than they've been for anyone else. People are pouring in from outside to join the party as she cruises through the second verse, and then the third, and I'm a *little* worried she's gonna go viral, and we're gonna get busted. But it'll totally be worth it, especially when she yells the last line and drops the mic, the place exploding as Chiara shrugs like it was nothing.

"*Yeah*!" I shout, overflowing with pride for her as Chiara blows a kiss to the bar and throws up a live-long-and-prosper sign, then runs off the stage in my direction. "That was amazing!"

She leaps onto me with a massive smile, and I stumble back with a laugh as I catch her, crashing into the people behind me, but I don't give a fuck. Everyone in this bar wishes they were me right now.

"Oh my God, I can't breathe," she gasps out with a laugh.

I squeeze her and set her down, perpetually dumbstruck in her presence. The next person takes the stage, the crowd giving Chiara another cheer as she blows a kiss to her fans and waves a final time.

When she leans toward me, she practically has to yell in my ear. "It is so hot in here." She fans herself. "Are you okay to go? I could really use some air after that."

"Yeah, that's fine," I yell back over the noise. "Come on. This way."

I take her hand and start to cut a path through the crowd, everyone gushing over Chiara on our way past and my eyes trained on the exit. Her fingers lace through mine, her other hand wrapping around my arm as people push in closer, shoving drinks at us and *who knows what's in them*. But I get us outside and Chiara into the warm night air, granting us some space.

"Oh, thank you." She tilts her head back, arms out like she's soaking in the sun instead of the moonlight. "That's so much better."

I laugh and take her hand, getting us back on the main drag. "That...was incredible."

Chiara beams at me, swinging our hands a little. "I told you I wanted to sing that song. So much better than the Lady Gaga one you suggested."

"I stand corrected."

She nods definitively my way. "As you should."

God, she's killing me. She's so *cute*. "You hungry? We can grab something if you want; soak up some of that crap we drank."

Not long before we got to the karaoke place, we raced an order of rainbow-colored shots at a drag bar. She won.

Chiara giggles guiltily. "I'm okay. Still full from earlier. But thank you."

"Okay. Just let me know if you change your mind."

We must've sampled every food cart on Petaling Street, trading bites of this and that while admiring all the knockoff designer swag. Then we started hitting the bars. Having a couple drinks and having more than a little fun dancing them out of our systems. Wandering around the city and marveling at buildings and taking so many pictures that Chiara's phone died.

I'm really looking forward to tomorrow—Chiara agreed that tonight just wasn't enough time to do all the stuff we wanted to, and I scored myself an encore. We've already got a plan in place, and I'm taking her to the *coolest* little indie comic store that I found the last time I was here. I think she'll like it. She seems to like a lot of the same stuff I do: sci-fi movies and video games, international travel, drinking and dancing, and flirting until you're edged from just the sexual tension *alone*.

Chiara speaks all my languages and probably a good dozen more, and it makes everything about what I have to do next a million times harder. So does the last two shots we had at that drag bar that were topped with whipped cream and went down way too easy.

"So…" I drawl, my world spicy with cinnamon and warm with her next to me, and I really, really don't want the night to end. But it's late enough that we're gonna have to make a decision about *where* it's gonna end, one way or the other.

Chiara is apparently able to read my mind. "We have to go back to the paddock?" She doesn't look totally disappointed, but she doesn't look thrilled about that prospect either.

"We could. Or...we could go to the hotel where I booked a room."

She bursts out laughing, a nervous blush painting her cheeks. I turn her toward me, lacing my hands through hers and clinging to the little bit of self-control I can claim.

*Make the right decision, for once in your life.*

"Honestly, though, it's whatever you want to do, Chiara. I had a really good time hanging out with you tonight, and if you're ready to go back to the paddock, that's cool with me. Just say the word, and I'll make it happen."

I'm almost wondering if something got lost in translation, because Chiara kinda sighs and melts my way, and I really don't deserve her looking at me like that. "Mason, I would like to stay with you."

My smile bursts so bright, my cheeks start hurting.

*I'm gonna stay the night with Chiara Martes.*

"Well then... Let's go make that happen."

# Chapter 10

*Mason King—February*

IT'S NOT FAR TO THE HOTEL, THANK GOD. AND I'M NOT EXACTLY sure what she was expecting, but her jaw hits the floor once the concierge opens the door and lets us inside. Gotta admit, it's even nicer than the pictures online. The ceilings are, like, impossibly high.

"What kind of phone you got again?" I ask her. "I wanna see if the front desk has a charger for it."

"Oh! Brilliant." She hands it over, and I take it up to the lady at the front desk while I get us checked in. Doesn't take long to get it sorted, and I head back to Chiara with a charger, couple complimentary toothbrushes and toiletries, and a room key, passing her the first one. "Thank you, Mason," she says. "I am such a mess sometimes. I never remember to charge my phone."

"Trust me, I'm a walking catastrophe. Mama used to call me a tornado of chaos."

Chiara laughs, retaking my hand and squeezing tight. "That is not very nice."

"Nah, she was just playing. And it's true. Elevator's this way."

It's impossible not to feel her watching me once we're in the elevator, Chiara standing there all tall and gorgeous, her hands playing with the long ends of her silky brown hair. My eyes rise to the screen counting up the floors to the rooms above us. I'm not sure why I'm so damn nervous—I have spent plenty of nights in hotel rooms with plenty of women before. Sometimes two at a time. *Get your damn head in the game.*

When we step off the elevator together, Chiara lets me lead her down a long hallway to a door that says *Suite with Terrace* on it in two different languages. I finally get it unlocked—stupid key cards—and swing open the door, letting Chiara go first.

She falls sideways against the doorframe. "Mason," she mutters, but in a really, really good way. She definitely hasn't been spoiled enough in her life.

"Yeah, it's nice." My hand on her lower back gently encourages her inside, and she takes off into the suite, turning the corner from the living area into the bedroom. My eyes widen a little at the mocha wall treatment and dark wood accents, the creamy carpet and deep gray curtains. The bedroom practically invites you into the king-size bed, a brown desk in the corner and a flat-screen mounted on the wall.

A cracked-open door gives a peek of a large garden tub in the bathroom, but on the other side of the room are two big glass doors with handles on them. City lights from the buildings outside sparkle just beyond, and Chiara goes right for them.

She pushes open the glass doors to reveal a wide-open terrace, the sound and air of the city rushing in past her and calling our names. I watch entranced as she wanders outside, where it's dark but well lit, a dinette ready for two and flowers lining the pillared railing.

Chiara leans over and looks up and down the street, but I've got the better view from here, no question. She finally turns, coming back inside and trailing a fingertip across the bedspread with a wicked smile on her face. "You went through a lot of trouble, Mason."

"Nah," I say, shifting my weight. "Anyways, it's worth it."

She's giving me all the signals for go—the red lights flickering in my mind and my whole being anxious to launch. But I can't tell if that's just me being me, or if it's her, or if it's all that crap we drank. I make my boots carry me to the side of the room where the luggage racks are before I crash and burn this thing by jumping the damn gun.

She crosses her arms and watches me with a curious smile as I sit and take off my Ariats, then set them aside. I really try not to wonder what she's gonna think about my new vertical limit in a minute. Don't matter when I'm lying down, that's for sure.

I head toward the bathroom and flip on the light. "You wanna find us a movie to watch?" I call back to her. "Or you wanna just crash? I didn't know how tired you might be after getting in from Italy this morning."

"Movie is fine," she says from the bedroom. "My hours are all off."

Story of my life.

The TV clicks on as I wash my hands, then brush my teeth. A lot. Should've thought ahead and brought my contacts case and my glasses, but I'll live. Not the first time I've had to sleep with them in. *Really* wish I would've brought my flask, but that's another issue.

When I can't make myself stall any longer, I come out to find Chiara leaning against the bed, her hands on the mattress behind her. My heart does about eight and a half backflips as I take her in.

Her hair is now tied up all messy and casual, Chiara wearing her T-shirt and no pants. *Zero.* Just...lots and lots of long, tan legs. And a tiny little anklet. She's gonna fucking destroy me wearing stuff like that.

With her gaze locked on mine, she curls a single finger toward herself, her entire focus trained on me. I clear my throat and walk toward her. *God,* she looks fucking amazing.

She straightens when I stop in front of her, then works her hands under the hem of my shirt before pulling it off me in one easy motion. "The scar on your shoulder," she says, tossing my shirt away. "What is that from?"

I glance at it, then try to brush it off, as though that's possible after the surgery I needed for tearing my rotator cuff. "World's most dangerous sport."

"Moto?" she offers. "Or bull riding?"

"Water volleyball."

Chiara laughs loud and clear, the sound encouraging me more as my hands settle tentatively on her hips, guiding her to lie on the bed. Her eyes track every movement of my hands when I unhook my belt and buckle, then slide off my jeans. Keep my briefs on—one thing at a time.

Her smile is a whole new definition of tempting when she scoots back, and I slowly crawl forward, then position myself directly over her before I lower to kiss her. I'm already infatuated by the way she tastes: spicy with cinnamon like the Fireball whiskey I love, hot as summer days spent blazing next to a swimming pond. She's a hell of a kisser and absolutely one of the hottest women I've ever seen in real life. But I can already tell that everything to do with Chiara comes with the shadow of Massimo behind her, and this is the last place I want him to be.

Chiara's nails start cutting into my skin as she moans and pulls me closer, her leg hooked around mine and her body moving in a way I'm sure to know *real* well in a minute. I pull back from her first, cradling her jaw softly in my hand and my eyes strict when they find hers.

"I'm not him."

She shakes her head, already pulling my lips back to hers. "I don't want you to be."

*Good enough for me.*

I kiss her deeper this time, rougher. In a way only I can do, with moves only I know. It's the same when I caress and massage my way down her body, reacquainting myself with all her supple curves before I reach my hand between her legs. I find her clit without any trouble, because once again, she isn't wearing panties. I really like this about her.

"Oh God, Mason," she moans on contact, and I really like that too.

I hook my arm under her neck and hold her to me as I get to work on the orgasm I owe her; tapping and touching, but just barely. Just her clit, with just one fingertip, rubbing and teasing and learning her, and not giving her anything else she's begging me for. She thinks she wants it, but she doesn't—the single focus of sensation is gonna work out so much better for her. I know it for sure when her nails clamp hard into my neck as her body locks taut, and I've got her coming for me before she even knows what the hell just happened.

*Score one for me.*

Chiara slurs something under her breath that I'm gonna take as an Italian "What the fuck," or maybe it's a "Holy shit," and honestly, either is fine. She needs to buck up, though. We're just getting started.

I slip two fingers into her, and she squeaks and clambers for a grip on my shoulders. Yep, she definitely came. Slip them back out and dip them in my mouth. Her eyes go hazy with desire as she watches me taste her on my fingers. Tastes fucking good too.

"Yep." I pat her thigh. "I'm gonna need some more of that."

She's still slack-jawed from her orgasm as I slide down the bed, propping that soft, tan thigh of hers on my shoulder. I smile and leave a kiss on her sneaky little tattoo that only the truly blessed will ever see, then take a real taste of her this time. She bucks a little, but not so much that I'm worried about it—just flatten out my tongue and slow down a bit, and she's good to go. Moaning and riding me, working with me and fisting her hand in my hair. Taking it all and pulling me closer, and I could do this all freaking night with her.

I bring her right to the edge, then back off and sit up before I let her get all the way there. She'll thank me for it in a minute, and I'm still not even close to done enjoying her. "On your knees."

God love her: she doesn't ask why or argue or nothing. Just turns over and props that ass up, and *damn* she's got a great one. I go in for a second taste of her, teasing her clit with my thumb as I draw my tongue over and around and inside her and right up to where it's not supposed to be.

Chiara jolts and bursts out laughing, looking back at me over her shoulder. "What are you doing?"

I smooth my hands over her legs and her lower back, squeezing the curves of her ass with a devilish smile on my lips. She knows exactly what I was doing. "Does it feel good?"

She blushes deep red, but there's only honesty in her honey-brown eyes. "Yes."

"You want me to stop?"

She thinks about it. But not for long before I get my answer. "No."

"Then don't worry about it." I jerk my chin at her, unable to stop smiling. She is so fucking sexy with her T-shirt all bunched up to her tits and her hair a complete mess over her shoulder. I am never gonna get over this. "Get your head down."

She smiles and goes back to hugging her pillow, and I kiss my way across her lower back and then go back to doing what I was doing. She's ready for me this time, and she's hot enough—just positively soaking—that she lets herself get all the way into it: riding my fingers curled deep inside her, bucking her hips back into me and making some crazy awesome noises into the pillow.

She sounds like she's gonna break something when she comes for me the second time, and I almost want her to. To come so hard that she fucking *breaks*.

But Chiara's fine: already trying to catch her breath as I ease her hips onto the bed that's…a little bit wet because I think she squirted. Hell yeah, baby.

I leave a kiss on her beautiful booty, then go get a condom from my jeans. Actually, I'm gonna need two with her, I already know it.

Chiara is still moaning when I come back to the bed, curled up on her side and her legs rubbing together like she's on ecstasy or something. I ditch my briefs on the floor—fitting myself with the first condom before flicking the second onto the bed. Position myself on my knees between her legs, letting her stay on her side so she's comfortable. But I toss one leg up so her ankle's at my nibbling pleasure, giving me the most control. She's still on another planet.

"Chiara, hey, baby, look at me."

She moans and glances my way, then cracks up laughing and covers her face with her hands. "Oh my God," she mumbles, then points at me. "That is a weapon! How do you fit it in your jeans?"

And that's why she gets a warning. "You let me know if it's too much, okay?"

Because it isn't just long. It's thick too.

"I don't care," she says with a grin, waving me on. "I need it."

With permission granted, I start slow and watch her expression really, really carefully.

She takes it really, really well.

"More," she complains—faster than most—already gasping a bit and her back curving for me, and I let her call the shots from here. *More, deeper. Give it to me. Fuck me, Mason.*

She reaches up and pushes against the headboard, rocking against me until she's got me buried to the hilt, and a breath strangles my throat—that's a rare treat for me. She feels so good too, so warm and impossibly tight. I stroke all the way into her and all the way out, just taking my time as I kiss her ankle and caress her body, letting all the endorphins bleed from my brain and cascade through me.

Chiara isn't having none of this slow stuff; she wraps her leg around my waist to lock me in deeper. *Fine, then.* With her body fully willing to accommodate mine, I go ahead and give her *exactly* what she wants.

She cries out at the first slam, and I pause, trying to keep myself in check. "You okay?"

She nods without hesitation, her hand smoothing up my arm and squeezing my bicep. "It's good. Harder."

I laugh, taking a tighter grip on her ankle. "Okay."

She cries out again the second time, but now that I'm learning what she sounds like, I'd definitely consider that in a happy way. She waves me on again. "Let's go, cowboy."

*Oh, she's getting it now...* I yank her closer and don't hold back this time, fucking her as hard as I want and as fast as I can, Chiara losing her mind and pretty much making all my dreams come true. She's so goddamn gorgeous to watch, and it steals my first climax without warning: thick and slow and seeping from me in long pumps and deep thrusts and going on for freaking ever.

It's a gift and a curse, because now comes the tricky part. It's time to make the switch, and I gotta do it fast, or we're in trouble.

As quick as I can, I grab the second condom and tear open the wrapper, then pull out and ditch my first. Tie it off, toss it on the floor, second one on, and I'm back inside. NASCAR pit crews got nothing on me.

I never stop moving as Chiara moans and runs her hands over my body, touching me everywhere she can reach and sending goose bumps surging across my skin. "Did you not come?"

Since I'm definitely back in the game, I go ahead and pull out to switch positions, turning her fully onto her back and draping her legs over my arms. "Yeah, I did. But we're fine."

We're also somehow sideways on the bed, and I hope she knows what she's in for. Because this is the fun part: it's gonna be a hell of a lot harder for me to come the second time, meaning it's down to me and my physical stamina. And physical stamina, I got a lot of.

I take control of her hips and push myself back inside her, loving how well and simply that works, even with my cock already swollen and aching for round two. Chiara moans and shifts so I'm sunk even deeper, and *fuck* she feels amazing. I don't know how I'm gonna ever leave this hotel room again.

"How are you still this hard?" she asks.

"How are you this sexy?"

She giggles until I slam into her, a moan crawling hard out of my throat and a pleased cry bursting from hers. I lean down and steal a thick kiss from her gorgeous lips, gathering her hands and anchoring them on the nightstand, because she's gonna need to hold on to something.

"You tell me the second it's too much, okay?"

But Chiara just smiles and arches her body up into mine. "Do your worst. I can take it."

And she absolutely does.

The lamp on the nightstand, however, *cannot*.

# Chapter 11

*Chiara Martes—February*

I AM IN SO MUCH TROUBLE.

I glance at Mason sleeping next to me, sunlight trickling in through the glass balcony doors and dancing over the smooth lines of his chest, right down to the sheet draped across his hips. My entire body is still tingling after all that happened last night and very early this morning. He is insatiable, and talk about stamina. But I just woke up to find it's nearly noon, and my phone is boasting multiple missed calls and a string of unread text messages. Why do I never remember to set an alarm?

As carefully as I can, I slip from the bed and search for my clothes. I need to go before Mason wakes up and freaks out that I'm still here. Or worse, *smiles* at me. He's just…he's too sexy, too tempting, way too much fun. And far too good in bed.

(It's fine, it's fine, it's fine. Don't get attached.)

Unfortunately, finding my clothes is a little more complicated than I expected. The room is a *mess*. The lamp from the nightstand is shattered on the floor, and I cringe at the thought of what it's going to cost him to replace it. Probably just as much as the empty little liquor bottles scattered everywhere else. He drank most of them during our naked dance party last night, but I had my fair share, and I've got the start of a headache to prove it. *Real smart, Chiara.*

I'm just stepping into my shorts when my phone starts vibrating again, and I hurry to answer the call from Lorelai before it wakes Mason. "Hey," I whisper.

"Oh my God," she says with a chuckle. "Tell me he was cute."

"He is totally cute," I breathe, trying to put on my shirt while turning down the volume on my phone because Massimo is being *very loud* in the background on her end. "And I kinda…overslept."

Too many orgasms will do that to a girl.

Mason moans and stirs on the bed, reaching toward the thick length swelling under the bedsheet. He runs his palm down it and tugs at the round tip, a shiver tingling down my spine. God, he's so huge… I don't know how I'm even walking right now.

"Mas, be quiet. I can barely hear her," Lorelai says. "He's been having a holy fricking meltdown that you didn't come back last night. He was convinced something happened to you."

Well, yeah. Something did happen to me—I had the time of my *life*. But as much as I wish I could talk to Lorelai about it, giggle and dissect every minute over a bottle of wine like we normally would, I just can't.

She may not see a problem with me dating Mason, but Massimo sure does, and I can't put a wedge between them when they're so happy. I won't do it. I *really* won't, because I'm not letting this thing with Mason go further than last night. Problem solved.

"Tell him to stop being such a grandma," I whisper to Lorelai. "I spent the night out with friends. I didn't get kidnapped." My shoes, however, have definitely been abducted.

I discover my Chucks under the bed, and I'm moments away from a cool, clean escape when Mason moans again and opens his eyes, a half smile curving his lips as he spots me from the bed. A blush instantly takes my cheeks, and I sort of wave at him like the tingly, giddy-from-sex dork that I am. So much for sneaking out.

"Lorelai?" he mouths, and I nod. He snorts, throwing back the sheet and getting up.

I bite my lip at his perfect naked body, Mason rolling out his shoulder in a way that seems more habit than anything else. But my jaw completely drops when he starts walking to the en suite bathroom. *His back…*

"Well, where are you?" Lorelai asks. "Do you need a ride? We can send a car."

"I…don't know yet," I admit. "I'm somewhere in Kuala Lumpur."

I follow Mason into the bathroom, waiting as he pees and comes out to wash his hands. His brow furrows at my worried expression, until I turn him so he can see his back in the mirror. Covered with angry red scratch marks from my nails.

He just smirks and turns toward me, holding up my shirt to reveal a rather large hickey on my stomach. *Oops.* I forgot that happened. Then he points at the zipper on my shorts, mouthing, "There too."

Awesome. He silently starts to chuckle, then runs the sink. I head back into the bedroom, tossing my messy hair. I've got walk of shame written all over me.

"She's in Kuala Lumpur," Lorelai repeats to Massimo. "I know, I know. Yes, I am aware of the time, Massimo, thank you." She groans, saying to me, "He's gonna come get you. Apparently, he had grand plans for us all to go to lunch today and is now getting hangrier by the minute even though he could just *eat* the PowerBar I gave him ten minutes ago. Fine, eat a banana then!"

That's going to be a big negative, Ghost Rider. "I took a bus here, I can take a bus back. I'm not going to make lunch though, sorry. Feel free to eat without me."

"Okay—she's gonna take a bus back. We'll do lunch another day. What is the big—you talk to her then."

*Oh joy.*

Massimo comes on the phone, his Italian mumbled around whatever he's eating. "You really don't want to come to lunch? I had something important I wanted to ask you."

He's got his nervous-excited voice, and it brings a smile straight to my face. "*Aw*, was this when you were going to ask if I would be your best man? I accept."

Massimo chuckles, totally busted. "Lorina told you."

"I honestly thought you were going to ask Dario."

Massimo chokes on his food. "Trust my little brother with the rings? Not a chance."

I start trying to straighten the horrific mess of our hotel room but stop when Mason comes out of the bathroom and waves me off. He sits on the edge of the bed and picks up the room phone.

I cover my receiver just to be safe, but he keeps his voice super low as he orders something I can't make out. "Coffee," he mouths my way. "Five minutes."

"Thank you," I mouth back. I would kill someone for a double espresso right now. Like straight up do a murder.

"No, I'm done. Yeah, we can go," Massimo says to Lorelai. "Well, when are you coming back?" he asks me. "You want to do something this afternoon? Maybe catch a movie, see some sights?"

"Um…"

Mason gets an evil smirk and crawls on the bed toward me, reaching over to tug me and my hips closer to him. A giggle sticks in my throat when he dips his head, a soft sweep of his tongue sneaking up my inner thigh.

He is so, so good at that.

"I'm not sure when I'm going to be back yet." My hand threads through Mason's hair as he keeps kissing me, keeps teasing me, a moan desperate to crawl its way through my body. Especially when he undoes the button on my shorts, the fabric dropping to the floor.

"So I guess we're *not* going to hang out while you're here."

Mason mouths my clit over my panties, the heat from his mouth delicious through the thin layer of silk and *oh shit, oh shit…*

"Dinner," I squeak out. "I'll be back for dinner."

Massimo sighs. "Fine. But you're buying dessert."

Mason flashes a grin up at me, then he hooks a finger into my panties and pulls them aside. He licks at my clit, and I nearly drop the phone.

"You sure you're okay?" Massimo asks. "You don't sound okay."

"Yep. I'm… I'll call you later." I hang up before Massimo can protest, letting my phone slip from my fingers and land somewhere on the floor. The moan I've been restraining pours out of me, my knees shaking as Mason growls and shifts closer, every lick and flick of his tongue soft and reverent.

"Good morning," he says to my overheated flesh, palming my hips and ass in a way that's nothing short of mesmerizing.

"Hi."

"In trouble?"

"So much."

He chuckles darkly, slipping my panties down my hips. Then he rolls onto his back, his cock fully hard and straining up as his head hangs off the bed. His hands guide my hips back toward him, and I let him put me where he wants me—straddling his face and riding the gentle lap of his tongue as he moans and hums, the sight of his thick cock before me absolutely making my mouth water.

He's got me gasping in record time, my breath just coming back into my body when there's a knock on the door. Mason pats my hip, shifting out from between my legs.

"Room service," he says, rolling up from the bed. Spares a quick swipe over his mouth.

"O...kay." I can barely think straight as he steps into his jeans, tucking his dick inside with a groan. Was the room always spinning?

"So what's the damage? Do I need to get you back right away? Or we still cool to hit the comic book store this afternoon?"

"We're okay." I crawl onto the bed, pulling the covers over my bare ass and hugging a pillow that smells deeply of his cologne. And sex. I could totally pass out again after that.

Mason chuckles, the bed dipping before I get a kiss to the back of my shoulder. "Sweet."

A smile sneaks onto my lips, my hand barely catching a whisper of his skin before he disappears and leaves the room. Moments later, the rich scent of espresso floods the suite.

This is fine. One more day with him doesn't mean anything, and then we'll definitely have gotten it all out of our systems. And as long as it's only one more day, then there's nothing to tell Massimo or Lorelai. No reason to rock the boat.

I've totally got this under control. (Yep.)

# Chapter 12

*Chiara Martes—March*

"Whatever you do, *don't move.*"

A nervous squeak pops from my throat, my whole face pulled in a wince that's supposed to be a charming smile. But my facial reactions are *not* working. Probably something to do with the very large, very angry falcon on my arm.

I barely risk moving my lips to speak. "Okay, but…I really, really want to move."

"Just…another…second," Mason says slowly, my cringe factor ramping up to eleven before the falcon decides he has had enough of this shit—that makes two of us—and starts flapping his wings while making the most god-awful noise.

"Mason!" I screech, holding my arm as far from my head as humanly possible because this huge-ass bird on my arm is thoroughly pissed the hell off and slapping my hair with its feathers. Any second, it's going to go for my eyes, I know it.

Why did we think this was a good idea? *Why?*

"Okay, okay! I got it."

I glance up enough to see him practically doubled over laughing, my phone limp in his hand and the falcon going bananas until the shop owner takes him from me. I ditch that leather sleeve thing and dart toward the safety of standing behind Mason's broad shoulders and, I swear, never have I felt so much relief.

Mason is still laughing, and I nudge his shoulder. "I'm glad you found that so funny."

He nods and wipes at his eyes as he straightens. "Sorry, but that was *hilarious.*"

"You are being a real ass today, you know that?"

"Hold on. Look though." He coughs and clears his throat, but he's still chuckling when he shows me the string of pictures he took, progressively more ridiculous from my strangled smile to my full-on freaking out, and it's not another second before I'm laughing too.

I look like I'm being murdered by the damn bird.

The shop owner coos in Arabic and pets the falcon, then glances around at the rest of the patrons, saying in heavily accented English, "Okay, who is next?"

I peek at Mason from the corner of my eyes, jerking my chin at the falcon. "Your turn, cowboy."

"No way," Mason says to me. "That thing is huge. You see his talons?"

I gape at him. "You ride bulls for a living!"

"And I still ain't fucking with that bird," he says, laughing as I start to push him out of the Falcon Souq. Mason waves at the shop owner guy over my shoulder. "Thank you, sir."

"And your bird is an—"

Mason clamps his hand over my mouth, laughing harder as he hooks his arm around my waist and spins me out onto the busy sidewalk. Probably for the best.

The elegant hum of Arabic and English and a couple other languages I can't identify floats soothingly over us, the bright Doha sun warm and welcoming after the thick stench of bird poop in that crowded little shop. I take back my phone and tuck it into my back pocket, then hook on my sunglasses. Mason's hand on my waist is a comforting kind of heavy that I'm quickly getting used to. Even though it was only supposed to be that one date, one time…

But when it became clear that our afternoon at the comic store was going to end in his bedroom, we very quickly struck a deal, putting clear rules in place. This is just casual. Friendship. No strings, no expectations, and some very big benefits. And considering Mason and I agree that we're *not* dating, we're just hanging out, then I guess I'm not technically doing anything wrong?

Massimo is uncomfortable with me dating other racers—okay, we're not dating. He doesn't want me to get emotionally invested in someone who I'll never see, and I can understand that. I wouldn't want that for him either. So I'm not. Getting emotionally invested.

Not that Mason exactly makes it easy. (It's fine, it's fine, it's fine.)

"Don't be mad," he breathes in my ear, sneaking a kiss to my neck.

Goose bumps shiver over my skin, and it's been a surprise to discover that even though we're still absolutely sneaking off the paddock to see each other—far away from the prying eyes of the moto press always following him with a camera crew—he's not afraid to be affectionate once we're in public. In fact, he revels in it.

We've been in Qatar for a couple weeks now, waiting out the time before the first race of the season. It's been beyond fun, spending every day exploring the market and strolling the Doha Corniche with him. Plus everything we do at night. In his RV. After Lorelai goes to sleep and I sneak over.

"I'm not mad," I tell him. "But the next dumb thing we do? It is your turn to go first."

"Looking forward to it."

I shake my head with a grin—I'm not sure I've ever met someone quite as competitive as Mason King. And while it's so nice to have someone to play with, to banter and constantly challenge each other, even I-Win-or-I'll-Die-Pouting Massimo isn't this bad. The one part I can't seem to figure out is why it isn't translating onto the racetrack.

Nearly every practice, every lap, Mason is two seconds behind his brother. Except he's quicker off the grid, faster through the turns, and he's built better for racing than Billy. But still, he's always behind.

I'm starting to suspect self-sabotage—especially with how often he tastes like whiskey when he shouldn't—but nothing provable yet. I'm also not convinced him double fisting careers is helping anything.

When everyone left Malaysia straight for Qatar, Mason went to Memphis for a rodeo. He came back a week later covered in bruises, and I honestly don't see the point of him risking his racing career for a single rodeo. But I'm definitely not talking to Mason about any of that—I would be so out of line, the line would be invisible.

"Speaking of doing dumb things," he says, "what do you wanna do tonight?"

"Hmm, what are our options?" He comes up with the best worst ideas *ever*.

"Well," he drawls, "I was thinking we could do the party crawl: drink some drinks, dance it off, find a place to make out, do our normal thing."

I can't help but smile as his thumb strokes over my side: *our normal thing.*

"Or," he says, "we could go to dinner."

There's something in his voice—a deepening of his country accent that spells pure trouble. "What kind of dinner?"

Before I get an answer, I get a tug on my belt loops. Mason takes my other hand, spinning me out with barely any effort on my part. Warmth takes my cheeks as he steps into me, his hand on my waist and a rhythm moving through him that isn't hard to follow.

I shake my head but still drape my arm over his shoulder, unable to stop smiling. The man reads far too many romance novels, and while he's great at playing the romantic hero, I am far from any kind of heroine. I'm the plucky sidekick at best. "What are you doing now, cowboy?"

"Dancing with you."

My eyes dart to the nearby shopping stalls, people parting around us. "We are in the middle of the market."

"So. That a problem?"

Most the people around us have stopped what they're doing and are openly staring, some *aww*ing while others wrinkle their noses, but I honestly don't care. It's worth it to feel him this close, to see that verge-of-chaos smile. Sometimes, I think he may be wilder than I am.

"Back to dinner," he says. "Some low lighting, soft music, a bit of ambience to go with an outrageously expensive bottle of red wine…"

"Mason," I warn.

"And then afterward, maybe, you'll let me put it in your butt."

I crack up laughing. Mason's smile stretches full-size.

"There he is," I say brightly, toying with the hair at the nape of his neck.

"Here I am." He grins and innocently bats his eyelashes at me—and what eyelashes he's got. "Seriously, though," he says a little quieter. "What's wrong with a little bit of romance?"

"It's...dangerous." Especially when I am trying to keep us friends with benefits *only*.

He levels a look at me. "I race bulls and ride motorcycles for a living, Chiara. I'm not exactly Mr. Safety."

"Other way around. Not race bulls, *ride* bulls."

Mason's brow furrows. "Huh? I didn't...I said ride. Ride bulls. Didn't I?"

I stop us, looking a little closer at him. He's typically very quick-tongued—not just in bed—and I've never known him to mix up his words like that. But right now, there's a little too much confusion in his blue eyes, an unmistakable trace of panic behind them.

My hand rises to his cheek, my heart speeding up to a full sprint. "Mason, are you okay?"

"Yeah, just...must be jet-lagged or something."

He's not, though. Not even close.

"Hey, I'm okay," he says with a wink. He covers my hand with his, pulling both away from his cheek so he can press a kiss to the inside of my wrist. Right before he nips at me, gah!

"I was not worried. I was making fun of you. Completely different thing."

Mason snakes his arm around my waist and hugs me up into him. "That's it," he growls, pretending to be mad. He may be quite the creative when it comes to role play, but he sucks at acting. "I'm cancelling the reservation, and we're having dinner at Burger King."

"No," I pretend to cry out. "My ambience!"

# Chapter 13

*Chiara Martes—April*

A WIDE SMILE STRETCHES ACROSS MY FACE AS I SINK MY FINGERS IN the chain-link fence, then tilt back my head and soak in the warm Austin sun. A wave of motorcycles rushes past on the track, the raw sound vibrating through my veins, dancing with my growing adrenaline.

After Qatar, our time in Thailand was a blur of unimaginable scenery that filled up my phone with awe-worthy pictures: hiking with Mason in the Khao Kradong Forest Park, visiting the Buriram Castle, and then partying at the night market at Sro Ground. I think I ate twice my weight in Thai food. And drank probably three times as much after Mason came in first place.

The hangover was brutal, but so worth it. I was so damn proud of him. And it was his birthday, after all.

The pack of women racers comes back around the track (practice, practice, practice), Lorelai leading and their bikes roaring louder as they battle to find more speed in the redlined engines. Tingles trickle over my skin and shimmer to my toes. I love that sound. The speed and the sex, the sex and the speed—I just can't seem to get enough lately.

"I thought you said there was nothing more boring than watching people ride around in circles," Massimo teases behind me in Italian.

I peek over my shoulder with a grin. "Only when it's you out there. You're nothing special, star."

Massimo chuckles, coming to a stop beside me. He bumps my shoulder with his, mine bare from my Starfleet Academy tank top and his hard from the pads under his Yaalon-blue racing leathers. He passes me one of the two samosas he's holding. "Peace offering?"

He must mean from last night, when he won our Monopoly game in record time. I swear he was sneaking cash from the bank. "Eh, mediocre attempt. But I'll allow it."

I'm freaking starving, and when I take a bite of the samosa, I catch Massimo watching me with a smile in the corner of his mouth. It gets even bigger when I can't resist a moan at the explosion of spices and flavors, and *holy crap*, this is amazing.

"Okay, you win," I say around a full mouth of beef and potato. "That's really freaking good."

"Yep. And you can't have mine." He eats half of his in one bite, turning around and leaning back against the fence. He slips on his sunglasses from where they were pushed up into his hair, the undercut a little shaggier than he prefers.

I'm kind of surprised to see him out here enjoying the endless ocean-blue sky. He usually spends all day in his garage, going over things with his crew to tweak and try on the bike or arguing with his manufacturer rep about all the ways they want him to default to Billy as the veteran Yaalon racer. If not, he's in Lorelai's garage.

"You need a haircut," I tell him, Massimo nodding as he shoves the rest of the samosa in his mouth. A piece of pastry is flaked on his lips, and I chuckle and reach over to brush it away. "You're so gross."

He smirks, then opens his mouth and shows me his half-eaten food.

"Ew! You're officially less mature than your little brother."

Massimo stretches his arms high above his head with a groan like he's exhausted. "Have you talked to Dario lately?"

"Yeah, yesterday. He's got a new girlfriend. Sent me a picture, and she's *cute*!"

Massimo yawns, but it's more of a grunt than anything. "He needs to break up with her."

"Right," I say slowly, "because that's the normal response to that."

Massimo gestures dismissively. "He's fifteen. He's too young to feel that way. He's just going to get hurt, or he's going to disappoint her. It's not like it's going to last."

I flare my eyes as I turn back to the fence, watching as someone tries to overtake Lorelai and she blocks them in the turn. It's just a practice, but she's *not* having it. She really is amazing to watch. Somehow even more ruthless than my "No Mercy" best friend.

"What's the word?" I tap my finger against my chin, then whisper toward Massimo, "Hypocrite. Because as I recall, when you met Lorelai—"

"Chiara—"

"You were fifteen. And you came home convinced you'd met the woman you were going to marry."

I wait for the pain to throb, but it barely comes. (I spent that whole weekend crying.) Honestly, I don't know why I was so surprised. He's always been so *perfect*, so beautiful, and ever since we were kids, every girl he ever met was desperate to lock him down and get between us. They would sit between us at church, walk between us at school, hanging on his arm and pushing me aside and out of the way.

(I've always been in the way.)

They'd scheme and they'd laugh and they'd lie to him about poor Chiara Martes with the drunk for a father. And I knew: Massimo may have saved me, but he was also stuck with me, probably sick of me, and I was forever a burden to him and his family until he was gone—surrounded by models and adoring fans. Then he was chasing after *her*.

"That's what you said anyway."

Massimo shakes his head, muttering, "That was different."

I reach over for the ticklish spot on his side, under the scythe he had tattooed over it. "Says the hypocrite."

"Well, it was," he grits out, dropping his elbow and keeping a mostly straight face. "And nothing happened."

I turn back to the fence. "Yeah, because she hated you."

For years and years, leaving me to pick up the pieces of his broken heart. All the times he wanted to give up and I wouldn't let him. Then it happened—she wrecked her moto, wrecked bad, and in her search for her lost confidence, she found him. That was that.

The pack of motorcycles comes back around, and I wonder what

Mason can see when he's going that fast or if it's all a blur? I'll have to ask him later. The trouble is whether I'll remember to ask once I see him. He just does this *thing* to my brain where I can't seem to recall important stuff once he smiles at me. After his shirt comes off? Forget about it. I'm *gone*.

"Thanks. I really wanted to remember that today."

There's an abnormally high amount of self-loathing in Massimo's voice, which I don't understand when he still got her in the end. Just like he wanted—I made sure of it.

"What's wrong now?" I fake a pout at him. "She use up all your favorite hair product again? Oh, wait, I know! You got in a fight with your mom, and Lorelai agreed with Maria."

"It's nothing."

That is so not nothing. "If you don't tell me, I'm just going to ask her."

He shifts his weight against the fence, crossing his arms and shrugging. Fully shrinking into himself like whenever he'd get lower marks on a school test than he expected. "I don't know. I mean, everything's fine, but what do I know about being someone's husband? I made you mad all the time when we were living together, and you're...easy."

I arch my eyebrow at that. He's called me a lot of stuff, but *easy* isn't one I've heard before. It's usually more along the lines of careless, irresponsible, dangerously impulsive. I may be the gravity, but he's always been the net. Maybe the bungee cord.

"Well, you are," he says. "Still, I just...I did everything wrong. I'm *still* doing everything wrong."

I stare at his profile, no idea where this is coming from.

I crack a small laugh. "Then make it up to me, asshole."

Massimo gives me the start of a smile, but it doesn't last long. Not the way Lorelai gets him to smile. "I'm trying."

I face him, fully intrigued. "Oh yeah? How?"

"I don't know," he mumbles. "I just...you should have been here. With me. You shouldn't have been stuck at home with Mom riding your ass about everything all the time."

I nod as I pretend to consider that. His whole career was launching; I would have only been a distraction. "And the fact that we were broke and couldn't afford it?"

"I should have found a way," he bites off, his words aimed at the ground. "I shouldn't have abandoned you."

God, he's really swimming in his guilt today. And it makes me super uncomfortable, but if I can't tease him out of this mood, I'll have to downshift into the truth.

I tuck my hair behind my ear, trying to keep my voice light. "So who stole motos to keep us fed and bought us our apartment? Because I'd love to meet whoever that guy was."

He looks away, tugging at the sleeves of his leathers. For a guy who loves to intimidate people, he sure doesn't know how to take a compliment. The cocky act is just that: an *act*.

"And how many years did it take you to scrape together your pennies until you bought my car? Three or four? I can't remember."

"You needed a car," he mumbles.

"Yeah? And what did you need?"

"For you to be taken care of."

I let out a loud groan—I swear, he is such a drama queen sometimes. "Massimo, that is all you have ever done. I'm okay."

"Are you?" He looks at me, and even though I can't see his eyes behind his sunglasses, I know exactly the look in them. All that Catholic guilt rotting his dark-brown irises. And his eyes are too pretty for that shit.

"Yeah." The roar of the pack of motorcycles grows louder as they come back around, and a smile starts to rise on my lips that I can't seem to control, images and moans echoing in my mind. A whole bunch of feelings flood my body along with them, everything from joy to excitement to lust and...a few things that shouldn't be there. But I'm ignoring those. "Things have been...pretty good for me lately."

Massimo turns a little more my way, and I shrug, resigned to telling him as much as he needs to hear to feel better.

"I've gotten to see some pretty cool places, meet some cool

people," I tell him. His jaw twitches, but I ignore that too. "And I've gained ten pounds just from stuffing my face with foods I can't pronounce. See?" I beam at him, batting my eyelashes. "Happy."

This earns me a bit of a smile. "Does this mean I get my favorite jeans back?"

"No. I'm just not buttoning them right now."

He chuckles, sounding a little more than halfway better. "Thief."

"Eh. You're the one with the record."

He glances around like he's worried someone heard that. But it's just us against the fence. "Yeah, because you're a terrible lookout."

I snicker, looking back to the track. "I told you that guy was dirty."

"Yeah, you did. I should've listened to you."

"Um, obviously. Kinda like when you wanted to grow your hair out into a ponytail. Freaking grunge stage was *so* not a good look for you." I pretend to headbang for a minute just to mess with him some more, and Massimo laughs. Like actually *laughs*. Score one for me.

"Oh, because the black lipstick and JNCOs were so attractive on you."

I dramatically flip my hair over my shoulder. "Hey, I rocked that shit."

Massimo goes quiet for a minute, just smiling at me, and it's the same look he gets when he buys my birthday present early and then has to wait to give it to me. He never lasts.

"What?"

He shrugs, then lightly kicks at my foot with his. "I've missed you. This. It's…" He blows out a breath, then glances around before he admits the real truth. "It's weird sometimes. Coming home to the house and you're not there."

"Um, yeah. That's what happens when you move out." I throw him a wink just to be safe. "You'll get used to it."

"And you have?"

"What's there to get used to? You weren't at the apartment that much to begin with," I tease him.

Massimo just stares at me. Jaw locked and eyebrow arched.

Because as much as he lets his feelings get away with him, he knows how much I deflect when mine try to take hold of me.

"I'm getting there," I answer more honestly. "It's...quiet. Living alone, in the weeks when we're home. Sometimes..." God, this is so embarrassing. "I come out of my room to say something to you and have to remember that you're gone."

Just saying it out loud...the damn throb comes up and hits me triple force, and it's been so long since I've felt it like *that*, my eyes start to prickle with tears at the sharp slice of all I've lost. He's such an asshole, always cutting through my defenses. Especially when it's the last thing I need.

"Any problems?" he asks quietly.

I don't have to ask him what he means—he went with me to therapy for years, listening as she told us what to watch for and for ways he could help. And it worked, it really worked.

"Sometimes," I whisper. (I try not to lie about this stuff.) "I, um, I get scared when there's a knock on the door and I don't know who it is. Like he's going to know I'm alone and show up, and you won't be there."

Massimo grabs my hand. Fast. "He won't."

"I know." I nod so he won't worry, though it's probably too late after what I just admitted. "It's just weird. I didn't think about it for years. All the time you were gone racing, I never even worried about it. But something..."

"Is different now," he finishes.

"Yeah. Like something expired, and he's going to know and try to take me back." My voice cracks, and Massimo reaches up with his free hand to wipe away a tear from my cheek. I shouldn't let him do that anymore, but right now, I need it too much to stop him.

"He can't. I won't let him."

A relieved smile sneaks onto my lips that I can't and don't try to stop. He is literally my knight in shining armor. "You'd come find me, right?"

"Always." His voice is strong and unflinching, everything I need to feel safe.

It almost works too.

"Well then," I sniffle. "I don't have anything to worry about."

He blows out a breath, lacing his fingers through mine. "Want to move into the guest house? Maybe for just a little while?"

I crack up laughing through my stray tears. "No."

Sometimes. But no. I'll just be in the way.

I've always been in the way.

Massimo half smiles at me. "Movie night, then? When we get home. You can crash on the couch. I'll make budino. I'll even let you eat some. Just a little, though."

"Wow, what an offer," I deadpan. "How Lorelai resisted you for so long, I'll never know."

He snorts, tilting his head and smoothing his hand over his jaw and face like a men's shaving cream ad. "I am pretty irresistible."

"Oh, *God*. Do I need to get out the grunge-era scrapbook? Because I can, and I will."

Massimo pushes off the fence and hooks an arm around my neck, pretending to put me in a headlock as I fake a punch to his stomach. "Your pictures are in there too, you know."

"Nope, because I burned them."

Massimo laughs as we start heading back to the paddock, his steps falling in time with mine. "So when are you going to tell me?"

"Tell you what?"

"Who the guy is you've been seeing."

My stomach drops straight to my knees, but Massimo doesn't seem to notice.

"And don't act like you're not. You're always busy on our days off, and you're smiling a lot for someone who's been indefinitely separated from their gaming system."

I fake a scoff that is hopefully more convincing than it feels. "Who says it's one guy? Could be a different one every night."

"Whatever," he says with a chuckle. "Just promise me you're being careful, whatever you're doing. Eyes open."

Guilt swirls in my stomach, blending sickly against the samosa. This is so not good. The last time I tried to keep a secret from

Massimo, I broke out in hives. "I promise I am being careful. I'm not doing anything serious with anyone you need to worry about. I'm just having fun."

That's what I'm telling myself anyway. Harmless, no strings, no worries fun. And there's no reason to upset Massimo when this thing with Mason is not going anywhere. Massimo is stressed enough as it is with racing and the wedding.

"Good. I'm glad you're having fun." He pulls me closer and brushes a kiss to my hair, his arm heavy and safe around my shoulders. As it's always been.

Walking next to him is all muscle memory, the foundation to everything I've always known. It should help, make me feel safe and loved and all I've been missing. The truest form of family. But when I lean my head to his shoulder, my mind is already skipping ahead.

Bounding across the other side of the paddock and racing toward tonight and wondering what terrible idea Mason has planned for us.

Can't wait to find out. (And hope Massimo never does.)

# Chapter 14

*Mason King—April*

I collapse on the bed next to Chiara, breathless and sweaty and my heart still pounding in my chest like my organs are at a rock concert. "We…" I pant out, turning my face from the pillow so I can at least try to breathe, "are getting really good at that."

Her laugh is soft and quiet, interspersed between deep pulls of air and the echoes of moans that I am completely addicted to. Sweat glistens on her neck and beads on her chest, and I can't resist crawling closer to kiss away a drop.

"Don't." She pushes me away with barely enough strength to move a feather. "Gross."

"Not gross. Sexy."

"Ugh." She rolls off the bed and slumps straight onto the floor.

I snort. "You okay?"

"Yes. I just…I need my clothes."

"Babe, you gotta pee first. I don't want you to get a UTI."

"Ew, super gross." Her head of tangled brown hair starts glancing around, then she crawls on the floor toward the pile of shirts and her lacy underwear. I roll my eyes where she can't see.

Chiara, as I'm learning, is a runner.

Not like Lorelai, who pounds the pavement every morning in her Nikes and black leggings. No—Chiara is more like an escape artist. Her trust issues run deep, and any hint of someone liking her or being *nice*, and she bails. Trying to take her to dinner is an endless battle, and cuddling after sex is out of the question. Usually about three seconds after she's got me spent, she's heading for the door. I normally wouldn't mind—I've never been one for lingering, and I've typically got my boots on before my condom is tied off. But *she's* the one who keeps texting me every day, asking what our plans are for that night.

I try to keep it light and expectations low, and I drop plenty of outs for her to take. But we always end up here. Usually her idea too.

"You're doing it again." I slide myself off the other half of the mattress, rooting around on the floor until I find her shorts. Hold them up on the crook of my fingers, barely looking up in time as she snatches them away.

"Do not start." She tugs them up her long legs, buttoning them with a vengeance. "We agreed from the start that this was only physical. Friends with benefits. Nothing more. And that does not include—"

"Yeah, I got it." I pull myself the rest of the way out of the bed, finding my boxer briefs and putting them on. Stretch out my lower back as I stand, and yeah, that's gonna be sore in the morning. She was bullying the hell out of me tonight—the slower I try to go, the harder she wants it. Surprised her back isn't hurting at this point too.

Chiara tugs her tangled hair out of the collar of her T-shirt, almost glaring at me. "I am not your girlfriend, Mason."

"I am aware of that, Chiara. And I didn't ask you to be."

"Well...good." She scoops up her Chucks and strides from my room, trying to slip them on her feet as she stumbles toward the door of the RV.

I'm following after her before I can tell myself it's a bad idea. "So that's a no to breakfast, then?"

"Yes. I mean, no."

"How you gonna say no to pancakes? Everyone likes pancakes."

"Not me."

I hook a finger in her belt loops and spin her back my direction. Chiara's guard is firmly up, her chin lifting higher by the second. Doesn't scare me a bit. "Tell me you didn't have fun."

"You are...always fun," she says reluctantly.

*Yeah, I am.* Because there's no denying that whether we're

exploring a new city or tumbling around in my bed, she always leaves with a smile. I've also gotten really damn good at giving her the orgasms she keeps coming back for. But that's just a bonus of me being able to read her moods, her moans, and learning what works best instead of just guessing because it's all new. Practice makes perfect, after all.

I take a step closer and Chiara's back hits the door, her body already sinking into her knees a little. Both of us are still riding the high from everything we just did. Twice.

"But that is not the point," she says firmly.

I lean my palm against the door above her shoulder, pressing a little bit closer as my grin refuses to quit. I'm drowning in the scent of cinnamon and rough, dirty sex and the faint trace of cologne on her skin that is 100 percent *me*. "So what is the point?"

"I…"

Her eyes search mine as she scrambles for her words. She doesn't find a single one when my fingertips tickle their way under the hem of her shirt and stroke slowly over her skin. Goose bumps erupt under my fingertips, and she grits out a curse in Italian, her hands seizing my jaw and tugging my lips to hers. Her kiss is sharp and hungry, kinda angry, and begging me to give her everything her words keep warning me against.

I give her back as good as I'm getting, and it isn't long until her body is crushed to mine: her nails digging into my skin to pull me closer, her moans rumbling deeper. I wasn't kidding earlier. We are getting really, *really* good at this.

"Just let me make you breakfast," I whisper against her lips. "One pancake isn't gonna morph into a ring on your finger."

She pushes me away, *again*, and turns for the door. "No."

"Fine. Don't call me tonight, then."

She halts in place, and yeah, I'm being a dick. But I don't know how else to get through to her. That just because I like hanging out and because I like doing stuff with her—and for her—it doesn't have to mean anything more. I'm not looking to hurt her, and not everyone is looking for forever. Some people just want pancakes. But she doesn't get that. With her, it seems to be all or nothing, and I'm not interested in all. So I guess that leaves nothing.

I turn and start walking back to my room.

"Mason..." she calls after me.

"Bye."

I straighten the tangled sheets and pull up the covers, then sweep up my glasses and the book off my nightstand before I flop onto my bed. Open up to my bookmark, skimming over the last page I read, and completely ignoring the sight of Chiara walking back to my room. Turn the page, scanning over words I can't begin to comprehend as she leans against the doorway.

"You are being really difficult."

My eyes never leave the page. "Thought you were leaving?"

She sighs, crossing her arms across her chest. "I am not trying to hurt your feelings."

"I don't have those kinds of feelings." Turn another page. "So don't worry about it."

"Oh, so now you don't have feelings? You are just a robot."

"Sex robot."

"That is bullshit."

My eyes lift at the heat in her tone.

"You are nice," she says. "And funny. And you don't give a woman orgasms like that if you don't care about how she feels. You wouldn't bother."

"How do you know?" I pop back. "I could be a total asshole who just happens to be really good in bed."

"No one is that good."

"I told you: sex robot."

"Mason," she says, exasperated, "I am trying to talk to you about this, and you are being impossible."

*Busted.* "So you *are* having fun then?"

"That's not..." she sputters. "I..."

I flare my eyes, looking back to my book and turning another unread page. "Uh-huh."

A tight sigh leaves her nose. "I just don't want this to get confusing."

"No chance on that happening."

Chiara tosses up her hands with a groan. "Fine. One pancake. But we have to eat it here because I don't want—"

"Yeah, yeah, yeah."

She doesn't want Massimo to know. I don't really either. It's none of his business.

I toss down my book, trying not to spring from the bed because *I won.* I stand and walk calmly toward her, past her, heading to the kitchen and getting out a mixing bowl and the box of Bisquick I keep stocked for emergencies. My pancakes are way better from scratch, but I don't have any baking powder in my RV.

I'm halfway through stirring the milk and egg and floury mixture when two arms slide around my waist, hugging my back as her cheek rests against my shoulder.

"Stop being so nice to me all the time," she whispers.

"Okay. I will work on being meaner."

"I'm serious. It makes me nervous."

My heart speeds up but I keep stirring slow, careful not to slosh over the sides. "Why would that make you nervous?"

"Because. People are nice, and then they..." She shakes her head, hugging me a little tighter. "They leave. Forget about you. It's easier when it's honest from the start. Nobody stays around forever."

Jesus Christ. He really broke her heart good.

*And she's still not over him.*

"Okay." I pour half a cup of batter onto the pan I've got heating on the small stove, then grab a spatula from the drawer. Spin it in my fingers as I wink at her over my shoulder. "One burned pancake it is. And don't even *think* about asking for a second one."

A smile finally starts to tease the edge of her lips. "Much better."

# Chapter 15

*Mason King—May*

THE WARM SPRING DAY IS BRIGHT AND BEAUTIFUL AND *PERFECT* for racing, and I'm happily lounging in my brother's pit box in Argentina, getting my report from him of what I did "wrong" in practice.

Even though *I've* got pole position.

We did have to switch to fishing code, though, because I think his crew doesn't like that we talk. I don't care. We were brothers first.

"Man, you're losing it," I tell Billy from my chair. "Sixty-pound lines are a waste. You only need to use a thirty-pound line for a thirteen pounder."

*Sixth gear is too fast, though. Especially when it's third gear for turn thirteen.*

Billy shrugs. "Fine, use the wrong line. But that's why the fish on my wall are bigger."

I flip him off, and he strolls back toward his crew, checking over the latest telemetry readouts. He's probably right, and I could push it faster in turn twelve, but it just feels risky with how sharp turns thirteen and fourteen are. *Fuck it. May as well go for it.*

I take a sip of water, half counting the minutes till tonight and wondering what Chiara's doing today. If she's hanging with Lorelai in her pit box or with Massimo in his. Hopefully, she's resting in the RV. We were up late again last night, and she's gotta be tired. I'm dragging serious ass. Still faster than Massimo, though.

I yawn and close my water, already down two energy drinks and a double espresso, and *speak of the devil*—Massimo storms in, looking ten shades of furious in his Yaalon racing leathers. For some reason, it makes me smile real damn wide.

"I want to talk to you," he says, practically growling his words.

"Talk to me?" I grin and clap my water bottle like it's a football, crossing my boot on my knee so I keep still in my chair instead of blasting up and getting in his face. I've got plenty I want to say, but I know damn well that if I pick a fight, it's only gonna end badly. For *me*.

Massimo is freaking *fast*, brutal in his textbook technique, and they should've branded him "Ice Man." He almost never makes mistakes on the track, doesn't leave gaps, and the last thing I want is him diving for me in turns over personal reasons. This is still my year, and they're all starting to realize it after my win in Buriram and my pole position today. Come Valencia, they'll know it for sure.

"No, not to *you*," he snaps at me. "You would probably only lie anyway." He leans closer, his eyes flaring. "I do not trust you."

"Ooh." I hold up my hands in surrender, looking over my shoulder at my brother and kinda enjoying the audience of his pit crew. Who are trying like all hell not to smirk as they keep working on my brother's bike. "Well, since we got that cleared up."

"What's going on, Massimo?" Billy comes over to stand beside me, towering over both of us and crossing his arms. I *love* when he does that to people. Hate when he does it to me. "We got a problem here?"

"You tell me," Massimo says. "We have been teammates for over a year now, and I thought we understood each other."

"Okay." Billy scratches at his stubbled jaw. He's using his big brother voice, and I can barely keep a straight face. "Remind me what I understand."

"We have talked before, yes? About certain things that we will *not* allow to be risked." Massimo's eyes dart my way like that threat was for me, and *yeah*, I'm sure it was. With the way Lori is about her 5:00 a.m. runs, I wondered if we were gonna get caught with Chiara not sneaking back until almost six this morning. Survey says: *yep*.

I *knew* we should've set an alarm. I'm normally...pretty bad at being on time to stuff. Chiara not only exacerbates that problem—a lot—but she's so bad about keeping track of it that she makes me look like the king of punctuality. It's kinda nice, though. Not only am I *not* getting judged for what most people consider my biggest flaw, but she's a bit of a motivator to work on it. And I've been doing a pretty good job of getting her home at a decent hour. Except for last night when she wanted to role-play pirates and Cap'n Relentless got to plunder the booty. *Aargh.*

"Massimo, I would love to know what you're talking about," Billy drawls.

But Massimo doesn't seem to care about what my brother's telling him. He's too busy watching me, scowling at the grin I know I'm wearing.

I wink.

A wave of fury flashes across Massimo's face, and okay, maybe that was a little far. Because now he looks like he's enjoying the possibility of catching me alone on the paddock, and *maybe* I need to watch my back. But I've handled bigger assholes looking to jump me for having a smart mouth.

He looks at Billy, stepping close enough to snarl in his face. "You come find me when you do."

Just to fuck with him a little more, I wiggle my fingers up by my smile in a wave. Massimo mutters something I can't make out, storming back toward his garage. I should probably start learning Italian, but that little translating bird kinda creeps me out.

Billy waits until Massimo is gone before he turns toward me, his posture slumping now that he's done playing Tallest Cowboy You Don't Wanna Fuck With. "You wanna tell me what that was about? What you've apparently done to jeopardize my relationship with my teammate?"

I bite my lip, my cheeks blazing because just thinking about her makes me smile. I take a sip of water, looking up at the boring ceiling of the garage. Nope, still smiling.

"Oh no," Billy groans. He glances back at his crew, still doing their best to pretend they're not listening to our conversation. He leans closer toward me, one hand on the back of my chair and the other on the armrest. I'm totally pinned in, nowhere to run. Still smiling. "Tell me you're not fucking around with Chiara."

"Okay. I'm not fucking around with Chiara." I don't get the words all the way out before I start laughing, because I can't even lie about it. Not that I really want to—makes me proud as hell.

"Oh goddammit," Billy curses again, but he sounds really upset about it this time. He pushes back from my chair to pace back and forth, scrubbing at his forehead, and I'm kind of surprised he hasn't pulled out his phone and called Taryn yet. It's his new favorite panic move. "But this is just…" he says, gesturing to me. "I mean you aren't…"

Oof. He is *stressed*.

I drop my water bottle on my lap, then lean back and lace my hands behind my head. "Aren't what?"

He bites the inside of his cheek and shakes his head, still looking shocked that I've dared to sleep with Chiara Martes. And okay, she is definitely way out of my league, but I'm doing my best to make up for that. And doing a pretty damn good job if I say so myself.

"And he doesn't know?" Billy says.

"I don't know what he knows. And I don't really care. As far as I can see, it's her decision and really none of his damn business. And by the way, I really appreciate you taking your teammate's side in this. Or did you forget we were blood first?"

Billy scoffs. "I don't have a side in this, because I'm not the dumbass playing with fire. You really have no idea what you're getting in the middle of, do you?"

"Oh, and you do?"

Billy stays quiet a little too long, watching me and flicking at his nose. Then he jerks his head toward pit lane. "Let's take a walk."

My eyes dart to his crew, who are still turning wrenches and huddled over computer readouts, but they're suspiciously not talking. They all report to the same manufacturer rep that Massimo's crew reports to, and maybe Billy has a point.

"Fine." I get up from my chair and grab my hat, then follow him out into pit lane. We both hook on our Stetsons against the afternoon sun, ignoring the random camera crews that are filming B-roll for tomorrow's race. This track is tough as hell, and there's a lot of debate about who's going to do best—what teams and whose bikes, which rider's style will prevail, and who is gonna punk out from playing it safe or pushing it too hard.

Whoever crashes, it isn't gonna be me.

The starting lineup is just how I like it: I've got first pole. Massimo is third. Billy is starting in fifth. Lorelai is leading the women's division, and she's going to win World Champion at this rate, no problem. The men's is still too close to tell. But I'm doing a hell of a lot better than anyone at Dabria really expected of me, and I'm happy to disappoint the naysayers. They just don't seem to understand that they're gonna be crowning me in November, not my brother. They'll figure it out eventually.

Billy glances behind us like he's making sure we're not being followed. There are a few people wandering around, but most everyone is busy in their respective garages. He scratches at his jaw when he starts to speak like he's worried a camera crew is gonna try to bring in a lip reader or something. "How serious are you about this?"

I wave him on, waiting for my enlightenment. "Serious enough."

"And she really didn't tell you about their history?"

I flip my water bottle in the air, catching it easily. "Nope. And I didn't ask. Because it doesn't matter."

"It does matter, and you need to ask her about it. Soon."

Okay, *now* I'm getting pissed off. "What exactly do you know that I don't? And why the fuck should I care what Massimo thinks? He isn't her father or her brother. He's her ex-boyfriend. That's it."

Billy looks hard at me, a warning in his eyes. "Mason, I'm telling you, if this is going where I think it's going, then you need to talk to her. It is not my secret to tell, man. And never mind your history of running your mouth, but this ain't a water tower kind of secret. This is a Cornucopia Exhibition kind of secret. Get it?"

My steps stutter—it's kinda hard to keep walking when your stomach bottoms out to your boots like that.

This is bad. Take it to your grave bad. He knows something he's not supposed to know.

"Well, who...who told *you*?"

Billy claps me on the back, steering us over to the fence. I lean my bad shoulder against it when we get there, staring at my water bottle, twisting it and flipping it in my hands. But he has my attention, and he knows it.

"Massimo was drunk after a race. We started talking about family and people back home." Billy shakes his head. "He called me the next day, asked me to never repeat what was said. Like I would. Shit gave me nightmares."

"You have to tell me, Billy," I say quietly. "I won't say nothing, but I have to know."

I need to make sure it's not as bad as all the stuff I'm thinking. And I absolutely, 100 percent can't ask her about this. It's not fair to put her on the spot like that, and it's way, *way* outside the rules. But it's going to haunt me otherwise.

Billy hooks his fingers through the fence, then stretches out so his mouth is hidden by his arm from any angle. There must be a camera crew filming us—he's got a sixth sense for that stuff, and I never notice until it's on ESPN. "Tell me there's a reason first. A damn good reason. *The* reason."

There's no room for levity in Billy's voice, and I can't quite look at him when I say it. The only answer that's gonna be good enough for him. The only one that would be good enough for me. "You'd have to know about Taryn, wouldn't you?"

His head turns my way, eyes wide at what I just admitted. I'm still having trouble admitting it to myself. But then the pity comes next, and there's so damn much of it that I almost change my mind.

"Then I'm sorry, Brother," he says. "Because this isn't pretty." He takes a deep breath, then spits at the ground, and I prepare myself as best I can for what's coming. But there's no way to prepare myself for this. "Her father drank…"

—⁓—

Billy was right: it gave me nightmares.

It's almost impossible not to think about. Her father's drinking problem. The physical abuse she suffered as a child. Massimo violently saving her from the situation when they were barely twelve years old—almost went to prison for her. How she's been living with him ever since.

How does a person just stop seeing those images behind their eyes? Makes me sick with rage. But despite everything, I'm trying *not* to let it affect me. I have to keep acting normal.

I don't want her to know that I know. She wasn't ready to tell me, and that is absolutely her right. I feel awful about it, like I betrayed her by letting Billy tell me her story. I wish I'd listened to him and asked her instead. Or maybe just had some damn patience for once and let it all go. But I didn't, and now there's no going back.

"Mason," Chiara says gently, pulling me from the dark swell of my thoughts. I glance up at her, stretched back and half sitting up against the pillows of my bed. She's barely covered with a bedsheet and in that calm, happy, quiet place she gets when I've done my job well. "You disappeared again."

"Huh? Oh, sorry." I tease another kiss to her ankle, lying on my side at the foot of the bed and very carefully painting her toenails.

Chiara giggles softly. "Where did you learn how to do this?"

"Goats," I answer. Chiara snorts, but I'm telling the truth. "Used to get drunk and go out back when I was bored, and I'd paint the goat's hoofs with glitter polish so they'd feel fancy."

Chiara laughs for real this time. "And here I thought we were reenacting *Bull Durham*."

"We can totally do that." I played catcher from Little League to high school, and I know that movie well. I blow a stream of air across the tips of her toes. Chiara squirms with a squeal like it tickles. "You gonna read us some William Blake or what?"

Chiara shakes her head. "No. I am too tired."

"Too tired?" I repeat, carefully painting the next couple of toes.

"Sì."

Yep—if she's slipping into Italian, she is tired. Go me.

"Speaking of," I drawl out, "I just got word from my guy in

Memphis. Looks like I got a rodeo right before Jerez, so I'm gonna be a day late getting there."

Something sharp flashes over her face, but she's quick to hide it. "Hmm."

There's something in that *hmm* too—something displeased. "That a problem?"

"No."

"So what's the *hmm* for?"

She rolls her eyes, yawning through her words. "I just don't want you to get hurt before Jerez. It's a big race for you. And the last time you had a rodeo before a race, you came back covered in bruises."

I shake my head. "That ain't hurt, baby. That's winning."

She shrugs, messing with her fingernails and avoiding my eyes. "If you say so."

I go back to painting her toenails. "Sounds like you got more to say on the matter."

"Except I don't."

"I'm open to hearing it, if you do."

She groans, the sound long and slow. "Fine. I guess if someone were to ask me, I would say you can either be the best bull rider in the world or the fastest moto racer. But no one can do both. Not when one interferes so much with the other."

I pause, looking up at her. "Billy did both."

"No, he did not. He quit bull riding when he moved up to MotoPro. You said it yourself. He only ropes now, and that is becoming less and less."

"Well, I'm not my brother."

Chiara looks at me with a devilish twist to her lips. "I know you are not. And I have never wanted you to be. But I do want you to win in Jerez. You deserve it, Mason. And I don't see how a bull ride is going to help you do that." Her words speed up, her tone lightening like she's getting uncomfortable and needs to laugh it off. "But I also really don't know anything about bull riding, so... You will make the decision you feel is best. And it will be the right one."

"Hmm." I go back to painting her toenails, thinking over her words with every red stroke of the small brush. She's right—Billy did quit when he moved up from MotoB to MotoPro. But that was only because of our father and the lie he told us about it being forbidden according to Billy's new premier racing contract.

Finding out the truth was just a double punch to the gut, because he said he did it to protect Billy. And he never tried it with me. In fact, he's been dead adamant about me doing both: racing and riding, no matter how hard it is to keep up. He doesn't care how much the schedule sucks when every minute I'm not at the track, I'm in an arena. Constantly injured from getting bucked and getting wrecked, and my body never quite fully recovered.

Frank's starting to grumble about it too. Says not being healed and rested is costing me seconds on my lap times and some of the wins I should've had. But bull riding has been my life for as long as I can remember. It was all I ever wanted to do—to stand in the lights and have the crowd call my name. The cowboys were my heroes, larger than life and death defying.

Most of them are dead now, though.

Once I started riding, I learned real quick what eight seconds can cost you. That the rush from beating the clock on a bull is the biggest you'll ever feel, until it's the last thing you ever feel. But it always felt worth it to me. Like it was the only way to ever really let myself *go* and be all I'm capable of. Until I started racing motorcycles at 210 miles per hour.

*Shit*, I don't know what to do. I can't even comprehend hanging up my ropes, but I hate how much sense she's making. How much something in me is heartily agreeing with her like it already knew racing and rodeoing just don't mix, but I didn't want to face it.

I still don't want to face it. I can't *quit*. That's just…not an option. I'd really be invisible then.

I close the bottle of nail polish and blow on Chiara's toes once more, then shift the right way on the bed. "Okay, you're all set." I reach over to set the bottle on the nightstand.

"Thank you." Chiara yawns behind me, her words mumbled. "And now, I should really probably go."

"Okay." I check my phone and the alarm I can't remember if I set or not, then add another just in case. Ditch my glasses, turn off the light, and try not to shiver so much when she ghosts her fingertips over my spine, calling me back to her.

I grab the comforter and pull it up over us. Chiara scoffs. "There is no way my toes are dry."

"So?" I shift onto my side next to her, then tug her into me so we're spooning.

"So I probably just got nail polish all over your covers."

"Sounds like you owe me some new covers then."

Chiara pushes at my leg with her foot.

"Gonna have to clean that up too."

"In your dreams," she says, shifting on her side and getting comfortable. "I really am getting up." She yawns again. "In, like, five minutes."

A victorious smile sneaks onto my face. "Okay."

I push her hair up out of the way, then snuggle a little closer in the dark room. Chances are it really won't be long before she'll push *me* away, get up, get dressed, and leave without a word. But for a couple minutes, she's right here—safe in my arms, satisfied and sleepy, and smiling against me. The world around us dark and quiet and full of secrets and space, the breakdown of barriers that lets me hold her like this and only exists somewhere between dreams and reality so we don't have to deal with all that it means come daylight.

The reasons *why* I want to hold her and fall asleep next to her and how much it means to me that she's letting me. Especially when I don't normally get to do this part. I'm not ever around that long. And until this moment, I have absolutely preferred to keep it that way.

Chiara's hand comes up and settles on my arm, her thumb sweeping over my skin as she lightly squeezes. I inhale the sweet perfume of her hair, press a kiss to the back of her long neck, and listen to the rhythm of her breaths change like she's already lost to the land of her dreams.

I don't know if I'm ever gonna get the guts to quit bull riding. But one thing's for sure:

I absolutely gotta quit drinking.

# Chapter 16

*Chiara Martes—May*

AFTER BINGEING ALMOST AN ENTIRE SEASON OF A RIDICULOUS reality dating show on Netflix, the RV I'm sharing with Lorelai is *finally* silent—sweet! With it now safe for me to bolt, I throw down the remote and nearly leap up from the couch, a bright smile on my face as I finger comb my hair.

Argentina was *incredible*. The fans, the weather, the chocolate, the *sex*. But the break before Jerez was barely long enough for me to stumble through my front door in Ravenna, wash all my dirty clothes, collect my gigantic pile of mail and dust my nasty apartment, catch up on some raids with Aria and Elena, and then run like hell to make the train to Spain. But I made it. Now, if I can make it to Mason's RV before he passes out.

He is almost impossible to wake up once he falls asleep. Almost worse than me. But that's only understandable when he had to squeeze in a whole rodeo in the small break. And came back covered in bruises, like I knew he would. He keeps saying he's okay, and they're mostly healed now, so...

I grab my Chucks and tug them on, and I'm halfway out the door when another one opens behind me. "And where are you sneaking off to?"

*Shit!* I look over my shoulder at Lorelai, coming out of her bedroom in her pajamas—a pair of MMW yoga pants and one of Massimo's old T-shirts.

What is she doing awake? She never stays up this late. Especially before a race. I gotta give it to her though: she is so disciplined in her training that it's no wonder she's been racking up the wins lately. Plus, she's just freaking *fast*.

"Going…for a walk?" I answer in English. "To get some fresh air."

Lorelai snorts and heads toward the mini kitchen, tossing long brown curls that are lying wild over a freshly shaved undercut. Guess the much-needed haircuts finally happened. "Well, before you go…*walk*, I want to say something."

Totally busted, I shut the front door and lean against it, watching as she pours a bowl of cereal with easy, methodic movements. Must be because it's so late. She's normally way more Road Runner with everything she does.

She shovels a bite into her mouth, then turns around and points her spoon at me. "Look, I'm all for…whatever you're doing. But you're gonna need to talk to him, Chiara. Soon."

I swallow and try to make my posture as casual as possible, but I'm still stuck against the door. Worse: now I'm *late*. Like that's anything new, but I really don't like to keep him waiting. Especially when I've got to let him sleep sometime. "Talk to him about what?"

Lorelai arches an eyebrow my way, then shovels another bite of cereal in her mouth, milk dribbling down her chin. "Now you're lying to me. Thanks a lot."

*Crap*. This is not the way I wanted this conversation to go. Even better would be to not have it at *all*. I hate that I'm keeping this secret from her; it's not the kind of friends we are. But keeping her in the dark is the only way to keep her out of the line of fire. "There's just…nothing to say," I tell Lorelai. "At least nothing you or he need to know. Definitely nothing to worry about."

"Yeah? You think he's gonna be cool with that? 'He didn't need to know.'" She gestures with her spoon, milk flinging all over the RV.

Total Massimo move. It's like they're becoming one person.

"It's not really his business," I say carefully. "He doesn't tell me everything about your relationship, you don't either, and that's fine because it doesn't involve me. Some things can just be…mine. Private."

Lorelai takes another bite of cereal. Chewing a *lot*. "Did he tell you when we met?"

I sigh, grumbling toward my crossed ankles. "Yes."

"Did he tell you when things changed?"

"Yes." I'm the one who convinced him to follow her to Memphis.

"Exactly," she says. "Because that's what best friends do. They tell each other stuff. They share the *important* things in their lives."

"Lorelai…"

"Look, your relationship with him is…your relationship. And I get that. I don't want to get in the middle of it, so please, don't make me." She slurps milk from the side of her bowl, *ahh*ing when she's finished. "But I can't lie to him for you, and I won't. So if he asks me anything, I'm telling him. And he's already suspicious. Like, *really* suspicious."

Even in the dark RV, I know she can clearly see it all over my face and…*fuck*. If she tells Massimo that she thinks I'm dating Mason, he's going to explode. And chances are it's going to land all over Lorelai before it even reaches me, which is exactly what I don't want to happen. She may have given me Mason's number and conspired to bring me onto the circuit, but she didn't do anything wrong, and I can't let something like this come between them. I can't be more of a problem. I'm in the way enough as it is.

She takes another bite of cereal, a smile growing on her lips. "So?"

"So…?"

Lorelai sighs, takes a last bite of cereal, then puts her bowl in the small sink. "Fine. But I've known Mason for a long time, a long-*long* time, and I'm telling you: this isn't nothing."

My heartbeat goes triple speed. "Who said anything about Mason?"

Lorelai goes stiff. "Now you're *really* hurting my feelings."

I swallow guiltily as she walks back toward her bedroom, shutting the door. My steps drag as I leave the RV, closing the front door behind me as quietly as possible, not that it really matters anymore.

Luckily, the RV I'm heading to isn't far, the Spanish moon shining bright overhead and reflecting off the handle that unlatches easily. Because he keeps it unlocked for me.

My steps are whisper quiet as I sneak down the length of the RV, past the dark windows with shades drawn. But when I open the bedroom door, all I see is Mason: sitting up in bed and reading under a swell of golden light, no hat and no shirt, and glasses on.

*Hello, Mr. Always Makes Me Feel Better.*

"You're totally right," he says when I come into the room and shut the door behind me. I flip the lock, just to be safe. "This book is, like, *exactly* like Pokémon."

"See?" I'm already halfway smiling again as I kick off my shoes, peel off my shirt, and drop my shorts on the floor on my way to his bed. I leave my bra and panties on, because he prefers to take those off me himself. He *also* prefers to steal my fantasy romance novels every chance he gets, because he's a full-out book hoarder. His ebook and audiobook collection is ten times the size of mine—talk about jealous.

At least the debates about me cracking spines and dog-earing pages have officially ended with an ice cream cone getting smeared all over *someone's* face (mine). Mason is steadily trying to convert me to the clear Post-it notes for margin doodles. Slim chance. What if they come unstuck?

Half the reason I even let him read my books before me is just so I can see what he felt was worthy of an underline or an all-caps *HOLY SHIT! THIS!!!* I love discovering his interpretations of the metaphors almost as much as the metaphors themselves, and I'm always losing everything already. I don't want to lose those too.

He slides the bookmark carefully between the pages, then sets the book on his nightstand with a sigh. "I want to be a shadow assassin. Plus, how cool would it be to ride Ocnolog? Need to find me a beast charmer."

I snort, pulling back the covers. "No spoilers. I have not finished that one yet."

"My bad." He rolls on his side to face me, propping his head in his hand. The hard muscles of his chest flex and shift while he adjusts the sheet across his bare hips, and *God*, his body is just...so good. "How's your day been? Did Elena figure out that new jump sequence yet?"

"She did." I slide underneath the sheets and instinctively take a deep breath to settle the last of my nerves, drowning in the scent of freshly washed sheets, just a hint of moto exhaust, and the clean spice of his cologne. "But..."

"What?"

I toss up a hand, no other way to say it. "There's been a recorded disturbance in the Neutral Zone."

Mason's eyes light up, his palm smoothing over my hip and tugging me closer until our legs are tangled under the covers. "Romulans? Or Ferengi?"

"Lorelai caught me sneaking out."

"Females," he growls in his best Ferengi impression. "What did she say? Were there threats involved? Do we need new identities yet? Because I want to be a shadow assassin, if we're choosing."

I laugh and shake my head at him, no idea where to start. Especially when he's a little manic tonight. But that's sort of typical before a race, and at least I don't smell any whiskey on his breath. (Not that I've been worried about it. Or noticing. *Nope.*)

"She says I need to talk to Massimo."

"And tell him what?"

"I don't know. I told her there was nothing to tell, and it wasn't his business anyway."

"Oh, I'm high-fiving that." Mason holds up his hand, and I chuckle when my palm meets his. "You know she's probably gonna tell him anyway, though, right?"

"I know." I collapse back on his pillows and hook out a foot from the covers, already hot from Mason's radiating body heat. Then I peek over at him: dark and gorgeous, sweet and passionate, and such a divine mix of all my favorite things. Danger and speed, sex and space, and all that lovely, relentless energy.

The last couple of months with him have been like living a reckless dream, bouncing from country to country and exploring the world without worries or restrictions. And despite my gamut of trust issues, he's become one of my closest friends. The person I can share my books with, my gaming, my terrible what-if-we-tried-*this* ideas. And it's so *fascinating*, watching him battle on the track with ruthless focus until at night when all those walls come down. When he becomes the gentle cowboy who holds my hand and slow dances with me under foreign stars—sometimes when there's not even any music playing.

A string of memories flashes through my mind—laughing and kissing and talking and playing with each other—and there's so much warmth surging through me that I can't deny it anymore. *Damn it.*

Lorelai is right. This isn't nothing; it's right on the verge of *something*. And if I take even one breath further across the line, I'm going to have to tell Massimo all I've been keeping from him. And I *can't* tell Massimo about this.

He won't understand—why it's Mason when he specifically asked me to date anyone else. Why I kept it a secret when he's always told me the truth, even when it's been hard. And I can't risk making things worse between us when we've never felt so far apart.

Right or wrong, Massimo is still half of my whole world. He's my past, my family, the only weapon against my deepest fears, and the one person who has never swayed despite my instability. I *can't* lose him. Especially not for a lawless cowboy who has never been in love and never hopes to be.

(Smart girls don't fall for fuckboys.)

Mason reaches over and runs a knuckle down my cheek. "Lot of thoughts behind those eyes tonight, trouble." He cracks a hint of a smile. "Tell me, there danger on the horizon?"

A blush takes my cheeks. I like it too much when he calls me trouble. Very occasionally, baby. Honestly, I like everything he calls me.

Just another sign that I'm already in too deep. I never should've allowed pet names. Even though I technically started it. "Not danger. Boredom."

"Well, we can fix that." He gives me an irresistible grin and leans over to kiss me, and it takes all my flimsy self-restraint to place my palm on his chest, stopping him.

"I need to go home, Mason," I whisper.

He stops instantly, but he still sighs. "You're bailing on me already?

You just got here. Why do you text me if this is what you're gonna do? *You* came to *me*."

I shake my head. "No, I didn't mean tonight."

"Then what are you talking about?"

"I need to go back to Ravenna. I need to get back to real life."

His brow furrows. "What? Did we cross into the Kitska Forest when I wasn't looking?"

"Mason."

"Okay..." He leans back, putting more distance between us. "Well, what's going on? Is everything okay?"

"Everything is fine, it's just... Look, hanging out with you these past few months on the circuit, it's been more fun than I ever could have imagined. Or would have known to ask for."

He gives me a funny look, and I can't blame him. This sounds suspiciously like a breakup speech, even to my ears.

"But it's not *real*, Mason. It's a holiday, and holidays end."

Especially for the plucky sidekick. Heroines, on the other hand? They get everything.

"Chiara, I don't understand. This isn't a holiday for me. This *is* my real life. Being on the circuit...it's what I do. Why is that so wrong?"

There's so much confusion in his eyes, and that's not fair. He doesn't need that from me when he struggles with his place in this world enough as it is. Will he ever be able to really beat his brother when it matters? What would happen if he did? And I have plenty of opinions on the matter, like how much Mason's holding himself back, self-sabotaging through a dozen different vices, bull riding included. But I have no right to sway his path. Even as a full-time friend and part-time lover. (Or is it the other way around?)

Either way, I can't be either of those things for him. Not anymore.

"It's not wrong. Not for *you*. But I am not supposed to be here, Mason. I'm supposed to be in Ravenna, working and spending time with my friends, and it's time I get back to reality."

"That's bullshit." He flops onto his side of the bed, scrubbing a hand through his dark hair. "You belong here as much as anyone else. And you *have* been working. I follow all your accounts, and you haven't stopped doing all his publicity stuff while planning their damn wedding, and your social media engagement is, like...really good. You're *good* at what you do, Chiara. And you do it better from here."

"I appreciate you saying that."

More than he'll ever know. He never makes me feel in the way.

"We were supposed to go to Le Mans after this," he says. "You're gonna miss Paris."

"I know." And as much as that really, *really* sucks, it's not even the worst part. Because Mason and I...we don't talk in the breaks between the races.

The circuit calendar is so full that it's only ever a week or two until we're back at the track and sneaking out at night, exploring the city and goofing off together. Coming back to his RV and having fun well into the morning, until his alarm goes off, and I have to sneak back into Lorelai's RV before anyone notices.

But when he goes home to Memphis and I go home to Ravenna, we don't talk. Don't text. I don't know what he does or who he sees, and he doesn't ask what I do or who I see. And it's supposed to be that way—no attachments, no jealousy, no strings. But if I don't cut this off right now, I'm never going to be able to hold to that.

I *will* want to know who he met in Memphis, who kept him so distracted that he forgot about me. If she understands his *Star Trek* references and knows what he means when he says the torque on his bike isn't quite right and it's freaking him out and costing him placements. I wonder if she'll ask him questions, if she'll be able to read him as well as I already do, to see his walls go up when he's being someone he thinks other people want him to be. If he'll leave notes in the margins of the books she knows he'll love, his true thoughts imprinted for the rest of time.

*God, I hate this.* It isn't fair that I have to give him up, and I already know I'll never be able to come back to the circuit—I won't be able to resist him. I'll fall the rest of the way I've already stumbled, and that cannot happen.

The only consolation I can find in any of this is that at least it won't hurt for Mason.

He's not there yet, and that's a blessing I didn't realize I needed. It'll be easier for him to accept it when I erase myself from his life. With any hope, he'll move on. Quick. (I hope it for me too, but I doubt it will work that way.)

Mason sighs and glances over at me, one of his hands finding mine and lacing our fingers together. I'm going to miss his hands so much—how strong and sure they are, rough with hard-earned callouses and his nails always clean and trimmed carefully short. But that's Mason: strong, sexy, and unpredictably, sweetly considerate.

"Look, it's whatever you want to do," he says. "And if you need to go home, then I get it. Sometimes, I need to be home too."

"Thank you, Mason." I mean it so much—he may challenge me and call me on my crap, but he never asks for more than I can give. And the most I can give him right now is a clean goodbye, leaving our memories intact.

He turns on his side to face me again, his voice soft in the dim light of his bedroom and as cozy as the sheets we're under. "Please don't thank me for stuff like that. For the way it should be." His palm comes up and cups my cheek, and when he leans over to kiss me, I don't stop him this time. I sink fully into the soft press of his lips and how they fit perfectly in the space between my own, layering and supporting me and teasing me with more to come.

I just hope tonight is enough to last me the rest of forever without him.

# Chapter 17

*Mason King—July*

MY FISTS ARE GRINDING INTO THE CONCRETE WALL AS I STARE AT my boots and try to breathe, the weight of my vest and chaps like anchors pulling me down, but there is no bottom.

She left. She really left.

I squeeze my eyes shut, a bead of sweat rolling down the back of my neck and under the starched collar of my black competition shirt. The crowd is screaming just past the tunnel, calling my name and their boots stomping in the stands shaking the ground, the walls, and the roof. My stomach flips with the sickly slosh of dread, my nose filled with the sharp scent of dirt and raging bulls, dried blood, but all I can think is *why didn't I expect it?*

But I didn't—I thought it was just a bad night at first. That maybe she and Massimo got into it about something. Or she and Lorelai were getting cramped in that RV. I figured she'd go home, get some rest, see her friends, and then be back across the paddock when we all arrived at Le Mans considering Paris was, like, a *really* big deal. But she wasn't there.

I came in eighth.

She didn't come to Mugello either, and that's only a short train ride away from Ravenna. But she no-showed the rest of May and all of June: Catalunya, Germany, the Netherlands, and it only makes it worse when my placements have been bouncing all around the damn leaderboard. And that's not the way to win World Champion.

"*May-son*! *May-son*!" The crowd claps over the music thundering through the arena, and I lean forward, the cold concrete wall pressing against my forehead. Their cheers swell into something unrecognizable when the announcers' voices cut through.

"And here comes the bull of the night, Jake. They're getting Hornet loaded up!"

I squeeze my eyes tighter shut.

I just can't fucking *concentrate*. Not when I'm racing, not when I'm rodeoing. The worst part is, I'm not supposed to care. It's not supposed to affect me. It's clearly not affecting her. She hasn't texted me once over the past two months. Not a text, not a DM. Nothing.

"Mason King?" a feminine voice says. "They're ready for you."

"He's coming, darling," my father replies, stepping closer from where he's been standing guard, watching me have a damn near nervous breakdown. Billy and Taryn are already in the stands, and I'm glad they're not here to see this. There's no way to explain why I'm shaking, fear tangled in my gut over whether to walk into that arena or out the door and straight to the airport.

*But why isn't she calling me?*

My father pats my back and clasps my neck, his hand so big it feels ear to ear. He holds out my helmet and rope to me. "You got him, Son. So get him."

I don't have a choice. There's no reason not to. No one to pull me back.

"Sir," the girl says, "we really need to get him in the chute. We're starting to run behind."

"Yeah, he hears you," my father says sternly. "*Mason.*"

I let out a gritted roar and push myself off the wall, steeling everything in my body from my thoughts to my boots as I stare at the dirty grout. Spit out my heart and take my rope and my helmet from my father. Then I turn and head down the tunnel, toward the lights and the bull and the crowd calling my name.

*Fuck it.*

—◆—

Even though it's dark out, the summer night is still hot enough to have sweat running down my neck, my shirt plastered to my back. I shift restlessly in my folding camping chair, Billy talking about the trucks in the parade floats with our father, sitting right next to him. Mama and Taryn are sitting shoulder to shoulder on the tailgate behind us with a blanket over their laps and beers in their hands. They'd probably be cold in a sauna.

The firetruck rolling by sends off its siren again, a sharp pain slashing through my head and making my stomach turn. The crowd lining Main Street cheers and blows their air horns in appreciation, and the first responder trucks give them exactly what they want. They honk their horns and let their lights flash and swirl in all their glory, the line of jacked-up trucks behind them strobing out and someone laying on a train whistle.

*Fuck.* I'm gonna be sick.

I lean forward and stare at the ground, my head in my hands. Press my thumbs over my ears and try to find whatever "still" is supposed to mean.

The last thing I remember from my rodeo this past weekend is my father yelling at me to hang on. I don't remember the second air horn—I was already unconscious at that point.

Hornet bucked me freaking *good* six seconds in. After landing on my head and neck, I was out for three long goddamn minutes. Taryn apparently had a total meltdown thinking I was dead. It didn't help that the bull nearly stepped on me while I was lying there knocked out, doing its best to dodge the bull fighters. He didn't step on me, though—just got close enough to brush my ribs and knock me away.

But I got lucky. *Damn* lucky. Luckier than some did that night.

A hand lands on my shoulder, and I glance back to find Taryn watching me with a concerned look in her eyes. I'm not exactly sure when we formed our new alliance, but I'll take what I can get at this point. Someone's gotta be on my side in this family.

"You want to borrow my sunglasses?" she says. "I have them in my purse. Billy, will you get my bag? It's on the floorboard of your truck."

My brother is already up from his seat when my father laughs. "Taryn, honey, I love you. But why would Mason need to wear sunglasses during a parade at *night*?"

Taryn's eyebrow nearly touches the stars above us. But it's Mama who says, "Because he has a grade-three concussion, Bill. Ease up."

"All right, all right. Y'all don't *all* got to get mad at me. He chose to come."

Yeah, because it's tradition. And there're certain things you do when you're from a country town: you support the high school football team, you go to church on Christmas Eve, and you attend the Fourth of July parade and firework show. And I knew it was probably a bad idea, but the guilt trip from not going would've lasted the rest of the year at least.

Billy looks between Taryn and his truck, parked right next to our father's, seeming confused over what to do. I wave him off, standing myself. "I'm gonna go for a walk."

Mama reaches across Taryn for me, grabbing my hand. Wearing her worried mama smile. "You're gonna miss the best floats."

I squeeze her hand. "Take some pictures for me."

When Billy nods next to me, his hand landing on my shoulder, she lets me go. She doesn't worry about me half as much whenever he's around. Nobody does.

Together, he and I wander through the stack of trucks and lawn chairs parked in the tiny strip center, if you could even call it that. It's just an old yellow building housing an old-time candy shop, a rustic furniture store, a computer repair place, and a hole-in-the-wall pizza restaurant that used to be a hair salon.

"Hey, man," Billy says once we're out of earshot of our family. "You okay?"

"No, I'm not fucking okay." I whip around to gesture angrily at our father, but I get so dizzy from turning that I stumble again—my boots catching on a crack in the pavement. My brother rushes forward to steady me by the shoulders. I shake him off. "Goddammit!"

"Hey, it's okay—"

"No, it isn't, man." I walk away but don't get far before I double over behind the hood of someone's Chevy, so fucking freaked out that I feel like I'm gonna cry. We never should've watched that Will Smith movie about concussion protocol. Knew it was a bad idea, right from the previews. "I still want to be me when I'm older, and this is, like, the third concussion I've had this year."

My brother's boots come to a stop next to mine. "Fourth," Billy says.

"Exactly. And you saw what happens to all those football players... It's bad, Billy. It's so fucking bad, man."

His hand lands on my back, then he hooks my arm and pulls me vertical. He walks us around the side of the building to the chain-link fence overlooking a pasture behind it, then hooks my arm over the chest-high rail for support. He leans his arms over it too, his shoulder pressed to mine so I don't feel like I'm gonna fall over. At least it's a little quieter back here, no flashing lights reflecting off glass windows.

I hang my head and do my *five-four-three-two-one* to calm my panic attack, trying to get my boots back under me. Billy doesn't say anything, just giving me a minute without hassling me about it. He really is a good brother—most of the time.

"I don't know if I can do this anymore, Billy," I quietly confess. And I never thought I'd say the words—not when it's the one place I come in first—but there they are. "I think...I'm done. Done with riding bulls."

Billy's already shaking his head.

"I'm tired of being scared, man. It just...it doesn't feel worth it anymore."

Not for the money, not for the call of the fans. Not even when I'll probably never catch him on the racetrack. Knowing Billy, he'll retire the very moment I start coming close.

He has the nerve to smile at me. "You don't mean that, though. You love riding bulls. It's always been your thing. This is just a stumble. You'll bounce back and—"

"Nah." I shake my head but stop when it makes me dizzy again. His cologne doesn't help. "I'm done."

"Mason." Billy clears his throat, checking over his shoulder and then leaning closer. "Look, man. I get it, okay? I don't ride anymore either. But you're only halfway through your sponsorship contract for the year. You made commitments."

"Excuse me, but do I look like Mr. Commitment to you? I don't give a shit about the stupid sponsorships. They can find someone else."

My everything-by-the-book brother just shakes his head again, still not hearing me. "Well, you don't have to decide right now. Just sleep on it."

"I'm scared to sleep, man! What if I don't wake up?"

"All right, all right," he says, hushing me and checking over his shoulder again like he's worried someone's gonna hear me. He turns us back toward the fence, patting my back. "You still getting sick?" he asks quietly.

I look out into the pasture, pulling my bandana from my back pocket and using it to wipe some of the sweat off my face. "Couldn't even get all the way through my ABCs last night without getting tangled up in the middle."

"Well, what do you wanna do about it? You want to go back to the doctor?"

"No," I mumble. "Already went for my follow-up. They say I'm fine."

"Well." He shrugs. "Just gotta…ride it out, then. We've been here before."

"Yeah." Too many times, and that's the whole problem.

I tuck my bandana back into my pocket. Flick at my nose.

I miss reading. Miss my books.

Miss having a reason to leave notes in the margins.

"Hey, man, it'll come back." He knocks at my chest. "Remember when I was convinced my name was Bubba for, like, a week that one time? And your dumb ass even had it monogrammed on my underwear just to fuck with me."

I can't help it—I start to snicker at the memory because I really am an asshole sometimes. And that was funny. I nearly had the whole town in on it. Damn grocery store checkout girl ruined the whole thing.

"You're gonna be fine," Billy says. "I promise."

He can't promise me that, though. Things don't just work out for me like they do for Billy. They go sideways. I make the wrong choice. Two seconds too late.

*I'm never gonna get another chance at Smashbox.*

I get all nauseous again, and as much as I know quitting is the right call, I don't know how I'm gonna resign myself to the fact that my brother got eight seconds on my nemesis of a bull, and now I never will. But no one knows that, because he switched places with me at the Cornucopia Exhibition—I was too drunk to ride.

Like he's been doing since we were little, Billy saved my ass, my contract and reputation. I may have the buckle, but he got the glory, and I get to live with the regret.

*I'll never beat him now.*

I blow out a breath, hanging my arms over the railing of the fence with a groan. At least if I puke, it won't hit our boots. "Can we talk about something else? Distract me."

"Okay…um…" He kicks restlessly at some weeds along the fence line, thinking. "Someone bought Duke Bricker's bowling alley and reopened it."

I wave my hand to keep 'em coming. I don't wanna talk about the bowling alley right now. Don't feel like being laughed at any more tonight. Besides, that's the whole purpose of having a shell company in the *first* place. I didn't buy it for bragging rights. I bought it because people in this town needed a place to blow off some steam, and I like going bowling. It's fun. Plus, everyone got their jobs back, and those people needed those jobs.

"Fine." Billy thinks again, then snaps his fingers like he's got it. "You know how me and Taryn were waiting a year to get engaged? Because of the cost of planning a wedding after buying the ranch and everything?"

"Yeah." Dumbest thing I've ever heard. They spent a good chunk of money on that land, but they're both professional racers, and they make plenty to cover that and a wedding too. They're just being skittish about it. Don't get why—it's not like Billy's gambling with his life on a bull once a month anymore. And it's plainly obvious that if I don't start placing better at the circuit, he's gonna win World Champion again—three years running.

"Well, the waiting year's over, but Taryn says we can't get married until after Lorelai does. Says she doesn't want to 'steal her thunder.' And because we don't want a long engagement, I'm not allowed to propose until Lorelai is on her honeymoon at least. And turns out she and Massimo aren't getting married until freaking December."

"That's so stupid," I groan, rubbing at my eyes. I think I put my contacts in backward this morning. I hope that's why my vision keeps going double. "You should do what you want. Lorelai can learn to get over it."

My brother scoffs. "Did your concussion wipe from your brain that Massimo is also my teammate? I know you don't care about starting fights, but it isn't exactly smart for me to start a beef with him. Dude's *fast* and already nipping at my heels."

I scoff right back—how nice that he's worried about Massimo's placements while completely ignoring mine. "Well, Massimo needs to get over the fact that he can't control the world. I don't remember anyone dying and making him king of the universe."

Billy squints at me from under his hat. "Did something go down between the two of y'all that I need to know about?"

"No."

*Not yet anyway.*

But lately, when I've been lying in bed at night and I'm too scared to sleep, I've been thinking about risking it. Thinking and watching Chiara's Twitch streams and her YouTube walkthroughs for games I don't even play. She doesn't have a big following or anything, but she's good, *real* good, and I like listening to her voice. The way she laughs when someone gets the drop on her. She doesn't rage, she just has fun, and it's taking everything I've got not to text her.

But she said she didn't want that kind of relationship. I didn't either.

It's getting harder to remember why, though.

Billy clasps my shoulder. "Come on. We gotta stay till the parade's over, but we'll skip the firework show and have Taryn check you over at the ranch. And if you promise to keep your smart mouth to yourself, you can even crash with me for a couple days if you want, okay?"

"Okay." I trust Taryn's opinion. Her and her sports medicine degree. And I wouldn't mind getting out of my parents' house for a few days. Even if it does mean cleaning out horse stalls in turn for use of the spare bedroom. At least Taryn's a really good cook. Billy can't make shit in the kitchen except a mess.

I push myself off the fence and follow him back toward our father and mother and Taryn, and I still don't understand why he ever agreed to wait to get married in the first place. Talk about choking the throttle—they already live together, and he's never gonna find someone better than her. But even with as perfect as Billy is, sometimes he really gets it wrong. Life's too short to wait for what you want. Especially when we risk our lives for a living.

"Hey, Mason," my father says when we get back, retaking our seats. "Hand me your flask, would ya?"

Billy leans back in his chair between us, crossing his ankles and acting like he doesn't hear nothing. Mama and Taryn keep chatting about flower beds and the best way to kill weeds.

*"Don't you think it's time we start being our own main characters?" I ask Chiara.*

*A wide smile takes her face as she considers that, then nods. "I do."*

*"Well then." I clear my throat, a grin curling the corner of my lips. "Let me know if you figure out how we're supposed to do that."*

I've had enough—tired of living a life that's going nowhere good and sick to death of disappointing people I care about. Heroes don't do that stuff. They take charge of their destiny, make changes, and figure out how to be better. Stronger. The man the heroine needs. The hero she deserves.

"I don't have it," I say loud enough that I know my father will hear me, even over the trucks and tractors rolling by in the parade. "I quit."

Billy's head snaps my way, both he and my father staring at me. Mama and Taryn go quiet too. But something in my chest is already a whole lot lighter just saying the words.

*I quit.*

"Cut the shit, Mason," my father says. "I'm gonna give it *back*." Then he shakes his Coke can at me. "Just want a little top off here."

"I told you, I don't have it anymore." I glance back at Mama before I say the next part. Make sure there's no anger, no judgment in my voice. "I'm moving out too."

Her shoulders fall a bit, but at least she doesn't start crying. And Mama always cries about everything. But for once, she actually looks kinda proud of me instead of worried.

I can't quite read the expression on Billy's face, but Taryn looks smug as all hell. I go back to staring at my boot, crossed on my knee, and try to enjoy the parade as best I can. My father just huffs and sits back in his chair, sipping his Coke. He knows there's no point in raising the subject again.

I said what I said.

# Chapter 18

*Mason King—August*

MOVING OUT WAS A LOT EASIER THAN I EXPECTED. ONLY TOOK ME a couple days to find an apartment, fill out the paperwork, put down the deposits, then pack up the few things I wanted to take with me and load them into my truck. Didn't ask for help from Billy or nothing—didn't need it.

Going to my first AA meeting, though… That was a lot harder.

Took me a couple weeks before I could say the words, but I did the thing, got a sponsor and a list of steps, and the clock is officially ticking on my sobriety. I've been going extra stir crazy ever since, but I've finally been cleared from my neuro to read, drive, and ride. Except books aren't doing it for me right now, and driving only sends me to places I don't want to go. At least the summer break for Moto is nearly over, but it ain't over yet.

Our race at Brno isn't for a couple days, and everyone agreed this was the perfect chance for me to get back in the rodeo arena. To face my demons and keep my sponsors happy. I had a better idea of what to do with my free time, now that I'm free.

I pace back and forth in the warm August wind, my heart beating outta my chest and my finger poised over the little green Call button.

My brother answers his phone on the second ring. "You get there okay? Blake said there was a hell of a thunderstorm on his way in, didn't think he was gonna make it for a minute. Oh and hey, who did you draw to ride? Hope it's not that grumpy old—"

"I…need to tell you something." My voice sounds guilty as hell, the same as it's sounded any other time I've called him for a rescue. But I don't need him to save me this time. Just cover for me.

Billy goes quiet. The TV in the background goes quiet too, some musical number cutting off in the middle of a high note. "Okay."

"I'm not in South Carolina."

Billy lets out a long breath that crackles through the phone line, still apparently giving me the benefit of the doubt. "Did your truck break down? You get stuck somewhere?"

I roll my eyes. Taryn says he's an enabler, and I'm starting to see her point.

"Honey, is Mason okay?" I hear her asking in the background. "He get caught in that thunderstorm? Holly said it was awful."

I lean back against the wall, the easy breeze full of salty air just enough to ruffle my shirt. "Sure, we'll go with that."

"Damn it, Mason. Where are you?"

A smile sneaks onto my lips. "Repeat after me: plausible deniability, Brother."

"Fuck." Then his voice changes like he pulled the phone away from his ear. "No, Taryn, he's fine…yes, I promise. No I don't need to go get him…yeah. Okay, I love you too. Call me when you're done shopping with your mom. Yeah, I'll come meet you. Bye, honey." A door closes in the background, and then Billy's voice comes back to the phone, low and gritty especially for me. "Look, whatever you're up to, just be careful and remember I'm not there to save your ass if you need it."

"Fully aware of that."

"Better be."

A lady comes up the stairs, looking me over like a bug she wants to squash before she keeps going up to the next level. "Look, if you really wanna help me out, then call Blake and tell him I'm sorry."

"Fuck no. Call him yourself."

*Damn it.* I knew he wasn't gonna want to do that. "Please, Billy? And tell Dad…I don't give a fuck what you tell him."

Billy huffs, I guess getting worried. "Okay, I'll bite. What's going on?"

It's a good thing he can't see the grin on my face; I'd be busted in a second. No way to hide it in my voice though. "Nothing you need to worry about. I'll see you in Brno."

"Mason—"

I hang up. Turn off my phone. Put it away, run a hand through my hair, then blow out a breath. My heart is pounding so hard it's throbbing in my temples, and this is without a doubt one of the riskiest maneuvers I've ever pulled. I honestly have no idea which way I'm gonna land, and it won't take me eight seconds to find out either. But walking away isn't an option. It won't fix what's been bugging me for months now.

I knock on the door before I chicken out.

*Be the hero, be the hero...*

It takes a few seconds—seven of them—before the door finally swings open.

My pulse sputters at the first sight of her, a wide grin snapping across my face and some kind of light lifting up my soul. It's been *way* too long since I've seen that smile. And she's wearing one hell of a damn smile.

Chiara recovers quickly, propping her hand on the doorway. She is unfairly sexy in a tank top and frayed khaki shorts, her long legs ending in a splash of hot pink toenail polish. "And where are you supposed to be?"

"Rodeo."

She giggles her naughty giggle, and after thirteen hours on a plane just to hear that sound in person, I can't wait anymore.

"C'mere," I growl at her.

But it's me that moves—I walk straight into her, and she's up with her legs around my waist like it's nothing, her laugh ringing out through the apartment as I kick shut the door behind me. *Cinnamon...*

Chiara wastes no time peeling off my hat and throwing it away, her hair raining down all over us with my jaw cradled happily in her palms. "Hi, cowboy." And with the way she smiles against my lips just before she kisses me, I know without a doubt that coming here was absolutely the right choice. No rodeo, no *anything* else could ever beat this.

I can't touch enough of her, and she tastes so good that she's already got me forgetting my plans by the time I set her on the dining table, dropping my bag off my shoulder so I can tug her closer and hold her a little tighter because I just fucking *need* her.

I've missed the way her jaw feels in my palms and how soft her cheeks are under my thumbs. I love the way she tilts her head and lets me take control even though she's taller, how she always hooks her hands behind my shoulders like she does when I'm on top of her. It's so *nice*, knowing how it works and not having to guess.

Chiara quickly shifts us up another gear, her moans getting lower as her hands drop to my belt, starting to search under my shirt. I don't want to stop kissing her for anything, but I really did have a plan, and kissing every inch of her gorgeous body was part two.

"Mm-mm. Wait, hold on." I tear my lips away from hers, and with the way she's looking at me, her lips already swollen from mine, I bet she's already completely soaking wet too. Makes this so much harder. Makes *me* impossibly harder.

"What? Why?"

I blow out a breath, tipping my forehead to hers and trying really, really hard to slow us down. It isn't exactly my strong suit. Especially when she smells this damn good. "What are you doing today?" God, I sound like I just ran a marathon. "You have any plans?"

Chiara snorts. "I do now." She hooks her leg around my waist, pulling me in closer. A needy groan rumbles from my dick all the way up to my throat, and when she turns her head to nip at my thumb, that smile of hers just keeps getting dirtier as she twirls her tongue around the tip and then starts to suck on it.

*Yeah… No!*

"Goddammit, hold on." I laugh and step all the way back from her, Chiara throwing her hands up in the air.

"What?" she says. "*You* came to *me*."

"Yes, I did," I agree, pointing at her to stay over there. "But do you have plans today?"

She huffs out a breath, but at least she's still smiling. "I was supposed to go to work, but I didn't want to go. So I stayed home and made bread instead."

"Okay, see? That's good." I blow out another breath, really needing to calm down. Because we're not staying in her apartment that long. Not if we're gonna make our reservation.

Chiara's smile grows delightfully curious, and it's one of my favorite things about her—how game she is for every bad idea I have, usually cranking them up another notch. But she's the only person who's ever made me feel like it's not wrong to be the way I am: typically restless and easily bored, aching for stimulants and stimulation wherever I can find them. Because Chiara is also wonderfully, terribly, exactly like me. Be it books or bikes, sex or space, we want to drown in it all. And we do it so *well* together.

"Why?" she asks, her voice sweetly drawn out with anticipation.

"Because." I can barely keep a straight face. "We're going skydiving."

"Are you *serious*?!" she screams, so much excitement on her face that she doesn't even get the words all the way out before she's across the space I set and jumping onto me.

I burst out in laughter as I stumble back, my hands wonderfully full of Chiara's curves and squeezing her even tighter against me.

*Absolutely the right call.*

# Chapter 19

*Mason King—August*

SKYDIVING WAS TOTALLY FUCKING WORTH IT. CHIARA HAD A blast, and I'm never gonna forget it—her cutting up and cracking jokes with me behind the instructor's back, and making bets about who could do the most somersaults. The crazy-hot kiss she smacked on me before she free-fell backward out of the plane. I dove out right after her.

But even the rush of skydiving can't compare to what I'm feeling now.

Chiara bites the back of my shoulder as I fumble to unlock the front door, her arms around my waist and already halfway done undoing my belt buckle. I don't know what the speed limits were on the roads back to her apartment, but I guarantee we broke 'em. Her egging me on in the passenger seat definitely wasn't helping. But Chiara gets off on adrenaline as much as I do, and there's only fast or faster when she's next to me.

I kinda want to get my hands on her transmission, but I've got other things to handle first.

Her fingertips brush my skin behind the button on my jeans, and fire blasts down my spine and lights up my veins. The door finally swings open. Thank God.

In one smooth motion, I pull her inside and turn us around, pressing her up against the door as it slams shut behind her. The wood groans as we fall against it, but Chiara just laughs.

"Record time," she says, her voice breathless and playfully impressed. "Incredible."

"Told ya." I lean my palms against the door, my cock swelling into iron as I kiss her as deep as I can, Chiara getting back to work on my jeans. I barely remember to flip the lock while kissing my way down her neck, relishing the sweet and salty taste of her tan skin. I am fucking *salivating* at how much I can't wait to go down on her, and I still can't believe it took me two months to get the guts to come here when this is what was waiting for me.

Slim fingers slip into my jeans, wrap around my cock, and squeeze, and I have no idea how I stay standing. She bites my earlobe, and my knees absolutely wobble that time.

I can't wait anymore.

With all the strength I can find, I straighten myself and pull off her shirt, letting it fall to the floor. Kill the bra, pink polka dots be damned. Take her gorgeous face in my hands and kiss her beautiful lips, then kiss my way down her chest and suck on a perfect pert nipple.

Goose bumps ripple down my back at her hands in my hair, holding me to her. Find her hips. Hook my thumbs into her shorts. Get the panties too. Peel them down her long legs and drop to my fucking knees.

"You don't want to go to the bedroom?" she asks.

I can't wait for the bedroom. Can't wait for the couch. We're doing this right here. "No."

She chuckles above me, playing with my hair. "Whatever you want, cowboy. I'm yours tonight."

*Oh my God.* But it isn't a fantasy in my mind this time when I trace my tongue up the inside of her thigh, then slip her knee over my shoulder, opening her up and taking a second to admire her. The slick sheen of desire waiting for me. That wonderful little tattoo.

I look up to watch her reaction, my heart beating absolutely wild in my chest. Her dark lashes are low, honey eyes hazy with want and her chest rising faster with every staggered breath. But she keeps her eyes locked with mine and never looks away as I slip my fingers over her, then dip them inside.

"You miss me?" My voice is low, gravelly and rough with how much I need her.

Have needed her.

Chiara gasps a "Yes" as I push deeper, curling my fingers and teasing her front wall and never touching her clit. A whimper escapes her lips as I find her G-spot and work it slowly, adoringly, growing harder in my jeans at every swell of heat that melts down my knuckles. Every brush of her fingertips as she sweeps my hair from my forehead. Every blink of her eyelashes while she never, ever looks away.

"You ready to come for me?"

Chiara nods, her body agreeing as she gets impossibly wetter for me.

"Good."

She squeaks out a noise when I duck my head and take my first taste of her, flicking my tongue over her clit. Her hips buck, but her palm instantly captures my neck to keep me where I am—not that I plan on going anywhere.

I stroke my fingers deeper into her, kissing her body and relishing in the slick evidence of how much she wants me. The tight fit of a perfect match and the explosion of sensation all bundled in one tiny place. I nibble delicate flesh and drown myself in everything about her that is uniquely Chiara until her nails go sharp, a flood of heat coating my knuckles as she throbs and locks me inside, moaning endlessly above me.

I love the way she tastes when she breaks.

Her grip on my neck slackens and my hand on her hip goes soft, but I linger a little longer than I'm strictly supposed to. Soothing everywhere she's sensitive, sweeping my tongue over each curve and into every dip, caressing her and savoring all I've been missing. Backing her down until she's revving up again.

Before I ever get her close, she stops me, panting out, "Your turn."

I groan, stealing a last taste between her legs.

She sucks in a breath, then tugs on my hair, arching my head back on my neck and her voice a kind of stern I only get when she really, really needs me. "I *want* your dick."

An evil grin curls my lips. "Come get it then."

The look in her eyes is positively carnal, Chiara sliding down the door and straight onto my lap with a slowness that is torturously sexy. But when her lips capture mine, the taste of herself on my tongue tears a hungry moan from her throat, her hands busily tearing off my shirt and pushing it over my shoulders.

She flings it away, and the second I've got my hands free, I'm grabbing her ass, turning us over and laying her on the floor. She gets settled under me as I kick off my boots, my eyes gorging on the sight I've missed more than any others. She pushes at my jeans, working them low enough on my hips that my cock springs free. *God*, just the air against it…

"Sit up, sit up," she says, her words rapid-fire. "On your knees."

"What?" No one's *ever* said that to me before. Not even Chiara. But I do as I'm told and sit back on my knees, and then I get it. Chiara swings around, lying on her side in front of me as she takes my cock in one hand, then positions me between her lips. "Holy fuck," I murmur as she kisses away the precum beaded on my head, then takes me all the way into her mouth.

A moan rumbles through my throat, matching the one in hers vibrating straight into my dick. I reach down and cup her cheek, losing more and more brain power as she sucks and licks and kisses me.

*I never should've gone to Memphis.*

*Should've come straight here the moment she left the circuit.*

I can't keep still once she starts stroking me too: rolling my hips so I can thrust deeper into her mouth, my thumb caressing her beautiful cheek as I feed her my cock. But I'm not done touching her yet. Not by far.

I let her go and reach between her legs, finding her soaking everywhere I want to be sunk inside. Chiara moans deeper, sucking me harder as she shifts so I've got a better angle. She squeezes my fingers when I dip them inside her, my thumb swirling around her clit. I match the rhythm she's giving me, her moans growing louder around my cock in her mouth until I've got her coming for me again. Coming *hard*.

It nearly pulls me down with her, but I'm saved when she rips her mouth back once she's done, panting for breath and her cheeks flushed. My cock glistening in her fist. Right next to her swollen lips.

"I need you," she says. "Now."

Don't have to tell me twice.

I lie beside her, getting rid of my jeans completely and throwing them away. Remember and have to get them back—because I'm a dumbass—so I can take out my wallet.

"Mason, hurry," she complains, her hands desperate on my skin.

"Just getting a condom, baby."

Another whimper comes from Chiara. "I'm on birth control. It's fine."

I stop, everything in me seizing when I look over my shoulder. That was never brought up while she was on the circuit. I didn't even ask because it didn't matter. I *never* go without a condom. It's the one rule I don't break.

But it's *Chiara*, and the more I look at her, the more my brain short-circuits at her bare breasts and soft stomach, long legs rubbing restlessly together and her brown hair fanned out on the floor. Woman's got a body like a racetrack, and I'm ready to *go*.

"Are you sure?"

"Sì. Yes." She nods quickly, her hand needy on my skin. "I am okay. If you're okay?"

"Yeah, I'm clean." Just got tested. Specifically.

"So?" She squeezes my arm, her eyes clear and full of need. Full of needing *me*. "Come be with me." Then she drops the bomb: "I trust you."

There is no saying no to that.

*Ah, fuck it.*

―⁓―

There's something so oddly normal about being in her dark bedroom, lying in her soft bed and listening to the bustling piazza outside the shutters. Chiara snuggles a little closer to me, her bare body pressed into my side and the long line of her spine stretching on forever, her head gently resting on my good shoulder. Her legs are all woven around mine, and her comforter barely covers our lower half. It was doing a better job of keeping us warm about five minutes ago, but she had to go and kick out one foot, and the rest was a lost battle from there.

My eyelashes flutter closed as my fingers pull again through her silky hair, massaging her scalp as I brush kisses onto her forehead, probably about ten seconds from passing out. "You still awake?"

I'm pretty sure she's good to go after our theatrics in the entry-way, bent over the back of the couch, and finally in the bedroom, but there's always the chance she's just giving me a ten-minute breather. I need to make absolutely sure I'm okay to fall asleep before I do— takes forever and a bulldozer to wake me back up.

"Hmm."

I brush another kiss to her forehead, Chiara groaning and then shifting like she's reaching across me toward her nightstand. *Staying awake it is*. I just…can't find the energy to open my eyes all the way.

She's back to her spot on my shoulder in a moment, but she seems more concerned with nuzzling her way into just the right spot rather than reaching toward the sheets. I figure out why when I hear the first punctuated click of her cellphone, then another, and I muster the strength to smile. Still can't seem to open my eyes though.

"What's the point of taking pictures of us *after* we have sex?"

"Because you are beautiful," she says, shifting a little like she's changing the angle of the selfie. "And I like the way we look together."

*I like the way we look together too*. We take a lot of pictures when we're together, not that we can show them to anyone or upload them to Insta or anything. But I like having them and seeing them in my camera roll every time I open my phone's gallery. Some of them are actually kinda sweet, but a lot are pretty fucking dirty, and it's been funny to me to discover which ones turn me on the most.

It's not the dirty ones.

"Lemme see." I peel open my tired eyes, and when Chiara turns the screen my direction, something tender fills my chest at the ones she just took. How warm we look under the black-and-white filter, how soft everything is despite the sharp focus.

"See?" she says. "You are just you. Not a moto racer, not a bull rider. Just Mason."

"If you say so." I clear my throat and shift like I'm getting comfortable. I have no idea if I actually move; I can barely feel my body. "Send me those."

"Okay." Her fingers fly as she pulls up her contact list, sends the photos, followed by a vibration of my phone on the nightstand. My eyes close.

*That's really how she has me listed in her contacts?*

I mean, I don't use her real name either, but... Damn.

*Let it go.* I'm too tired to say anything about it now. At some point though, we're gonna have to talk about that.

Chiara reaches across me once more, followed by the soft thunk of her phone being put down. She snuggles into me, and I hug her closer, dropping another kiss to her forehead.

"How have you been?" she asks quietly. "Really."

I shrug, my fingertips drawing circles on her back. "All right. Busy."

"Your last bull ride..." She ducks her head to my chest. Holds on to me a little tighter.

A deep sigh falls from my lips—I wish she hadn't seen that. "It looked worse than it was." I pull her closer, breathing, "I'm okay. Cleared to ride again and everything."

She nods, dropping a kiss to my chest before she looks up at me. I trace away a lock of chestnut hair from her cheek, and there's such depth to her eyes tonight—a raw intensity between us that's only gotten stronger with each time we've been together, magnified by all the months we've been apart.

It should scare the shit out of me: seeing all that's been driving me lately reflected in her eyes. It does scare me. But not so much that I'm willing to walk away from it.

That's exactly the kind of scary I like to run *toward*.

"You really have to leave tomorrow?" she asks, and just like that, I already know I'm gonna miss my flight tomorrow afternoon.

The summer break for Moto Grand Prix is officially over. And not only am I crazy freaking thankful that I got cleared in time to race again, but I've really been looking forward to racing Brno. I've missed my bike, the speed and the vibration and the blur of the world as I pass it all by. I've also got some placements to make up if I want a prayer of topping the World Champion podium, and I *want* that goddamn podium. But the first day back to the circuit is all press conferences and photo shoots anyway... It's not, like, *practice* or anything.

I hum again, shifting my head deeper into the pillow as a grin sneaks onto my lips. "I don't know. Maybe."

Chiara softly giggles, nipping a kiss to my chest before she shifts on top of me. "Good."

*Man, is Frank gonna be pissed...*

# Chapter 20

*Chiara Martes—August*

"LITTLE MORE," MASON ENCOURAGES FROM BEHIND ME, HIS hands steadying me by my hips and his breath tickling my neck under the collar of his shirt, since I stole his. He hasn't worn more than jeans for most of the time he's been here, and I think shirts are now going to be banned for him in my apartment. Forever. God invented pectoral muscles just for Mason King, I swear. "One final twist should do it."

I bite my bottom lip and grip the pliers with all my strength, the rest of me balanced precariously on the edge of the tub between Mason's legs. I start to turn the twisty piece on the pipe to the right, then stop when I think better of it. "You promise it's not going to spray me?"

He chuckles, tickling his fingertips down my bare thigh before smoothing his palm back up. "I promise it's not gonna spray you. We turned the water off."

I turn forward and eye my target warily—I hate these pipes. Massimo hates these pipes. Mason's been here for twenty-four hours, and *he* hates these pipes. But he found some old tools (of Massimo's) under the sink, and he swore it wouldn't be that big of a deal to make the gurgling stop. He also insisted on me doing it myself.

To be fair, he was half-naked and I was still coming down off my last orgasm; I had no idea what I was agreeing to. And he did loosen the first turn for me because it was too tight.

Step by disgusting step, he's walked me through how to turn off the main water line, take it all apart, clean it, and put it all back together. And oh my God, the crap that came out of that pipe... I was gagging for my life. Mason was practically talking dirty to it. At least he wasn't totally grossed out, but I guess he's seen worse while working ranches.

"One more turn, and then we'll turn the water back on and check it," he says. "I'll even switch you spots so I'll take the hit in case it blows."

I whip around, my eyes huge. "What do you mean it could blow?"

I knew I should've called the plumber.

Mason rolls his eyes, reaching around me to grab the pliers. With his hands on top of mine, we make the final turn, though he instantly checks it over with his left hand like his bare grip is stronger than the tool. Actually, it might be. His hands are freaking *strong*.

"All right, moment of truth." His grip on my hips guides me to stand, and I pull my leg from the tub as he scoots forward to the spot where I was. I bite my lip, hugging the pliers to my chest and wincing as he reaches around the tub to turn the main water line back on.

Nothing happens.

Mason glances back at me, chuckling. "You look genuinely scared right now."

"I don't want it to explode on you! These pipes are not to be trusted, and I do not want to have to explain to your sponsors that I maimed their prize rider three days before a race. I can't handle that kind of insurance claim."

He snorts. "What in the world are you talking about?"

I stare at him—sometimes I really don't understand how he can look in the mirror and not see the man I do. "You're the third fastest moto rider in the world right now. And after Brno, you could be the second."

He could've been the first already—but he's been finishing all over the place since I left in May. It's just a coincidence, though. It can't mean what I think it does. I'm just reading into things.

"But instead of packing to leave like everyone else, you're here, fixing my jerk pipes. And now you're telling me they could explode on you? Sorry! Not thrilled by that prospect."

Mason sits up, smiling at me as his knees bounce with restless energy and looking annoyingly at home sitting on the edge of my bathtub in his Wranglers. But he fits perfectly in my bed too, and stretched out on my sofa, at my kitchen table, and it's so *frustrating* how easy it is to be with him. How natural everything feels despite how long we've been apart.

It's just going to make it so much worse when he goes.

"First, you fixed the pipes, not me," he says. "And second, I'll be fine. This isn't by far the most dangerous thing I've done on the break, Chiara. We kinda went skydiving yesterday."

"I am aware of that," I snap, even though I'm not really mad at him. Especially when yesterday was a truly amazing, once-in-a-lifetime event that I will never, ever get over. I'm so glad I got to experience it with Mason too, because he makes everything a thousand times easier and way more fun.

I'm just...still a little freaked out by what happened at his last rodeo. Even worse was being halfway across the world where information was nearly impossible to verify. For a good six hours, I thought he was dead. Landing on his neck like that...

I repress a shudder.

*He's fine*—here and smiling and operating in prime condition.

"Are you gonna let me turn on the water?" he drawls. "Or are we just *not* gonna shower for the foreseeable future? 'Cause that's gonna get real interesting, real quick."

I toss a hand up. "Fine. But I take no responsibility for what's about to happen."

"I'll enter it in the log." He flares his eyes and turns back to the pipes, propping his ankle on the edge of the tub before he turns on the water. It runs happily from the spout into the tub, no gurgling whatsoever. "See?" He turns toward me. "Everything's—" A blast of water erupts from the twisty piece, nailing the side of his face and spraying his shoulder and chest. "Ah, *fuck*!"

"*See*?!"

He tries to cover the leak with his bare hands. But water is still spraying everywhere. He reaches toward me. I take his hand. "Wrench, baby, wrench!" I hand him the pliers, which are apparently called a wrench, before I retreat farther back while water continues to coat *everything* in my bathroom, Mason included. "The hell is wrong with this thing?"

"Oh my God," I mutter, mortification rampant through me as he grits his teeth and twists and twists it, getting wetter and wetter as water soaks his jeans, speckling the back of his arms and shoulders. He's really never going to call me again after this.

"Come on," he growls, the muscles in his back flexing as he puts all his force into the twist. I can barely watch. *Please*, don't let him hurt his shoulder. "*Turn*, you son of a…"

There's a sharp pop of metal against metal, and then the water stops spraying, *thank God*. Mason lets it go and sits back, turning off the spout and taking a couple of centering breaths.

"That," he says, looking back at me with a laugh, "was not your fault."

"Oh sure."

"This fitting is stripped." He shakes out his wet hair. "Probably just old. We'll get a new one. It'll be fine."

I clear my throat, reluctant to remind him… "You're leaving tomorrow."

Mason winks. "Then I'll get one this afternoon. It'll take me five minutes."

There's no point in arguing. Not that I really want to. I grab a towel instead, waiting as Mason stands and sets the wrench on the counter beside the sink. I start to pat off his chest, but it's basically a lost cause. His jeans are *soaked*. I guess it's not really the worst thing in the world when we originally came in here to take a shower, then got distracted by the whole pipe issue. But I just…don't want to be remembered as a bad time, a nuisance.

"What?" he says quietly, a smile in his voice as I start toweling off his shoulders.

"You are so wet."

Mason snorts, pulling the towel away. He sets it on the counter, his blue eyes locked with mine as he cups my cheek in his hand, running his thumb over my lips. "Pretty sure that's my line."

Heat flames my cheeks, Mason leaning close enough to kiss me. His lips are still wet, soft and sinfully delicious, and a flush of desire tingles through me when he moans and wraps me in his arms so he can kiss me softer, slower.

Everything with him is so different this time: the way he hugs me, the way he looks at me and touches me...

He made love to me last night. *Late* last night, when everything was dark and quiet and the world was asleep. I don't know if he realizes, but I damn well know the difference, and he...*yeah*.

I'm trying not to dwell on it. He isn't going to be here long. Might never come back—but that's tomorrow's problem, after he leaves for Brno.

"We gotta have sex in the shower more," he whispers against my lips, still sipping kisses from me that I can't get enough of either.

"Hmm, we could do that *now*..."

He moans deeper and sneaks his hand under my shirt, cupping my breast, and I'm only too happy to stroke my hands through his wet hair, letting Mason back me into the wall so he can do what he wants with me for as long as he pleases.

He's just hooked a hand behind my knee, lifting my leg to hug his waist, when my phone starts vibrating on the counter. For the third time this morning. *Goddammit, Massimo.*

"He can leave a message," Mason breathes, his lips trailing to my neck.

I sigh, frustrated. "If I don't answer, he's eventually going to come over here."

Mason tilts his hips deeper into mine, letting me feel *exactly* how much he wants me. "Let him come over here then."

I roll my eyes at myself in the bathroom mirror. *Oh yeah, because that's going to end well.* But then I notice my messy bun and the loose sleeves of his shirt, dangling at my wrists as I grip his shoulders, the roll of muscles in his back as he palms the back of my thigh—*damn*, watching us is *hot*. We don't need to just have shower sex before he leaves, we need it in front of a mirror too. Actually, I wonder if he'd let me film us?

"Just give me five minutes," I whisper.

Mason groans, nipping at the sensitive spot above my collarbone that makes my nipples go instantly hard.

"Three minutes?"

He groans again, lifting his head and letting go of my leg so I'm back to balancing on ten toes instead of five. "It's fine," he says. "Take twenty, whatever you need."

I smile and pepper kisses across his lips until he laughs and kisses me back, then I duck under his arm and grab my phone. *Jesus, Massimo!* Four unread text messages, three missed calls, two voicemails, and all from one super needy best friend.

"I'm gonna put on some dry clothes," Mason says behind me, heading out of the bathroom with a wink.

"Okay." I trail my fingertips down his arm on his way past, then head into the kitchen to call Massimo back, trying to calm my raging hormones. Like that's possible right now—if I manage a slow simmer, it'll be a miracle. "Hey, star," I say in Italian when he answers on the first ring.

"She's alive," he teases. "I can't believe you slept this late. Up all night streaming again?"

"I didn't sleep *that* late. And as a matter of fact, I've been running errands all morning," I answer sort of honestly.

Mason and I went out for an early cappuccino, then to the grocery store because my fridge was empty and I had nothing to feed him. We came back here and unloaded everything, had some kinky as fuck sex in the living room, then fixed the pipes...

"Uh-huh. Sure." Massimo chuckles like he doesn't believe me. "Is that what you're calling grinding now?"

I lean back against the kitchen counter, propping up a foot. "Who taught you that word? Do you even know what grinding is?"

"Yes," he says, feigning indignation. "Dario explained it to me."

Oh my God, those two, I swear.

Mason picks that moment to come around the corner wearing a dangerously sexy smirk, a dry pair of jeans, and a shirt! The nerve! I pretend to glare at him until he stops in place, his brow furrowing and hands held up in surrender. But I curl my finger toward myself, and his smirk comes right back. *Much better.*

I hold my phone between my ear and my shoulder as Mason stops in front of me, a devilish arch to his brow and his hands on either side of me. Time to get started on undoing the buttons. "I can't believe you're taking gaming advice from your little brother," I say to Massimo.

"Not advice. I just asked him what he was doing and he explained it. Anyway, now that you're awake—"

"I wasn't sleeping."

"—you want to come meet me for lunch? Thought we could hit the grocery store afterward. My flight out isn't until four."

I swear, how does he always know? "Who said something? Aria or Elena?"

I push the shirt over Mason's shoulders, tugging it down his arms and throwing it toward the kitchen table. I give him a warning glare, along with a stern finger, then shoo him away. He grins and presses a lingering kiss to my cheek before he heads toward the refrigerator, pulling it open.

Massimo snorts. "Lorina. After she was over there the other day."

Ah. We were planning the boudoir photo shoot she's giving him as a wedding present. And I get to photograph. I'm weirdly excited about this. She had some really good inspiration pics and she really loved my ideas. We make a good team.

"Anyway, she said your fridge was empty."

"Tell her she's a traitor."

"She's just worried about you."

Mason closes the refrigerator, setting on the counter a lone tomato, a package of provolone, and some sliced ham, looking back at me and mouthing, "You hungry?"

I nod. Freaking starving.

He very quietly washes his hands as Massimo clears his throat. "How's work?"

"It's fine," I singsong lightly. "And I went grocery shopping this morning. I'll even send pics as proof, okay?" I point to the cupboard for the piadina I made yesterday morning. Mason opens it, looking right past the plastic container I use after making a batch for the week.

I push off the counter, reaching past him to take it out and peel off the plastic lid, revealing the flatbread. "My bad," Mason mouths. I wink and hip-check him out of the way, turning on a burner under a nonstick skillet. Take out a piadina and swirl it around the pan, Mason waving me off in the universal sign for "I got it."

"Chiara," Massimo says, "I'm just—"

Worried. "I know. But you don't need to be." I snatch up the tomato and the provolone, opening the fridge and exchanging them for arugula and stracciatella. The prosciutto can stay.

"Fine, then you can pay for lunch," Massimo says lightly. "Come meet me."

"I, um, already ate."

Mason sets out the first flatbread on a paper towel, shaking off his fingers like it's hot enough to burn. I grab a spoon from the drawer, waiting as he places another flatbread in the pan before I scoop out a bit of cheese and hold it out to him to try.

He licks it off with a dirty flick of his tongue, mouthing an appreciative, "Oh *fuck* yeah." Then he leans closer, grinning wickedly as he taps his lips and mouths the words, "Kiss me..."

I push him off, trying to hide the smile in my voice as I tell Massimo, "Elena and I met up earlier. I didn't know what time you were leaving today. I figured you'd be busy."

Massimo huffs out a breath. "Okay, well...dessert, then. Espresso."

"Don't you have packing to do?" I start spreading the stracciatella over the warm piadina, then sprinkle fresh arugula. Layer the prosciutto, fold and hand to Mason. Tease my nails down his back as he takes a bite with a nearly silent moan, then takes the second flatbread out of the pan. I cross back to my counter. "Or is something going on with you and Lorelai that you're avoiding?"

"Really?" Massimo deadpans. "It couldn't be that I'm about to be gone for a month, and I've barely seen you over the break?"

"You never want to come out when I call you." Apparently becoming engaged means you no longer enjoy live music and the occasional drink with your best friend. He shows up for all the wedding stuff, but that's always with Lorelai.

"That was one time."

"Twice," I correct.

"Whatever. I'm grabbing food and heading over there to fix the pipes before I leave. You really don't want me to bring you anything? Bacon cheeseburger from America Graffiti?"

My heart slams in my chest. I am the worst best friend ever.

He sounds so normal—so happy and so *him*. Exactly like my best friend of twenty years is supposed to sound. Everything I was scared I would lose when he moved out. But so much more has changed than just our living arrangements, and it's not just Massimo who's different.

I watch as Mason moves silently around my kitchen, the ease with which he recreates the sandwich I made before he starts putting everything away. I didn't quite understand before, how Massimo was able to propose to Lorelai without telling me. But it's starting to make sense. How it could happen. That it wasn't meant to hurt me, it just...wasn't about me. And that's okay.

It has to be okay.

"I, um, already had the pipes fixed. For good. The guy was amazed they'd even worked this long." I try to laugh, but it sounds fake even to my ears. "But they're, uh, they're fine now."

Mason turns around and leans back against the counter, taking a bite of his sandwich. He nods toward the counter and the matching one he made that's sitting on a paper towel for me.

I don't know how I'd eat anything right now with the way my stomach is flipping more and more the longer Massimo stays quiet on the other end of the line. When he finally speaks, I can barely hear him, he's so quiet. "You really don't want to see me, do you?"

"Of course I do. But you should enjoy the day with Lorelai. Like you said: you're about to be on the road for a month, and you should take advantage of having some privacy with her while you can. I'll see you when you get back."

He scoffs, but it's gritty with bitterness. "Right."

"Don't be—"

"I'll call you later." The phone clicks, and I glance at the screen, and yep, he just hung up on me. *Awesome.*

I set down my phone, trying not to make it too obvious what just happened. It'll be fine. We've had worse fights than this. I'll FaceTime him tomorrow, and everything will be *fine*.

"He still coming over?" Mason asks quietly.

"No."

Mason nods, finishing the last bite of his sandwich. He chews and swallows, crossing his arms over his bare chest and watching me when he's done. "You need to go meet him somewhere?"

"Why would I do that?" I say in English. "We're hanging out." I force a smile, extending my hand like everything is okay. "Can I have my sandwich?"

Mason sighs. He does not hand me my sandwich. "Are you okay?"

"I'm hungry."

"Chiara, I don't have to speak Italian to know that he just hung up on you for blowing him off. He's your best friend, and he's leaving for the circuit today." Mason picks up the paper towel, sets it on the counter next to me, then goes back and leans against his opposite counter. "I'm just the guy labeled 'Fuckboy' in your phone."

# Chapter 21

*Chiara Martes—August*

I DO MY BEST NOT TO REACT, AND I COMPLETELY FAIL—*HOW DOES he know that?*

"When you texted me those pictures last night," Mason says, his words aimed at the floor between us, "I, um, I saw the name on the contact."

I glance over my far shoulder to hide my face, *but fucking fuck!* I did that right in front of him. I didn't even think, and I...

*Oh God.* He's been so sweet to me all day, suffering all sorts of domestic errands while knowing it was there the whole time.

He made love to me last night, knowing it was there the whole time.

"If that's what you think of me, then...I guess that's fair." He chuckles, but it's quiet and thin and doesn't sound right coming from Mason. "I guess that's who I'm supposed to be where you're concerned, right? That's what I'm good for?"

I'm nearly faint with shame—I did that for *me*. So that every single time I wanted to text him, I'd be forced to remember that he wouldn't want me to. "Mason, I didn't mean—"

"Are you seeing other people?"

My heart lurches in my chest, and I grip the counter behind me for support. This kind of conversation only ends one of two ways, and neither is good. Neither survivable. "Please," I whisper. "Don't ask me things like that."

"Why not?" He tilts his head. "Because it breaks the rules?"

I can already see what's coming all over his face, and *this can't happen.* Not from him.

He was the safe bet, the loose cannon I could rely on not to complicate things. The lawless cowboy who had never been in love and never hoped to be. But it doesn't matter how lost I've been in the fantasy of having him here. He's about to ruin *everything*, and there will be no coming back from this. No way to keep things casual. No way to keep things safe.

(No way to keep my heart safe.)

"Look, I'm not seeing anyone else," he says, shifting his weight and his voice cutting clear through the apartment. "Haven't been out with another woman in months. Haven't even thought about it. And I haven't slept with anyone else since, like…March. Maybe April."

Jealousy flares hot through my stomach at the thought of him with another woman, even though I've been sleeping with other people too. And a lot more recently than April. But I refuse to feel guilty when I did what I needed to keep my guard up, the boundaries firmly between us.

Self-preservation is not a crime when he's been at the circuit, at rodeos, surrounded by models and adoring fans, and I haven't heard a word from him. So yes: I firmly expected him to be doing…what he normally does. What his reputation said he would do.

Exclusive was never on the table for us. I didn't think it was.

"You don't have to tell me those things," I say carefully, swallowing when my voice wobbles. "And I wish you wouldn't."

"Why?" he says again. "You know me, Chiara, and you know I don't bullshit about this kind of stuff. I'm tired of pretending there isn't more going on here than what you're saying. So I'm gonna say it: Why haven't you called me once over the past couple of months, huh? Why haven't you texted me?" He shakes his head. "You don't think about me? Ever? Because you are *all* I fucking think about."

My breaths start shrieking into my lungs, and *how did I let this happen?* I knew the signs, I followed all the rules, and it still happened anyway. "Please stop."

"So that's a no."

"It's a…you're leaving," I sputter. "Which is exactly why we agreed we didn't want that kind of responsibility," I remind him. "We don't want a relationship."

Mason scoffs. "I hate to break this to you, but I think we're already *in* a relationship."

"No, we're not!"

"We've been sneaking around for eight months now. Wait— November! Nine months! And that's longer than I've ever been interested in anyone."

I cover my face with my hands, wishing I couldn't hear him. That I could make him stop. He has to *stop* before I forget why we're terrible for each other, a toxic mess of bad decisions that no one will ever accept.

*Massimo will never forgive me.*

"Chiara...I *miss* you when I'm not with you. And it appears that I will do just about anything to get back to you, missing rodeos and being late to races included. And I know I'm not, like, Mr. Relationship over here, but you're really telling me this is all just me? That you don't feel this too?"

I squeeze my eyes tighter shut. Of course I feel it—there's no way *not* to feel it. But it doesn't matter what I've long suspected of myself, even before I left the circuit in May. I can control my heartbreak. Savor it slowly, cherish the small time we had together, and not ask for more. I am a goddamn expert in how to love him, let him go, and accept that if he never comes back, it's because he's doing the right thing, the more important thing.

What I cannot handle is the unpredictability of Mason loving me *back*.

It wasn't part of the plan, and he said it himself: he's a tornado of chaos. He wrecks everything in his path, and I can't be his next victim. My heart will never survive it.

Mason pushes off the counter and crosses the distance I've put between us, and I'm locked in place as he pulls my hands away so he can cup my cheeks in his hands, his touch so tender that it nearly breaks me all over again. He's always so careful, so considerate of my space and my body, and he doesn't even know how badly I need that from him. How much I trust him, despite all the reasons I probably shouldn't. But he's never failed to give me exactly what I need, and that's exactly what scares me the most about him.

With the way he makes me feel when we're together...

I already know it would take absolutely nothing for my rebel ass to flip the tables on my nothing life and follow him everywhere if he asked.

It's why he *can't* ask.

"I don't want to worry about when I'm gonna talk to you again or see you next," he says. "I want to *know*. And I know I'm asking for a lot, that it's..." He takes a deep breath, his voice soft and private for my sake. "I know he hurt you when he left. And that pain, that's never really gonna go away. But I'm not him, Chiara, and I'm not going anywhere. Not unless that's what *you* want."

I can barely breathe to gasp out his name. "Mason—"

"I can do this, Chiara. I swear to you, I won't fuck this up. But you gotta let me in first, baby. You gotta let me *try*."

I can't do more than shake my head. I don't trust my voice. It's the only hope I have of resisting his blue eyes, the way he smiles when he sees me for the first time since the last time. I'm not prepared to say no to him when he's been here, making me laugh and making me feel safe and important and kissing me senseless every moment in between.

I'm emotionally compromised, and *he can't do this*.

"No, you won't let me try?" Mason says. "Or no, you're not in love with me too? Because I'm sorry to say this, but you're definitely not in love with him anymore."

Tears rush into my eyes before I can stop them, my body trembling and all my instincts at war over whether to push Mason away or to kiss him and never let go. Between the fights and the circuit calling, it already feels like I'm on the verge of losing both of them, and I can't lose both of them.

"Yeah, I bet that does hurt to realize," Mason breathes, tipping his forehead to mine. "And I really am sorry for that. I know we didn't mean for this to happen." His thumbs sweep tenderly over my cheeks, and it makes it all so much worse with how much that simple move undoes me. How many times I've dreamt of him and made bargains with myself I knew I'd never uphold: if I could only see him one more time, it would absolutely be the last.

His hands fall to my shoulders, trailing lightly down my arms, and it's not fair when I'm shivering under the influence of how much I've missed him. He's all I think about too, worrying about him when he's racing or getting bucked from riding bulls. Wondering how badly his shoulder is bothering him and if anyone is taking notice. If they see how much he has to offer, if they would only ask instead of telling him what to do. But no one sees him as they should, how capable and intelligent and brave he is. That all he needs is a chance.

(I never stood a chance.)

"I have to leave tomorrow," he says, his hands finding mine and our fingers tangling together. "And I'm gonna be gone for a while. I don't have a choice in that. But I really don't want to go with anything left unsaid between us. Especially if it's the last time I'm ever gonna see you."

A new wave of tears breaks free from my eyelashes at the thought, stealing their way down my cheeks, and I don't have it in me to fight anymore. I'm so tired of being apart. So tired of waiting for the ends of Novembers. Tired of making excuses about why it's wrong to care about him when it doesn't *feel* wrong when we're together.

It feels like fate, as though he can decipher the metaphors of me as easily as he can in all those books. And the stability of never knowing what he's going to do...it's *exactly* that twin flame of escapism that makes me feel safer with him than I ever knew was possible. Because with Mason, I will never be trapped, and there's no one else I'd rather run away with than him.

Just like that, the dam breaks. And as the first wave of acceptance rolls over me, it sends goose bumps rushing across my skin—the freedom from the fear, from all the lies I've told myself about all the ways he'd hurt me if I wasn't careful. How much he'd take and demand and what it would cost me.

Everything. The last of all I have to give.

But that's not Mason. It never has been.

"If you want me to go, Chiara, just say the word and I'm gone." His voice is more serious than I've ever heard from him. And it's absolutely heartbroken. "I won't bother you again."

It's the easiest decision I've ever made. I shake my head, whispering, "I don't want you to leave. Not today, not tomorrow. Not ever."

A shocked breath huffs from his lips. "Really? Are you sure?"

He sounds *so* surprised—I can't help but brokenly chuckle as I let his hands go so I can reach up and wipe away my tears with my shirtsleeve. "Um, fairly sure…"

"Sorry, I just…I thought for sure that you were gonna tell me to go."

"Why?" My voice is destroyed from crying, but there's nothing I can do about it now. My hands settle on the warm strength of his chest, and I find my smile, because I finally get to tell him the truth. But I should've known better than to think I could keep a secret this big from him. He's been calling me out since our first date—he sees me better than I see myself.

"How would that help anything when you are right?" I take a deep breath to steady my nerves, absolutely beaming when I tell him, "Han Solo was a better hero than Luke Skywalker, and I am terribly in love with you."

A bright grin rushes across Mason's lips, a look I've never seen from him shining in his eyes. "Chiara…" He swallows hard around my name, his grip tightening on my hips. When he speaks again, his voice is completely choked like the words are coming straight from his heart. "I *never* thought I'd be this damn happy hearing someone say that."

There's no stopping my smile, riding the adrenaline from free-falling into wild love sewn by seamless harmony. "It was the Luke and Han Solo part, wasn't it?" I playfully roll my eyes. "Boys and their *Star Wars*."

Mason cracks up laughing. "You are so much worse!"

I am so much worse. He's still laughing as he takes my face in his hands and crashes his lips to mine, his kiss rich with passion and fierce with adoration, and it's like an explosion of joy in my heart as I let myself feel it all: no brakes, no rules, no fear. The endless realm of possibilities before us to make the absolute best worst decisions we could ever conceive of because wonderfully, or maybe disastrously, it turned out to be *Mason*.

And I can't wait to never know what we're going to do next.

# Chapter 22

*Mason King—August*

I KNEEL NEXT TO THE BED, SOAKING UP THE SIGHT AS MUCH AS I possibly can. Memorizing the placement of each tangled lock of hair over the pillow, the few freckles that only show when she's not wearing makeup. The curl of her eyelashes.

I reach out and run a knuckle down her cheek, waking her up as gently as I can. She moans and *hmms*, a smile starting on her lips before she ever gets her eyes open. "It's so early," she whispers.

"I know. And you should definitely go back to sleep. But I gotta go."

Her eyes fly open. "What?" Chiara scrambles to sit up, reaching for her phone to check the time. "No, it can't be—"

"Noon, yeah."

"No, no, no!" She throws down her phone and runs her hand through her hair, bunched in her fist in pure panic before she reaches for my chest. "I was supposed to make breakfast, make you coffee. Help you pack and screw your brains out. *No!*"

A chuckle ripples from my chest as I take her hand, nipping a kiss to her wrist. "That sounds amazing. But we kinda overslept."

We being her. I've been up for an hour. Showered, packed, cleaned the kitchen, and made coffee. And a sandwich. Made a second cup of espresso before I couldn't wait anymore and finally had to wake her up.

"Mason—"

"It's okay." I tap my lips. "Gimme a kiss."

Her hands find my jaw and she leans down, kissing me soft and deep and like I'm the most important thing in her world. In my heart, I know I'm not, but it almost feels like it.

"See? That's all I need right there."

*If only that were true.*

I smile but she doesn't. Her face only falls further when I stand and slip my bag over my shoulder. Hook on my hat. Take her chin under my thumb and steal one long, last look.

She's so damn beautiful. And I'm gonna miss her so much.

"Bye, trouble."

A breath of air escapes her lips that I'm never going to forget, and I make myself walk out of the room while I still can. Every thud of my boots on the floor sounds like the loudest mistake I've ever made, but I don't have a choice.

I *have* to go.

I'm already a day late, and I can't risk fumbling my racing career when I need it more than ever. By the end of this year, I'm absolutely gonna be done with bull riding, and for the first time in my life, I'm actually a little worried about money. About being able to take care of myself and possibly someone else. Maybe even more than one someone someday.

"Mason, wait."

I turn at the door to find Chiara running after me, wrapped in a bedsheet and trailing half of it behind her. I barely catch her in time as she hugs me desperately tight, my lips falling to her shoulder and breathing in the sweet smell of cinnamon. I'm never gonna get enough.

"Promise you're going to call me," she says.

God, that she even asks me that... "I'll call. You answer."

She nods, hugging me closer. "I hate this. You just got here and you already have to go. It isn't fair."

"No, it isn't fair," I agree. "But at least..."

"At least what?"

"Nothing. I got nothing."

A small laugh breaks through her lips, but she only holds me tighter. "I am really going to miss you."

"I'm gonna miss you too." I squeeze her once more, then start to let her go. I hate that I'm the first one to do it, but someone's gotta. "Don't work too hard while I'm gone, okay?"

She nods, her lips trembling as I steal one last kiss.

"There's espresso for you on the counter." Then I turn and unlock the door. Slip out into the hallway and start for the stairs before I never leave Italy again. Look back at the last minute because I can't help it, and my heart stutters in my chest at Chiara in the doorway: tall and perfect, brown and beautiful, and wrapped in a crisp cotton bedsheet.

I touch my hat and she half smiles, closing the door a little more between us. But not all the way. *Not all the way.* And for now, that's gonna have to be good enough.

Five weeks.

# Chapter 23

*Mason King—August*

My heart is pounding with *FUCK YEAH* adrenaline under the clear Czech sun, and I grin in my helmet as my bike rumbles beneath me, locked in place while my fingers fly over my phone screen.

> **Mason:** What do you think the racing commission would say if they knew you texted me nudes while I'm being broadcast on live TV?

Chiara texts back right away:

> **Chiara:** They'd probably be horribly jealous

I text back a string of emojis, one at a time, enough to fill the screen so the picture is no longer visible to Marco or my crew or anyone else buzzing around me. Doesn't change the fact that she took it, sent it, and I saw it, and she risked it even though cameras are sweeping high and low on cranes, catching all the regular chaos of the prerace grid: crowded with bikes, riders, crews, managers, sponsors, and—

> **Chiara:** Besides, my ass is so much better than your umbrella girl's

I can't restrain a snort, tilting my screen away from the sponsor model holding an umbrella over me and her to shield us from the sun. She probably needs the shade more than I do considering I'm in leathers and a helmet and she's wearing a red crop top with teeny-tiny shorts that aren't covering her teeny-tiny ass.

I think her name is Alicia? Maybe Allison. She's modeling her way through veterinary school; I remember that much from our single bad date last year.

    **Mason:** Absolutely better, no contest

"Mason, you're up," Alli-something hisses at me. I glance up as she goes back to flirting with the camera being walked directly toward us, propped on a bearded dude's shoulder. *Shit.*

I act like I'm blowing a kiss to the camera, wave for a second, then look back to my phone like I'm studying the telemetry of the track or something. I really probably should be…but I've got these turns down backward and forward since Chiara and I have been racing each other online at night.

    **Chiara:** Aww was that kiss for me?
    **Mason:** Yep. And why aren't you my umbrella girl?

It's not unheard of for girlfriends and wives to do it as a supportive thing. It's not like they have to wear the skimpy outfits either—there are T-shirts and jackets to wear with jeans. Though Chiara could rock the shit out of those little shorts…

    **Chiara:** The grid can't handle me. Whole track would fail to launch

I roll my eyes. More like she still isn't ready to face him. That's what she said anyway: that she needed more time, a moment to tell him alone, face-to-face, and we aren't gonna be home for *weeks*. So until then, I'm under the strictest of instructions to keep quiet.

"Mason, thirty seconds," Marco says, my crew pulling the warmers off my bike's tires. I glance around, and the grid is clearing, Billy flipping down his face shield ahead of me. Frank says something to him and smacks the back of his helmet, but in a good way, while Massimo is ready to go in second place, his weight shifted for the launch and his crew already cleared. Santos is checking his gloves in the third pole, Giovanni checking on Santos from the fourth.

**Mason:** Gotta race, baby

**Chiara:** Yeah, yeah ;) Nice subject change

"Ladies and gentlemen," the announcers boom through the stadium. "We welcome you on this fine August afternoon to Brno, Czech Republic." They stop to repeat everything in Czech, then Italian. "In a few moments, the red lights will go out and we will officially start the race for the MotoPro division of Moto Grand Prix. If you'll please take your seats."

**Chiara:** Oh shit you're serious—YOU'VE GOT THIS!!! I LOVE YOU! FUCK THAT ARTICLE CALLING YOU AN UNDERDOG—YOU'RE TOP DOG! AND FULL THROTTLE IN T2!

I snort. *Top dog?* What a freaking dork. I'm so giving her shit about that later.

**Mason:** Call you in an hour

I lock my phone, handing it over to Marco. "Good race," he says, rubbing the top of my helmet for good luck. My crew takes turns doing the same, finishing up as Frank comes jogging over from where he's been giving Billy his pep talk.

"You good?" our manager pants out. "It's all about the elevation changes, which you're more than used to from home. Just don't—"

"Choke the throttle in turn two. Yeah, I got it."

He rubs the top of my helmet. "You got this, Mason. This is *your* year." He gives me a last clap on my shoulder, then clears the track with everyone else, numbers counting down on the clock tower and the sun blazing on the track. The green flag is the next to go, and we take off for the sighting lap, trying to get every last bit of heat into our tires and warming up the brakes. But even over the announcers and the call of the crowd, Frank's words are echoing in my ears, Chiara's last text burning behind my eyes.

*Don't choke the throttle, don't choke the throttle…*

We come around the last turn and retake our places on the grid. Engage launch control, my eyes narrowed on the gray track ahead of me and sweat trickling down my back.

Thirty-nine minutes, twenty-one laps, and three places on that podium.

Billy can't win them all. Massimo either.

*Time to ride.*

The red lights disappear. I fly off the grid, ducking low as my Dabria bike growls hungrily under me. The opening straight is long and wide, the pack spread out as we fight for position. The crowd is already on their feet and cheering as we fall in line before the wide right of turn one—my brother in first and taking the hole-shot, like always, followed by Santos, Giovanni, Massimo, and then me.

My body lies flat only hundredths of a second after theirs, my right knee sliding on the blistering pavement as the nearby motorcycles whine and scream at being restrained. My front forks are inches back from Massimo's tailpipe, and when we come out of it, I downshift and dart past him on the inside, using a move that Lorelai's been kicking his ass with for as long as I can remember. *A move I'm not supposed to know about.* But former teammate codes from when she hated him and all that…

I hear a muffled curse in Italian as I slip ahead, full throttle for the touch left of turn two and barreling down the long straight toward the hard left of turn three. The crowd roars from the stands, waving multicolored flags that speed me along—Billy is already in turn three, Santos and Giovanni swapping positions behind him, but they ain't gonna hold them for long.

*My year. Mine.*

My speedometer hits 196 miles per hour before I downshift twice and tap the brakes, leaning clean into turn three and dipping right into a cleaner turn four. I'm fast as fuck on my way out, the roar from the stands deafening as I slam the throttle and overtake Giovanni, aligning behind Santos for turn five.

I spare a glance back at Massimo, ducked low in his attempts to gain back his position, and I can't help but chuckle.

*Come and get me, asshole…*

———

A deep yawn rumbles from my chest as I sit back in my chair at the dinner table, tugging a hand through my hair before I lace my hands behind my head. I'm all full of tangy grilled chicken and sautéed broccoli, and there's something about England that always makes me extra tired. I think it's the weather.

Frank takes a sip of water, the ice clinking as he sets it on the table. But he keeps twisting the glass in his fingers, his eyes darting between me and Billy. "So we all clear on that?"

"Yep," Billy says.

"Mason?"

"Forward all inquiries to you." I shoot him some finger guns. "Got it."

"Good." He jerks his chin at me. "Mason, it's your turn to do the dishes."

"What? Why?" I glance between him and Billy, pushing my plate farther away. "I cooked. It's Billy's turn."

"*Well*, I need to talk to him," Frank says. "About a…uh, Christmas present. For Taryn."

Liar. That's code for secret contract stuff, and you'd think he'd be better at coming up with excuses on how to talk to Billy alone after so many years. I wonder what it is now: another lifetime achievement award? Some new way to promote him?

I look at Billy. But for some reason, he doesn't look any happier about being pulled off cleanup duty. He's silently tapping his fork against his empty plate and not looking at me.

"Someone wanna tell me what's going on here?" I ask them. "Am I about to get fired?"

Fuck, I cannot get fired. I need to start upping my bring-home cash if I'm gonna build some kind of stability for me and Chiara, not lose my damn job a few weeks into being together. She has a hard enough time trusting me as it is—I'm not taking it personally, but she's been screwed over and abandoned too many times—and the last thing I want is to rock that boat by going broke. She deserves the world, and I mean to give it to her, but if I lose my contract...

"I told you I don't know anything about the—"

"No, it's nothing like that." Frank chuckles, waving me off. "You're doing fine. Keep doing what you're doing."

I sit back in my seat. *Okay...* That's a relief, but still. I guess that's what we're calling winning now—I barely beat Billy in Brno, but I beat him, and I busted up Massimo something bad in Spielberg. Crossed the finish line almost a full thirty seconds before him. I also have every intention of doing the same here in Silverstone.

"I'll clean up after we're done talking," Billy says. "Mason can go."

"*Thank* you." I stand and push in my chair, grabbing my water and taking it with me as I leave the conservatory.

This little cottage we're staying in is cool as hell—two stories, five bedrooms, an attached glass conservatory with a large dining table overlooking the garden, and just the three of us here for the next four days before we transition to the paddock. We'd normally stay in something smaller, but Frank booked it because Lorelai and Massimo and Massimo's manager, Vinicio, were supposed to be here too. They ended up staying somewhere else nearby. I'm heartbroken.

I take the stairs up to my room two at a time, kicking shut the door behind me and dropping off my water on the dresser. Haven't had a drink in over thirty days now, and I'm doing all right with it. Not always great, but it's getting easier, and sometimes I don't even think about it. My sponsor, Tank—a long-haul truck driver who's ten years clean off pills and alcohol—says that's normal for now, but the real test will come when I'm not living on top of the world.

We'll see if he's right. Kinda hope he's not. In the meantime, I'm Zoom calling into meetings and FaceTiming with him three times a week. Sometimes more. Chiara's been more than supportive about the whole thing. Told me all about her dad—*all* about her dad—and how proud she was of me for taking the first steps by myself. Made it clear that she stands with me even if I don't end up adopting their abstinence-is-the-only-way lifestyle.

She doesn't like the word *powerless*, and I think that's fair. I don't like it either.

Mostly, I think she can tell I'm not super gung ho on all the God talk—thought it was supposed to be AA, not church—but it's still nice to have Tank to talk to about stuff. There is less than zero judgment for all the shit I've done as he helps me work through my steps. It's also really nice not to be hungover all the time, and I think it's shaving a couple seconds off my lap times. I've been *killing* it in practice and pole positions lately.

*God, I can't wait to kick Massimo's ass on Sunday...*

I ditch my clothes on the floor of the small connected bathroom, sort of rushing through my normal shower routine and debating whether to jerk off. Decide against it just in case she's up for a little extra phone time tonight.

As soon as I'm out of the shower with a towel around my waist, I dial her number. She answers right away. "Hey, cowboy. Did Frank finally explain that weird phone call he had earlier today?"

"Yep. Says he's getting hit up from reporters left and right, wanting to do some kind of exposé on me and Billy."

Chiara snorts, taking a bite of something crispy. Maybe juicy.

*God*, I miss her lips.

"I knew that was coming," she says, her voice smug. "Are you going to do it?"

"Uh, probably not," I say with a laugh. "Frank never lets us talk to the press. Thinks it gets in our heads." We're not supposed to watch sports shows or read the articles, none of it. "Why, do you think I should do it?"

"Hmm, depends. Did they say what the angle was?"

I tuck my phone between my ear and my shoulder, getting started on taking out my contacts. "What do you mean the 'angle'?"

"Well, is it about you both being bull riders and now moto racers? Is it because you are brothers on different teams? Or is it because you are going to beat him for World Champion?"

I roll my eyes, shaking my contacts case. "We ain't there yet."

"You're favored to win on Sunday. Three to one."

"Don't tell me that!" I hook on my glasses, my head lifting until I can see my confused face in the mirror. "Wait—am I really?"

She eats something new. Definitely juicy. "Yep."

*Huh...*

Whatever. I gotta change the subject before I think too much about this. Silverstone is tough, and I need to bring my A game. But I've been studying, and Chiara and I have been racing it online, and I'm ready. More than ready. *Ready to kick Massimo's ass...*

I dig through my Dopp kit for my facial moisturizer, squeezing a small amount onto my fingertip before I start smoothing it in. It's a new one she sent me with a higher SPF sunscreen, and it smells like tangy oranges. "On a more interesting note: how goes the linen emergency?"

"*Ugh*," she groans. "Finally over. I'm only just now eating dinner."

"Oh yeah? What's for dinner?"

"Hmm, olives," she says, chewing sexily on what I guess is an olive. "Then caprese; farfalle with spinach, mushrooms, and pancetta; braciole; fried zucchini flowers, and maybe some gelato."

I smile, switching my phone to my other ear. "Really?"

"Nope. I'm eating a bacon cheeseburger from this place called America Graffiti," she says with a laugh. "But I *could* make all that, just so you're aware."

I head out of the bathroom, flipping off the light and dropping my voice. "You vacuum in pearls too?"

"Heels and a thong."

I dissolve against the wall, hitting the base of my fist against it because *Jesus Christ.* "Why aren't you here?"

"Because. I have to work."

I pivot on my bad shoulder, trying to ignore my empty bed. Not that there's much else in this room to look at. White walls, tiny nightstand. Rug. Windows. Plenty of space to fuck on the floor. *Oh God...*

I massage and tug at my aching dick, swollen under my towel with missing her and unfairly encouraged at the sound of her voice. "You have three jobs, and only one of them has to be done in Ravenna. So I think you should quit that job and come to the circuit."

She scoffs at me. "I don't have three jobs."

"You're a publicist, a waitress, and a wedding planner," I count off. "That's three."

"The last one is not a job. It's a gift."

I gesture, frustrated, at nothing. "It's basically another full-time job, and I don't understand why you're not getting paid for it with all the crap you have to do."

"Because that is part of the deal." She pauses, ice clinking in the background like she took a drink of something. "They are my friends. It made me uncomfortable when Lorelai offered, and I thought we already talked about it?"

"Fine," I grumble.

"Don't be mad." Her voice dips into that soft place that absolutely cuts me to the core. The one she only uses when it's dark, and we're alone, and we're not anyone but ourselves.

"I'm not."

Not really. The whole wedding planner thing just feels weird to me, like they're taking advantage of her because she's nice. But she's right: it's her call, and I need to shut up about it. I've got other battles to pick tonight—way more important ones.

I head over to my empty bed and sit on the edge, my knee bouncing restlessly. I lean forward to pick at a loose thread in the carpet. "Quit your waitressing job. You hate it anyway."

"Mason," she says with a laugh. "Stop tempting me. I have bills to pay."

"I'll pay your bills. Quit and come see me."

"Oh my God." Her words are garbled like she just took a monster bite of her burger. "Hang up the phone, jerk off, then call me back."

"What? Why would I do that? If anything, I'd rather do that with you on the phone with me."

She snorts and takes another drink. "Well, at least you being sexually frustrated means you're not cheating on me, which is nice to know."

I roll my eyes, even though I guess I kinda deserve that based on my reputation. "Wanna switch to FaceTime and see my empty room for yourself?"

She sighs. "No. Sorry, I shouldn't have said that."

"It's okay."

"You're just...not thinking straight tonight."

But I am thinking straight. For the first time in my whole life.

I *love* Chiara, her spirit and her jokes, her laugh and her legs. She's the first person I want to talk to in the morning and the one I'm not afraid to share all my weird, random thoughts with. She doesn't judge me; she just *gets* me. And more and more, it doesn't make sense to me—how love ends up translating into linen tablecloths, why people wait a whole damn year just so they can pay for ugly flowers and a crappy band.

I abandon the snag in the area rug I just made worse, then push up from the bed and walk over to the window, peeking past the curtains. The dark garden below is lit with draped Christmas lights, and I'm not all that surprised to find Billy sitting on a lawn chair, leaning forward with his elbows on his knees. Probably talking on the phone with Taryn, telling her his good news, whatever it is.

He hasn't been talking to me much lately, ever since I beat him in Brno, and it's been hard. I could really use his advice right now: how he was able to stomach walking away from bull riding and how he and Taryn handle being apart so much while making it look easy. How he copes with the pressure of supporting him and her financially and what it's like to live with a woman full time. Especially how he deals with Taryn's constantly meddling mother, who Billy hates almost as much as she hates him. But for the first time in my life, he's the one person I can't ask about any of that stuff. I'm gonna have to figure it out on my own.

"At least tell me you're gonna be in Rimini," I ask Chiara. The racetrack is, like, an hour away from her apartment. On a Sunday, when she definitely doesn't have to work.

"Yes, Mason, I will come to the race in Rimini."

I turn away from the window, smiling as I fist-pump down by my side. "Yeah?"

"Of course."

I hug an arm over my chest. "You gonna be my date to the gala Saturday night?"

The other side of the line goes quiet—not a great sign. "I am not sure that would be a good idea."

I toss up a hand, sitting on my empty bed. Freaking knew that was coming. "You said you were gonna tell him when we got back."

"And I will. But I don't think going to the gala and rubbing it in his face is the best way to do that."

Of course, because Massimo's feelings always come first. "And I am supposed to do what exactly?"

"Go," she says. "Have fun. Like you would've anyway."

My eyes narrow. This has *trap* written all over it.

"Whatever," I mumble, going back to pulling at the thread in the carpet. "Probably wouldn't have made it there anyway."

Chiara takes another drink of whatever she's drinking. "What does that mean?"

I shrug, even though she can't see it. "Got a rodeo first."

A tight sigh comes through the phone line. "Okay."

"Okay," I repeat, just waiting, because based on—

"You know what? Not okay," she says, her voice getting sharper. "I thought you said you were quitting?"

"Retiring."

"So retire then. Stop doing this to yourself. Because I can tell you the chances of winning Rimini with a broken neck, Mason. They're zero."

I let the snag go and scrub a hand over my face. She just said it, gave it a name. "Chiara, we already talked about this. I have to finish the season, baby. I made commitments."

"So? Screw the commitments. The only reason you are doing this is because you are trying to prove that—"

"I don't have anything to prove," I cut in. "And even if I did, I already proved it."

She waits a beat, then says, completely smug, "Exactly."

*Damn it.* I walked straight into that. This is why I hate arguing with her—she always gets me to admit stuff I don't wanna. Usually to her advantage.

"I just don't understand why you would risk everything for a job that you don't want to do anymore," she says. "You are retiring for exactly this reason."

"Chiara," I say slowly, "I am going to be fine. I promise."

But we both know that promise is bullshit. There's no way to know I'll be 100 percent able to walk away unless I just...don't ride at all. And I don't know how to do that yet.

"You better be," she says. "Or I am holding you personally responsible."

"I'll enter it in the log."

She *hmpfs*, taking another drink.

A smile sneaks onto my lips. "Tell you what, trouble. I'll skip the rodeo if you quit your job and come to the circuit. Right now."

"Are you—? You are *such* an asshole." Then the phone line goes dead.

I snort and shake my head, then push myself up to standing, wandering over to the dresser to grab my bottle of water. No point in calling her back; she won't answer. But she'll call me back as soon as she calms down. Always does.

I take a long swig of water, trading my towel for a clean pair of boxer briefs, then turn off the lights. Get into bed and get the covers halfway pulled up when my phone starts vibrating in my hand. "Assholes-R-Us, how can I be of service?"

Chiara lets out a breath, her voice soft. "I love you. And I don't want you to get hurt. I want you to come home and be with me and for everything to be like it's supposed to."

"I know, baby." I tug at my pillow, settling in for the night. I honestly have no idea how I'm going to last not seeing her until we race Rimini. But we've made it this far—three weeks down, two to go. "But you gotta trust me. I'll know when to walk away."

"That is exactly what worries me, Mason. That by then, it will probably be too late."

I hug my pillow closer, wishing it was her. *Yeah, that worries me too.*

"It won't be."

It can't be.

# Chapter 24

*Chiara Martes—September*

"WE'RE NEVER GONNA MAKE IT," LORELAI SAYS FOR THE fifteenth time, now standing at her naturally lit vanity in a silk lavender robe, aggressively blending the contour over her cheekbones I just spent thirty minutes delicately applying. "The car's gonna be here any minute…"

"We're fine. Blink." She abandons the foam egg and goes stark still so I can apply a final layer of mascara to her curled eyelashes, then switch to the tinted lip gloss. A large crash echoes from their bedroom. "Massimo, my phone!"

He falls back against the door to their bathroom, pretending to be stabbed by the foam sword tucked under his arm. "Argh, ugh…" he groans out, wailing and moaning and clutching at his chest as his other hand extends my phone toward me.

"Thank you." At least he's ditched his jeans and T-shirt for his tux, although his shirt is still open and his jacket and tie are mysteriously missing.

"Healing…spell…" he grits out in Italian.

I roll my eyes and flick my fingers at him.

"On guard!" He launches from the door, apparently magically healed, and goes after his little brother once more. Boys, I swear.

I look to Lorelai, bringing over the padded stool we pushed aside a while ago. "Sit, look into the mirror, and hold this, but don't use it, and relax your face."

She takes the open tube of lipstick that isn't actually the color I just applied, closes her eyes, takes a deep breath, then pops open those thick black eyelashes and tilts toward the mirror. I snap a couple of quick pictures and actually get the shot in record time.

"Perfect. Pee, then dress. Massimo!" I call out, heading into their bedroom to find him preparing to cut his little brother's throat. "Parlay, or whatever. I need to do your cuff links."

"Ha! Loser." Dario sneers up at his brother. Massimo's tie is looped around Dario's forehead like a bandana with the ends dangling by his shoulders. Awesome—it's going to be all wrinkled now, but nothing I can do about that.

Massimo sneers identically down at Dario, dragging the foam sword carefully across his brother's throat so it doesn't interfere with the cords of his oxygenator. Dario pretends to gurgle and fall dead, his hands limp by the sides of his wheelchair.

Massimo tosses the sword away with a smirk. "Fine. I'm done now."

"Dick," Dario says, his head popping up before he starts rocking back and balancing on two wheels. I can't believe he's almost sixteen already. Every day, he looks more and more like Massimo did at that age. Acts more like him too.

I grab the cuff links off the dresser, Massimo meeting me in the middle of the room and holding out his wrists. "You going to wear your hair like that?" I ask as I start buttoning his shirtsleeve. Dario snorts. Massimo arches an eyebrow at me. "Okay," I drawl, hooking through the first cuff link. "It'll only take me a second, but fine."

"Why aren't you coming tonight?"

I fumble the cuff link, my head popping up. "Huh?"

"Tonight. The gala. Why aren't you coming with us?"

"I never come to the galas," I answer, going back to his wrist.

Massimo grins. "Or you have a date with the guy you're not telling me about."

I drop the second cuff link, scrambling after it. "You've lost it. Officially have cracked."

"Mm-hmm. And you haven't been staring off into space all day, smiling like a beauty queen in the Miss Universe pageant."

"I have not."

"Have too," Dario chimes in behind me. Then he starts making kissy noises and moaning in a way that he is far too young to know. "Oh, Man of Mystery, how I love—"

Lorelai comes out of the bathroom, her dress on but not fitting her right for some reason. She reaches around to her back like she's having an allergic reaction. "Dario, can you zip me?"

He rocks forward on his wheelchair, slamming down all four wheels and popping out a helpful, "Yep!"

Massimo kicks his leg out, blocking him. "Don't even think about it."

I snort—she's been Dario's favorite racer for as long as anyone can remember, and his room was practically a shrine of her marketing posters before she and Massimo started dating.

"I got it," I tell Massimo. "But don't button your shirt yet, and go stand by the bed. We still have to take your pictures."

"Why do mine have to be with an open shirt?" He gestures toward Lorelai, switching to English even though she's halfway to fluent. "You are okay with this?"

Lorelai shrugs, holding her hair to the side so I can zip up her gown. "It depends on the pictures. And Chiara's not gonna do anything weird or distasteful, so what's the big deal?"

He grunts something under his breath and storms into the bathroom, fussing with his shirtsleeve.

"Where are you going?" I call out.

"To fix my hair," he snaps back at me from the bathroom.

I share an air high five with Dario, then do the last clasp on Lorelai's dress. "Okay, *now* you're ready."

"Shoes," she gasps out, hiking up the hem of her gown and starting to search around the messy bedroom. I swear, they need a damn housekeeper. There are clothes freaking everywhere.

"The car is going to be here any minute," I yell at him.

"*Fuck*! Okay." He comes out the bathroom, and yeah...his hair has looked better. But anything is better than the limp nothing he was doing with it before.

I steer him toward the unmade bed, fluffy with soft ivory sheets and a plush white down comforter. The pillows are piled toward the middle of the headboard, and I absolutely do *not* see the ends of some bondage straps that are not quite tucked down behind the mattress.

I sit him on the edge of the bed, snapping my fingers toward Dario. "Tie." He slips it off his forehead, flinging it at me.

"Found one," Lorelai declares, hooking the shoe on her foot before she goes back to looking for the second.

"Lorina." Massimo points to the other side of the room. I pull the tie loose from its knot and drape it around his neck. "Over there, behind the door." There's a funny smirk to his lips that I am *also* not going to think too much about.

"Shit, you're right." She abandons the laundry-filled armchair for the pile of shirts and pants behind the bedroom door. (Not thinking about it, not thinking about it.)

I slide over the nightstand and take up the lamp, remove the lampshade, then hop up and hold the lamp high overhead so it hits his cheekbones the right way. Then I whip my phone out of my back pocket.

"Oh my God, go, Chiara," Dario says with a laugh.

"Ten years," Massimo grumbles. "I made it ten years without doing anything shirtless, and all of a sudden, it's totally fine—"

"Button your damn shirt then," I snap at him.

"Di-va," Dario singsongs.

Massimo grabs a pillow off the bed, flinging it at his brother. I crouch down on the nightstand to fix a couple hairs in the back he missed in his rush to do it but will absolutely show up at this angle. He's half done buttoning his shirt by the time I straighten, starting to swipe through filters. "Seriously, though. You are seeing someone, right?"

"Oh yeah. In all my free time?"

"Fine, keep it a secret. But it's been nice, seeing you smile more. You seem happy."

I plaster the fakest grin ever on my face. "Like this?"

"Pretty much. So when do I get to meet him?"

"Car's here," Dario announces.

"Shit!" Lorelai hooks the second shoe on her foot. "Purse, purse…"

"Black clutch is on the kitchen counter with your phone and ID already inside," I call out, then let my phone start snapping photos of Massimo because I never know when he's finally going to stop scowling for all of half a second. "Don't even think about moving…"

Shit, he is wearing his shoes, right? I peek down, and yeah, they're on.

"Vogue, vogue," Dario chants.

Massimo sighs and looks toward the bed, taking a deep breath and blowing it out slowly like we've practiced, and *there it is.*

"Got it!"

He bounds up and starts tucking in his shirt, getting about half in before he reaches the dresser, grabbing his phone and wallet and keys and stuffing them into his pockets. He glances back over his shoulder. "You have your house keys?"

"Yeah, of course."

Lorelai appears in the doorway. "We gotta go. We're gonna be late!"

"Shit." He double-checks everything he just put in his pockets, patting his chest. "I feel like I'm missing something…"

"Yeah, the top half of your brain," Dario says.

Massimo dives for his brother, ruffling his hair with a laugh as Lorelai calls out, "Mas! Time!"

I break up the boys, pushing Massimo toward the door. "Okay, okay, you're both the coolest swordsman in the land. Now go!" Oh shit, I know what he forgot. "Star, hold up."

I go back to grab his jacket, still hanging on the door to the armoire. Massimo curses under his breath when I run back with it, but I'm spared his normal tirade about the futility of black-tie events and the ridiculousness of tuxedo protocol. He simply turns toward me so I can help him put it on, shrugs it the rest of the way up his shoulders, then turns back toward me so we can get his lapels straightened out and the tie in place under the collar.

"We're probably gonna end up staying at the hotel," Lorelai rambles on, "so feel free to stay here if you don't want to drive back tonight—"

"She can't. She's got a date with Mr. Mystery," Massimo interrupts.

"Do not!"

"—and help yourself to anything you want and *oh*! Can you put the pizza up before you go? It's still out in the—"

"Lorelai, I got it." I laugh, letting go of Massimo's tie so I can hug her and double kiss both her cheeks. "You look beautiful. Have a wonderful time."

She lets out a relieved breath, barely touching her fingertips to her forehead because she wants to touch her face but doesn't want to mess up her makeup. "The wedding is gonna be exactly like this but a thousand times more hectic, isn't it?"

"Probably," Massimo says, trading a kiss to my cheek before he opens the front door. "Oh, *fuck*!"

*It's raining? Shit!*

"Bummer," Dario says behind us, but there's a wicked smirk in his voice like he already knew it was raining. I look back at him, balancing on two wheels, and I love that kid but sometimes he's a real twerp. He could've warned us.

The driver emerges from the town car with a big black umbrella, jogging up the front walk that's pretty much just a puddle-infested front yard. I told Massimo he needs to do something about that, but they're never here enough to put time into stuff like landscaping.

"Fuck," Massimo mutters in Italian again as the driver hops over puddles, mud splashing up and painting his pants regardless of how careful he's trying to be. Massimo looks at Lorelai, then shrugs off his jacket and hooks it over her face.

"Really," she deadpans from underneath the black fabric.

"Yes." Then he scoops her up into his arms, carrying her out the door under the protection of the driver's umbrella.

"Bye!" Lorelai calls back.

The driver is totally getting soaked as he carefully holds his umbrella over Massimo and Lorelai, and I take out my phone and snap a couple photos of them for evidence, because *oh my God*, the things men will do to keep Lorelai Hargrove from stepping in a puddle.

"Please tell me you got that on video," Dario says behind me, switching back into Italian now that Lorelai is gone. I turn back and show him the photos, waiting as he chuckles. "Classic."

"Right?" I shut the door. "Ten minutes, then we're blowing this nut hut."

"Phrasing! And I'm driving."

I chuckle to myself as I head back to the master bedroom, starting a fast and shitty process of tidying up. They'll be in Rimini for the night at the biggest sponsor gala of the year, with maybe a quick stop by the house tomorrow before they go to the paddock for the next couple days. And after the race on Sunday, they're having dinner with his mom for about two seconds before heading to Bruges for the next two weeks. For his birthday. They haven't started packing for any of it either.

I pile up everything in the main armchair as best I can, straightening the stuff on the dresser and then going into the bathroom. Pick up the damp towels off the floor and hang them over the railing, separate the counter back into his and hers sides, pack up the makeup I brought over, then unplug the curling and flat irons and flip off the light.

Grab the pillows off the floor and fling them back onto the bed, tug up the blankets and put back the nightstand and fix the lamp, and you know what? I'm done. I'm not their freaking maid.

"You about ready?" I call out as I close the door to the bedroom, then stop by the kitchen to put away the pizza. And the milk apparently.

"Yeah. And I'm stealing his copy of *Modern Warfare*."

"You can't." I head down the ramp into the living room, telling Dario, "Because I already stole the disc and left the box."

He pretends to gasp, clasping his hand over his mouth. "Op!"

I can't help but laugh as I double-check the back door is locked, and it's only another few minutes before we've got the house fully secured, Dario in the passenger seat of my car and his wheelchair in the trunk. He changes the radio station six times before I'm at the end of the driveway, finally settling on a rap station and barely grooving his head to the beat. I catch the shadow of a couple dark hairs on his jaw, and it's *so* hard not to see Massimo.

"So how's the girlfriend?" I ask him, changing the speed on my wipers.

Dario shrugs it off. "Missing me, probably."

"Oh yeah?" I turn off one country highway onto another—they really do live out in the middle of freaking nowhere.

"Yeah," Dario says. "She met some guy in her cancer support group. I told her that cystic fibrosis was way sexier, but he's got the good chemo drugs, so...whatever."

I snort, even though it's not just cystic fibrosis. "Her loss."

"Damn straight." He holds out his hand for a lateral high five, our palms sliding together before our fingertips snap apart, Dario wiggling his fingertips at me as I flick my hair.

We both start laughing, and he's such an awesome little twerp *sometimes*. I taught him too much about how to get away with stealing his brother's stuff and the best way to prank people. Especially their mom.

He goes back to finding a new radio station for us to listen to as I settle into the drive, and we're fine like that for most of the hour ride. But Dario and I grew up together too, and I was the one home with him after school when Maria was working and Massimo was... busy. Working his dad's shop. Practicing racing. (Stealing motos to sell to black market buyers.)

"You're still going to come over, right?" Dario asks when we cross into Ravenna, the traffic starting to pick up on the highway. "After they're married?"

I swallow, checking my mirrors. "I still come over now, and they're engaged." I check on Dario, and he's watching me like his brother does. Dark-brown eyes trained directly on my soul. I smile at him as comfortingly as I can. "Nothing's going to change."

He nods, looking through the windshield. "Okay." Then he tilts his head. "Maybe after they have a baby, you'll finally get the hint."

"What makes you think they're going to have a baby?"

"That's what people do," he says like it's obvious. "They get married and start having freaking babies."

I try to keep my face neutral as I switch lanes, preparing to exit. (Not if the vasectomy Massimo had in July has anything to say about it.) He still hasn't told his mom, and while it should've been obvious that Lorelai was never the motherly type, Maria is going to be *pissed* when she finds out.

I reach over and muss Dario's hair. "Baby or not, you're not getting rid of me that easily, punk."

He pushes me off. "Whatever. Just admit you're still hanging around because you're in love with me. We both know the truth."

I cough out a laugh. "Maybe in another ten years. Once your voice changes."

"It's totally deeper now!" he says, but his voice breaks in the process, and it's impossible not to laugh even harder at him. "Whatever."

"Don't be weird. You're going to get over this girl and meet someone new, I promise."

He throws his hands up in the air. "That's what Vinicio keeps saying."

"Well, there you go. And when has Vinicio ever been wrong about anything?"

Dario slowly turns his head my way, blinking at me, and I keep a straight face for about two seconds before we both crack up. Their stepfather is actually a really good guy, but he has his moments.

We're both still chuckling by the time I pull up in front of their mom's house, and it's almost enough to calm the nerves in my stomach at being here. At least it stopped raining.

"When are you going to be done with *Modern Warfare*?" Dario asks as I walk him up to the front door.

"Like, next week, maybe? I'll bring it by. We'll get pizza or something."

"Cool. Can you, uh, bring Aria too?"

"She's gay," I remind him.

He looks up at me. "Elena?"

"Gayer."

"Fuck," he mumbles. *Ah*, teenage hormones.

Maria opens the front door, hugging a cozy sweater around her shoulders and looking up at the sky like it's my fault her son was out in inclement weather.

Dario rolls right past her, calling back, "See ya later, loser."

I turn on my heel, heading back down the front walk.

"Chiara," Maria calls after me. I stop and half turn her way. It's more than enough to see the annoyed look all over her face. "Are you coming for dinner on Sunday?"

"I assume so." There's only been one year that I ever missed Massimo's birthday dinner, and she knows that. Because it wasn't long afterward that I came to live here. Followed by my first of many failed attempts to run away.

It's not that she was mean or anything. Living here was like heaven on earth after the horrors of my house. No one drinking, no one yelling. Hugs and kisses and sweet dreams and lunches made with fresh fruit and handwritten "Have a good day!" notes. But I didn't trust it, and I always knew that I was putting more stress on a family that already had plenty.

Massimo's father was old and sick; he died not long after I moved in, and things were just…rough. But every time I tried to run away, she always brought me back.

Then grounded the holy hell out of me.

"Don't be late," she says. "And try to find a pair of jeans without rips and holes in them, if they even make those anymore." She goes back inside and shuts the door, then turns off the outside lights.

*Love you too, Maria.*

I turn back to the street, but I'm only halfway to my car when thunder cracks and the sky opens up—*perfect*. I don't even run. I just stand here and let the rain fall on me, soaking through my shirt and jeans and matting my hair, because *this* is my freaking life. And I still have to upload the goddamn pictures when I get home. Plucky sidekick, party of one.

It's thankfully only a short drive back to my apartment, but I'm chilled to the bone and shivering by the time I park my car. I get out and get soaked by the rain all over again on my way to the stairwell, jog up the stairs, then fumble to unlock my door. It's going to take the longest, hottest shower ever to thaw me out. But it's fine—Mason said he wouldn't be back from the gala until the early hours, and he knows where my spare key is. I told him he could keep it.

Although, it might not be necessary for either of us to have a key when I can apparently never remember to lock my damn door. *Really, Chiara? Again?*

The wood is swollen, and I have to shove with my shoulder to get it to move. It bangs open, and I barely get my squeaky shoes across the doorway before I stop in place, my keys and phone slipping from my numb fingertips and crashing to the wood floor.

"Hiya, trouble."

I blink at Mason standing next to my sofa in a sleek black tux, black Stetson, black boots, and a single sunflower in his hands. His suit is so dark, his eyes so blue, the flower so yellow that I can't make sense of what I'm seeing. The colors are so *bright*.

This can't be happening. Not to me.

I glance toward my kitchen. The dishes that were piled in the sink are gone, the stack of mail on the counter put away. My laptop and books and all the normal junk have been cleared off my table, and in its place are flickering tea light candles, place mats, dinner already laid for two and smelling richly of creamy garlic.

I look toward Mason and the trail of pink rose petals sprinkled down the hallway behind him. (Mother fricking pink rose petals!) "Are...you real?"

He quietly chuckles, shifting his weight. "Yeah," he says, his voice low and rumbly and perfect. "I'm real."

I swallow thickly. Shut the door. Make my feet slowly carry me toward him, the rest of me still shivering from the rain and pure romantic shock. "Aren't you...supposed to be at the gala?"

"What would I wanna go to that thing for?" His eyes search mine as I stop in front of him, Mason taking my hand and placing his other on my lower back. "The only person I wanna dance with is right here."

He gently pulls me into him, his cheek to mine, and he slowly starts leading me with a rhythm that's never been hard to follow, not since the marketplace in Qatar. Just like that, I let it break and wash over me, a shaky breath flowing from my lungs as I relax into his arms, his cologne, the feeling of his hands on my body, and his warmth, and he's *here*.

He's finally here.

My jaw starts quivering from the strength of it, and I hug my arm tighter around his neck, unable to resist letting my second arm join my first because I need to hug him, more than I've ever needed anything. The last five weeks have been the longest of my life.

"When do you have to be back?"

"Early," he breathes. I squeeze my eyes shut, holding him impossibly tighter against me—that's not enough time. He drops a kiss to my shoulder, his palm wide down my side. "I drew us a bath, but you...kinda seem like you already took one."

I can't help but chuckle, leaning back to savor a single first kiss from his lips. "Yeah. I was helping them get ready, and I got caught in the rain."

Mason nods, tracing a lock of wet hair away from my cheek. "Did you tell him?"

A guilty sigh nearly sinks me to the floor. "No."

Mason has made it more than clear that he's willing to do this with me, but I told him I wanted to talk to Massimo alone. When he'll be my best friend and not the guy competing against Mason on the racetrack. It's complicated enough without bringing all that into it. And with how happy Massimo has been lately, the last thing I want to do is to ruin it by telling him I've been lying to him. He's going to be so upset with me, and I know I deserve it, but I just can't face it.

Not when I've been so happy too.

"There hasn't been a good moment," I tell Mason. "We've been so busy with the wedding and the gala, and now they're going out of town for two weeks after Rimini..."

Mason watches me. And watches me. And I know he's going to

be pissed when my not telling Massimo *also* means I'm not coming with him to Asia for the last leg of the circuit. It's going to be another month apart, at least. But I just couldn't find the right time to talk to Massimo. The right way to break his heart.

"After Valencia," I promise. "I'll tell him after that." When they're no longer racing, and I don't have to worry about them diving for each other on the circuit.

I have no idea how I'm going to do it, but I have nearly two months to figure it out.

(Please, let me figure this out.)

"Okay." Mason grants me a forgiving smile, then leans in and brushes a lingering kiss across my lips—*thank God* he's not too upset. I'll find a way to make it up to him. Not that he'll let me, but I'm going to try anyway.

He tips his forehead to mine, smelling so good that I barely even notice my wet clothes sticking to me. Except *crap*, I totally got his tux all wet.

"So," he drawls wickedly, "they're gonna be gone for two weeks, huh?"

A wide smile takes my face. "Yep." I gingerly start undoing his tie, slipping the black fabric from his neck and dropping it on the floor. "Probably will be out of cell service too."

Mason tosses the sunflower toward the sofa, then takes my hands and starts walking backward, bringing me with him down the trail of pink rose petals. "Whatever are we gonna do with that kinda time?" he asks, an innocent twist to his voice.

"I don't know," I play along.

I've got a couple ideas. His will probably be better.

# Chapter 25

*Chiara Martes—September*

"Mmm," Mason hums next to me, his steps relaxed as we stroll down the sidewalk on Rue de Sèvres. The weather couldn't be more perfect, sunny and warm with just a slight morning breeze ruffling the shop canopies. "We have any more of the Mimolette?"

"Um…" I cover my mouth, but my words are still garbled around the Selles-sur-Cher goat's cheese I'm ready to pledge my existence to. "I think so." It takes me a second to dig through the bag we stuffed full from Fromagerie Quatrehomme. But I finally find some, trading a cubed sample of the aged cheese for a piece of bread from one of the many loafs he's carrying.

"God, that shit's so good," he groans. "We should've got more."

"Mason," I say with a laugh. "We have enough cheese to last us to the end of time."

"Not if we're sharing." He winks and steals another cube of cheese from the bag, sneaks a kiss to my lips, then hugs his arm around my shoulders and pulls me in close enough to drop a kiss to my hair. I don't know if it's possible to be any happier than this, but I doubt it.

We lasted about a week in Ravenna before Mason tempted me with Paris. As if I could ever say no to that. And while Paris is intoxicating, Mason in Paris is a whole new kind of chaos.

Erratic. Shameless. Ruthlessly romantic.

We've only been here for three days, and we're not supposed to leave for another four, but I don't want to leave *ever*. It's so wonderful, being free with him to live at our own pace—sleeping in and staying up late, taking long naps in the afternoon between running wild all over this gorgeous city.

We've done so much already: left tubes of lipstick at Oscar Wilde's grave, made friends with a cat on Jim Morrison's grave, went shopping on the Champs-Élysées, and had dinner at Les Ombres, watching the Eiffel Tower sparkling like a diamond. We spent an afternoon going to the Île Saint-Louis and eating ice cream at Berthillon, bought way too many books, and then did the dinner cruise and had too much fun laughing at the waiter making fun of our accents.

Today, our entire morning agenda is to eat cheese and bread. And so far, we're killing it.

My phone starts vibrating in my back pocket as we dodge a couple with a baby stroller walking the opposite way on the sidewalk. When I pull it out to check who's calling, Mason groans.

"You're on vacation," he singsongs.

"It's just the florist." I send the call to voicemail and tuck my phone back into my pocket. "And she can leave a message."

"Yes, she can. Along with everyone else."

I slightly narrow my eyes at him, then hug an arm around his waist. "So grumpy today."

"Not trying to be grumpy. I just want you to be able to take five minutes for yourself. I doubt they're fielding calls from the dress designer while in Bruges, so why should you be doing it in Paris?"

"Uh-huh." I tickle the sensitive spot over his hip. "And your hatred of weddings has nothing to do with it."

"I don't hate weddings," he says, slightly squirming because that spot is really, really ticklish. "I just don't get the whole wedding *thing*. Buying dinner for four hundred of your closest friends, just so they can turn around and give you some fancy silverware that you're never gonna use. Like seriously, what is the point of that?"

"It's how some people show their love. They want to share it with everyone." I reach over and tear off a piece of bread, letting out a low moan at how warm and delicious it is. I swear, we are just walking carbs at this point. "Like me publicly making eternal vows to this fougasse," I say with a full mouth. Holy crap, this stuff is so good.

Mason looks at me, a smirk growing in the corner of his lips. "That what you want?"

"Fougasse? Yes."

"That, and…to do the chicken dance in a big white dress in front of a bunch of third cousins?"

I crack up laughing. "Oh yes, how did you know?" He laughs with me until I shake my head, passing him another cube of cheese. May as well eat a piece myself—I have to wait for a loud moto to go by before I can continue anyway. "I would get married in my Chucks if I could. And I'm much more the eloping type than planning a grand anything. Two people being there is more than enough for me. *If* I even get married."

Mason looks genuinely confused by my answer. But most people probably would be. "You know you can do whatever you want, right? That it's totally fine to elope in your Chucks?" He winks at me, then pops another piece of cheese in his mouth. "*If* you even get married."

Warmth flutters through me, and I can't stop beaming at him. "You know what? You're right." I grasp his jaw and lift a sweet kiss from his lips. "Thank you for that."

"Anytime." Mason hugs me into his side, and I lean my head to his shoulder, an easy silence falling between us as we walk along the storefronts but never bother to go inside.

"Are we heading back to the hotel soon?"

"We can." His hand on my shoulder drops to my waist, lightly squeezing. "Tired?"

I nod slowly. "Too much cheese." Mason squeezes my waist again in agreement. I love taking naps with him. We always have the most delicious sex before we go to sleep, and it's a foolproof method to waking up blissfully happy and utterly refreshed. "Did you have anything you wanted to do tonight? Apart from *not* buying dinner for four hundred of our closest friends."

Mason is kinda quiet, and when I look at him, he's got a look on his face that spells pure trouble. The really fun kind.

"*Oooh*, you had an idea."

"It wasn't an idea, it was just a thought," he deflects. "And it was a really bad one. Trust me, we're just gonna"—he lets out a sharp whistle—"let that one go."

Oh, this is going to be good. "Now I really want to know what it is."

He half shrugs, but it's getting harder and harder for him to restrain his smile. "Could be dangerous."

"Well," I say, bringing his own words back to him, "isn't that for me to decide?"

Mason playfully rolls his eyes, but he's also never looked more eager when he stops and turns toward me, tracing a lock of hair away from my cheek. "You're sure?"

"Absolutely. But this bad idea better be truly awful, because now my expectations are very high."

"All right." He bites his bottom lip, his neck getting a little red—why is he so nervous? It's just me. "Hold the bread?"

I snort as he passes me the bag containing three half-eaten loafs and two more we haven't even touched yet. This must be big if he needs both hands to explain it.

Mason takes his time tucking my hair behind my ears, then takes my face in his hands, his eyes searching mine. "You can always say no," he says quietly. "It won't change anything between us. I promise."

"Okay..." Now I'm starting to get a little nervous. What in the world does he want to do?

Maybe this *is* a bad idea. But it sure doesn't feel like it when he tips my mouth to his, kissing me so tenderly that it leaves me a little dizzy. How could anything bad start with a kiss that great?

He lets me go. Smiles his verge-of-chaos smile. Then he kneels down.

My brain short-circuits as he looks up at me from one knee, people sitting outside at the nearby café pausing their conversations to watch us. A few camera phones come out, and a nervous laugh bubbles in my chest. (Play it cool. This can't be happening. Not from Mason.)

"What are you doing now, cowboy?"

His grin is impossibly big, eyes sparkling with mirth. "What does it look like I'm doing?"

I mean, he's *kneeling* in front of me. So yes, it looks like he's...

My pulse takes off, anticipation and surprise daring to flutter through my veins. "Is...your shoelace untied?"

"Don't have shoelaces, baby."

The patient gravity in his voice makes my eyes start to prickle with tears, though I'm not quite sure how that happened so fast. My brain can't seem to catch up to what my heart already knows. "You don't?"

Mason's smile goes soft when my voice cracks, and he reaches out and takes my hand, his thumb stroking over my knuckles. "Nope."

The sight of him blurs before me, but his voice is clear and calm, an anchor in the storm of joy. This is happening. He's really doing this.

"You wear the Chucks in our house, trouble. I wear boots."

# Chapter 26

*Mason King—September*

I SHIFT IN THE CHAIR BY THE WINDOW, MY ANKLES CROSSED AND MY body naked except for my boxer briefs and my hat tipped low, watching the sunrise by watching Chiara sleep: the glow of French light that brightens and changes as it comes in and settles on her skin, illuminating her long arms hugging her pillow. Her dark hair is spilling everywhere it can above, but it isn't touching her back: bare all the way to the white sheet draped across her hips and covering her legs. Except for the one foot that snuck out and she hooked around the covers, like she got hot at some point in the night. She usually does.

In all my life, I have never seen anything as beautiful as her.

Never found something that scares me as much as the possibility of losing her.

In all the books I read, the guys always say in their grand speeches how they can't seem to remember life *before* her anymore: wondering why they did half the shit they did or what they thought they were escaping. But the problem is, I remember.

I can perfectly recall every night of being that restless, selfish guy…and the idea that at some point very soon, I may have to change back, it scares the living shit out of me. Because what the old me never could've guessed was just how much I would want to keep something like this once I found it. The lengths I would go to make sure of it.

Turns out, there is no limit.

Chiara moans and stirs, a low roll starting at her hips and curving up her spine, because her body always wakes up long before her mind does. She's still on her stomach, but her breaths are getting deeper, more controlled like she's thinking about them. Feeling the air come into her body and satisfy all the space of her lungs.

Won't be long now. Then I'll know: who I'm gonna be for the rest of my life.

With slow, tired movements, she lets her pillow go with one arm, sliding her palm out toward my side of the bed. Her muscles go strict and her head lifts.

"Here," I tell her, my voice gentle but clear through the dark room. "I'm right here."

She melts back into the bed, just breathing for a second before she pulls the sheet up to her chin and rolls over to face me, brushing the sleep from her eyes. "You couldn't sleep?"

"Nah." The start of a smile is daring to pull at my lips. *She's so calm.* I wasn't sure that would still be the case come sunlight. "How are you doing?"

She pouts at me, snuggling in the bed like this is any other morning and all the shit that went down last night didn't happen. "I'm cold."

Well, that won't do.

I nod toward myself. "C'mere, then. I'll keep you warm."

She rolls her eyes with a smile, but she still gets out of bed, wrapping the sheet around her like an oversize beach towel. I can't help but chuckle at how cute she is, all burrito'd up and kicking at the ends of the bedsheet on her way over to me, having to take care not to trip over our clothes scattered across the hotel room floor.

"I need a triple espresso and a double espresso with an extra shot, so fast." She gets settled on my lap, but turned to the side so she can face the windows and our postcard view of the Eiffel Tower. I nod as I hug my arms around her, because I know she does. I'll call for room service in the next few minutes.

Chiara doesn't enjoy the view for long; she looks at me, her eyebrow arched like she can read in my expression all the things I told myself to be prepared for when she woke up: the apologies, excuses, and the start of pulling it all apart. But not only is Chiara a damn architect at calculating all my walls, she also knows exactly how to break them down.

She frees her arms from her bedsheet robe, peeling back my hat and setting it on the dinette table beside us. I swallow, feeling more vulnerable than I ever have when she cups my jaw in her hands, then brushes a soft kiss against the scar on my temple. Freshly healed from my last rodeo. "Stop worrying," she whispers.

My eyes close, my grip on her tightening. I don't have to do it—any of it.

I don't have to let her go.

"Good morning, my love," she says and kisses me again, and it's like I can finally breathe after the panic I woke up under, pressing on my chest and tearing me from the bed. But it's gone now, every trace of it absolutely disappeared as I melt into the promise of her voice.

Chiara yawns and loops her arm around my shoulders, leaning her head against mine and sighing contentedly. I shiver with goose bumps.

"Do we have plans today?" she asks quietly. "Or are we winging it?"

"No plans." I can't even think to come up with a good suggestion right now. "Unless there was something you wanted to do."

"No." She half shrugs, then looks at me, combing her nails down the back of my hair. "I think we should stay here. Make love all day."

My smile dares to come fully to life now. "Oh, you do?"

She nods firmly. "Yes. It's important."

No arguing with that.

"Well, where exactly are we doing this?" I tease her. "You wanna move to the bed? Or you wanna give that couch a workout? Lady's choice."

Chiara considers that, glancing around at our hotel suite before she answers. "We had sex in the bed last night." *Yeah, we did.* "And the sofa has buttons... I think here is fine."

I can barely keep a straight face.

"I'm serious," she says.

"I see that." And then I burst out laughing, because I can't keep it in. The surrealness of having this conversation with her. This morning of all others. But Chiara and I have always called it straight, and knowing that sends such a lightness through my veins that I'm not sure how I'm ever gonna stop smiling. Because this woman loves me.

Actually, *really* loves me, and she wants to be with me as much as I want to be with her. Forever, unconditionally, till death till we freaking part. And that…that isn't something I ever expected to happen.

I mean, I knew one day I'd probably fall in love. Odds were stacked against me from the start. But I never expected someone to love me *back*, to see me for someone I'm not sure I can be but I absolutely want to try to be. To worry and notice and dream for me. But Chiara isn't just that…

She's not a pedestal. She's the goddamn sky shining down on it.

"You are being a real dork this morning." She hooks a fingertip under my chin and pretends to glare at me. But there's a lightness in her eyes too, something soft and safe where there used to be fear.

"Sorry."

"No, don't apologize for that." She leans down, a smile in her lips poised a breath from mine. "I love it when you are this happy."

"Are you happy?"

"Oh, I am very happy." With the way she kisses me afterward, I would have to agree. There's an unmistakable joy in the slowness of her lips against mine. Just feeling me, knowing me, and knowing I'm hers.

When she breaks the kiss, I can't help nuzzling my way into her neck, breathing her in and just feeling her. She smells so good, so warm and so soft from sleep. It just makes me want to hold her closer—my arms locked around her body as tight as I possibly can.

There is nothing in the world I wouldn't do for this woman. No distance I wouldn't travel, nothing I wouldn't give up. All she has to do is say the word.

She runs her hand down the back of my hair, feeling everything I feel and silently promising she knows. Because we may not hold back our words, but we don't always have to use them either. She hears me, especially when I just can't find them.

I press a kiss to her neck, her jaw, under her chin and up to her cheek, Chiara trembling and holding me tighter against her. But it's still not enough when it's today—the first morning after last night. Not the last but absolutely the first.

My hand starts massaging her beautiful body over the bedsheet everywhere I can until it finds a way inside and touches bare skin. Goose bumps light up her silky leg, my cock hardening into action. Chiara turns and captures my lips with hers, her palm on my jaw ensuring she can kiss me as deep as she wants, and she wants it deep.

I tug at the white sheet she's wrapped in. Don't have to for long—Chiara stands and opens it, presenting me with her perfect naked body before she straddles my lap and wraps her arms around my neck, draping us both in the cotton fabric this time. But it doesn't hide the fact that there's nothing else between us when I free myself from my boxer briefs, taking my cock in my fist and sweeping my thumb over the bead of precum.

Chiara positions herself above me, her palms on my jaw and her kiss locked with mine as I guide her hips low enough to tease her clit with my cockhead. She gasps into my mouth, always ultrasensitive in the morning. Sometimes too sensitive.

"Too much?"

"Yeah," she breathes, taking another ravenous kiss from my lips. "I just want you."

She drops her hips, slipping around me, but not all the way. It's too early, and we had too much sex last night. Rough sex.

"Slow, baby. Slow." I take a tighter grip on her hips, my palm soft on her stomach as I guide her just a bit lower, nudging but not pushing, and just letting her warm up to me. Spare a swipe of my fingers over my tongue, then smooth them over my cock to help and reposition myself to start again.

She slips around me more easily, a moan rumbling from her throat and into mine as she starts working me in, her kiss getting more heated and Chiara getting wetter with every measured thrust until she finally, carefully, sinks fully onto me, plunging me to the hilt.

I can't think to move other than to hug her body onto mine with all the strength I possess—she's so fucking warm, so deliciously tight—and I can't stop feeling her everywhere, kissing her everywhere.

"I love you so much," I whisper, my hands roaming for purchase and my heart so fucking humbled that I get to be inside her even though I still can't get deep enough.

Chiara nods with her cheek against mine, the movement slow and euphoric. Then her teeth scrape my earlobe. "Show me."

Desire flashes down my spine—it's not a taunt, it's a plea. A secret she trusts me with, and only me. And I will always do everything in my power to give her what she wants.

What she *needs*.

"I can do that better from the bed."

She shakes her head again. "I don't want to move."

I don't either, but I can't do much except enjoy her when she's on top of me like this. I tease my fingertips down her leg, caressing my way back from her ankle to her hip so I can pull her closer. "Call the ball, Topper."

Chiara moans and hides her face in my neck, and moving it is.

"Hang onto me, baby." She already is, but I figure a warning is safest. I secure my grip on her, then stand, carrying her back to the bed. Lay her down as carefully as I can, one knee at a time on the mattress until her head is cradled by the pillows and I'm safe to let her go.

I never want to let her go.

The look in her eyes is every reason why as I crawl forward and she pulls me down, her legs wrapping around me to guide me back inside her. My fingers find hers, lacing together and sinking into the bed as I refind my home inside her, Chiara arching up into me as her legs squirm outside mine.

I nip at her collarbone. "Be still."

She shakes her head, her voice breathless. "I can't."

"Try."

A squeak melts from her lips as I run my tongue down the trail of freckles on her chest, pausing to enjoy a soft kiss to her breast, letting it fill my mouth and my teeth scraping faintly over her nipple. It stands at attention when I pull back, glistening and gorgeous, and I can't resist a second taste.

"Mason, please."

I curl my hips and press myself firmly into her, giving her exactly what she's asking me for. But I'm still in charge here, and I can't risk going at the speed she wants quite yet. She's not the only one who's sensitive in the morning, and with nothing between us, she's gonna break me quick once she gets going.

So I keep the throttle slow, relishing each thrust inside her, inch by delicious inch. Kissing her deep and holding her to me as I make love to her like I should've done last night, but we were high on adrenaline, and we devoured each other without a thought to hold back.

I don't regret it—it was *us*, raw and unfiltered as we get.

But this is us too, my palm soft on her cheek, my thumb caressing her jaw as I kiss into her lips a thousand dreams and a million promises. It's us when she accepts them with every pull of her hands, flat on my shoulders. And it's us when I pull back to watch her eyes, deadlocked with mine when I go still, then slam into her.

She gasps and clings to me tighter, one hand on my neck and the other moving so she can sweep her thumb over my lips. *More.*

I drop my forehead to hers, soaking her up and making myself wait as long as I can before I surprise her again. Let her catch her breath, watching her needy pulls for air before I lower down, kissing her torturously slow and pressing myself back into her even slower.

Get lost in the blur: palming soft flesh and crawling closer in search of more heat. Drowning in moans that I don't know if I'm making or she is. My lips trailing over parts of her body I can't even name, but I know I need to kiss them. Aching, always, for the redline.

She faintly pushes at my chest, and I take my command. Turning onto my back as Chiara shifts on top, then sinks down easily on me again, sitting up and pinning me low with her palm flat on my chest. "Your turn to be still," she says.

"I'll do my best."

She takes my hands and settles them on her body, smoothing my palms from her hips to her breasts as we start to touch her together. There's no way not to marvel at her above me.

She moves and I don't deserve it, rocks and moans and makes love to me like I'm her king even though I'm unworthy to kneel at her feet. But Chiara also chose *me*, and I will give her anything, everything I have. She can take it all and leave me with nothing, I don't give a damn. She's the whole reason I even exist, that I am the way I am. I'm convinced—we fit together too perfectly for it to be wrong.

I sit up when I can't keep still anymore, sink into every kiss she blesses me with as she claims my jaw for hers, drawing her nails down my cheek with a sharpness that should draw blood but doesn't. Tilt my hips up into her to find a better angle, and it isn't long before she cries out in climax with her head thrown back. *There it is.*

I hug her closer and keep her steady on my lap as her inner walls throb and hug me tighter, silky warmth painting me as hers and turning me on even more. I lean her farther back and take a nipple into my mouth, my palm splayed wide between her shoulder blades to support her, and I never want to stop, unable to decide how to enjoy her next.

I crave her laid out and legs open, squirming and screaming at every hard thrust until I flip her over and take her from behind. I want her to come for me when she's on her knees, watch it drip onto the bed as my cock swells into iron, thick with desperation. I want to watch the contours of her face change as I slip it into her ass, stroking into her deep and slow as she whimpers and calls for me to fuck her harder, her hand between her legs petting greedily at her clit.

I *want* her. Every way you can pleasure a person and be pleasured by a person.

And she's *mine*.

A blast of desire pools in the base of my skull and rips down my spine at the thought, taking over my best worst intentions and undoing the last of my resolve. I cry out through gritted teeth as I hold her to me and come deep inside her, the strength of it so much that I can't think or breathe or feel anything else.

Chiara melts forward onto me, and I carefully fall back to the safety of the pillows, her head on my shoulder and my fingertips drawing circles on her spine as we search to find our breath. We don't move for a long time, the thought of space between us torturous.

"Say we never have to leave," she whispers, her lips tickling the skin over my heart and the words sinking directly underneath. "That we can stay here forever."

"We never have to leave," I promise, even though we both know it isn't the truth. But that's the problem with me and Chiara: we just don't fucking care about right or wrong as long as it means we get to be together.

And after this, nothing is going to keep us apart, not ever again.

# Chapter 27

*Mason King—September*

"EVERYTHING IS GOING TO BE OKAY," I TELL HER AGAIN. "WE'RE gonna figure this out."

Chiara nods at me for the dozenth time, the final call for her flight back to Bologna blaring overhead, but she still won't let go of my shirt. We stayed in Paris an extra day because I needed it, and she asked me, and I can't say no to her. But I have to go deal with some legal bullshit back in Memphis before I book it to Aragon.

Some asshole thought it would be a good idea to get drunk and drive his truck through the wall of my bowling alley, and now he's suing *me*. I do not need that place to go belly-up. That's my backup plan, what's gonna cover all I'm not gonna make from bull riding. And once I retire from moto racing too. I have to make sure that no matter what, I can take care of not just me but Chiara too, and anyone else who comes along in the future.

Chiara glances over her shoulder at the gate again, but she doesn't want to go, and it's written all over her.

"You really have to go to Ravenna?"

She nods, tossing her hair. "I've been trying to get an appointment with this makeup artist for Lorelai for months. They're coming back early specifically because of it. I have to go."

"Well, what if…what if we just call them? Right now? They gotta understand—"

"No." She shakes her head, her voice panicked. "I can't do this over the phone. It has to be face-to-face. And I am still not sure you should even be there when I tell him. He's going to be so…" She cringes, and I really try not to take it personally.

I keep telling myself this isn't about being ashamed of me. That it's about him being a dick and having her too afraid to tell him the truth. And I don't know what kind of friendship that is, but it feels really fucking wrong to me.

"Signora!" the attendant barks. "This is the final call."

"Yeah, she's coming," I call back. The lady *hmpfs* and crosses her arms, and I cup Chiara's cheeks in my palms. "Four weeks. Then we're gonna fix it. I promise."

She tries for a smile, but it doesn't get all the way there. I kiss her as sweetly as I can, breathing in cinnamon as deep as I can get it into my lungs, and it's never gonna be enough. I'm sick to fucking death of leaving her to get on planes and waking up without her. This isn't fair.

"I love you," Chiara whispers, then takes one last taste of my lips before she pulls away and walks toward the gate. My heart breaks at the sight of her back, her long hair swinging down her leather jacket, and her hand coming up to swipe at her eyes as she turns the corner onto the Jetway.

It still doesn't feel like a mistake to me.

# Chapter 28

*Mason King—October*

I FLIP MY WATER BOTTLE IN MY HAND, STROLLING PAST THE BROOM closet Chiara and I made out in earlier this year—finally back at the Sepang circuit. A smile sneaks across my lips even though I've missed her horribly the past few weeks I've been gone. Like, *really* missed her. More than I was really prepared to deal with. But I'm dealing with it. I wish she would've come back with me, but all that's almost over, and she'll be here next year. No doubt about it.

We're so damn close to being free; I'm halfway through the last leg of the circuit with Aragon and Japan down and only Australia left after this. Then it's two short weeks before we slingshot back to Spain for Valencia, and not only can I *not* wait to get home to Chiara and enjoy three glorious months of the winter break, but it looks like I might be coming home a World Champion too.

Spain, Japan...I've been at the top of every pole session, the first on every leaderboard. And with me and Chiara doing better than ever, everything is coming up roses for me.

*Pink roses.*

I round the corner to the garages, striding down the sunny pit lane in my red Dabria leathers and kinda messing with a camera crew that starts to follow me. But they let me go when I keep walking past my pit box and head instead to my brother's garage.

"Hey, dumbass," I say when I find him with his crew, going over the latest telemetry readouts. "You see the fishing tournament last night? It was one for the books."

*What did you think about my practice earlier?*

He claps his crew chief on the back, then heads to the other side of his pit box, grabbing his water bottle and squirting a long stream into his mouth. "Nope," he says when he's done. "I'm done watching that. And stop asking me for the best fishing spots when we're home."

*I'm done giving you advice.*

"What? Why?" I cross my arms with a snort. "Because I don't like the same shitty lures that you do?"

*You think I don't listen to it?*

"Not that." He flicks at his nose. "Pete Willis has been catching some big fish lately, and now the talk about Brad Finley retiring is getting serious."

I stare at Billy, stunned, my stomach dropping somewhere around to the bottom of my boots. Because I'm Pete Willis. He's Brad Finley.

"He can't do that," I tell Billy. "That isn't fair to Pete Willis. It's not his fault... And Brad Finley...he's the best."

Billy shrugs. "He's old. Slowing down."

"The fuck he is."

Billy's crew glances my way, and Billy laughs it off, clapping my shoulder. "It's just fishing, man. Take it easy." He flares his eyes at me where his crew can't see. "You got any Tums in your bag?"

"Yeah, I do."

I definitely wanna talk about this—what is he thinking? He can't retire. The people pressuring him about this for the last couple years are nothing more than assholes, and so what if I've been winning? That doesn't mean he gets to just cut and run. He can deal with it, like I always have. The fuck!

He follows me out of the garages, down the sunny and humid pit lane, and through the tunnel back to the paddock. Clouds are lazily swirling across the sky as we cut through the crowds of crew people getting food and hanging out in the paddock, people laughing and talking around tables, and it's too pretty a day for this kind of shit to be happening. Shouldn't it be raining during the apocalypse?

We head toward the line of parked RVs where there are barely any people. He checks around, and once we're clear of the straggling fans and the skeleton camera crews, he jerks his chin at me and quietly says, "You remember that talk Frank had with me before

Silverstone? When we were staying in that cottage and I said I'd do the dishes? Well, it's because Yaalon's been talking about you."

"No, uh-uh." I wave him off. "Don't put this on me. You're the one bailing."

"You wanna know what happened?" he growls. "Then *listen*. They're impressed—not with you missing sponsor galas and skipping press conferences. But with how you're riding this year? They've taken notice. A lot of people have."

This is, like, the unfairest thing that's ever been unfair. That should be music to my ears, and all I can do is glare at him. "So? I ride for Dabria."

"So now Yaalon wants to retire me into being a test rider for development while offering you my spot on the team. They think I'll be able to handle you. For them."

I sputter out a scoff. Hearing it a second time doesn't make it any better. First, what the hell does "handle me" mean? And second, for them to pull him off his bike, the machine he's spent years perfecting for Yaalon, so they can give it to someone else to race during the season while only trotting Billy out for practice and testing and *that's it*?

And worse: they want to give it to *me*? Like we aren't blood.

Fuck them. Fuck *that*.

"Yeah, I was pissed at first too." He crosses his arms, shrugging as he walks slowly beside me. "But the more I think about it, I don't know."

"You can't be serious. A *tester*?"

He glances toward me. "It's salary."

I roll my eyes. Of course, he wants to go for the safe bet.

"And the schedule...well, it isn't bad, man." He clears his throat, scratching at his jaw. "I could see Taryn more. Maybe make it to some of her races more than once or twice a year."

Fuck, there's gonna be no arguing with that. And I can't even pretend anymore like I don't understand how important that is, what I would trade to spend more than a couple weeks with Chiara at a time. And Billy and Taryn, their schedule is even worse because whenever he's not racing, chances are *she is*. They're hardly ever at their ranch together, and I honestly don't know how they make it work. They do, but I know it's been pulling on him.

"Could be good for you too." He knocks my chest. "They'd probably offer you more money than Dabria, and you'd get to ride the Yaalon."

I shake my head even though he's right: I'd be fast as hell on his bike, with all that lovely engineering behind it. He's definitely right about the pay raise. And God knows that would make me feel better about all that it would mean for me and Chiara, but still. "Well, why didn't anyone say anything to me about it? Frank hasn't said nothing."

Billy shrugs. "I guess they wanted to see what I was gonna say first. It's not set in stone."

Well, that's even more annoying. That a whole group of people decided it wasn't even worth bringing it up to me, because my career depends on what *he* decides. Screw that—the decision is made as far as I'm concerned.

No matter what Billy does, there's no way in hell I'm moving to Yaalon. I *might* be able to use their offer to sweeten my deal with Dabria, but that's as far as I'm going with that. I was already gonna try to renegotiate after this season anyway—my wins are up, and I had fully planned on beating him for World Champion. But now...I don't know what to do.

About the race tomorrow. About Australia after it, and Valencia. I *want* those goddamn podiums. The glory and the chance to bring it home for the underdogs. I want World Champion for Chiara, who believes in me. I want it directly in Massimo's smug-as-fuck face. But I don't know if I want it more than my brother—for him to go out a champion, one last time.

I don't know if I want it more than for Billy to stay in MotoPro and kick my ass every Sunday, bossing me around in the paddock and pissing me off in the pit boxes and just...being my big brother. My shadow.

But if I keep beating him, and they retire him into a test rider because of it...

*Not yet.*

I stop and turn toward my brother, poking him in the chest. "Fuck that. Your knee's doing fine, your ankle's healed, and you don't get to retire at the top of your game. You were our star pitcher since Little League, first in track and 4-H, starting varsity quarterback and captain of our football team. You're a champion tie-down roper, a hell of a good dancer, and you were the best damn bull rider Tennessee had ever seen." I lean closer, growling, "You're Billy Fucking King, and you tell them that."

He peers down his nose at me, still crooked from me breaking it with a hard right cross when we were in middle school. Then he scoffs. "You realize who *you* are, right?"

"Yeah, I do." I turn and walk away, calling over my shoulder, "I'm your little brother."

—◊◊◊—

I don't know how the world keeps turning when bad shit happens. But it does—people keep moving, talking, eating. I guess it's easier to pretend like everything's fine than deal with all that's crumbling apart. But I'm not great at pretending. Not like Billy is.

*Billy*, who finished ten long seconds after me in Sepang, five seconds after Massimo. Billy, who is starting in fifth position tomorrow here in Australia. Billy, who keeps making us play poker every night like everything's fine and this may not be our last season together.

Chiara says it's just his way and I should try not to worry about it. *Yeah, okay.* She's also not convinced I should turn down the Yaalon bike if they offer it to me. Says I'm letting my ego get in the way of hard-earned opportunities, and Tank had the nerve to agree with her. But they don't seem to understand that taking over Billy's ride is just going to make everything *worse*.

Every win I'd take on it, people would say it was because of him, the work he put into the bike, and I just can't live with wondering if they're right. If they've been right all along, and my whole life has been blessed by his damn coattails. Just the idea of it makes me want to drink—*a lot*. But I still haven't touched a drop. Tank's probably sick of me calling him all the time. It's, like, three times a day at this point. Almost as much as I talk to Chiara.

*God, I fucking miss her...*

It's like my skin is on fire from needing her touch, her hugs. But one more week, and then she's in my arms. And I ain't letting go this time. Not for the circuit, not for Massimo, not for anything. Everyone can just freaking deal with it.

"Lorelai, you're the big blind," Billy says. But my ex-teammate doesn't move to react, staring off into space at something behind me.

I take a sip of water, then set the bottle beside my chair leg, peeking back just in case. There's nothing there except the rest of the dark Phillip Island paddock. The few crowds of people hanging out after a long, hot day of practice.

"Lorelai. You're the big blind." My brother's voice rumbles a little more loudly the second time, drawing the attention of a few people nearby. But it finally snaps Lori out of whatever reverie she was in.

"Huh? Oh!" She pops up and glances around, pushes up the sleeves of Massimo's jacket that she's wearing, then throws in another chip. "My bad."

She's usually more on top of her betting than she's been tonight. But Chiara says she's been stressed about the wedding, and she's racing harder than ever. Like she's out to prove something, but I don't know what. We don't talk as much since she moved to MMW.

I throw in my ante, the clink of plastic on plastic muffled against the low chatter of racers and their crews. Billy does the same before he starts dealing out for five-card draw. Starting with Massimo to his left. "Deuces wild."

"You always want to play deuces wild," Lorelai complains. "Why not do sevens wild? Or eights?"

Billy scrunches up his nose at her. "Because that's just weird. Massimo."

Massimo tosses in a chip, his eyes trained on me as he adds two more. I still can't tell if Billy's told Massimo about the offer from

Yaalon yet. He hasn't officially decided on what to do, but they are teammates...

Probably not, because I'm sure to hear about it once he does. Massimo would probably raise holy freaking hell at the idea of me and him being teammates. Not that the idea fills me with butterflies either, but I can be professional about it. He's mostly just been pissed because I've got pole position for tomorrow's race. He's also not as good at poker as he thinks he is.

Billy jerks his chin at Lorelai. "How's the wedding planning going? Taryn says the caterer has been giving y'all all sorts of issues."

"Yeah, it's been a nightmare." Lori settles up, the big ol' teardrop diamond ring on her finger practically blinding me under the paddock flood lights. "There's a million moving pieces that I never realized were so important, and I'm kind of ready for it to be January already."

Massimo scoffs at her. "The last time I said that? I got yelled at."

Billy chuckles as he and I settle up. "Isn't that always the way, buddy?"

"Sorry." Lorelai winces, then leans over to press a kiss to Massimo's cheek. He smirks and folds his cards flat to his chest while she does it too.

Billy nods at Massimo. "All right, No Mercy. How many you want?"

"Two," Massimo tells him, sliding over his cards. His eyes flick back to me. "Lorina, I forgot to ask you: did you ever give Chiara's number to that guy?" Massimo shrugs innocently while I absolutely do not react. "Whatever happened with that?"

Her eyes shift my way. But just barely. "Which guy? Two," she tells Billy.

"Two for Wreckless."

"The good-looking one," Massimo says. "The DJ."

*Don't react. Don't react. Don't react.*

"One," I tell my brother.

Billy slides a card my way. "One for Relentless. Dealer takes two."

"He...already has her number," Lorelai says to Massimo, shuffling her cards around in her hand because she probably doesn't have shit. Loves to bluff, though. "Because he's the DJ, and Chiara hired him."

She sure did. And she said his mixes were okay, but his original stuff was pure shit.

"Did they hook up?" Massimo looks right at me when he says it. I blink so slow and calm, it feels way too obvious. He picks up his cards, looking through them. "I thought they looked good together. And you know how she is about music."

"I have no idea if anything happened," Lorelai says. "You should ask her the next time you talk."

"I will."

Billy taps his cards against the table, stacked together. "Your bet, Massimo."

Massimo considers his chips, then bets modestly, still trying to draw me in instead of just going for it. When he's done, he stretches comfortably back in his chair, putting his arm around Lorelai. He looks over at her with a smile and brushes a kiss against her hair, just because he can.

"Call," Lorelai says, matching his bet.

"I'm all in."

All three of them look at me, but it's Billy who says it: "We just started playing."

"Don't matter." I stare at Massimo. "I'm all in."

Massimo smirks at me, still stroking his fingertips down Lorelai's shoulder.

"Well, I fold then," Billy says. "Since you're gonna ruin the game."

Lorelai tosses down her cards, looking at Massimo. "Me too."

Massimo taps his cards against the table, his far hand now twirling a lock of Lorelai's curly hair around his finger. "Call."

*Yeah, you did, motherfucker.*

"Ah hell," Billy mutters, scrubbing a hand over his face before he sits forward, lacing his hands together. "Okay. Let's see 'em."

My pulse is racing like I'm on the last straight of a track, staring down the finish line with nineteen men behind me, charging for the gap between us. I don't show any of it on my face as I lay down my hand, my stare deadlocked with Massimo's. "Flush."

He cringes. Then he fans out his cards and turns them over, showing me before he flicks them onto the table. "Full house."

*Fuck!*

Lorelai stares at the cards, breathing hard as she swallows thickly. Then her big brown eyes lift to me. Billy doesn't say shit.

I nod, getting up. "See y'all tomorrow." Gently push in my chair, grab my hat and hook it on, then start walking toward the RVs. A couple people nearby glance my way, but it's hopefully not too obvious what just happened.

Massimo snorts from our table. "We will wave at him from the podium, more like."

I turn and stride back to the table at twice the speed as before.

Massimo rockets to his feet, his dark eyes blazing and his left hand held low in front of Lorelai. My brother leaps up right after him. Lorelai stares up at us, her hands gripped to the arms of her chair.

"What?" I drawl coolly, coming to a stop next to my chair. I bend to grab my water bottle, flipping it in the air and catching it easily once I straighten. Massimo glowers at me. "No need to stand on my account." I wink at him, then pivot and head back toward the RVs, taking a sip of water that doesn't begin to quench the temper raging in my chest.

*God, I can't wait to rub it in his face so fucking bad...*

Starting with my win, tomorrow afternoon.

"Hey, Mason," Billy calls after me with a laugh, "I told you not to eat those tacos, man. Come on. There's some Tums in my bag."

I flip him off over my shoulder. I don't want to talk about it. Not with him, not tonight. There's only one person I want to talk to, and she better not be talking to some fucking DJ.

Billy jogs a little until he's beside me, catching me by the arm and his voice low. "The hell is going on with you? You're really gonna let Massimo get to you like that? Before a race?"

I shake myself loose. "He's the dick who started it."

Billy leans closer, growling, "Then fucking finish it. Before it gets out of hand."

"Don't worry," I sneer at my brother. "I'm going to."

# Chapter 29

*Mason King—October*

TWENTY-SIX LAPS, TWO TURNS TO GO, AND MASSIMO IS RIGHT ON my ass. But I've had this race since before the red lights went out, and I'm not going home with anything less than first place.

*Come and get me, asshole…*

The sky is crystal clear and liquid blue as we cross under the Melbourne archway, the gray track rippling like smoke in the humidity as my bike roars in sixth gear, my speedometer reading a brutal 187 miles per hour, 189…190… Top out at 193, then tap the brakes and drop it into fourth, redlining it all the way as Massimo drops into the third behind me. But I know I can hold it, g-forces sucking my stomach up into my throat as we pull ninety degrees to the right, heading for turn two, the Southern Loop.

Drop into third gear, breathe, and don't overshoot it.

Slow in, fast out.

Watch the fence through the long left turn. Blue and white, flashing in the sunlight and guiding me left until it disappears. *Now.* Hit the throttle and bump into fourth. Fifth. Turn three: Stoner Corner. Hold it for the left in fifth gear and don't choke it, *don't choke it…*

I glance over my shoulder, and Massimo is dead on my tailpipe, my brother's matching blue Yaalon directly behind him. Followed by the bright orange of Santos Saucedo's Hotaru. And they're all coming for me.

I look forward and wait to brake until I see the marker. Fourth gear, third, second, first. Massimo's engine screams at me as I lean hard right, leading them through one of the best places to pass. And the easiest to crash. But I'm not fucking around today, and I hold the line and push into second as I leave the turn, take the kink to the right for turn five, lining up for Siberia.

He can't catch me in there. And safe-play Massimo won't risk it.

Sure as shit, I hoard the apex and hear his engine struggling all through the left turn, mine growling louder with clean air in front and nothing to slow us down. But when I come out, I can't stop my eyes from lifting to the archway covered in Wild Turkey logos—because why wouldn't one of our sponsors be one of my favorite brands of whiskey?

Massimo's transmission redlines, and I realize my mistake too late. I punch it into third, but it's already done. He sneaks up beside me, our front forks side by side as we battle into fourth gear and pull left for turn seven.

The gust of wind hits from the right.

I barely miss him as it swerves his bike toward mine—*son of a bitch*. I knew better than to approach there. Phillip Island is always super windy, and three guys got blown off the track yesterday during practice. We had to have a meeting this morning on whether the conditions were even safe to race, and I voted yes. Massimo voted no.

I check behind me and Billy got blasted too, his tires farther on the left side of the track than he likes to be, but he's already working it back and dealing with Santos trying to take advantage and cut around. Good luck with that, dude.

I look forward, and Massimo has my line into the apex for turn eight. Damn it, there's almost no way to pass in the right turn, and all I can do is wait for my moment. Wait, but don't choke it.

*Don't choke it...*

I train my eyes on the road just past his wrist, watching every adjustment of his throttle. Control my breathing, duck into his slipstream, and let him do the work for me. His Yaalon whines under the strain, his tires chewing hard track while my Dabria eases through, because he went for a soft back tire when I went on the medium, and we both know he's got nothing left. The skyline curves as we come around, and *go*.

Pop the clutch and redline into third, my heartbeat thundering at the surge in speed. Duck outside his slipstream and use it to push me faster as I pass. Massimo curses—*dumbass*—my RPMs screaming while I use him to slingshot up through the steep loop of turn nine.

I'm not fucking losing this race—no matter what. But he just isn't getting that.

We're side by side when we crest the hill, the fans in the stands at the bottom roaring when they see us. Massimo's helmet peeks my way, but I duck lower and don't take my eyes off turn ten. Sharp and hard to the right, it's where legends are made and heroes die.

Third gear, second. Wait for first. *Wait for it, wait...*

But the need and fury are too much, and I can't resist. I glance at Massimo next me, daring closer even though the turn is coming. Dude needs to back the hell off and get in line, or we're going to have a problem. Except that's been the problem with him from the start: he just doesn't know when to back the fuck off.

I look forward, the sun raining down and a white canopy glistening in the distance that's getting closer, too close, and he can do whatever he wants. Just like his bad tire choice, it's his mistake.

I hit first gear and lay her flat, my knee and elbow sliders grinding against the ground and *shit*. I let him bully me into waiting too long, and it's too damn fast. Too hard, too much speed and too much force, and there's no way I'm gonna make it through this turn...

A gritted yell pours from my throat. My back tire skids, hot and worn from twenty-six grueling laps. But I don't let go, *don't let go*, touching the throttle as the sky moves and then the turn ends.

I'm gasping for breath in my helmet as I straighten, letting my body settle back in the saddle to where it's supposed to be. Second gear, third. But that's when I hear it: the crowd hissing and *ooh*ing.

I spare a glance back, and there's a cloud of dust ballooning up.

Massimo isn't behind me anymore.

My head whips forward, a cold sensation shrieking through my chest.

*Fuck!*

"Crash at turn ten," the announcers blare over the loudspeaker. I climb into turn eleven, nowhere to go but up. "Number Thirty-Two for Yaalon Motorsports, Massimo Vitolo."

Come out of the turn and straighten, my tires getting chewed to shreds as I prepare for turn twelve, but all I can think is that he crashed. He fucking crashed.

"Rider okay."

I take that announcement and force it down, force myself to blink and shake my head as I push into fourth gear. Lean hard to the left in turn twelve, my left knee scraping the track as I hug the inside line at 95 miles per hour, keeping it steady. Green grass flashes top left in my field of vision until the track bends, and I level out. Open her up to 120 miles per hour, 145. Shift.

The crowd is wild in the stands when they see me in the Gardner Straight, people on their feet and cheering me on from just beyond the Melbourne banner. It's the same down pit lane, waving flags and signs as cameras swoop and broadcast it all over the world. To everyone who's watching at home.

I spare a look back at Billy, blue and ducked low and coming cleanly through turn twelve, his technique perfect as always. Santos is still right behind him, Giovanni hot on their heels. One lap to go—one more race in the circuit to go—and they're never gonna catch me now.

I'm going to win today, then take Valencia too and win World Champion. But there's no joy in my chest. No sense of victory or validation.

Because constantly-ruining-my-life Massimo screwed up and crashed out today, and I already know: with how protective she is about him, there's a really good chance she's gonna be pissed at me about it.

# Chapter 30

*Chiara King—November*

"This is getting ridiculous," Aria grumbles in Italian. She's currently sitting on my couch next to Elena while running her warlock through the new *Nightfall* map. "Where are you hiding, jerk?"

"It's supposed to be up here on the right." I lean over the back of the sofa, pointing because I can't sit still anymore. The anticipation is too much—Mason's spent the last thirty-six hours flying in from Australia, and he should be here any minute. I can't wait for my friends to meet him either.

Aria and Elena know everything about everything, have from the start, and it's important for this to work. But I'm not worried about it—they're going to love him. And he already likes them from all the stories I've told him, so…easy. (If only telling Massimo would be this easy.)

I still don't know what his problem was, challenging Mason in a turn like that in their last race. Mason hasn't said a word about it. And when I talked to Massimo, he said he saw a hole so he went for it, and anyway, he's fine. The moto is mostly fine. So it's all apparently fine.

*Yeah, right.*

Elena pauses the YouTube walkthrough on her phone, jumping up as she points at the TV. "There! Right there. See it?"

"Got it." Aria redirects and slides through the hidden doorway, her warlock creeping down a tunnel that should lead right to a—

"Bingo!" Elena high-fives me, and I push off the couch, heading to the dining room to double-check everything is ready. No dishes in the sink or any dust to be found. Not that he cares, but still. I woke up bursting with energy and cleaned the hell out of my apartment, currently sparkling with the scent of fresh flowers because Mason is the *sweetest* man alive.

He's sent me flowers at least once a week while he's been gone racing. Which has been *forever*, and I have been stuck here working and finalizing everything for Massimo and Lorelai's wedding. (Come on, caterer! Pick up your phone! You can do it!) But thank God and every other deity, the end of the circuit is almost here, and that means I get the best present ever: Mason is on his way here for the two-week break before Valencia, and I don't know what we're doing after tomorrow. If we're staying in Ravenna or going somewhere else, and I seriously do *not* care where we end up as long as I get to be with him. I'm trying to prepare for any and all possibilities. For now. For after the circuit ends.

I lean over the dining room table, tucking my hair behind my ears and breathing in the roses that were delivered yesterday morning. Pink roses.

"I'm still not convinced this guy is real," Elena says behind me with a chuckle.

I straighten and peek over my shoulder, finding her twisted around on the sofa and watching me. Aria is fighting some trash mobs, muttering curse words under her breath. She jerks to the side as her warlock blinks out of the way, her pink ponytail bobbing with the movement.

I nod firmly at Elena. "He is very real." And very mine. "You'll see."

"Is she making the face again?" Aria hisses under her breath when her warlock blows her super and misses.

"Almost," Elena teases.

"What?" My smile bounces right back, unstoppable under the certainty of seeing him soon. "Being in love is not a crime. Especially with someone who respects me, believes in me, completely gets me, puts me first, and treats me like a freaking queen. He...being with him...it's the *one* thing I don't have to worry about, that I can completely trust in. It's just *done*, it *is*, and I don't know how else to explain that we just..."

"You love him," Elena says.

I nod quickly, a whole bunch of air swelling in my chest because *God*, I do. I really do, and I can't count the ways I've missed his voice, his hands, the way he rolls out his shoulder when he first gets out of bed in the morning. The nearly silent caress of paper against paper when he turns a page in whatever book he's reading. The kisses he whispers against my cheek when we're snuggling in bed and how deeply he breathes me in when he holds me...

And okay, maybe she's right and it's a little bit ridiculous how infatuated we are with each other. But I *love* it. No one has ever made me feel less like a burden. With him, I'm definitely not the plucky sidekick anymore. Main character all the way, baby.

Elena snickers at me, Aria cursing again. "Shit! I'm dead." She sets down her controller with a sigh, then turns to glance at me. "So where's Mr. Perfect? I thought he was supposed to be here by now."

"I don't know," I whine, literally fidgeting in place I'm so ready for him to walk through the door. "His flight landed on time...he should be here."

"Ten bucks on a train running behind," Elena says.

"You're on," Aria replies.

"Ugh." I toss my hair, and I would give anything for a shot right now to settle me down, but I'm not drinking. I figured it wasn't fair when Mason's been working so hard to stop, and I firmly support what he's doing and why, and I don't want to make it harder, so...no alcohol for me. Not even wine. Or mimosas. It's okay. He's worth it.

Especially when there's *a knock at my door*! *Yes!*

I let out a giddy squeak, Elena laughing and gesturing at me. "Shh! Down, girl."

"Oh, fuck you." I skip over to the door and swing it open with a beaming grin. "You're home!"

"We're home!" Lorelai squeals, her arms thrown out to the sides and her MMW bag hooked on her shoulder.

My stomach plummets straight through to the center of the earth, taking my reality along with it. I'm so shocked, so terrified, I can't even move when she hugs me, revealing Massimo standing right behind her.

A strangled breath huffs out of me, his expression quickly downgrading from tired and irritated to super suspicious.

*Oh my God, please let this be a nightmare.*

*Wake up! Wake up!*

Lorelai lets me go and walks straight into the apartment. A waft of lemon slices through me, and I sway in place. "We would've been here earlier, but the trains were—Hey…"

Her voice trails off, Massimo tilting his head at me because he knows something's up. (He knows, he knows, he knows.) He's been after me for weeks over whether I've been seeing someone, because I apparently sound so happy on the phone all the time, but he's sounded so happy *too* and I just…I don't want to be the reason he stops smiling. Ever.

I swallow. Tuck my hair behind my ear. "Hey," I mutter to him. "Hi."

I still can't even conceive of the catastrophe that is about to occur. But it's already in motion, and it's as though time has slowed, every torturous moment preserved so I can feel it all. Mason is going to be here *any second*, and it's so goddamn petrifying how much my whole life is on the edge of a knife. And I knew it was coming, but I…

I wanted to do it on my terms. My time. When I was ready and knew how to apologize for all the secrets I've been keeping. When I knew what to say.

(I have no idea what to say.)

Massimo heads around me to follow Lorelai inside the apartment: the home he picked out for us and brought me to see and drank champagne with me on the living room floor on our first night here because we had no furniture. Who stayed with me, every single time I was scared.

With numb hands and a seized heart, I shut the door. God, here we go.

"Hey, Massimo," Elena says casually. I look up to find her leaning over the back of the sofa, seeming perfectly comfortable.

Aria is back to playing, but there's a visible tightness in her shoulders. "Plot twist," she mumbles. Elena elbows her, still smiling at Massimo.

I feel like I could puke.

"You two just get in?" Elena asks.

"Yeah," Lorelai says, a smile in her voice before she looks back at me. Currently melded to the door. "Y'all having a girls' night?"

Nod head. Make words. "Mm-hmm."

"Well, we won't stay too long and spoil all your fun. Our cab is actually still running downstairs. We're just stopping by on our way to the house because we probably won't see you again for a couple weeks."

Light. Hope. "Oh?"

"Yeah," she says. I make the mistake of checking, and Massimo is watching me. Closely. I keep my eyes locked with Lorelai, pretending he doesn't exist. "We're going to Memphis in the morning. Apparently Mason has some big rodeo, and I thought it would be nice to go support him before he retires, so..." She sighs, heaving her bag higher on her shoulder like it's gotten heavier in the three minutes she's been here. "Back to the airport it is."

The most strangled, awkward chuckle ever leaves my throat. I cannot breathe.

"That okay?" Massimo says in Italian, his eyes peering deeper and deeper into my soul. "Or did you need us here for a wedding thing?"

I shake my head. Don't trust my voice.

"So we'll see you when we get back," he says slowly.

I jerk a nod. "Mm-hmm. Yep."

"Great." He smiles at Lorelai like everything is totally normal, then comes over and takes both my hands in his, forcing me to meet his eyes. I wait for him to ask who I was waiting for. Who I expected to see once I opened the door, because we both know it wasn't him.

In my mind, I practice the word *You.*

"Call me tomorrow?" he says.

"Of..." I have to say it twice before my voice works. "Of course."

His eyes are X-rays as he sweeps his thumbs over the backs of my hands, then carefully kisses both my cheeks. I shudder, knowing I don't deserve any slightest bit of affection when I'm outright lying to him.

*How am I ever going to explain this? He has never lied to me. Ever.*

Massimo lets me go, then gives me a forgiving smile like *he knows* I'm keeping a secret but still loves me anyway. He promised he always would, no matter what, and I believed him. I still do. I just...don't deserve it.

He passes me off to Lorelai when she comes over to hug me good-bye. "Sorry to barge in on you like this," she whispers. "I'm so glad you're having a girls' night. You deserve it." She squeezes me again, then lets me go and turns for the door, Massimo already there and holding it open for her. "Oh hey," Lorelai says at the last minute, "any word on the caterer?"

*Any minute, any minute, any minute—SPEAK!*

"Still, um, waiting for a call back," I choke out. "I'll let you know when I hear."

"Hmm. Well, okay. Thanks, Chiara! Love you!"

She blows me a kiss as she heads out the door. Massimo takes one last look at me, a dozen questions in his eyes as he shuts the door, and then they're gone.

A massive swell of breath rushes from my lungs, and I grab the back of a chair in my kitchen to stay standing.

"Dude, are you okay?" Elena says, her voice low and serious.

I shake my head, my heartbeat thudding in my chest.

Definitely not okay. And everything is about to get so, so much worse.

---

It's twenty minutes until Mason shows up. Twenty long minutes of me freaking the hell out and pacing in my kitchen, biting off three of my manicured fingernails and Aria twice trying to convince Elena they should leave. Then the key slides into the lock.

The door pushes open, and my nerves are so shot, the regret so sickening that I can barely make sense of Mason in my doorway: unzipped leather jacket over a pearl-snap shirt, Wrangler jeans and black Stetson and red Dabria bag and a bouquet of burgundy calla lilies in his hand.

He stops half a step into the apartment, his blue eyes locked on my face. "What's wrong?"

"Do you have another rodeo coming up?" I'm a taut ball of energy, my arms snapped across my chest to keep me from bursting into flames.

He blinks a couple times, then comes the rest of the way inside, setting down his bag. Lays the flowers on top. Not his hat. "Yeah," he drawls warily, straightening. "I was gonna talk to you about it tonight."

I nod, but all my movements are jerky. I feel like I could start bawling at any minute. "Did you tell Lorelai about it?"

I can see him thinking in the slow lick of his lips, the controlled work of his jaw. "We were all having a meeting with Frank when I got the call, so yeah, she knows. You wanna tell me what's going on here?"

"She's freaking out," Aria says.

Mason startles, his head whipping toward the living room. "Holy shit! I didn't even see y'all there. I'm sorry." He clears his throat and walks over to the couch, holding out his hand to Elena. "Mason King. Nice to finally meet you."

"Elena."

"That must make you Aria," he says to Aria, who nods and shakes his hand too. He covers it with his other one. "Can I just say: your void warlocks are freaking *sick*."

She gasps with a surprised grin, glancing at Elena and then back to him. "Thank you!"

"Sure thing." He pats her hand, then lets her go and turns back to me. Takes enough steps that he's closer to the kitchen than the living room but still leaving plenty of space between us. He must sense how volatile I feel. "Okay, so tell me what I missed here."

"Lorelai and Massimo are going to your rodeo." My voice starts to crack. "They were just here, telling me they're now leaving for Memphis in the morning."

His eyes go wide. "Did you tell them? How'd it go?"

"No, I didn't tell them!"

The wideness in his eyes narrows back into slits. "Why not?"

"Because, I…" I can already feel it, the tears prickling their way from my cheeks to my eyes, and I can hear it in my voice. The hopelessness, the fear. The cowardice.

Mason crosses his arms, jerking his chin at me. "Call him. Tell him to come back."

I steel myself under his gaze. I will not fall victim to his blue eyes or how they look when shaded under his black hat. I will not forget that Massimo has been my forever, and he doesn't deserve the rain of hurt I'm about to bring down upon him. The windfall of betrayal.

"Hey, so we're…uh…going to head out."

I startle at Elena's voice, finding the TV off. I don't even remember hearing them shut down my PS4. But she and Aria are already on their way to the front door. I nod, reaching out and taking a soft squeeze of my hand from Elena. Aria just gives me a pitying look with those sweet green eyes of hers. This is going to take so much explaining, and I am not looking forward to it.

"Bye, Mason," they echo each other on their way out the door. "See you tomorrow."

"Nice to meet y'all." Mason touches a finger to his hat their way, then goes back to glaring at me.

When the door shuts behind them, I'm breathing hard, but I don't move for my phone. "Well, that was awkward."

"Yeah," he agrees. "More awkward since I've been gone a month and you won't even say hi to me."

I don't know how to respond to that. Because he's right. But I can't act like everything is okay when it's such a horrible, horrible mess. So I go straight for the heart of the matter. "Mason, you have no idea what you are asking me."

"I know exactly what I'm asking you. Call him. Let's do this."

I shake my head. "You can't be here when I tell him. Especially not after your last race."

"Goddammit," he mutters, his jaw popping tight. "I knew. *I knew* the second he crashed, you were gonna be all over my ass about it."

I take a steadying breath, making sure my voice is calm. Now I know why he hasn't talked to me about it. "I do not blame you for what happened last weekend, Mason. I know it wasn't your fault."

"Well," he says, gesturing my way, "that's something."

"But I do still think you're letting our personal life interfere with your racing. And the very last thing I want is to make it *more* dangerous for you out there."

He throws his hands up in the air, exasperated. "You know?" He laughs cruelly. "I honestly don't know what else I can do. Winning isn't good enough, I guess."

"It isn't about that."

"Then what's it about?"

The edge in his voice is right there, and I head toward the kitchen and yank open the refrigerator, taking out what I need to start on dinner. I'm not hungry, but I need something to do with my hands. Something to keep me busy in case I start crying.

I grab an onion from the basket. Along with my biggest, sharpest knife. I chop off the ends, peel off the skin, then start dicing with a vengeance. I don't even like onion in this dish. "Everything is a competition with you, Mason. *Everything.*"

He comes over and stands next to me, but leaning against the counter so we're facing each other. "Not everything. But some things? Yeah."

I bend to grab a skillet from the cupboard, placing it on the stove and clicking on the burner. "Is that what I am?"

"Are you what?"

I scrape butter into the pan, then lower the flame. Preheat the oven, then do it again when I set the wrong temperature. "You once asked me if I was using you to get back at Massimo. But I think it's the other way around." I slide the diced onions into the skillet, then set down my cutting board and knife before I turn to face him. "I think you are using me as a way to beat him, because you want to beat him on the track."

Mason flares his eyes, a darkness shimmering over him. "I don't have to use you, because I'm already beating him. Check the god-damn leaderboards if you want."

"See? That is exactly what I'm talking about."

"You're the one who brought it up."

"Yes, because I cannot handle you fighting with him all the time!"

Mason shakes his head, waving me off. "Stop trying to turn this around on me. You're the one not coming to Memphis."

I turn to the sleeve of chicken breasts.

"You're *really* not gonna come?" he says again, leaning around me so he can better see my face. "I can't believe this."

I run my knife along the cellophane for the third time, but this shit just won't cut. How are people supposed to cook when they can't get past the packaging? "How can I go when they are going to be there now?"

"Well, you could call him, tell him to come over here, take a stand, and we could get this shit out on the table once and for all."

I shake my head. "Tonight is not the night. He is already in a bad mood from the wreck and being exhausted and—"

Mason chuckles darkly, cutting me off. His jaw is gritted as he looks away, the vein in his temple starting to throb. "He's exhausted. That's just great."

I swallow thickly at my mistake. But I don't look away when Mason's eyes come back to mine. He deserves that much.

"You're really not coming to my last rodeo? It's Smashbox, Chiara. It's fucking *Smash*, and you're not coming?"

I bite my trembling lip. But I don't know if that's because I'm about to disappoint him more than I'm sure he's capable of handling or because of what he just told me.

*The* bull. Smashbox. The one that haunts his dreams and has nearly killed him twice before. And the last time, scared him *so much* that he got too drunk to ride at all. So Billy swapped places with him, and Mason has grieved over it every day of his life since.

I've seen the videos. Of that rodeo, of the others with Smashbox, and I can't blame Mason for being terrified. I could never do something like that. And I can't wait for the day that he stops.

He swipes a hand over his mouth. "Okay," he says throwing his hands up. "I'll go, you stay. I'll have someone let you know if I end up dead."

He turns and starts heading for the bedroom, and I give up on the chicken, setting down my knife. Take a couple deep breaths and make sure I'm in control. But I can't help glaring at his back, unable to find any of the emotions that were rampaging through me when I was waiting for him to get here. "You are acting like a child."

He whips around, his hand pressed desperately over his heart. "No, I'm acting hurt. Because you're *hurting* me, Chiara. Why are his feelings more important than mine?"

"They're not."

"Then *show me*!"

"He's all I have left, Mason!"

The words are like a bomb. His name echoing in the apartment as he stares at me, and I feel every single stab of regret. But there's no way to take it back.

God, if I could only take it back.

Mason scoffs. "Guess I'm back to invisible again."

I open my mouth but find no words. No breath. The shame is too heavy, the guilt too big.

What did I just do?

He crosses over and grabs his bag, flips the lock on the door, then turns and heads toward my bedroom. He never looks my way.

The tears come fast and hard, and my eyes fall closed when the door shuts softly behind him. I don't know how any of that could've gone any worse. And I have no one else to blame.

My wobbly knees give out as the first tear falls off my cheek and lands on the floor, and I sink down until I'm sitting in it, my knees hugged to my chest and my heart torn in two.

I can't keep hurting Mason like this—*I can't*—but I don't know how not to hurt Massimo either. I just…I don't want anyone to get hurt. But with the two most important men in my life on the brink of war, I don't see how this is going to end any way but bloody.

# Chapter 31

*Chiara King—November*

My dreams are all nightmares.

I'm in traffic, but I don't recognize the city. I'm in the back seat of a car, on a highway with endless lanes, stopped in gridlock. I can't get out of the car. The driver has dark hair, his face obscured, and I hate that I can't tell if it's Mason or Massimo. He never turns around.

I'm still screaming at him, kicking at the door and beating wildly at the handle when I wake to an empty bed. My body is motionless, supported in the pitch-black room, silence ringing out through the apartment. Until I hear a *clack-clack-clacking, click-click-clicking* sneaking past the cracked open door.

I take a centering breath and wipe a hand over my face, then check the time on my phone. 2:53 a.m. A worried sigh settles in my chest as my fingers fall from the edge of the nightstand—his hours are so off, he's barely slept in days. And he needs to be rested for tomorrow night.

I have no idea how I managed to fall asleep. I don't count on it happening twice.

At least we got through our first big fight okay—talked it out, had passionate makeup sex, and kept our appointment with Aria and Elena the next afternoon before we caught a late flight to Memphis. An easy compromise to make for my not coming to the rodeo, and I didn't want to spend more weeks apart anyway. Everything is mostly back to normal, except for the fact that he's not sleeping.

With a quick flick of my wrist, I throw back the covers and grab my hair tie from the nightstand, tying my hair up into a messy bun. I love his bed, the padded headboard and plush mattress and big square pillows, but I can't get used to the smell of fresh paint and staleness in the rest of the Memphis apartment. He's hardly ever here, and it's like someone staged it: the pieces are all in place, but there are no signs of life.

As quietly as possible, I pad my way out of the room. Like I expected, he's sitting on the couch, shirtless and in jeans, bathed in artificial light. Endless lines of text are reflected in his glasses as he leans forward, hunched over his laptop. He hits a single key.

"You couldn't sleep?"

His head pops up. "Hey, sorry." He gives me half a smile, then goes back to reading. Types in a couple words. "I'll be right there."

No, he won't. Because I'm not the only one having nightmares.

I head around the counter into the dark kitchen, half watching him continue to read and peck at the keyboard as I grab a small glass from the cupboard and rinse it out in the sink. Everything is dusty. Fill up the glass halfway and take a sip as I go to stand next to him.

Mason sits up, taking the glass when I hand it to him and drinking nearly half of it in one gulp—he never drinks enough water. He smooths his other hand over my lower back and around to my hip, pressing a kiss to my stomach. I cup his cheek and hold him to me as I read the words on the screen, my heartbeat speeding up more with each one. "This is necessary?"

"Just a precaution." He kisses me again, looking up with a wink. He hands me the water glass, then goes back to the laptop, reading over his last will and testament and the instructions in the event of his death. He moves the cursor and clicks on a line, then changes a semicolon to a comma. "It'll be all right."

A breath huffs out of my chest—nothing about this seems all right. "Mason," I say quietly, sitting next to him. The gray leather sofa is soft and creamy and surprisingly warm against the backs of my bare thighs. "Explain this to me again."

He stops and sighs, looking over at me. But his words are laced with patience, infinitely gentle. "It's my bull. My ride, Chiara. And it's my last chance to do this, forever." He coughs out a scoff. "Hell, just to do it sober."

I run a knuckle down his cheek, along the line of his jaw. "I think that is all very true. But I also think this has a lot to do with Billy." He rolls his eyes, but I reach over and take his hand. "You think he's always going to be better than you," I start quietly, "that you will never catch up, but that's not true, Mason." I look him over, full of love and pity and the bitter sting of frustration. "You are just as good a man as he is, and you are fully capable of beating him on the track, if you would only stop holding yourself back."

"Chiara—"

"And I understand that you are scared that it will change things between you, because it will. Things *will* change. But he is your brother, Mason, and I promise you: he will love you even if you finish first. There is room for both of you in this world."

Mason pulls his hand from mine. "Even if what you're saying is right, he was fine."

"He broke his ankle riding Smashbox."

"I know what happened."

"Then *stop*," I say strongly. "Walk away while you can, while *we* still can. You were going to retire anyway. So why not retire now, wait one more week, then win World Champion in moto? You are *so* close."

Mason watches me, fire and frustration burning in his blue eyes. "Are you really telling me not to do this?"

I wish that I could. That there was *any* way to make him understand.

"I am asking you to think about the decision you are making and why you are making it," I tell him carefully. "I am asking you to remember that I love you, and I don't care if you are a bull rider or a moto racer. I just love *you*."

He sighs, then reaches over and retakes my hand, squeezing tight. "I love you," he says. "And I hear what you're saying. But I still have to do this." He shakes his head, his jaw gritted and the words pained. "I can't live with the regret of missing my chance. Not again."

The fear, the sense of failure is so strong, so cold, it sends goose bumps rushing across my skin. It feels like I'm already mourning him. My cheeks prickle with the start of tears, and I lean over and press a sorry kiss to his cheek. "You know I will always support you. And I will wait for you, no matter how long. But I cannot watch you do this."

His head hangs as I pull my hand from his and get up, going back to bed. I set the water glass on the nightstand, then lie on my side and pull the covers up to my shoulder. I blink away my tears in the dark, listening to the stretch of silence in the living room until he resumes his *clack-clack-clacking*, his *click-click-clicking* until the light finally shuts off a long time later.

When he comes in, he shuts the bedroom door completely, leaving his jeans on the floor and his glasses on the nightstand before sliding under the covers until he's behind me. His hand rests on my arm, his lips on my shoulder, and I squeeze my eyes shut. He's always so warm.

"I'm sorry," he breathes, hugging me to him.

I'm sorry too. Because nothing I say is going to be enough to save him from himself. From this damn bull. And I'm not ready to lose Mason.

Not now. Not tomorrow. Not ever. Not for anyone.

His lips brush the back of my neck and I shiver, a dark tinge of desire that feels closer to grief warming in my belly and crawling down between my legs. It's calling for things that I know are wrong in this moment but I still want anyway.

I need to feel him. The tickle of the hairs on his legs and the softness of his skin, the strength of his hips and the broadness of his shoulders. I need his body to cover mine and swallow me up. That way, I can be with him, always. Wherever he goes.

With a gentle movement, I tilt my hips back against him. Mason ducks his head to the back of mine, his arm over my chest tucking me in tighter but not moving closer anywhere else.

I rock back again, purposefully skimming my ass against his cock, silently begging for what I need. He sighs, whispering, "We don't have to, Chiara. I know you're upset."

I shake my head, my voice broken. "That's exactly why I need you."

Before he's gone forever and I'll have missed my chance to enjoy him one last time.

He sighs again, but then shifts so my head is resting on his arm, his fingers finding mine and tangling them together on the pillow in front of me. "Okay." His other hand smooths its way over my side, tugging my hips back so he's pressed firmly against me, already stiffening and swelling thick. Goose bumps rush over everywhere he's touching me, Mason slipping his palm under the hem of my shirt and massaging me everywhere: my hips, my stomach, my breasts. Down to my thighs, over the curves of my ass and back around, under the thin strap of my panties.

He peels them low enough that his skin meets mine, the head of his cock searching and pushing against me. I push back harder. Mason hisses through his teeth, a low growl in his throat following behind as he bites a kiss to my shoulder. Then he moves—rolling away from me and reaching into his nightstand. I don't shift, don't look, don't do anything but wait impatiently for him to come back.

It doesn't take long, listening to his thumb pop open the bottle of lube, then the click when he closes it. Another stretch as he puts it away. He's slick and cold when he finally comes back against me, but he warms quickly, his palm on my ass guiding me to make space for him. The thick steel of his shaft is already intimidating, but I don't care. I almost want it to hurt. (He'd never hurt me, though. Never.)

He massages my body gently, like his hands can't touch enough of me as he nudges his hips closer. Shifts a little like he's getting a better angle, then nudges my ass again. I gasp at the first hard press, feeling my body stretch and strain even as I push back harder. But he's too big, and my heart is breaking, and it's just...

His palm takes up all the space on the back of my thigh, guiding my legs apart. He tries again, not getting far, and I whimper, frustrated at needing him and not being able to take him, at how cruel our whole life has become.

"Turn over, baby," he whispers, gently encouraging me onto my stomach. He never goes far, one arm still wrapped around my shoulders as his chest covers my back, his legs settling between mine.

He guides one of my knees out to the side, kissing the back of my neck and nibbling at my shoulder. But when he presses against me, I can't contain my wince and he stills.

"Do you want to stop?" he breathes, but I shake my head. I don't want to stop, I don't want him to go, I just don't want...any of this.

Mason sits back, a swell of hot tears glistening in my eyes as I hide my face in the pillow. He trails his fingers down my back, watching me, deciding. I pray he doesn't give up on me. I just need another chance. I can do this. I want this. I just need my body to understand that.

Thankfully, Mason must hear me, silent though my words are. He carefully pushes my T-shirt up my body, waiting and helping as we get my arms free and slip it over my head. He pulls my panties off next, easing them down my legs and throwing those away too. The air is freezing against my skin, but he gathers the comforter around us so I'm snuggled and warm, only my spine exposed as he gathers more lube, then lowers down on top of me.

He slips against me so much easier this time, his breath tickling my neck and his knees shadowing mine. He presses forward, and I feel myself melt around him, a low moan escaping from Mason as he carefully rocks inside me and I dare to push back. I steal a solid inch of him that sends lightning through my veins, and I need another hit. He's still going so slow, so careful, but I can't take the anticipation and I reach up, pushing against the headboard.

He slips in deeper, growling deeper, working himself in deeper with easy rolls of his spine that soon have me gasping for breath. He reaches for my jaw, calloused fingers gentle on my skin as he kisses my cheek, the corner of my lips, resting his temple to mine and slowly thrusting into my ass until he's buried inside me, and I can finally breathe. Arching my body up into his so there's no part of us that isn't touching, listening to his heavy breaths as the world gets fuzzy and hot and tumbles clean away, leaving only Mason.

The caress of his lips. The grip of his hands. The hard rod of his cock and the sensations flowing through me from feeling him move inside me.

He reaches between my legs, and I tremble, grasping for a hold on anything I can when his fingers find me soaked for him. It's too intense, but I've never felt more *alive*, more real than when he touches me. Like I'm not just a person to take pleasure from—I am the pleasure. I am sex incarnate and the goddess of desire, and I sink into the freedom of being a muse. His muse. Letting him fuck me hard and dirty and slow because it's what he needs. It's what I need.

To know and remember him this way. When he's perfect and strong, and he's got me on my knees but I'm still bringing him to his with every little noise I make, every part of my lips and every thrust I make against him. But he's not without his own tricks, and he knows me well. So well. Knows my body and what makes me scream the loudest, and he's not playing it safe tonight.

He works every single one of my buttons until I'm gasping and shaking, slamming my fist against the headboard as I try to control it and can't, coming hard for him without making a sound. But he feels it—the hard throb as my body squeezes where it wants him—only growing stronger as he pumps his cock into my ass and then breaks along with me, coming hard but keeping his voice to himself.

I reach back and cup his cheek in my palm, regret sinking through my chest because I wanted to hear him, but it's too late now. Too late as he lowers down, breathless but still breathing kisses all over my skin. Too late as he pulls out and lays beside me, tucking me into him and the covers around us, and holding me so, so tight that I'm already getting hot. But it's just...

It's too late.

For the life we could've had if we hadn't been so scared.

For the future we wanted.

The life I wanted with him.

It just all feels so...over.

—∼—

I wake up a little after dawn. Alone.

He left without waking me or saying goodbye, and my hands won't stop shaking. It's been the longest day of my life, pacing back and forth in his tiny apartment. Peeking out the windows into the gray parking lot of his complex. Watching TV and never noticing what I'm seeing. He's not far: the annual Cornucopia Exhibition is taking place in Memphis this year, but the cell phone reception in the arena is a nightmare—according to Twitter anyway.

Taryn's been texting me info as it comes in:

> **Taryn:** Hi! This is Taryn. Mason asked me to text you. I have his phone.
> Anyway I wanted to let you know we're here
> **Taryn:** All checked in
> **Taryn:** Press interview at 3 pm
> **Taryn:** He rides at 7:45
> **Taryn:** Lorelai and Massimo just got here

The last text only makes me a million times more nervous. He doesn't need Massimo in his face, messing with his head right now. He needs to concentrate, to be confident, and…

*I should be there.*

I collapse on the couch again, my head in my hands and my knees bouncing as I shiver and wait for time to tick by. I hate this, so freaking much. The danger, the secrets. The hiding.

I can't stop checking the clock:

6:23.

6:43.

7:17.

7:19.

7:37.

7:41.

7:45.

7:46.

7:47.

7:49.
7:52.
7:54.
8:01.
Then it comes in:

**Taryn:** Eight seconds but he's hurt. Transporting to First Presbyterian ER

A broken breath bursts from my lips, and I leap up, blistered from all my worst fears coming true.

*Mason.*

There's no time to panic, to wonder what "hurt" means. It's not perfect, not healthy and strong and safe. My heart is rampaging in my chest, and I can't feel my body except to know I'm cold. Nauseous. But there's no time to be more afraid than that. I wasted it all already.

I swipe at my blurry eyes and pull up the directions to the hospital. Snatch up my earbuds from the kitchen counter. Plug them in and start the navigation. Run to the closet by the front door. Jacket, helmet, keys.

"Turn left onto North Magnolia Avenue," the woman's robotic voice tells me. "You will reach your destination in thirty-nine minutes. You are on the fastest route there."

Run back to the room for my wallet. Hit the light but leave the TV on and then I'm out the front door, down the stairs, and thanking God he took his truck this morning because I don't know if I can drive that thing. But I sure as fuck can drive his moto.

"Turn left onto…" The woman's voice disappears as I start the engine and swing a leg over, the blood red Dabria growling at me like it knows I'm not him.

Or maybe it just knows he's hurt.

*Don't cry. You can't cry and drive.*

I pinch away the wetness blurring my eyes, then flip down the face shield on his helmet and kick up the stand. Try not to breathe in the trace of his cologne and sweat swirling on his jacket and in his helmet, because it's a battering ram to my heart. Walk back the moto from its parking spot, then gun it and peel through the mazelike buildings and endless parking lots of the complex, dodging stupid speed bumps until I get caught up at the gate—tall and iron with spikes on the top and not catching the moto on the sensor to open.

*Come on!*

A jacked-up Jeep pulls in behind me, blocking me in. Another car, old and rusted, pulls in the entrance and stops as I rock it forward and walk it back over where the sensor should be, and I can't *believe* this! He's in a goddamn ambulance right now!

"Hey, Mason, it's broken again," the guy in the car yells at me, half hanging out his window. I look over at him, my long hair tangling in the wind. "What the—Hey, Jimmy!" he yells toward the Jeep. "Someone's stealing Mason's bike! Call the cops, man!"

*Fuck.* I don't have time for this.

I pop the clutch into first and use the torque to swing around in the small driveway. (No time, no time, no time.) Rev the throttle as I swerve around the open-door Jeep, dodging the bearded guy scrambling toward me from inside yelling, "Hey! *Stop!*"

Hit second gear and veer around the landscaped concrete divider between the iron gates. Duck low and fly down the entrance driveway, past the open gate and the passenger side of that goddamn car.

"Call the cops, man! She's getting away!"

I spare a quick glance for traffic. Hang a sharp left that nearly lays me flat, the engine barking as I slam it into third on the empty road and rev it up into a faster fourth, leveling out before I downshift and let her redline, then hit fifth gear. Sixth.

"In eight miles, take a right onto Smoky Mountain Way." The GPS voice is clear over my shaky breaths, the Dabria roaring continually louder. "You are on the fastest route there."

# Chapter 32

*Mason King—November*

"Get this shit *off* me." I tug at the leads reporting my vital signs to the stupid beeping machine, ripping the stickies off my chest and throwing them away.

A nurse blows around the corner, skidding to a stop in her white sneakers and Captain Marvel scrubs. "What are you doing?"

"Checking out."

"Sir, I will restrain you," she warns as I get out of the bed, but I don't give a fuck. Let them try it. "Janey," she calls out of the room toward the nurse's station. "Page Dr. Navarro. We got a runner."

I glance around for my shirt, then remember they cut it off me in the ambulance. What a bunch of overreactors. I do find my boots, tugging them on with my one good hand. Billy has my wallet and my hat and my truck keys, so at least those are safe. But Taryn has my phone, and I need to call Chiara. I need to get home. *Now.*

"Mr. King," the doctor says as he jogs into my room. "Leaving us so soon?"

"Yeah. It's been real fun."

He sighs and looks at the nurse, and she is *not* happy about what we all know he's gonna tell her. "Go ahead and take out his IV. I was gonna discharge him in an hour anyway." Then he looks back at me. "You'll be sure to follow up with your ortho and your neurologist within a week to make those appointments."

"Yup," I say through gritted teeth.

I can't fucking believe I was dumb enough to jack up my shoulder again. Probably gonna need surgery, and the buzz from the painkillers isn't enough to erase the fact that there's no way in hell I'm gonna be able to race Valencia in a week.

I may have gotten my eight seconds on Smashbox, but I just lost MotoPro World Champion.

*And maybe Chiara too.*

My stomach flips at the thought, panicky fear rippling through me again that's ten times worse than what I felt climbing the gate into Smashbox's chute. She made it perfectly clear last night that she didn't want me doing this, that there was too much at stake. But I didn't fucking *listen*. I put my ego first, and the fact that she never showed up to the arena says it all: I went too far. I crossed the line, and I've read enough books and watched enough movies to know what happens when that happens—women *leave*. And they aren't all like Taryn; they don't all come back.

My whole self is vibrating with nerves and itching to *go* as the nurse stands there and scowls at me in her scrubs, then finally goes over to the sink and cabinets and pulls out a pair of blue plastic gloves, getting what she needs to take the IV out of my hand.

"Thank you," I tell her as she takes care to remove the needle without hurting me. Even though I've been the worst patient ever, all night.

She still scowls at me. "Mm-hmm."

It isn't another two minutes until I'm rushing down the hall, my head throbbing more with every step and my sore arm cradled in a sling against my bare chest. The emergency department is a maze of gurneys and identical doors, arrows pointing to the exit leading to more arrows until I finally get to a set of double doors and slam the button to open them.

They slowly create a gap, my father's voice the first thing I hear. *Great.* I slide through the doors, then stop in place when I see them. Billy and Taryn are sitting next to each other in ugly blue chairs. My brother has his fist to his mouth, Taryn holding his other hand as his knee bounces. My father is standing next to them, his long arm holding my mom into his side, her face hidden in his chest. Lorelai is pacing back and forth.

*Damn it*, there's no way I'm gonna be able to get outta here without them wanting to talk to me and discuss everything that happened to freaking death. And I don't have time for that shit. I need to go.

Maybe I could slip back inside the hallway and find another exit before they—

"Mason!" Taryn says.

Everyone looks my way, but I'm blinded when a headlight flashes through the windows behind Taryn, the loud growl of a motorcycle speeding to a stop on the sidewalk. The rider drops the kickstand and rips out the keys before they take off toward the entrance. Then they blast through the automatic doors, tearing off their helmet and glancing around.

*Chiara.*

I let out a sharp whistle, and her head whips my direction. The rest of the hospital melts away as she takes off running toward me, blowing straight past everyone in the waiting room until she's crashing into my arms, her body trembling as she tucks her face into my neck and chokes out a sob.

I rock back with a gasp that's pure relief, gathering her against me with my one good arm as I breathe in cinnamon and press a kiss to her hair and try not to start crying too, just fucking wrecked with guilt. *God, I really thought I'd fucked this up for good.*

"I'm done," I promise, holding her tighter as she nods, still shaking from head to toe and *Christ*, what was I thinking putting her under this kind of stress? "I'm fucking done, and I'm so sorry. I should've listened to you."

"I'm just glad you're okay," she whispers, her voice broken. "That's all that matters."

I press another kiss to her hair, just holding her and wishing we were alone, already home. But we've got a full audience, and the shit is going to hit the fan in about three seconds.

Maybe less.

"What are you doing here?"

Massimo's voice is the first to cut sharply through the chaos, sending a stiffening chill through Chiara, still locked in my arm. I can barely look at his face, barely breathe, my adrenaline so redlined and my pulse pounding so loud in my chest. I didn't even see him standing there, leaning against the wall with his arms crossed.

"I texted her," Taryn says quietly. "Mason asked me to."

Chiara leans back, wiping at her eyes but not looking at the group of people behind her. All their eyes are trained on her back.

Massimo glares at Taryn, then looks straight to Lorelai. "You knew she was here in Memphis. And you did not tell me." He scoffs, gesturing harshly at her. "What happened to no more secrets? We are getting married in three weeks!"

"I didn't know!" Lorelai bursts out. "I mean, I kinda suspected something was going on but...I didn't *know* anything."

"I asked you just the other night!" He turns to Billy, barking, "Did you know they were together?"

Billy nods.

"Fuck you."

Chiara shudders, and I tighten my arm around her waist. Lean my temple to hers, wishing I could give her strength or peace or anything, just *anything* when I know how badly she's gotta be freaking out right now. She never wanted it to come out this way. *My fault again.*

"Dude," Billy growls, holding up his hand toward Massimo. Taryn hugs his other arm tighter, like she's trying to keep him in his chair. "Not now."

Massimo and Lorelai start whisper bickering, and I ignore them.

"Mason, are you okay?" Taryn asks. "Is it another concussion? What did they say about your shoulder—"

"So this must be Miss Move Out," my father interrupts. I look over to find his and Mama's eyes trained on me, taking in me and Chiara. They've never seen me hold a woman like this, and I damn well know it. But while my father looks full throttle suspicious, Mama just looks scared and tired, smudges of black mascara around her eyes and her fist clenched in my father's pressed shirt.

"What does that mean?" I ask him.

"Miss 'I'm moving out.' Miss 'I'm going to AA.' Miss 'I'm gonna start missing rodeos and cutting out on my responsibilities.'"

My heart is raging in my chest, and I can't believe he's going to do this now of all times. But I'm not sure why I'm surprised. He's always had the most backward priorities.

I open my mouth, but Chiara gets there first.

"Every decision he has made has been because *he* has made it," she says, pure ice in her voice. "I do not tell him what to do or where to go, ever. But I don't expect you to understand this."

My father looks like he just got slapped, his eyes are so big. Mine too.

Billy looks up at me, his brow furrowed. "You're in AA?"

"Yep," our father drawls, still staring down Chiara. "Just hit sixty days."

"No one told me that," Billy mumbles, glancing at Taryn.

"Well, you didn't tell me he was dating some Italian girl, did you?" our father says to him. He curses under his breath, then looks back at me. "So how long has this been going on?"

"Bill," Mama cuts in, "now is not the time."

"Now's the perfect time," he says to her. "We're all here. Let's get it all out."

My voice is as cold as Chiara's was. "A year."

Massimo silently shakes his head behind her, eyes trained on the ground.

My father scoffs, crossing his arms. "A *year*? Well, that explains a lot."

My brother scrubs a hand over his face, then reaches between his boots and picks up a bottle of water, taking a long drink.

Chiara huffs, saying to my father, "It has only been serious for the past few months. Before that, it was just sex."

Billy chokes on his water, spilling half of it all over Taryn. "Shit! I'm sorry!"

"Billy!" She leaps to her feet, dusting off the water from her jeans. I'm too stunned to react. But my mother flares red, looking toward the hospital hallway like that'll erase what they all just heard. Maybe the sirens from the ambulance outside covered it...

But nope: my father absolutely heard her, looking hard at Chiara for a long time with a curious smile growing in the corners of his lips. He tilts his head, trying to stall us out. It's not going to work on her. "You don't bullshit, do you?"

"No, I do not," she tells him, her chin lifting. "I am honest. Just as Mason is, like you raised him to be. And I will tell you something else: I don't care about your approval or what you think of me. It is not going to keep us from being together, so hate me all you like."

He smiles now, half nodding his head even though I feel like I'm about to have a fucking heart attack. This is not going well. "Yep, this is starting to make a lot of sense."

"I don't care what you think," she repeats, his resulting chuckle only pissing me off more.

"Can you stop?" I snap at him.

"Bill," my mom says. "I swear to God, you will leave this until tomorrow."

He shrugs, hands help up. "All right. Just curious how serious 'serious' is. But I guess it can wait."

Chiara looks at me, angry and defiant, and I can see it reflected in her eyes that she's ready. I'm so relieved—I'm sick to death of hiding in the shadows. And I'm not even close to ashamed.

I trace a lock of hair away from her face, caught against the tears drying on her lips. "Well, we eloped in Paris in September. So it's pretty serious."

There's an echo of gasps, though I'm not sure who from. Probably all of them.

"Oh my God," Taryn mutters, covering her face with her hands. Chiara winces, scooting closer to me and hiding her face from their view.

"What?" I ask Taryn, but she doesn't respond. Billy won't even look at me.

"Is that even legal?" Lorelai cuts in. "Eloping in Paris? Don't you need, like, paperwork and shit?"

Finally, a reasonable reaction. "Yeah, you do. It wasn't legally binding."

A wave of breaths being released—practically in unison.

"Well, thank God for that," Taryn mumbles. Mama just shakes her head.

"Hold on." Dad takes a step closer, pointing at us. "Say that last part again?"

"It wasn't legal." I can't help but practically smirk when I say it. "But the civil ceremony we had in Ravenna three days ago was."

"Oh my God!" Taryn bursts out.

"Son of a bitch!" my father curses. "Is that why you asked for your birth certificate? You said it was for legal stuff!"

"It was for legal stuff," I tell him. "We wanted to be married, so we did it twice just to make sure it took. I needed to make sure she was gonna be okay if something happened to me, and I wasn't interested in waiting around because of some stupid stepping-on-toes bullshit."

"Wait…" Lorelai rocks back a step, her brow furrowed. "What does that mean?"

Shit. There goes me and my big mouth again. "Nothing," I tell her. "Forget I said it."

"Mason," Lorelai growls at me, "what did that *mean?*"

There's no point trying to put her off; I've known her long enough to know that. I jerk my chin at Taryn but tell Lori, "She and Billy have been waiting to get engaged until after your wedding because she didn't want to steal your thunder or whatever."

Lorelai looks at Taryn, the color draining from her face. "Is that true?" she whispers. "Did I delay your wedding?"

"No," Taryn rushes out frantically. "We were already waiting, and once you were engaged and everything, I just—"

"Are you pregnant?" Massimo interrupts.

Chiara sniffles and finally looks over her shoulder at him, her voice gentle and absolutely unapologetic. "Does it really matter?"

My mom sucks in a harsh breath. Six heads whip my direction, twelve eyes in different shades of furious, and none of them watching as Chiara looks back at me with the slightest shake of her head and half a wink, and I'm actually a little disappointed. God knows we've rolled the dice enough times that it wouldn't really have come as a shock. And she's terrible about remembering to take her birth control. Even with the alarms I set on her phone.

Billy stands, crossing his arms and glaring at me like I'm the most irresponsible person who's ever lived. My father looks so pissed he apparently can't even speak.

"Oh, because it would be the worst thing in the world," I sneer at my brother.

"Yeah, it would!"

I glare back at him, full of disgust. "You're gonna talk about your kin like that? Your little niece or nephew?"

"Goddammit, Mason!" is all he can say.

"*No*! I have fucking had it with all of you trying to tell me how to live my life!" I look at Taryn, starting with her. "I may have made some mistakes when you and Billy first got together, but I apologized for that, and I have never gotten in the way of your relationship since. Have I?" Taryn looks away, and I look at Lorelai next. "We were teammates, and we were friends before that. You're the one who gave Chiara my phone number in the first place. But where is the support now?"

"Hey!" she yells at me.

"Massimo doesn't control the fucking world, and he doesn't control me or Chiara."

I don't see the left cross coming—I don't even remember seeing him move. But I sure fucking feel it when Chiara gets ripped out of my good arm, and Massimo's left fist connects hard with my face.

My knees hit the ground and everything goes dark. Quiet. Pain is blasting through my jaw, and when the sound comes back on, there's a lot of muffled yelling. Mostly my brother. A couple strangers I don't recognize. Someone is saying the word "cops" a lot.

The light comes back next, and I realize Taryn and Mama are standing over me, or maybe kneeling, because I think I'm on the floor.

"Mason, open your eyes," Taryn says again, but her voice is choked with tears.

I reach up and find her hand on my face, then pull it away. "I'm okay." I test my jaw, and *holy fuck*. That's gonna leave a mark.

"No, you're not," she says brokenly, then yells over her shoulder, "Billy, let him go!"

There's more yelling, more scuffling, but I can't hear Chiara in the mix, and I don't know where she is. I roll over and push myself up, Taryn and Mama helping me to stand, but everyone is gone. Except for a few pissed-off nurses and a security guard with his hand on a walkie.

"They're all outside. Come on." Taryn keeps her arm locked with mine, my mom on my other side. They hurry us outside, the world spinning and impossible to control. The lights of the parking lot, the stars, it's all swaying like a roller coaster.

I try to focus on the ground, my boots bouncing up at me like a bad 3D effect. Swivel my head on my neck up enough to see Chiara standing opposite Massimo and Lorelai in the pull-around driveway. Billy and my father are standing protectively over her, my father's arm between them as Massimo goes on and on, yelling and gesturing.

"You don't talk to me. You don't tell me anything. I never see you. You don't answer my texts or my calls..."

"That's not true," Chiara cries. "I call you all the time. We talk every day. I've been planning your wedding for months. What do you mean we don't talk?"

"And you *lied*!" His voice blasts through the parking lot, drawing the attention of the few people outside talking on cell phones and coming in from their cars. "For a *year*, Chiara! All that time, and you've been keeping this from me." He shakes his head, his voice so gritted it sounds like he's on the verge of crying too. "I have never lied to you. You have known everything about me and Lorina, every step of the way. There is no part of me that is not open to you: my life, my house, my family. Anything you have ever needed, I would have given you. But *this*..."

"Massimo, I wanted to tell you, believe me." She takes a hasty step toward him but gets blocked by the arm of my father. "You think it was easy for me not to be able to share this with my best friend? It's the biggest thing to happen to me *ever*, and I couldn't tell you. But I can't talk to you when you don't listen to me because you think you know better."

"How do you know what I think when you tell me nothing!" he shouts at her. "Where is the trust? Where is the honesty? I feel like half of me is *missing*."

Taryn and Mama and I come to a stop next to them, Billy stepping back to make space for me. I reach out and rest my palm on Chiara's shoulder, her hand coming up to cover it. Squeezing tight.

"Half of him is missing," I say to Lorelai. "And you're okay with that?"

She turns her teary-eyed scowl on me, her voice razor blades of impatience. "Mason, I don't know what you don't understand. I fell in love with Massimo. And Massimo came with Chiara. That's... what I got. And in order for him to work"—she gestures between him and Chiara—"*that* has to work. She is part of who he is, and he is a part of her, and if you break that, they break. And not seeing that is *exactly* where you fucked up. If you really loved her, you would've been honest with Massimo about it."

"It does not matter anymore, Lorina," Massimo snaps at her. Then he zeroes in on Chiara, standing stock-still with tears running down her cheeks, the long ends of her hair blowing in the wind. "Keep what other secrets you have, and tell your lies to someone else. I'm done. I'm fucking *done*," he growls at her. "I don't want to talk to you. I don't want to see you. You no longer *exist* to me. You're fired. Stay away from my family, and don't you dare come to the wedding. This is over."

"Massimo—" Lorelai says breathlessly, her eyes huge in horror.

"No!" He looks back to Chiara. Looks her over from top to bottom. Then he grabs Lorelai's hand and walks off toward the parking lot.

He doesn't say goodbye.

I barely catch Chiara in time as she doubles over, sobbing with her hand clasped over her mouth. I wrap her in my one good arm and tuck her into my chest, but her knees are starting to buckle, and she's so goddamn broken—*fuck, what did I do?*

"Breathe, baby, breathe," I tell her, but she ain't breathing. She's gasping between sobs, and I've never heard a person sound the way she does. It's like someone died.

Our knees hit the pavement, Chiara crumpling forward until her forehead is on the ground. I lay my cheek to her back as she cries and cries, my father and brother watching us with pity plain on their faces. Especially when a motorcycle roars to life, then speeds out of the parking lot with two riders ducked low.

It peels onto the highway with a sharp squeal of the tires before the engine revs and a car honks, and I hate that son of a bitch so much for doing this to her. Almost as much as I hate myself because I already know: Lorelai was right.

All the fighting, the anger, all the people being hurt by this…

This is my fault.

I didn't understand what I was getting in the middle of, and I should've…

I should've talked to him. Man to man. Right from the start. I should've listened to her when she said this was complicated and hard, that it required a delicate touch. When the time was right. But I didn't think, didn't listen, and now she's heartbroken, and I don't have the first clue how I'm ever gonna fix it.

I'm not him.

# Chapter 33

*Mason King—November*

THE APARTMENT IS DARK WHEN I GET HOME FROM MY DOCTOR'S appointment. Dark and deathly quiet. My keys clink on the counter when I set them down, my phone a hard thunk and the crinkle of the brown bag of food right next to it. Light is struggling to come in through the blinds, casting weird shadows across the dusty screen of the TV. There's no music coming from anywhere.

I take off my hat and head toward the bedroom, my heart in my throat. But there's a shape in the bed that sets the world right, if it can be right, right now. I don't turn on the light, don't say anything as I walk around to my side of the bed, slip off my boots, then crawl under the covers next to her. Her eyes open right away because she wasn't sleeping, even though she's snuggled under the comforter up to her nose.

"Hey," I breathe, trying to find a comforting smile for her. "Today a bed day?"

She nods, her eyes closing.

Yesterday was better. She ate. Showered. Drank her coffee, then made me take her grocery shopping because she wanted to cook a big dinner for whatever reason. We ended up riding horses with Billy and Taryn in the afternoon and eating dinner there.

She smiled. She laughed.

But not every day can be a yesterday.

I scoot a little closer, whispering a kiss to her forehead. "I got us some lunch. You hungry?" She shakes her head. "You mind if I eat in here with you? Maybe watch some TV?"

"I don't mind."

"Okay." I leave another kiss on her hair, then roll up out of the bed.

Two days ago was the worst it's been. So bad, I panicked, and I asked if she wanted a divorce, maybe a separation. Whatever it would take so she could talk to him, earn back his friendship. She accused me of pulling an Edward Cullen in *New Moon* and I quit talking. Nobody wants to be that, and neither of us wants to do it. Separate. Divorce. It all felt wrong as soon as I said the words—felt wrong even as I was thinking them—and I was selfishly glad when she said it would only make everything a thousand times worse. But I didn't—*don't*—know any other way to help her through this.

She said time. Closeness to me. *That*, I'm more than happy to give. The rest of my life, if that's what she needs. Was already planning on it anyway.

Heading to the kitchen, I grab two bottles of water from the fridge, then hug them into my chest with my sling and grab the bag of food. When I get back to the room, Chiara hasn't moved, but that's fine. I dump everything onto the bed, grab the TV remote off my nightstand, and turn on *Star Trek*, but I keep the volume low. I sit next to where she's still lying, digging my sandwich and pickle out of the bag, then hand her one bottle of water.

"I'm not thirsty."

"Can you open this for me?"

Chiara sighs, her hands coming up through the covers to unscrew the cap. "Sorry."

"Well, I'm super pissed, so ya know..." I wink at her, and she snuggles a little closer into my side, taking a deep breath like she's breathing me in. Then she reaches for my pickle.

I take a drink of water, then set the bottle on the nightstand and unwrap my sandwich, taking a bite.

"I hate this episode," she mumbles. "Deanna Troi is so annoying. 'I have to find you! I have to tell you something!' Why doesn't she just *say* it instead of saying that instead?"

I snort, shredded lettuce escaping out the back of my sandwich and falling onto the wrapper because I can only hold it with one hand. "Trouble, if that ain't the truth."

She grumbles more and sits up, tucking her hair behind her ears and kinda sighing at the TV. She looks at the brown bag, then reaches inside and pulls out the second sandwich. "Where is this from?"

"Schlotzsky's."

"Huh? What language is that?"

I shrug, taking another bite. "I don't know. But they got bacon grilled cheeses down pat." They put avocado on it too, and that shit's amazing.

Chiara leans closer to me, peering at what's in my hand. "That doesn't look like a bacon grilled cheese to me."

"It's not. Mine's a Spicy Turkey BBQ Bacon Smokecheesy. You got the grilled cheese."

Chiara blinks at me. She reaches out and takes my sandwich, looks it over, sniffs it, takes a bite, then hands it back. Her hand covers her mouth, her eyes wide and words mumbled. "I don't know what you just said. But that is…"

"Really damn good, yeah."

She picks up the second bottle of water, cracking the seal easily and drinking nearly half. Something loosens a little bit more in my chest. Especially when she unwraps her sandwich, then takes a bite, moaning a little at the soft bread and crispy bacon, the slice of tomato and splash of mayo. And those perfectly diced bites of avocado layered in between. "*Mmm*, but this is better."

She takes a second bite with a little more life coming back into her cheeks, and I pick up the remote and change to a new episode. *Knew that was the right sandwich.*

I jerk my chin at Chiara. "You gonna give me a bite of that?"

She leans away, scowling at me.

I playfully roll my eyes. "You eat my whole pickle too?"

She searches the bedding before handing me the wax paper bag. I finish it off except for the last bite, which I give to her. Tuck the wrapper into the brown bag and go back to my Spicy Turkey. Shit's so *good*. And something about doctor's offices always makes me hungry.

"You know…" Chiara kisses pickle juice off her fingertips. "I have always loved that Dr. Crusher and Captain Picard have breakfast together every morning."

"Well, they're friends. And she's the only one who calls him Jean-Luc."

"Do you think her husband knew that Picard had a crush on her? And that's the real reason they lost touch?"

"I don't know." I consider that, reaching for my bottle of water. "I mean, probably? Most men usually know when another man is interested in a woman they like. So yeah. I'm guessing he did know."

She looks back to the screen, picking a piece of avocado out of her sandwich and eating it with a sigh. "I'm glad they still got to be friends in the end."

"Yeah, me too."

She takes the bottle of water when I hand it to her, drinking almost a third and then passing it back to me. I take another sip, then twist on the cap and set it on the nightstand.

"How was your appointment?"

I shrug, taking another bite of my sandwich. "Same old stuff. I'll be fine, take it easy, call if there's problems, blah blah blah."

She nods, then quietly says, "Mason?" and I do everything in my power to be as calm as possible. Totally normal. Just sitting, eating, watching *Star Trek*, and waiting patiently for the bomb to finally drop.

That she's had time to think it over, and maybe I was right. Maybe we made a mistake. That the consequences are too much to bear and leaving me is the simplest solution to putting her life back together. Because I fucked it up. Just absolutely tornadoed it in a whirlwind of chaos. And I really, really didn't mean to, but either way, I did.

*Maybe she should leave me.*

But I can't bear the thought of it.

"Can I ask you for a favor?"

I nod, swallowing. It takes a long time to get it down. "You say it, I'll make it happen."

She leans her head onto my good shoulder. "Can we go home to Ravenna?"

My pulse stutters like it slipped into neutral, RPMs revving before I find the right gear and everything thumps calmly back to the speed it's supposed to be. Make sure I'm breathing okay, because I really wasn't expecting that. I barely turn enough to press a kiss to her forehead, inhaling the sweetness of cinnamon. "Flight out is tomorrow morning, ten a.m."

Chiara straightens enough to look at me. But I'm having trouble reading the words in her eyes right now. Been struggling with that for days, ever since...

There's just too much darkness. Too much pain.

And it's my fault, all my fault. *Some hero I turned out to be.*

"I've...had our tickets booked for the last three days," I confess. "Kept pushing it back. Figured you'd tell me when you were ready."

I know she's scared to go back to Italy. To the apartment they used to share, where there are memories on every corner. But Memphis isn't her home—Ravenna is—and I knew it was coming. That soon, we were gonna have to go back and face everything we couldn't deal with the first time around.

I'm just glad she isn't asking me to send her on alone.

"I'm ready now," she says.

I nod. I'm ready too. Half of her is missing, and I won't rest until I put the pieces back together. That's what you do when you break something. You fix it.

I wink at Chiara, then pout dramatically. "You're really not gonna give me a bite of your sandwich? My shoulder hurts..."

"Oh my God," she mutters, rolling her eyes. "You are such a big baby."

She gives me a bite of her sandwich, though.

*For better or worse, she still loves me.*

———

Billy won World Champion.

Massimo came in second. Santos, third. Giovanni, fourth.

Because I missed Valencia, my zero points at that track dropped me all the way to eighth in the final rankings. To top it off, instead of happily renegotiating with Dabria for more money, Frank is now trying to convince them to let me finish my three-year contract instead of buying out my last season and dumping me.

I get it—they're concerned about my shoulder, my reliability. But I've got surgery scheduled in two weeks and plenty of time to rehab it before practice in February. As long as I'm smart about it. And I'm gonna be smart about it.

I wait for the espresso machine to finish its gurgling, back home in Ravenna though I'm not sure when home and Ravenna became synonymous. Probably because this is where Chiara is happiest, even though I've never seen her so depressed. It's not constant, but when it hits, it hits hard.

Last week, she tried to convince me that we should move out. I shut that shit down fast—she *loves* this apartment, the windows and the light, the blue tile backsplash in the kitchen and the shitty pipes in the bathroom. The balcony that overlooks the piazza. Besides, I'm not giving up yet, even though she has.

Three weeks, and she hasn't heard from him. Not on her birthday, nothing.

The espresso machine wheezes to an end as the front door opens, keys jingling when Chiara comes in, finally off work for the day. I told her she didn't have to work if she didn't wanna, but she said she likes the distraction, and it's her call. Really, I think she's just freaked because of Massimo firing her, which was, like, 75 percent of her income.

"Hey." Her smile is almost normal, unlooping her favorite purple knit scarf and hanging it on the hook by the door. "That for me?"

"Nope." I pick up the pink espresso cup and lean back against the counter, bringing it up to my lips as she gapes at me. I chuckle and hold it toward her. "Yeah."

She tosses her keys and phone on the table on her way toward me, unzipping her leather jacket and glancing around at the quiet apartment that I just finished cleaning from top to bottom. "Where is everyone?"

"Out."

Chiara stops in front of me, taking the cup from my hands. She takes a sip and moans, then sets it on the counter, a funny twist to her brow as she repeats, "Out?"

It pulls a wicked smirk onto my lips. "Yep."

Chiara giggles her naughty giggle, leaning forward to brush a kiss against my lips. My good arm slips around her waist, pulling her closer against me as she moans and reaches up to cradle my jaw in her palms.

Even with my bum shoulder, our sex has been hotter than ever lately, and I cannot *wait* to have full use of both of my arms again. I will do just about anything, any time, any place that will help her feel better. Even if just for twenty minutes. And sometimes in public.

"We should go into the bedroom, just in case," I whisper against her lips. But even that wasn't quick enough—the front door opens, my brother and Taryn and my parents all traipsing inside while talking over each other.

"I don't care if they sell it at Walgreens—"

"Billy, do you have that card from that guy? I can't find it..."

"Yeah, in my wallet."

"—it's not the same when you buy it in Italy," my mom says.

"Yeah, except for the duty tax," my father grumbles, shutting the door behind them.

Chiara turns around and leans back against me.

"Oh, good! Chiara, honey, you're home," Mama says with a bright smile, because she has become adamantly concerned about the hours that Chiara works. *Aren't we all?* She and my dad are only staying here for a few days, Billy and Taryn are in a hotel nearby, but that's been enough for my mama to completely fall for Chiara. My father too.

We had dinner with them in Memphis before we left, and I really wasn't sure how all that was gonna go when Chiara wasn't in the mood for bullshit and my father was champing at the bit. Sure enough, that Sagittarius in her came to play, and she kinda ran her mouth off on him, telling my father everything she thinks about him and the decisions he's made about my life—college included—and I came within seconds of fully stroking out. Until he started laughing.

Hugged her, welcomed her to the family, clapped me on the back, and that was that.

They're, like, weirdly bonded now. He gives her shit, she gives it right back, and he may actually like her more than he likes me. Like that's hard, but still.

My brother jerks his chin at me, already helping Taryn with her jacket and then hanging up both his and hers by the door. We're cool. All dust settled.

"How was the basilica?" Chiara asks my mom. Bless her: she actually sounds like she gives a shit, even though I damn well know she'd rather go in the bedroom, have sex, shower, then put on her pajamas and game for an hour before she crashes. Just makes me feel like even more of a jerk—she's been such a good sport about my parents taking over the guest room, sucking up all the air and energy in the tiny apartment.

I was rooting for a hotel room. But Chiara sent me for a massive guilt trip, saying family is important and my family is all we have. So I caved, and they got the invite. But the reality of dealing with my relatives might be why she's pulled some extra shifts lately.

They'll all be gone Monday, and life will go back to normal. Just me and her, and usually Aria and Elena too. After the Saturday wedding everyone's here for, and Chiara and I have been absolutely *un*-invited to.

"Oh, the basilica was just *divine*," my mom tells her. "You were so right."

My father scoffs, heading into the kitchen to wash his hands. "Yeah, if divine means loud and crowded."

Chiara chuckles as he dries off his hands. Until he picks up her espresso cup and takes a sip. "Hey," she says with a laugh, taking it back. "Get your own."

"Mason won't fix it for me," he complains to her.

"Then maybe you should ask him nicely." She smirks at my father, then sweetly kisses my cheek. "That's what I do." She heads past Billy with a smug sip from her cup, joining my mom and Taryn in the living room. "Show me all your pictures."

My dad looks at me, then makes a bunch of kissy faces. *Dick*.

I scowl and get started on making a second cup for him, Billy leaning against the other counter and twirling his hat around his finger. "How'd it go?" he asks me quietly.

"No go," I tell my brother, the espresso machine sputtering to life. I turn back around, double-checking Chiara isn't watching me or listening in. Scratch at my jaw as I say it, just in case. "They've still got me blocked, and I can't get through. I'm gonna have to go over there."

My father shakes his head. "Maybe some things are better left alone, Son."

"Not this. It's her family."

"You want some backup?" Billy asks.

"Nope." I turn around to get the now-filled espresso cup, handing it to my father. "I need you to hold down the fort for a couple hours."

He nods, spinning his hat in his hand. "Can do."

My father sighs, taking a sip from his cup. "*Damn*, that's good." Then he walks into the living room like everything is fine. "Honey, come on. She's seen all that stuff before. The real question"—he picks up the TV remote, turning it on and flipping through the channels—"is exactly what Chiara here knows about football, because I'm guessing Mason ain't told her shit."

Chiara snorts. "You're right. I have never asked him anything about it."

"Well, see? We gotta fix that."

Billy rolls his eyes, pushing off the counter and turning toward the living room. I follow behind him, leaning over to brush a kiss against Chiara's cheek. "Gotta run out. Borrowing the car."

"What?" Her eyes narrow—from day one, she's been able to read me even better than I can read her, and I'm giving myself a fifty-fifty shot of getting out of here. "Where are you going?"

"To run an errand. I'll be back in a couple hours."

"A couple *hours*?"

"Hey, Chiara, honey," my dad says, "can you help me? I can't find the football."

She huffs under her breath, giving me a suspicious look before she stands and goes over to help him. "Bill, I don't think we have that channel."

"Sure you do. Come on. I bet you can find it for me."

My mama is watching me warily, Taryn too, but I ignore both of them and head toward the kitchen table, snagging Chiara's keys. Step into my boots by the front door, grab my hat from the hook, then slip out into the hallway.

Please, let this work.

# Chapter 34

THERE'S NO REACTION TO THE SHUTTING OF MY CAR DOOR. MAYBE because it's pitch-black out here in the sticks. Maybe from the music. It's loud—Italian rap coming from the open garage. The villa beside it looks exactly like the pictures Chiara has shown me: two-story, brick and ivy-covered, and semi-lit with golden light pouring from the open shutters. Not exactly what I expected from him, to be honest. But the garage sure is.

I score a better view as I walk up through the dark yard, and the whole space is just as perfectly organized as our professional ones at the track: shelves and pegboards, racks of tools, and cubbies of spare parts. Bright white lights illuminating everything that you'd ever need and more.

*Virgos gonna virgo.*

Massimo finally lifts his head and spots me, straightening from where he was elbows' deep under a jacked-up bike. Looks like he's putting on an aftermarket muffler—probably for Lori. She always liked 'em loud.

"You can stop right there, turn around, and leave the way you came," he says. He rolls up to standing and grabs a towel to wipe off his hands. "I have nothing to say to you. And don't even say her name to me. I do not want to hear it."

Lorelai comes through a side door. "Mas, what was the name of that comedienne from that movie—" She stops when she sees me, her jaw dropping and eyes growing meaner. "What do you want? Do you know what you've done? The family you've broken up?"

*And we're off.*

"I do know," I tell her, making sure to keep my voice calm. "It's why I'm here."

Lori deflates a little, but not all the way. She's a champion grudge holder, though Massimo seems to be giving her a run for her money.

I look back to him. "Look, man, I'm sorry for showing up here like this, and I'm not trying to wreck y'all's night. But I've been trying to get in contact with you for weeks. You didn't leave me much of a choice."

"No, you had a choice." He throws the towel onto the table of tools. "You made yours, she made hers, and now I have made mine. You can go."

Fuck. This is not starting off good. "Look, you don't want me to say her name? That's fine. Because I'm not here to talk about her. I'm here to talk about me and you."

Massimo trades a confused look with Lorelai. Can't really blame him.

Here goes nothing.

"I'm sorry," I tell him plainly. "Man to man, I'm really sorry. We've known each other a while now, and you're not a bad guy, Massimo. I've enjoyed racing against you. Hell, at one point, we were almost friends. But I fucked all that up, and I didn't give you the respect of being straight with you. I'm sorry. That's not how I usually like to do things. This one is on me. All on me."

Massimo watches me for a minute, just letting me squirm with how uncomfortable that was. Billy does the same whenever I'm coming clean, and I'm not all that surprised Massimo's doing it to me now. He's a big brother too, after all.

He turns his head and says something to Lorelai, low and in Italian. Her eyes dart my way before flicking back to him. "You sure?"

"Mm-hmm."

"Okay." She stretches up to brush a kiss to his cheek before she heads for the door, glancing back at me just before she shuts it behind her.

Massimo watches every step she takes before his gaze swivels back to me. "You have two minutes."

Two minutes? *Two*? "Okay, well, what else do you want me to say?"

He pretends to consider that. "How about what the fuck you were thinking coming into my apartment and sleeping with my roommate—"

"Lorelai cleared it," I tell him, one hand up because my other is in my sling. "I'm not trying to bring her into this, I swear, but she did and I thought you knew."

Massimo's jaw is locked tight. When he doesn't say anything else, I decide to roll the dice and walk farther into the garage, then squat down to see where he's at with the muffler. He's already got everything oiled and removed the U-bolt. Old muffler should slide right off. But when I test it, it's not budging.

Massimo grabs a pry bar and points it at me. "And after you left, that first night in Ravenna, who took the next step?"

I'm not quite sure the significance of that question, but I make sure to answer it honestly. "Me. I texted her." He lets me take the pry bar, then start to work off the old muffler. Isn't easy with only one good arm, but it's not impossible. "We talked once, but you were kinda in the background, and she got uncomfortable, so I cut it off. She wasn't ready to move on."

There's a pop of metal on metal, and the muffler slides loose. Massimo pulls it the rest of the way off, setting it on the table. "Then why not leave it alone?"

"I tried to, man. But then, ya know…" I check the rubber straps, uncomfortable as all hell.

"She came to the circuit, and you started sleeping with each other," he fills in.

"Yeah."

"See, this is where I get upset." He hands me enough rubber straps to replace all of them. Only one actually needed changing, but he probably doesn't let stuff like that go. Not on Lori's bike. "Because you had every chance to come talk to me, to be honest, and you chose to lie."

"It wasn't supposed to go anywhere, man. I'm sorry. I know you probably don't want to hear that, but it wasn't." I reach around from under the bike to tap the tank. "It's ready."

He grabs the new muffler, slipping it on. "Yes, but then you kept sleeping together, and still, you said nothing."

I swallow, everything about my words entirely serious. "I wasn't just sleeping with her, Massimo. I fell in love with her."

He growls under his breath like he can't quite stomach the thought.

"I, um, I need the U-bolt."

He shifts toward the table and comes back, handing me the bolt and the wrench. I'm glad I have something to work on while I do this; it's a lot easier than trying to look him in the face.

"We tried to stop it," I tell him, gritting my teeth as I make sure to tighten the bolt beyond question. "She left, and we didn't talk for months. But it was torture, man. Pushed me right to the limit." I shift to check the back, and he hands me the second bolt it needs. "I, um, cleaned up, got sober. You can call my sponsor if you want to. And then I went after her. I had to."

One last turn, then I check the muffler to make sure it's secure. It doesn't budge a bit. He'll probably redo it anyway, but for now, he takes the wrench when I hand it to him.

"No, you didn't have to."

"Yes, I *did* have to." It's awkward as fuck to try to stand up from the ground with only one arm, but I get there, straightening to find him glaring at me. "I *love* her, Massimo. I asked her to marry me, and she said yes. *Twice.*"

"Don't talk to me about that," he growls, pointing the wrench at me. "You stole that from me too."

"I'm sorry," I say again. "It's what she wanted."

He scoffs, tossing the wrench onto the table. "She said that? That she did not want me there?"

"No, not like that." Damn it, how am I making things worse? "I'm sure she did want you there. But she just couldn't tell you. She was scared."

"Why should she be afraid of me?" He starts to make a show of packing up all the tools and bolts and rubber strips. "She *chose* not to tell me. There is a difference."

"You're right," I agree. "We chose not to tell you. We fucked up." I debate whether to push it, and actually, yeah, I'm going for it. "Totally justifies you blowing up on her in a hospital parking lot and delivering a life sentence, right there."

He doesn't have anything to say to that. Not for a while anyway. After he puts everything in its designated drawer, he grabs the old muffler and carries it to a box on the other side of the garage, sliding it inside with his back to me. His voice is quiet, most of its edge gone. "How is she?"

"How do you think she is?" I say carefully. "She's heartbroken. She's in shock. She's working overtime to try to distract herself, and she really wants to run."

He stops, his eyes lifting to mine over his shoulder. "Run where?"

"I don't know. But she keeps talking about moving out of the apartment."

He rolls his eyes, muttering under his breath in Italian as he closes the tab on the muffler box, then slides it into place on a higher shelf. "There is no reason for her to do that."

"I agree. So can you please call her and tell her that? Because she would really like to talk to you."

"No." He snatches up the mat from under the bike, tossing it into the corner. Then he starts working on reconnecting the battery.

I throw up my one good hand. "Why won't you let her apologize? She wasn't trying to hurt you. The exact opposite in fact. And no one's denying that we were in the wrong here, but you're really gonna spend the rest of your lives apart because I got in the middle?"

He pauses what he's doing to stare at me. "You could leave."

I stare right back. "I offered. She said no."

Massimo scoffs and shakes his head, going back to the battery and looking so angry he could spit. "This is exactly why I did not want her to date you. I knew you would be out the door at the first sign of trouble."

My temper rumbles in my chest, but I keep myself calm as he

straightens and grabs the key, turning it over to make sure the lights come on. "Dude, I'm not the one who has her blocked right now."

"Because I am not interested in hearing any more of her lies." He starts the engine all the way, a roar of noise filling the garage. Christ, that thing is loud. But it ain't rattling, because it ain't loose, that's for damn sure.

"Then give her a chance to tell you the truth!" I yell over the ruckus.

"The truth?" He scoffs, shutting off the engine. Takes out the key and walks over to a pegboard, hooking it in place next to a couple others. "The truth is that she and I had an agreement. She knew it, and she broke it."

"Yes, she broke your agreement," I admit. He gets to work on putting back the battery cover, followed by the upper right fairing that hides it. "Yes, she fucked up. And I understand you have concerns about her being with another racer, that it gets in the way and can be distracting. It's half the reason she didn't tell you—she didn't want to put you in danger. So…fine. I'll quit. Whatever it takes for you to forgive her and get past this."

Massimo stops and blinks at me. "You would quit racing? So I would forgive her?"

"If that's what it takes." I don't know how I'm going to explain it to Frank and my father and everyone else, but I don't care. She comes first.

He shakes his head, checking the fairing is secure before he straightens. Tosses the Allen wrench onto the table. Glares at me like he wishes I had never been born. "You could have been with anyone else. Anyone. *No.* It had to be my best friend."

"I didn't do it to spite you." I hold the bike steady as he goes around to the jack, lowering it down. "And she can still be your best friend. It's just now, she's my wife too."

His eyes flare my way, and yeah, he's not used to that word yet. He mutters under his breath the whole time he lowers the bike, then pulls away the jack and rolls the custom Dabria over to its spot:

backed in and glistening under a poster of Lorelai in her leathers, flexing her bicep like Rosie the Riveter.

He sets the kickstand, then heads back to the tool table, grabbing up the towel he threw down earlier and wiping off his hands again.

"You can hate me as much as you need to, for as long as you want," I tell him. "It's more than fair, and I don't even blame you for it. Just please, punish *me*, not her. At the very least give her the chance to apologize. She misses her family. She misses *you*, Massimo. Chiara needs you. And I know I didn't get that before—"

"Your two minutes are over." He crosses his arms over his chest. Not an ounce of forgiveness on his face. "This conversation is finished."

My heart sinks. "Really, man?"

"Yes."

He's not joking either. He turns on his heel and strolls into the house, the lights turning off just before the door shuts behind him. I'm plunged into darkness, too stunned and too disappointed to move.

I can't fix this. She's going to be missing him for the rest of her life, and it's my fucking fault. Just like Lorelai said, I broke up a family. Their family.

I turn and start heading toward the car, no idea how I'm going to make this up to her.

The garage lights turn back on behind me. "Mason, wait," Lori calls out. Her voice is about ten times nicer than it was earlier, and I turn toward her, standing in the dark yard as she comes to the edge of the lit garage. "Is Chiara okay?"

"Yeah, she's…" But I stop right there. Because that's not the truth. "No, she's not okay."

Lori hugs her arms around her chest, her brows downturned. "Can you tell her I miss her?"

I nod. At least there's some hope with her. "She misses you too."

Lorelai looks back toward the house, her voice dropping a little quieter. "Just give him some time, okay? He's mad, but he'll come around. He has to."

It's been weeks already. How much more time does he need? This is killing her.

"You sure?" I peek toward the open shutters when I catch a shadow of movement. I don't see anything, but that doesn't mean he's not in there, listening. "Seems pretty set in his decision to me."

"I'm sure," Lori says. "They don't know how to live without each other. He misses her more than he's letting on."

I look back to her, genuinely curious now. "How do you know?"

She gives me a funny little smile. "Mason. The playlist never lies."

# Chapter 35

*Chiara King—December*

I twirl my fork in the whipped cream, then abandon it to my plate, no longer hungry though I haven't eaten much. The day is perfect and sunny and beautiful, and I'm not sure that I've ever been this miserable at a café on a Friday afternoon. Well, half-miserable.

Mason sits forward, tangling my fingers with his and bringing them to his lips. A smile tugs at the corners of my mouth—he's been so sweet, so patient through all this. I'm putting on a good face for his parents, but I'm...

I'm not okay.

Massimo was right: it feels like half of me is missing. Something in me...broke.

The only, *only* thing that's gotten me through this is Mason. How steady he's been, how calm and understanding, and all the silent ways he's picking up the slack where I'm dropping the ball. His family staying with us is kinda driving me crazy. I miss my privacy, my gaming time, and my showers with him. But it's also been a little bit nice: the noise and the busyness, the hugs from his mom and the ways I mess with his dad. Billy doesn't say much, but Taryn is actually very sweet and not nearly as fake as she seems. She's fun to cook with. And the men always make a fuss of appreciation, no matter how simple the meal.

I like his family. And they're starting to like me. And now that the initial shock is past, they all seem pretty much on board with the fact that Mason and I eloped. Billy's still kinda freaked out. But that may have more to do with Taryn *not* being as freaked out as he expected her to be.

I'm giving it six months before they're married. Maybe less.

"What do you wanna do tonight?" Mason asks gently. "Wanna go see a movie?"

He's done his best to distract me all day, but it's impossible to ignore. Especially when both the florist and the caterer did *not* get the message that I'm no longer their point of contact. Yesterday was the linen company and the venue and seven different guests texting me for directions to the church. I guess seven out of four hundred isn't bad, but zero would have been infinitely better.

"Whatever you want to do." I try for a smile. "Whatever you want to see."

He nods, pressing another kiss to my fingertips. "Okay." But neither of us gets up to leave.

We linger at the café through another espresso, talking about everything and nothing. I'm mostly just listening to the noise of the piazza and the traffic in the streets. Watching the setting sunlight, tasting the salty air on my lips and ignoring the passing of time.

I need a lot of air right now. Space. Room to let this pain in my chest ripple out without pressing back into me. But there is no way to run from this.

I lost my best friend.

Mason says it's his fault. (I don't see how.)

He says he wants to try to fix it. (I don't think that's his job.)

But sometimes, I'm almost tempted to let him try. It just *hurts*, so much.

"You wanna get some ice cream?" he asks me. "Or you wanna maybe go somewhere? I hear Egypt is nice this time of year."

"Whatever you want to do."

He lets out a sigh through his nose, but he doesn't go off on a rant about how unfair this is to him; he simply slips his phone out of his pocket, checking the screen. Lets out another sigh, but this one sounds different. Like he got good news he's been waiting on. "I'm gonna go use the men's room, then we'll figure out our next move. Okay?"

I nod, staying in my seat as he gets up, leans over the table to drop a kiss to my cheek, then heads inside the café. It's starting to get colder now that the sun has gone down, and I blow a stream of hot air into my hands, then tuck them into my jacket pockets. A guy drives by on a moped that reminds me a little of Massimo when he was younger, and I wonder what he's doing right now. How his stag party went last night.

If he's panicking about his wedding tomorrow, pacing back and forth. Maybe he's joking with his brother or rolling his eyes at Vinicio. Possibly bickering with his mom, or just giddy at the prospect of finally marrying the woman of his dreams. Just like he's always wanted.

The wind picks up as I sniffle, and I get slammed with the faint trace of cigarette smoke.

"This seat taken?" a male voice asks in Italian.

I look up, everything in me seizing when I find Massimo standing across from me. Black shirt, leather jacket, black sunglasses, and a smug smirk on his face. Like he totally hasn't been stress smoking.

I can barely get my voice to work. "Mason's going to be back any second," I mutter.

Massimo looks pointedly toward the bar, and I follow his gaze. Where Mason is sitting, nursing a glass of water. He glances over his shoulder at us, touches his hat, then turns forward again. *He knew?*

That text message…

What a sneak.

My heart is rampaging in my chest as Massimo takes the seat across from me. He looks over our table but seems unsure what to do with his hands. Whether to rest them on the cloth or keep them in his lap.

I open my mouth to say something, but I'm not quite sure where to start apologizing—at the beginning or at the end and work backward. Massimo starts talking before I can decide.

"You missed your birthday dinner at my mom's house," he says. "Everyone sat around yelling at me and not eating in your honor. You would've enjoyed it."

*Don't cry, don't cry, don't cry…*

"I've been busy," he continues, glancing around like he's making sure no one nearby is listening. "I, um, I went to confession."

The words are so *weird*, so the absolute last thing I expected him to say, I can't keep my response to myself. "Willingly?"

"Yeah." He scoffs and looks down, starting to fidget with a napkin. "I, um, I told the priest that I'd broken a promise. A big one. That I made a long time ago. And I...I've been struggling with it. With losing my best friend."

I look away, blinking my eyes in the wind to dry them.

"He said that I was asking for forgiveness from the wrong place."

A shock of air bursts from my lungs. "No, he did *not*."

Massimo cracks a hint of a smile. "No, he did not. He said to say five rosaries and to start coming to Mass."

I choke out a laugh, wiping the tears from my face. He's such an asshole, always making me feel better even when I don't deserve it.

"I'm sorry," he says quietly, his voice raw as he sits forward and reaches for my hand. "I'm so fucking sorry, Chiara."

I dissolve into a fresh mess of tears as his hands clasp around mine, something so familiar about it and yet so far away now. He'll always be the boy who saved me, my first everything, and the man who worked so hard to support us. But it's not his hands that I need anymore. Just his willingness to talk to me, to share space with me. To be in my life. And I hope that will never change.

"I'm sorry too," I promise. "I never meant to hurt you. And I know I should've told you. I wanted to, so many times. But I didn't want to worry you when it wasn't supposed to go anywhere, and then it was *everything*, and by then, it was too late—"

He shakes his head. "It's never too late. Never."

"But it was, Massimo. It was too late... I had done everything wrong, and I didn't know how to disappoint you like that. To tell you that I fell in love with the one person you asked me not to date. I was terrified I might lose you over it, and that's exactly what I did. I lost you." My voice gives out, because even after living through it, it still feels unthinkable. "And I know I deserve it, that you've always been honest with me, and I was the one who lied, but I just... I wish you could forgive me. Maybe not today, and maybe not tomorrow. But someday."

"Chiara, I was *worried*, not disappointed." His voice cracks as he lets me go with one hand to hold his palm to his chest, pressed desperately over his heart. "And I know I made it too hard. You shouldn't have to be scared of how I'm going to react or what I'm going to say. You should be able to trust that I will always hear you out. I...I love you. You're my..."

I nod, my voice wrecked. "I love you too."

"I hate so much that I made you feel that way," he says, the words tight with bitterness and heavy with guilt. "Like you couldn't come to me when something this big was happening to you. You can *always* tell me anything."

I can't even speak anymore. All I can do is nod, desperately wiping at the tears streaming down my cheeks.

His jaw is quivering as he shakes his head. "I'm mostly just sorry I missed it. That I haven't been here for you. I would've liked to have seen that: seen you fall in love with someone. To be that happy."

I'm sorry he missed it too. Watching him fall in love with Lorelai, as hard as it was at times, was wonderful to witness. To know your best friend is as happy as they could ever be...to see them light up with love and comfort...it's a gift. To know they're taken care of. Their heart is safe.

"That's just it, Massimo." My voice is ruined as I tighten my grip on his hand. "I didn't get to share the beginning with you. But this is my forever, and I don't want you to miss the rest of it too. I want you there. With us. But I'm really, really scared you won't want to be."

"I want to be there," he says quickly. "And I want you with me. I'm..." His voice cracks, hand trembling in mine. "I shouldn't have yelled at you like that, said those things. No matter what, I had no right, and I'm so fucking sorry if I scared you. It will *never* happen again."

I know it won't. And I wasn't scared. Not of him—just of losing him.

"It's okay," I whisper.

"No, Chiara, it's not. It's not fucking okay." Massimo's voice breaks, quickly followed by the rest of him: his hand over his heart now covering his face as his shoulders rack with silent tears he won't let me see. But I can feel the tremor in his other hand, clasped tight around mine. I can hear the staggered breaths he's pulling in and the single sniffle that confirms exactly what I'm seeing. And while I may tease Massimo about being emotional, I can count the times I've seen this man cry on two fingers. And this is the second.

"Hey, come back, star," I breathe quietly. "It's not as bad as all that."

He pulls our hands over and presses a kiss to the back of mine, then lets me go. Sits back and pinches at his eyes under his sunglasses, his posture suddenly relaxed. *Such an actor.*

"How have you been?" I can't help but ask. We've never in our lives gone this long without talking, and I miss everything: his thoughts and his frustrations, the news of his family.

He shrugs. "Oh, you know. Lorina says I'm not allowed to listen to Guns N' Roses in the garage anymore—headphones only—but otherwise, I'm okay."

It takes everything I have to keep from cracking up laughing—he was totally pining. I am going to be smug about this for the rest of forever.

"How have you been?" He nods toward the bar. "This is going okay?"

I can't help smiling toward Mason, soaking in the image of him making idle chatter with the bartender and sipping on his water. When I look back to Massimo, it's still a little weird to be talking openly about it, but hopefully that will get easier. With time. "It's perfect."

"Can't believe you're married." He scrubs a hand back through his hair before pushing his sunglasses up into it. Don't mention how red his eyes are. The shadows under them. "That you eloped in Paris."

*Yeah*, we did, and it was beautiful. Maybe not like his wedding will be, but it was beautiful all the same. And it was absolutely the right thing for me and Mason.

I wink at Massimo. "Says the guy getting married tomorrow.

Weren't we supposed to be in the Bahamas by now, scamming tourists and living on the beach?"

"That's right," he says with a grin. "Whatever happened to Project Piña Colada?"

"I don't know. But we definitely screwed up somewhere."

Massimo laughs, a steady kind of calm in his eyes as he jerks his chin my way. "You still going to come stand up there with me tomorrow?"

I was supposed to. My best woman suit is now hidden in the very back of my armoire where I can't see it. "You won't need me. Dario's got it covered, and you'll be fine."

He scoffs. "Chiara, you may be okay with eloping on your own, but I am not." He trains his puppy dog eyes on me. "I'm the selfish one, remember? And I need you with me. Plus, I am not trusting Dario with the rings. He will lose them. On purpose."

A long sigh melts from my chest. Dario would do that, twerp.

"Please?"

"I don't know... What does Lorelai say?"

"She says I'm an asshole, and I'm lucky we're still getting married after I cut you off."

My eyes pop. "No, she didn't."

He makes a face that only makes my jaw drop further, because *oh my God*, she totally did. "By the way," he says, chewing on a fingernail to hide his grin. "Are you, um, busy tonight?"

"I don't know," I tell him, playing coy. "Why?"

He shrugs. "Nothing, just...it's the rehearsal."

I know it's the freaking rehearsal. I made all the arrangements and booked the restaurant reservation for after it. "Fine. *Maybe* I will make an appearance."

"Fine," he says back. But that damn grin is growing in the corners of his mouth as he stands, pushing in his chair. "And I'm giving you your birthday gift tonight."

I gape at him. "That's not—"

"It is totally fair," he says. "But if you wanted, you could always wear the jeans with all the holes in them. That would help a lot."

My suspicion meter ramps up to eleven. "Why?"

"Because. Mom found out about the vasectomy, and she's pissed. Like *really* furious."

"*Ah*. So you want me to take some of the heat off you and Lorelai." I smirk at him, batting my eyelashes. "Not a chance."

"Should've known." He rolls his eyes, then stands a little straighter and holds out his hand to the cowboy who just appeared beside him. "Mason."

Mason glances at me but still shakes Massimo's hand. "You heading out already?"

"Yes," he replies in English. "But maybe I will see you tonight."

Mason glances at me again, and I shrug. "Maybe," I tell Massimo. "We might be busy."

"Okay," he says with a smile. He steps around the table to drop a kiss on my cheek, whispering, "Ripped jeans."

I snort and smack his shoulder, Massimo straightening and heading off.

Mason retakes his seat, watching him walk away before he looks back to me. "You all right?" he whispers now that we're alone. "That looked kinda…intense."

I blow out a breath, tossing my hair. "It was intense. But everything's okay."

"Like…*okay*, okay? Or just okay."

"*Okay*, okay."

A bright smile cracks across Mason's face. "Good. So, um, how much trouble am I in exactly?"

I flare my eyes at him. "Lots."

He bites his lip, leaning closer and whispering, "Any way out of it?"

"Still deciding."

He groans, sitting back and tossing his hand up. "I'm really sorry, okay? But I couldn't stand seeing you hurting like that, and so yeah, I went over there and talked to him. And I know I should've told you about it, but I didn't know if he was gonna come around or how long it would take, and I didn't want to get your hopes up. I will also *not* apologize for standing up for you and for us when I love you, and you would've done the same for me."

I prop my chin in my hand, just watching him. He's right. I absolutely would've done the same for him, any day, any time.

He scowls and toys with his napkin, then pushes it away. But his teasing voice gives away his theatrics. He's such a terrible actor. "I guess this means we gotta go to the rehearsal dinner tonight."

"We don't *have* to do anything we don't want to. But it would help things a lot."

He nods, looking over our table. "Well, I guess Egypt can wait another day."

I can't keep it in anymore, and a laugh trickles from my lips as I shake my head, utterly full of love and peace as I stare at Mason. The sweetness in his blue eyes and the strength in his heart. The warmth in his smile, his hands, and the comfort from knowing that whatever may happen, he's with me, all the way.

I stand, pushing in my chair. Then I hold out my hand to him. "Follow me?"

He doesn't hesitate to answer. "Anywhere."

He stands and takes my hand, lacing his fingers through mine and letting me lead him through the café. For the life of me, I don't know how I got so lucky with Mason King. To marry a man who never asks me for more than I can give but always finds a way to give me everything I need: passion, adventure, honesty, and security. A family. And of all the mistakes I've made in my life, falling in love with him is my absolute favorite one.

"Trouble," he teases when he sees where I'm going, dropping his voice so it's just between us. "You are going to get us banned from every single restaurant in Ravenna."

I smile and push open the door of the ladies' room, checking to make sure it's empty before I tug Mason inside and lock the door behind us. He doesn't go far: his arm around my waist hugging me to him, his lips on the back of my neck and his breath as warm as his skin when we fall asleep at night. And there's no safer feeling than that—no matter where we are in the world, as long as we're together, we're home.

I spin in his grip, my palm on his chest backing him against the wall and soaking up the flame of desire in his eyes. The spark of anticipation, the depth of his devotion. His back hits stone and my hips crash to his, a needy moan falling from his lips as he swells thick between us. I grip his jaw and tease his mouth with mine. "Only if we get caught."

# Epilogue

*Mason King—Back at the Circuit*

I pull Chiara against me, drowning in the deliciousness of cinnamon as I hook a hand into her hair, then tease a kiss onto her smiling lips. She looks so goddamn beautiful today, more beautiful than any man deserves, and I've been dying to kiss her for hours. But the press conferences took *forever*, and then came the pictures and the meetings and blah blah blah.

She dissolves into me with a needy moan, so I feel absolutely no guilt whatsoever about searching for the zipper on her jeans as my lips trail to her neck.

"Are you crazy?" she teases. "Actually, never mind. I know the answer to that question."

I nip at her earlobe. "Crazy about you."

She laughs as I untuck her shirt, sneaking my palms underneath and smoothing them over her skin. *God*, she's so soft. "Mason..."

"Nah?" I bump her nose with mine, nuzzling kisses against her lips. "You don't wanna be a little bad? Have a little fun?"

"Stop tempting me," she says with a look that means she absolutely wants to. "You think because you're leading the World Championship right now that you can get anything you want?"

"Damn right," I playfully growl at her. "It was in the fine print and everything."

Chiara cracks up laughing again, starting to unzip my leathers. She pushes them over my shoulders as I free one arm, then another, goose bumps streaking across my skin when she presses a kiss to the scar on my shoulder. I pull her body closer against mine, everything only made more intense when she works her way up to my neck, wrapping her long leg around my side and threading her fingers up through the back of my hair.

I drop my hips and press myself harder against her, swollen thick with lust and love and absolutely lost to the way she makes me feel. Because coming home to Chiara is all the proof I need that it doesn't actually matter where I finish in races or that I don't rodeo anymore.

No matter where I place or how I finish, being married to her makes me the best version of me that I can ever be. And that in itself is absolutely a win worth celebrating.

I get back to kissing my way across her neck and down to the sweet spot over her collarbone. She hisses and moans as I smooth my hand over her body and pull her a little tighter against me, slipping my hand into her jeans. I'm just reaching her tattoo when there's a hard pound of a fist on the door of the broom closet.

"Three minutes," Santos growls through the door. "Or we're launching without you."

"Fuck," I mutter. The Hurricane from Spain is more like the alarm clock from hell.

Chiara only laughs. "See? I told you we didn't have time."

I push myself away from her with a groan, zipping my leathers back up.

"You owe me later after getting me all wound up too."

"Yeah, yeah, I know," I agree. *Can't wait.*

I take her face in my hands and kiss her lips, then flip off the light. I'm first out of the broom closet, checking left and right before I slip out and hook on my hat, hauling ass down the hallway, into my pit box, and out onto pit lane where my crew already has my bike set and waiting for me. The roar of the stands is like starting my truck with my radio volume cranked, my hand waving toward them even as I jog toward the people scowling at me on the ground.

"Mason," Marco growls when I jog up to the grid, swinging a leg over my bike.

"I know, I know! I'm sorry."

"Late again," Billy calls over from first pole, Frank standing on one side of him and Taryn on the other, holding his Yaalon umbrella.

Lorelai is doing the same for Massimo, one pole back, but she's in leathers from the race she just ran for the women's team. And *won*.

I was honestly more than a little stunned when Billy told Yaalon he had decided *not* to retire. And while Taryn wasn't thrilled, I'm glad we have another year racing against each other, even if it ends up being our last season with MotoPro. We started this together. I guess it's only right we should finish it together.

"I'm not that late," I tell my brother, checking over my bike.

"You are late," Billy says. "You're also wrong."

"I'm not wrong either."

Chiara comes running up, then whips out her phone, already getting started taking pictures of my bike and me before she goes to cover the other Dabria rider, then down the poles toward the satellite team—she's no longer anyone's *personal* publicist.

Once word spread that she and Massimo had professionally separated, her phone started ringing off the hook. And after an auction of multiple offers from multiple manufacturers, she now works for Dabria directly, managing the profiles of eight different racers.

She's kicking *ass* at it too. So fucking proud of her.

I have to raise my voice over the sound of my bike rumbling beneath me. "*Last Crusade* was the best Indiana Jones movie they made. No question."

Massimo *hmpfs* from the third pole, but I'm not sure who that means he agrees with.

"I always like the one with the girl with the hat," Lorelai says.

"That was *Last Crusade*," Chiara calls over to her. "Alison Doody. She was *so hot*."

Taryn snorts from her spot next to Billy, planting a hand backward on her waist. "Hot girl's name is Doody?"

"Oh my God, Taryn," Lorelai says emphatically. "She wears this white shirt and black leather pants, with gloves and a fedora..."

Massimo stops talking to his manager long enough to flip up his face shield. "Who?"

I smirk at my brother, his crew pulling the warmers off his tires. Mine start doing the same, my adrenaline growing more with the steady clap of the crowd, the heat rippling on the track and flags blowing in the wind. "You probably like *Kingdom of the Crystal Skull*," I tell Billy.

Frank claps Billy on the shoulder, then starts walking my way. "What's wrong with the Cate Blanchett one?" he says. "She's a damn good actor."

Massimo claps in Frank's direction, the sound muffled from his racing gloves before he gives him a thumbs-up. "Marissa Wiegler, *Hanna*." Then he goes back to talking to Vinicio in rapid-fire Italian. I honestly don't know how Lorelai picked it up so fast—it's taking me forever. And Chiara is constantly teasing me about my country accent, but I talk the way I talk.

"Thank you." Frank turns to me. "Mason, you ready to go?"

"*Last Crusade*," I repeat. "Final answer."

"And that," Chiara calls back, "is exactly why I married you."

We share an air high-five. My manager snorts and hands me my gloves, checking over my leathers and kinda massaging my shoulder. "How's it feel?"

"Good. No problem."

Hasn't always been the case lately, but I'm getting better. Stronger. All thanks to Chiara—she took amazing care of me all through my surgery and recovery, and while she may still be terrible about remembering to take her birth control, she had my rehab scheduled within an inch of my life. Had me back on a bike before anyone could believe it, myself and Frank included. But I made it back. Been racing better than ever with her by my side.

The announcers' voices blare on the wind, announcing the start for the warm-up lap in less than a minute, and *time to ride*.

"*Raiders of the Lost Ark*," Billy says, a smile on his face as he glances at Taryn. It's a look I know well and down to the tips of my soul—it's exactly how I was looking at Chiara the whole first week in Paris after we got married. It's only been a month for my brother, but considering how long he waited for Taryn, I'm not giving him too much crap about it. "That's the one I like."

I arch my brow and don't say nothing.

Massimo lets out a low whistle, shifting his posture on his bike like he's getting ready for the launch. "Karen Allen."

Billy tugs on his helmet. "See? Who didn't like her?"

Massimo lets out a low chuckle. "Scary."

Billy points at him, his big brother voice fully out in play. "Shut up."

The paddock starts to clear, cameras pulling back and reporters retreating to pit lane. Chiara comes running up from where she's been taking pictures, holding out her hand toward me. "Hat."

I pass it over, Chiara hooking it onto her head.

"Kiss." She gives me my good luck kiss, though it's never long enough. "Earplugs," she tells me next, handing me a pair. I hook in my left one, but she stops me from putting in the right, leaning closer to whisper in my ear. "By the way…"

"*What?*" I exclaim, already halfway to standing up to hug her because if what she said was true, I really, really need to hug her. Right fucking now.

But Chiara pushes me back onto the bike, kisses me soft and sweet with a sweep of her thumbs over my cheekbones. Then she pulls back with a wink, hands me my helmet, and starts backing away while blowing me a kiss. "I love you."

"Are you *serious?*" I call out, the pure joy and excitement in my voice causing Billy to look my way. But I don't know if Chiara can hear me over the roar of the engines on the track and the wild call of the fans in the crowd.

She laughs and nods, then mimes for me to put on my helmet, and that's my answer.

*Holy shit! Like…holy shit!*

I blink and hook on my helmet, my heart thundering in my chest and the movements all muscle memory as I buckle the strap and look toward Massimo, needing to scream and celebrate with someone else who will actually appreciate the beautiful magnitude of what she just told me.

He waves me off. "I do not want to know. Not until after the race."

He points forward where the green flag is being walked off the track, the safety car already pulling out, and it feels like I'm never gonna stop smiling when I duck down, waiting for the lights to go out on the warm-up lap.

I can't believe she's—

The lights go out, and I launch from the starting line—revving it up as fast as I can to pop a wheelie, a raw cheer bellowing from my lungs that matches the one in the stadium before I slam my front tire back to the hot earth of the track. Pop the clutch and down-shift, then lean hard into the first turn, taking the hole shot with my brother and Massimo falling into line right behind me. Come out and punch it, shifting up quickly into third gear.

Between falling in love and loving racing, I don't know how life gets any better than this.

# WRECKLESS

THIRD GEAR.

The cool night air screams past me as I downshift in my approach to turn fourteen, a hard right corner on the Losail International track. A smile rushes across my lips as my Dabria lies deep into the tighter-than-tight turn, my knee scraping the Qatar track rippling past my helmet.

I tuck in my elbow and control my breathing, harnessing all my anticipation into crisp, unbridled focus. Twenty-one laps down, two turns to go, and then I will fly over the finish line: the first woman in history to win a race in Moto Grand Prix. The first woman ever to race in MotoPro. And all I have to do is what I've done for ten years: beat Massimo to the finish line.

Fourth gear. I tilt my bike vertical and charge toward the sharp left of fifteen. Fifth gear. Sixth. Golden dust flashes on my right, black pavement and gray bailout gravel rushing by my left. The stars of Doha are sparkling above me, but the stadium lights of Losail lead the way—a lit path on the dark track guiding me home to the checkered flag, riding the glory rained down on me from the thousands of screaming fans I can't hear over my engine.

They want it—for me to win—and I can't wait to give it to them.

*Time to deal with Massimo.*

I fade left, forcing my oldest rival farther inside the lane than he wants to be. As far as I'm concerned, that's what he gets. Massimo peeks at me over his shoulder, and I don't care how sexy his stubble is. Today is the day I'm going to make history.

Fifth gear. Fourth. Third, and lean.

My body lies flat, my bike flexing under ruthless speed and gravity pulling it further down. It takes everything I have to stifle the primal fear that wants to creep in, screaming how I'm going to crash and die because I'm going too fast to hold it. There's too much speed, too much weight, and the laws of physics don't mean crap, because they don't exist.

I swallow the lies and bury them under the truth: even though looming death is on my left, my body is caught in the middle of a love-and-war affair between gravity and centrifugal force, and it's the only place I want to be. But when I lean harder into the turn, Massimo's blue chassis and front tire are all I can see around the curve, blocking my view of the finish line. And I'm *sick* of him taking my finish line.

His right knee is closer to my helmet than my own gloves, the space between us growing dangerously closer. When I check, I'm clear to move: there's at least a four-second gap between us and the rest of the field.

*See ya, sucker...*

With the first hint of victory swirling through me, I let off the accelerator so I can duck around behind Massimo. He should push dangerously right, but the jerk slows down with me. I curse in my helmet and speed up, over the games and ready to secure my win. He stays with me, then starts to drift outside and directly into my left knee and elbow. He's out of the apex and taking me with him.

I'm already calculating my options, none of them good. Once again, he's risking my win, my bike, and my life. It's crap like this that made me realize it doesn't matter how intoxicating his smile is. The cold truth is we both need to win more than anything else, and if he's going for the kill every chance he gets, so am I.

I can't afford to downshift into second gear and lose any more speed to get around him. Hard way it is. Gritting my teeth, I hold the turn, my arms and abs bellowing in anguish from the G forces, but I refuse to cower. I won't drift farther right and toward the gravel bailout. I know I can hold it...

My heartbeat thuds in my ears, my breathing fast and increasing. Blue paint and black tires are inching closer to my bright red fairings, and survival instincts tell me that if I don't move over in the next half second, he's going to hit me and crash me out, and... *Shit!*

I let off the accelerator or risk losing it all, my engine slowing as I careen right, my tires bumping on the curbstone and the bike wobbling in the gravel. My breath cascades into my lungs as I grapple for control, my reflexes throwing a glance to my left to make sure I won't run over Massimo and kill him. He should be sliding on the ground in front of me. Maybe tumbling down the dark pavement. There's no way he held that turn at that speed when he was so far out of the apex. Except when I look, Massimo's gone.

He's just freaking *gone.*

A roar rises from the stands as my head whips forward, and blue paint is meters ahead. He didn't crash, somehow pulling off that screwed-up apex without hitting the gravel.

I swerve back onto the racetrack, my determination screaming as I shift up fast from third gear to fourth. Massimo's transmission roars deep in sixth, and his helmet peeks over his shoulder. When he sees the space between us on the last straightaway, the asshole pops a freaking wheelie as he takes the win.

The stands explode, booming his name as green, white, and red flags billow from every direction. Television cameras rise on cranes as fireworks light up the night sky, and I curse where no one but me can hear it, soaring across the finish line behind him two seconds too late.

Bye-bye, history. And first place.

—⁓—

I step down off the podium, squinting from the lights and my cheeks hurting from smiling as I pump my silver trophy in one hand and a bottle of champagne in the other. A new wall of screams erupts from the fans in the stadium, all shouting every translation of congratulations while waving signs with my name and picture and #77.

The whole place is a massive party waiting to explode. It always is after the night race in Qatar: the first Grand Prix of the nineteen-race circuit that takes us all over the world from March to November. There's also nothing quite like the capital city of Doha—spicy desert air, the hum of Arabic tickling your veins as you sit in traffic, staring up at a skyline that beats New York any freaking day of the week. Especially at night, when the buildings are lit up so the world is a neon rainbow reflected in the Persian Gulf.

It's a hell of an upgrade from my family's ranch in Memphis, where the horses are treated like kings and farmhands come and go like seasonal allergies. But partying in Doha isn't an option for me when my diet is on lockdown, I've got a plane to catch for the next race, and really, I'm counting the minutes till the cameras are off me so I can cry in private over my first MotoPro loss.

*Everyone* expected me to win this one. Which I know because they didn't have a problem telling me beforehand—my mom, my dad, even Billy King. The reigning World Champion's ankle is still healing from his brush with a bull, and he whispered to me on our flight from Memphis that I need to enjoy every minute of Qatar. Because after that, he would be fine and was coming for me. But taking advantage of Billy being slow didn't even matter when Massimo was still too fast.

After one last wave, a smile and flirty wink to the crowd, I head toward the door that leads to the pit boxes where our crews will meet us. I tuck my trophy under my arm to haul it open. But I get knocked aside when Santos Saucedo brushes past me, whistling his way down the hall with his third-place trophy propped on his shoulder. Jerk.

I follow him into the hall, the sounds of the crowd and the stadium disappearing behind the door. Even though I shouldn't, I drink deeply from my bottle of champagne. I knew it wouldn't be easy to be a woman in the racing world. I certainly didn't expect the guys to take turns braiding my hair between practice and qualifying sessions. But I never expected the ostracizing to last all the way from the Rookie Cups to MotoPro.

"Lulu," an Italian accent drawls behind me, and I lengthen my strides away from the worst of them. It doesn't do me any good. Two seconds later, I have Massimo in my face. Then he drops to his knees.

My patience is already nil and quickly creeping into the negative as Massimo smiles up at me with his arms outstretched, the champagne we sprayed on the podium still sparkling in his black hair: shaved brutally short on the sides, long and thick on top, and all slicked back in that weird Italian bouffant thing.

He's been wearing the same bad haircut since we were fifteen, and I refuse to tell him. It's the best running joke I can think of. Although it'd probably be a lot funnier if he didn't pull the look off so well, balanced against the controlled stubble darkening his cheeks and nearly black around the line of his jaw.

Taryn swears I called him "damn hot" one night when she and I went swimming in a bottle of tequila. But I have no memory of saying that, and I'm betting she made it up just to mess with me. She knows that is not—and never will be—an option.

"Marry me, Lorina," Massimo says in his thick Italian accent. I roll my eyes, so not in the mood for his crap right now. This is no less than the fifth time he's done this. Usually, he's drunk, but sometimes, his wins pull out his proposals. Like beating me to the flag is the way to get me to the altar. Yeah, okay. "Today is the best day of my life. Marry me."

I shrug, wondering if there's a path of least resistance here that I haven't tried before. "Yeah, all right."

His smile stretches wider. "Sì?"

"No!"

I walk around him, but he's back in an instant. Guess that didn't work. "Why are you always so difficult, Tigrotta?" He leans closer, whispering, "You know you love me."

I elbow him out of my personal space, tucking my trophy under my arm and turning to face him. He's still freaking smiling as I jam my finger into the front of his leathers. The plate underneath protecting his lungs and ribs is like a block of cement, and I wonder if his heart beneath is made out of the same stuff. "How could you do that to me today? I don't care what the win is. We aren't supposed to try to hurt each other."

His dark eyes flash and burn a little more fiercely, a dangerous smile curving his lips. Like that's supposed to scare me. "No?"

I push my finger harder into his chest even though it makes my knuckle ache and he probably can't even feel it. "No." Of all the people I figured would wager a win against my life and still dive for the flag, I never expected it from him. He knows what it's cost me to be here, how hard I've had to fight to be on the grid beside him. "You crossed the line, Massimo."

He swallows, but he doesn't apologize. He never has, whether I deserved to hear his "Mi dispiace" or not. I grit out a frustrated huff and storm around him. I'm barely past his shoulder when he snatches my hand, tugging me back into his chest.

My eyes fly wide, adrenaline from the race still pumping strongly in my veins and surging even faster at the regret sinking the corner of his mouth. I check around for anyone else in the hallway who could report to the world that one of Moto Grand Prix's most talked about rivalries filters a little differently behind closed doors. But luckily, or maybe not, we're completely alone.

Massimo's grip on my hand loosens to just a gentle press of his palm covering mine, keeping the back of my hand flat against his leathers. It's too much—how close he is, how his eyes seem to peer straight through me and see it's not the loss making my eyes want to prickle with betrayal. It's the fact that he thought five points were worth me possibly ending up broken in the hospital, never able to race again.

*Stay focused, Hargrove.*

"Well?" I do my best to keep my voice steady under the intensity of his stare, his bottle of champagne dangling forgotten in his other hand and his trophy gone, possibly on the floor. "Are you going to apologize to me or not?"

"You want me to apologize for crossing a line? Sì, it is true. I did, Lorina, and I will not lie to you and say I did not."

His grip on my hand tightens, and my eyes drop to where he has them secured against his chest. His personally crafted version of my first name isn't new, nor is the softness in my chest when he says it. But when he leans forward to whisper in my ear, his lips are so close that I can almost feel his stubble scrape my cheek, and I'm no longer the fearless moto racer from fifteen minutes ago. I am now completely frozen.

Talking is one thing. Whispering, alone, while he's holding my hand, is another.

"I crossed the line," he breathes, and a shiver I'm not proud of trembles through me. "I crossed the finish line, first."

I reel back, my gaze narrowed as Massimo puckers a kiss at me. I snatch my hand away from him, Massimo throwing his head back in laughter as he turns, striding down the rest of the hallway. Once he's a few steps away, I pick up the tattered shreds of my dignity and stuff them back into my racing boots.

I should be used to it by now: his jokes that aren't funny, his pranks that only serve to piss me off. But it still hurts.

As soon as we're in pit lane, Massimo's manager and crew rush over to hug him while screaming victory accolades in Italian. Basically treating him like the God's gift to racing he thinks he is. So he won here at Qatar—big deal. There are eighteen races left in the circuit, and the competition is far from over.

Heading into my garage, I leave Massimo for where my own crew is waiting by my bike.

"Lori, gimme some sugar, girl!" our manager, Frank, bellows before he runs over to wrap me in a hug, even though I probably smell like pure Pennzoil.

When I pull back, I give him a sweet smile as I hand him my trophy. "You know your old gut can't handle no sugar."

Frank bursts out laughing as he drops a kiss to my forehead.

Nudging my way past my constructor and crew, I head for my bike and our customary postrace ritual. I squeeze her tight, petting her fairings and thanking her for keeping me safe until an unmistakable whistle catches my attention.

I rise and turn to find Massimo leaning against the open door of my garage, the strangest look on his face like he wants to try to smile, to talk to me again, but can't decide whether he should. I'd *almost* bet my bike it's because even though he just messed with me, the truth is, he's not-so-secretly worried about the damage the near hit caused to our *already* strained relationship.

He'd never admit it, but he really can't seem to stay away from me. Which wouldn't be the worst thing in the world except that he also doesn't know how to apologize for the crap he does. He's probably never apologized for anything in his life.

The part that kills me is that as angry as I get, I can't really claim any innocence in this situation. I've gone after him too. Attacked him too. Even though there have been so many times when I thought there could be something more between us than just rivalry. At the very least, I wondered if somehow, someday, we could be friends.

"All right, Lori," Frank says, shaking hands with my crew. "You about ready to hit the road, girl? I need to get you and Billy and Mason to the airport. Oh," he adds, "Taryn called to say, and I quote, 'Way to go, bitch.'"

I snort at my best friend's message, wondering when she hung up with Billy long enough to leave it for me. But I can't seem to muster more of a response than that. Because without saying anything, Massimo sets down a clean, white towel at the entrance to my garage. When he straightens, dark eyes locked with mine, I cross my arms and stand a little taller. It's not the apology I want, not by a long shot, but it'll do for now.

The smile he was restraining breaks free, and with nothing more, he turns and heads the other direction, leaving me to wonder what words would have come from him if we were alone instead of surrounded by the watchful eyes of hundreds of thousands of fans, on top of the ever-nosy press.

Mostly because the younger, naive part of me wants to hold close the idea that this silent, private ritual—the clean white cotton, soft, carefully folded, and laid at my door—is the safest language in which he can communicate that he'd never try to hurt me. However, the twenty-five-year-old professional racer me says I also don't need him to tell me to brush myself off and keep going. Not to get discouraged just because today, he beat me to the checkered flag.

I've been doing this as long as he has, and I don't need his help.

Frank's massive barbecue-filled frame knocks into me, shaking me into awareness. I chuckle as his arm comes around my shoulders, squeezing tight. "You okay?"

I nod absently. But really, I'm still wondering if Massimo's white towel of truce would carry the scent of him. That familiar spicy sweetness of exhaust and that stuff he puts in his hair. The aroma that's never been far and I'm drawn to breathe more deeply than I should... It's as comforting as a promise from my crew, as familiar as a scolding from my conscience.

"Yep," I tell Frank. "Just thinking about that apex in sixteen." And whether Massimo would've had nightmares about me dying on the way to the hospital if he'd crashed me out. The way I did when he wrecked in the Netherlands last year.

"Aw, don't sweat it, Lori. You'll get it next time." Frank winks. I glance over my shoulder at my bike, like I always do when I have to leave her between cities. At that towel, left where Massimo laid it.

It was only six weeks after the Netherlands that Massimo came back to the circuit following his biggest wreck to date, and the nightmares eventually stopped. I've come back after my own crashes, and I'm sure I would've even if I had crashed today. The extra weight of my chest and back plates on my body, the restriction of my elbow and knee sliders, and the imprint on my chin from the strap of my helmet say so.

But after all the races, all the close calls, and all the times I've challenged him...

After all the almosts and all the fights, all the times when I've wondered and hoped and had those dreams come crashing down...

After ten years of racing against Massimo, I have to accept the truth: it's too late for anything to change.

# ACKNOWLEDGMENTS

This story was written during the COVID-19 pandemic, right as the world was locking down. It seemed so silly and surreal to be writing about crowded racing paddocks and eating in restaurants while everything fell apart, and it even felt wrong at times. But disappearing into this story is what kept me going, and I hope the joy Mason and Chiara found in each other grants you some bit of the peace it brought me.

My heart goes out to each family with an empty spot at the dinner table. There is no way to replace what was lost.

All my thanks to my amazing agent, Kelly Peterson, for supporting me in a dozen different ways and always knowing just what to say. I'm so blessed to have you have my back.

I am continually grateful to Mary Altman and the entire team at Sourcebooks for bringing my dreams to life in the coolest way possible. I love what we've created together.

Michelle Hazen…I don't know how I got so lucky to have you in my life, but I would be lost without you. Thank you for every email, every text, every reminder, and all the times you kept me climbing.

The world's biggest bag of M&M's to Denise Williams. Meeting you was an unexpected blessing of 2020, and I am so grateful for every DM, page swap, card in the mail, and inside joke. Eagles!

Margaret Torres, Maxym Martineau, Lindsay Landgraf-Hess, Shanna Alderliesten, Dakota Shain Byrd, Tauri Cox, Briston Brooks, Meryl Wilsner… I love y'all. You make me feel like I can do anything, and everyone should be so lucky as to have a cheer squad like y'all.

Grazie mille to Marisa Escolar for gushing over Chiara and Mason and for correcting all my Italian coffee details more than once. You are a lifesaver.

Everyone else who had a hand in this through years of querying and writing contests and teaching me pretty much everything I know (though they may not know it): Shira Hoffman, Shannon Powers, Kat Kerr, Lisa Rodgers, Michelle Hauck, Amy Trueblood, Sun vs Snow, Query Kombat, Brenda Drake, Pitch Wars and PitMad, and the Fellowship. Y'all really know your stuff. (And I probably forgot a lot of people. I'm sorry! I love you!)

I am incredibly lucky to have the support of an adoring father and doting stepmother. Thank you for making books such a big part of our lives. And for not freaking out when I called and said I was going to be a romance author.

To my mother in heaven: Mason is still not Billy, Mom. You really may wanna go back to Billy.

My Sagittarius goddaughters: You two are going to take the world by storm, and I can't wait. But please let me grab an umbrella first, and I promise to make lots of macaroni and cheese.

My wonderful son: you are the joy in my heart and the reason for everything I do. Thank you for every hug, and I'm so proud of the young man you're growing into. Dimension Badass.

And finally, to my darling husband: I still need five more minutes. Though I doubt forever will be enough time with you.

# ABOUT THE AUTHOR

Katie Golding is a sports fan with a writing problem. Based in Austin, Texas, she publishes contemporary romance novels with the support of her loving husband and son. She is currently at work on her next romance novel, unless she's tweeting about it. Visit her website at katiegoldingbooks.com.